Engaging the Enemy

Rachel Rowan

Please visit www.rachelrowan.com to sign up to Rachel Rowan's newsletter and for more information on her books.

Edited by Libby Patrick, Headlight Fluid Press

Engaging the Enemy

Published 2023

1st Edition

Contents

Author's note	VI
Dedication	VII
Epigraph	VIII
Prologue	1
1. ONE	4
2. TWO	14
3. THREE	22
4. FOUR	31
5. FIVE	39
6. SIX	45
7. SEVEN	54
8. EIGHT	62
9. NINE	67
10. TEN	77
11. ELEVEN	88

12. TWELVE 99

13. THIRTEEN 108

14. FOURTEEN 119

15. FIFTEEN 126

16. SIXTEEN 135

17. SEVENTEEN 144

18. EIGHTEEN 152

19. NINETEEN 159

20. TWENTY 167

21. TWENTY-ONE 181

22. TWENTY-TWO 188

23. TWENTY-THREE 196

24. TWENTY-FOUR 207

25. TWENTY-FIVE 219

26. TWENTY-SIX 229

27. TWENTY-SEVEN 237

28. TWENTY-EIGHT 245

29. TWENTY-NINE 253

30. THIRTY 257

31. THIRTY-ONE 262

32. THIRTY-TWO 272

33. THIRTY-THREE   280

34. THIRTY-FOUR   292

35. THIRTY-FIVE   305

Epilogue   317

Thank you   325

Have you tried...   326

Acknowledgements   328

Author's note

This book uses British English spellings, e.g. "realised" instead of "realized" and "travelled" instead of "traveled". I promise they are not typos.

For everyone who's fallen heart over head.

There are some situations of the human mind in which good sense has very little power.

Northanger Abbey, Jane Austen.

The boy cried out 'Wolf, Wolf,' still louder than before. But this time the villagers, who had been fooled twice before, thought the boy was again lying, and nobody came to his aid.

The Boy Who Cried Wolf, Aesop's Fables.

Prologue

I N AMELIA'S DEFENCE, SHE was a little drunk. And she had dreamed of this moment for years. So when Hugo Blackton led her off the dancefloor, she let him.

But the problem with dreams coming true is that it's hard to believe they're real. And the problem with any kind of dream involving Hugo Blackton is that he was as insincere as he was attractive. And Hugo was unfairly, irresistibly attractive. He had dark hair, navy-blue eyes, and a wicked, lazy smile. And he had never meant a single thing he'd ever said.

Except now he was saying, "You're beautiful."

Not just saying it, but *whispering* it, his mouth grazing Amelia's jaw. And she knew it was a lie—*had* to be a lie—because this was Hugo, the devilish friend of her childhood, the boy who never played fair, who couldn't laugh without it being part of some teasing game. And also, it couldn't be true because it was exactly, *exactly*, the very dream she'd had for years.

And this sort of thing didn't happen. Not to her.

But he'd appeared in front of her on the dancefloor at her sister's engagement party and said, "Hello, Little Amy. It's been a while." Then he'd smiled one of those wicked, lazy smiles, blue eyes almost black in the dim light, and taken her hand.

He'd pulled her up against him, his other hand on her lower back, and they'd swayed and turned together, a mockery of a

1

dance, Hugo smiling all the time. Because of course he didn't mean it. And even in her dreams, Hugo was never quite *nice*.

He was just humouring her, dancing with Little Amy at the party because she'd been out there all alone. So he danced with her, laughing in that way he had, as though everything was a game, his lean, hot body pressed against hers, alcohol on his breath as he dipped his head to her ear and said over the thumping music, "How long has it been since I last saw you? Nearly a year? Far too long. I want to talk to you properly. Let's go somewhere quiet."

And he'd led her off the dancefloor.

He took her to a quiet room, not switching on the light. Moonlight was coming through the tall windows, and the pounding music of the party was distant. They were at Redbridge, her family's ancient home, and though it wasn't quite as large as the stately home Hugo's family owned, it was large enough to almost swallow the sounds of a hundred-person party. To let them find an empty room, where they could be secluded and alone.

Amelia had no idea what Hugo could want to talk to her about. In the twenty-three years she'd known him, he'd never once said anything really worth saying. She might be the victim of a helpless infatuation, but it didn't blind her to his many, many flaws.

But Hugo didn't speak for a moment. He leant back against a desk, still holding her hand, and played lightly with her fingers while she tried not to choke on her own heartbeat. This was not the sort of thing they usually did. This was different. Hugo was being...different.

"I missed you," he said.

He looked up at her then, blue eyes sea-dark in the half-light.

"Oh," she said.

"Amy... I realised..."

He let out a slow breath, and if it had been anyone else, she would have said it sounded like it carried the weight of his soul with it. But this was Hugo, and he'd probably left his soul behind somewhere, forgotten down the sticky back of a sofa booth in a too-expensive bar.

He straightened, standing up from the desk. The movement brought them almost as close as they had been on the dance-floor. He still held her hand, held it loosely in his long, strong fingers. And his other hand came up and traced a marvelling line down her cheek.

"Hugo... What...?" Was that her voice? That weak, breathless thing?

"You're beautiful," he said, whispered it against her neck, his mouth grazing her jaw...

And she was lost. Had been lost for twenty-three years.

Until she heard the laughter.

ONE

H UGO BLACKTON HAD NEVER been a fan of consequences.

For instance, he'd once had a Physics tutor at Harrow who had lectured long and hard about cause and effect. About how every action has an equal and opposite reaction. Hugo had mostly ignored all this, stared out of the window, and graffitied the corners of his textbooks.

Because to Hugo, consequences had never seemed as inevitable as his tutor insisted. They could be laughed off. Ignored. One could simply get too drunk to notice them. Or, failing that, leave the country and escape their reach.

These tried and tested techniques had served Hugo well for almost twenty-seven years, but now, he had a sinking sort of feeling things were catching up with him—that even he might be subject to the laws of nature. Or of society, at least.

It had started with a phone call from his father. Hugo had been in the Italian Alps, spending a rather enjoyably debauched few weeks with friends of recent acquaintance. Then his father had called, telling Hugo they had something important to discuss. And he'd said it in that tone of voice that had Hugo dragging himself regretfully from a hot tub and the wandering hands of...Whatshername...and wrapping a towel around his dripping hips, phone pressed between his ear and shoulder while he tried to hear his father over the sound of music and laughter.

"It's best if we do this face to face."

"Sure. I'll fly to London."

"Meet me at Conyers."

So here Hugo was, in deepest, darkest Lancashire at the family estate. And his father—the current Earl of Carnford as well as the founder, owner, and CEO of BlacktonGold, one of the country's largest asset management firms—had inevitably gotten held up at the London office by business far more important than the son and heir he had peremptorily summoned home.

Which left Hugo to endure a week of solitude in the rattling silence of that enormous house. A week where he had little to do but think about things he rather wouldn't. And, even worse, as the days slowly ground by, he was forced to confront one of the first major consequences of his life. He was bored. And it was all his own fault.

Normally when he was stuck at Conyers he would go next door and annoy the Banberry-Thompson sisters. It was a course of action as familiar to him as breathing. Return to Conyers, walk through the garden to the neighbouring estate, find a B-T sister, preferably Amelia because she was easier to wind up, and annoy her. But he couldn't. Because Cassie B-T was out of the country, and though he was fairly sure Amelia was at home, he was too scared to show his face after what he had done the last time they met.

Too scared to see Amy B-T.

Hugo shook his head with a small, incredulous laugh and turned away from his bedroom window. His window looked towards the Banberry-Thompson's house. And if his laugh held a slight tremor of despair, he did his best to ignore it.

For the first time in his life, he was glad when the butler knocked on his door to let him know his father had arrived. Finally, he would find out what all this was about. And then he could leave Conyers. And avoid seeing Amelia. Ideally forever.

Hugo walked through the house from his suite of rooms to his father's office on the ground floor. He would have been able to tell his father was home even without the butler's message. Something had shifted in the air. The staff walked more quickly. The reflections in the mirrors seemed to sharpen.

Not that his father was a tyrant. He was merely the sort of respected, successful man everyone sought to impress, and whom Hugo never did.

And his word was law.

He found his father standing at his office desk, briskly sorting through a stack of mail, tossing most of it into the wastepaper bin. The older man looked up as Hugo tapped lightly on the open door and flashed his eldest son a brief smile. "Hugo."

"Father."

He was dressed as usual in suit trousers and shirt, a tie and jacket presumably abandoned at some point on the journey up from the London office.

"Is Mother with you?" Hugo asked, his father's attention having already returned to the documents on his desk.

"No, I believe she had some function or other in town."

Hugo cast around for something to say. His brother Roscoe would no doubt have had a million things to discuss about the family company. His sister Evie would have prattled on about her latest do-gooding charity venture, heedless of anyone's disinterest. What could Hugo say? Complain about the party he was missing? He knew how well *that* would be received.

"Roscoe is here though," his father said.

"Really? Can the firm spare him?"

The sarcasm of his question was noticeable only to himself. He actually got on well with his younger brother, but Roscoe's determination to follow in their father's footsteps was irritatingly sycophantic—in Hugo's opinion, if not anyone else's.

Roscoe was slavishly devoted to his internship at BlacktonGold. Given he barely got paid, Hugo couldn't fathom quite why he took it so seriously.

"I asked him to come up. I decided that what I have to say, I may as well say to both of you at once."

He finally looked up from the letters on his desk. His blue eyes—several shades lighter than Hugo's—fixed on his son's face with the thoughtful but determined look that always made Hugo's chest tighten. It was the sort of look that preceded announcements like the hiring of a maths tutor when Hugo's grades in that area had proved unsatisfactory. Or the decision to make him a full boarder at Harrow with no weekend visits home. Or the repeated delaying of Hugo's promised appointment to the board of BlacktonGold...

"It concerns both your futures," his father continued. "So it seems right to hold this conversation here at Conyers. I had thought to have a proper dinner first... But we may as well get it over with. Call Roscoe for me, tell him to meet us here."

Feeling an acute sense of foreboding—the kind that dug sharply around in his gut—Hugo took out his phone and called his brother.

His father stepped around the desk, and sat back against the front edge of it, arms crossed, watching Hugo make the call. He was much broader in build than Hugo, but not quite as tall. Roscoe was their father's spitting image—they were both strong-looking men with pale blue eyes and light brown hair, though his father's was going grey. Built like rugby players rather than Hugo's leaner build. He took after his tall, slim, dark-haired mother. She had been a model.

Call made, Hugo put his phone away.

"You've been here five days?" his father confirmed.

"Six." *Waiting for you,* Hugo could have added but didn't.

"And how is Andrews getting on?"

7

Hugo paused, knowing this was a test, and knowing he was about to fail. Who the hell was Andrews? The name sounded familiar. Was it the head gardener? It couldn't be his father's driver, because he had been in London. The housekeeper? Surely not the cook. He was French. Or possibly Swiss.

"Um... He's well. I believe."

"Really? That's interesting. I heard he was still in hospital after that accident with the tractor."

"Ah. Yes... And he's doing well."

"Hm."

Luckily, Roscoe arrived and put a halt to any further questioning. Twenty-five years old and often irritatingly cheerful, Roscoe clapped his brother on the shoulder and said, "Still alive, huh? Haven't mouldered away up here just yet?"

"You need a haircut," said Hugo, eyeing Roscoe's tousled brown hair.

"Nah. Poppy likes it this way."

"Remembering a girl's name? You're doing well, Ross."

He shrugged, palms up. "Pippa? Poppy?"

"Use one nickname for all of them, that's my advice."

Their father ignored this rather ignoble exchange and gestured for them to sit on the armchairs gathered near the fireplace as he poured them all a scotch from the crystal decanter on the sideboard. It was late March, and the fire was unlit, but these were the traditional seats for discussions of importance.

Hugo sat down, his long legs stretched out and crossed casually at the ankle, though he took a large, fortifying mouthful of his drink. It still felt like there was something twisting around in his gut.

Their father cleared his throat.

"Well, boys," he said, looking at them in turn with something approaching sentimentality in his voice. He soon cleared it away with a sip of whiskey. "As you have been since the day you were born, you are the future of this family: of the Earldom, of Conyers, of the company."

Dimly, a small part of Hugo protested on his sister Evie's behalf for being left out, but it was only a small voice, and easily pushed aside. He certainly wasn't going to mention it now, not when his father was looking at him with something approaching fondness.

"Hugo. My heir. And Roscoe—"

"The spare?" quipped Roscoe.

"That's my line," drawled Hugo.

"Too slow, brother."

Their father sighed, but only a little. The boys had always known he liked their unruly spirits. Perhaps they played up to it.

"I'll get to the point, shall I?" he said, and proceeded to dump about twenty-seven years' worth of consequences at Hugo's feet.

⸺◦⸺

"A year? Here?" railed Hugo, pacing up and down the drawing room—or a portion of it, anyway. The room was far too large to pace the full length effectually. That would have been more of a stroll.

"A year managing the estate? And then he will review—*review*—my position, as though I work for him! As though I'm just another lackey, not his son, not the heir to the whole damned place!"

Roscoe just smiled in a grimacing sort of way and held out the whiskey tumbler he had refilled. Judging from the decanter, he had snagged it from their father's study. Hugo had stormed from the room, and Roscoe had followed him, though Hugo wished he hadn't.

"And you, golden boy! A full position at the company!"

"Come on, Hugh. Don't take it out on me. Besides, it's probably just as well you'll be living quietly up here given the other...ah...stipulation."

Hugo stopped pacing long enough to snatch the glass Roscoe held out to him. Some of it spilt on his hand, but he ignored it and took a burning mouthful.

"This Belgravia fund," said Hugo. "What's the dividend?"

"Currently? It's healthy. Stable. Enough to live on. If you're here—no travelling, no big purchases. Nothing, um, excessive."

Hugo snorted at that. They both knew *excessive* was his entire mode of life.

"I can't live on pocket money, Ross."

"And you don't have to. Don't you see? This is Father's way of getting you to prove you deserve a job at BG. By cutting off your allowance and making this fund your source of income for the next year, he's forcing you to learn how to invest it. There'll still be a job for you at BlacktonGold if you can show you know how to do it."

"There was always meant to be a job for me at the company, regardless."

"It was the board who voted to only appoint one additional family member. Nepotism doesn't have a great public image right now. You're the heir to the title, Hugh. There's no...um...line of descent when it comes to the company."

"Knowing you've been given the position purely on merit isn't much comfort."

Roscoe grimaced a little more. "I did the internship, Hugh. I *have* worked for this. And you... Well. You didn't."

"Prick," said Hugo, though with more fondness than venom. More quietly, he mused, "I didn't think I needed to." He turned away, sighed, and drank some more whiskey.

A year managing the estate. A year living at Conyers. A year to prove himself as responsible and capable and...*grown up*.

He'd rather be anywhere else in the whole world. Especially given he might bump into Amelia any time he stepped outside.

"You need responsibility, Hugo," his father had said, attempting to present it as an opportunity rather than a punishment. "A chance to prove yourself. Because I can't, at this point, risk taking you into the firm. We manage people's money, and that means we manage relationships. Our reputation for trust and responsibility must be maintained, and you have—I'm sorry to say—not convinced me that you are someone my clients will trust with their assets. Last summer, for example, whatever happened at Cassandra Banberry-Thompson's engagement party... Well. I've allowed you to maintain your silence on what happened that night. You're a grown-up, and so is Cassandra, and I consider it beneath all of our dignities to pry into your private affairs. But rumours do reach me. I know you were involved in the breakdown of her engagement. And the breakdown of a centuries-long friendship between our families. People talk, Hugo. And in a business like ours, where reputation is everything..." He had trailed sadly off while Hugo squirmed and glowered. "Do I need to remind you that Cassandra's ex-fiancé's father is one of my biggest clients? Not to mention a personal friend. How would it look if I made you responsible for investing his assets? It's difficult enough to get people to believe I'm appointing Roscoe on merit, but as you know, his grades from Cambridge were exemplary, and his internship performance has been first-rate. Whereas you..."

His father had paused then. As though doing him a kindness, when really he was searching for words sufficient to describe the depth of his disappointment.

A difficult task, clearly.

"You need to grow up, Hugo," he had said at last.

Hugo walked over to the fireplace and rested his forearm on

the mantelpiece. He dragged his other hand roughly through his hair and down his face.

"I kissed Amy," he said, a flash of her dark eyes haunting him.

"What?" said Roscoe.

"I kissed Amy!" he said more loudly, annoyed at having to repeat the confession. "I kissed Amelia B-T. At Cassie's party."

He practically felt Roscoe's frowning stare between his shoulder blades.

"No... You kissed *Cassie*. At Cassie's engagement party. Hence the whole marriage being called off thing."

"And I kissed Amy. After I kissed Cassie." He turned back to his brother, waving the hand that held his glass a little wildly. He would have spilt his whiskey if he hadn't drunk it all. "I kissed Cassie. And *then* I kissed Amy."

Roscoe boggled. "Both B-T girls? On the same night?"

"That was the dare."

"The...*dare?* Dare I ask about this dare? Do I want to know, Hugh?"

Hugo laughed darkly and sat down heavily in one of the armchairs, forearms on his knees, glass clutched between his hands.

"It was just a bit of fun."

"Clearly," said Roscoe, somewhat drily, given his brother's forlorn posture.

"The gang put me up to it."

"Biffy? Jay? But they weren't there."

"No, the B gang."

"Tristan and those idiots? Why would you listen to anything they said?"

"It was just a dare. Get Cassie to kiss me. I never thought she actually *would*. It was her bloody engagement party, for fuck's sake. But...Ross...it wasn't even *difficult*."

He thought back to that night, the cold, gritty feel of her silver sequinned dress under his hands, the sweet cloying taste of drink in her mouth. Not that she'd been drunk. Or not too much. She wasn't drunk enough to not know what she was doing. Red lipstick and dyed honey-blonde hair... And the way she had started laughing halfway through, then pulled his head back to hers for more...

"I think she was *glad*... I think she wanted a reason to end it."

Roscoe looked at him thoughtfully, seeming to weigh up his brother's attempt at an excuse.

"It *was* rather a rushed engagement. I never did think David was quite right for her. They're such a stuffy family. Cassie B-T would have been bored in a week."

"I honestly think I did David a favour."

Roscoe laughed, then, like the annoying little brother he was, he fixed Hugo with a merciless smile and said, "So... Amy?"

Hugo groaned and refilled his glass.

TWO

A MELIA BANBERRY-THOMPSON WRINKLED HER nose at the smell of mildew and damp, surveying the room with a dragging sense of despair.

"I do one upstairs room a month," the housekeeper was saying. "Just dusting and what-not because that's all I've got time for. So it's been a few months since I was in this room. I don't know when the leak started. I'm sorry, miss."

"It's not your fault, Sarah," Amelia said, suppressing a sigh as she stepped further into the room and gingerly lifted a mildewed book off a pile. There were dozens of ruined books, all stacked haphazardly on an old desk that had been pushed against the far wall. The dark stain on the ceiling was directly over the desk—a big black and brown spreading stain, at least a metre across, the ceiling paper buckled and bulging.

"Are all the books ruined?" asked Sarah.

"I think so. But they're only old paperbacks. The valuable books are mostly downstairs in the library."

The desk was damaged though, the antique mahogany veneer peeling. And the old rugs lying in rolls on the floor were covered in blue and white blooms of mildew.

Amelia looked up again at the ceiling. "I think it's the roof rather than a pipe. I'll get someone out to take a look."

"Shall I send Lee or someone from the garden up to clear all this lot out?"

"No, don't worry. They all have their work cut out already. Could you bring me up some bin bags, please? And perhaps some gloves? Thank you, Sarah."

Amelia stood for a moment, looking reluctantly at the stacks of mouldy things, then walked over to the window while she waited for Sarah to return.

The mid-morning sky was a silvery-grey, but there were dark clouds along the horizon where the coarse brown hills of the moors began. Fifteen or twenty miles to the north was the grander landscape of the Lake District. But here in the northern part of Lancashire, the land had a more workmanlike feel. A terse, blunt landscape, prone to rain. Rather remote in places, with scattered farms and small villages of stone houses surrounded by fields dark with mud. And to the west, out of sight from this window, was the estuarine sea and the muddy cockle beds of Morecambe Bay. A hard-working landscape, but with its own heedless beauty.

Amelia frowned at the clouds on the horizon. It seemed they were in for more rain. Exactly what they needed, with a hole in the roof and so much work to be done in the garden...

So much work always to be done.

It was late March, and the Easter weekend event that would kick off the open season at Redbridge Grange was only two weeks away. The gardens and house were still far from being ready for visitors.

And they needed visitors. They needed twice as many as the year before, because they had barely broken even. And the list of repairs and jobs and things that really ought to be done but *not quite yet*—not until there was a bit more money, not until the absolutely essential things had been paid for—that list was growing crushingly large.

She turned at the sound of the door opening, but it wasn't

Sarah, the housekeeper. It was Janson, the butler and general head of everything to do with the house. He had worked for them for thirty years, and he was as tall and straight-backed as ever, despite the silver in his hair.

"Viscount Leighton is here to see you."

A rush of heat set Amy's cheeks flaming, then just as quickly deserted her, leaving her feeling cold and slightly sick.

She half-turned back to the window, fiddling with a bit of flaking paint on the frame as she said in a light voice at odds with the heaviness in her chest, "Call him Hugo, Janson. You rescued him from the pond when he was six. You cleared up after him when he raided my father's drinks cabinet at eleven. And, more to the point, you know as well as any of us that he's a terrible, awful excuse for a human. Let's drop the title, shall we?"

Janson chuckled. "He was the one who used it." He then did a remarkably good impression of Hugo at his most pompous, drawing up one eyebrow, standing straight, shoulders back. "'Tell Miss Amelia that Viscount Leighton is here to see her.'"

Amelia snorted. "Well, tell *Lord Leighton* that Miss Amelia is not at home."

Smiling, Janson winked and left the room.

Amelia waited a while longer, frowning out of the window but no longer seeing what was in front of her. She dwelt miserably instead on unpleasant memories. On her own stupidity. On what happened the one time she stopped being the sensible one and threw caution to the wind. Because until that night, she had spent her whole life being the voice of reason, of caution, of restraint.

They called her Little Miss Good.

Not just the Blackton boys, though it had started with them. Everyone had caught onto the joke, everyone had always found a reason to laugh at her ways. As though wanting to do the right thing, as though that nagging sense that certain things were indefinably *good* and *right*—and that other things definitely weren't—was just a silly childish foible.

Somehow, she was the most sensible person around yet never taken seriously.

And maybe everyone was right, and she *was* just a naive child after all, because why else would she have let Hugo lead her to a quiet room, and why else would she have shivered, breathless, at the things he whispered against her neck—

Only an idiot would have believed them.

Especially knowing what Hugo was.

Clearly, she was an idiot.

But she already knew that. Because she had loved Hugo Blackton her whole life.

Amelia eventually gave up waiting for Sarah and went downstairs, finding the housekeeper busy dealing with a hallway radiator that was leaking unpleasant-looking brown liquid all over the antique parquet floor.

"Shall I get more towels?" asked Amelia.

"Someone's gone to get some. Sorry about the bin bags, I'll get them in just a minute—"

"No, no. Don't worry. Has someone called a plumber?"

"Yes, Janson's doing it now."

Amelia nodded, trying not to think about the bill that would follow in the plumber's wake—just as she was not thinking about the bill to fix the leaking roof—and went into the family's private kitchen in the small corner of the house they used as their living quarters.

Her mother was at the kitchen table on her laptop. She looked up excitedly as Amelia walked in.

"Guess who's going to Peru?" she asked, grinning like a

17

schoolgirl.

"Erm, you?" guessed Amelia, given it certainly wasn't her.

"Your father just called me! One of their guides got bitten by a spider and nearly lost his foot and the insurance won't let them do the next leg of the trip without a qualified replacement, and that's going to take a couple of weeks to arrange, and there's some issue with permits, so the whole film crew are stuck in Lima doing nothing—well, except for getting some location shots." She paused briefly for breath, tucking her shoulder-length dark hair behind her ears—a similar shade to Amelia's, but a little darker since she had started dying it to hide the grey. "But *mostly* with nothing to do. So your dad suggested I could come out and visit. I haven't seen him in two months! And I never get to go on location with him. Well, not anymore. Not since you girls came along." She turned back to the laptop, though her eyes had a far-away look as though she was seeing something else entirely. "Did you know I went to Thailand with him once? And to Mexico—one of his first-ever documentaries. They still show it sometimes on the Discovery Channel."

Her father was a documentary filmmaker by trade, but it was merely an excuse to spend half the year abroad—the heavy pull of Redbridge Grange, the title, the land, the history, none of it holding any real sway over his heart. Amelia often thought he had been born in the wrong era. He ought to have been discovering South America or attempting to reach the South Pole with Scott and his crew.

Instead, he made documentaries. And he was often gone, and for quite some time.

He used to make that quip before leaving on his trips—"I'm just going out. I may be some time..." Until the girls had realised he was quoting Captain Oates's final words before the man sacrificed himself in a blizzard on Scott's ill-fated expedition. And then it always set Cassie off into hysterical tears—she had a macabre imagination, fuelled by a diet of books she probably wasn't quite old enough for. Amy saved her own tears for her room, not wanting to upset anyone and knowing he needed to go, however much she wished he could stay.

"You don't mind, do you?" asked her mother, sobering a little. "I'd suggest you come too, but with the Easter opening coming up and you needing to hand things over to Cassie..."

"No, of course. I'm going away too, remember?"

"Of course! Your European trip with Evie! Well, that's good. I don't have to feel guilty at all."

"When are you leaving?"

"Soon. I'll stay until Cassie gets back because I'm desperate to see her, and then I'll be off."

Amelia nodded, going to the cupboard under the kitchen sink and looking for bin bags.

"You'll be back from Peru before I leave, won't you? Because leaving Cassie in charge of everything over the summer..."

"Of course! I'm sure I will. It'll only be a week or two, and then the film crew will be off into the mountains. I'll have my adventure, and then you'll have yours. Everything will work out perfectly."

Amelia nodded, and tried to look optimistic. Maintaining a dementedly unfounded sort of optimism was often the only way to survive the day at Redbridge.

Later that afternoon, when all the most pressing emergencies of the day were more or less dealt with, Amelia finally sat down in the estate office to go through her emails.

She needed to contact some suppliers for the Easter event. The event was the beginning of the estate's open season and was supposed to both advertise Redbridge as a tourist attraction and bring in some funds. Last year, the year after she graduated from university, had been Amelia's first time fully in charge of it. It had been a learning experience—that was one way to put it. Another was 'barely controlled chaos'. But she had enjoyed it, sort of. And it had *almost* been profitable. This year she was absolutely determined it would be.

Because it had to be.

There were other events planned for the summer, but for once Amelia wouldn't have to worry about them. She would be travelling with Evie Blackton, finally doing the post-graduation trip they had been planning for ages. There hadn't been time at the start of last year, with Amelia trying to get to grips with everything and her father out of the country. Yet again. Then there had been the rush of Cassie's engagement, the party to plan, and the mess after it.

So Amelia hadn't been able to go away last year. But this year, nothing would stop her, and she would finally get to *go* and *see* and *do*. Because she had inherited a little of her explorer father's soul.

Or maybe she just needed a break.

But at that precise moment, she was studying a portaloo catalogue, reading the enticing line '*Our toilets come with full ventilation, internal privacy door lock and coat hook.*' Which felt about as unexotic as it was possible to get.

There was a knock at the door, and she looked up to see Janson. She tensed, fearing another sortie from Hugo, but Janson said, "There's a Mr Patrick from the running club here to see you. He said you're expecting him?"

Amelia swore softly under her breath. In all the chaos of the day, she had completely forgotten the appointment. Some of the local running clubs wanted to work together to organise a large 10K run, and they had asked if it could take place on the estate.

"Yes, of course," she said, shutting down the toilet catalogue. "Show him in."

She stood up from her desk ready to shake the man's hand,

but froze.

The young man who walked in was fair-haired, disordered curls tumbling across his forehead and softening a rather rugged, ruddy face. He was wearing a plaid shirt and green cargo trousers with leather boots. And he was extremely attractive. But that wasn't why she froze.

"Toby!" she exclaimed.

He smiled warmly. "Hello, Amy. Long time, no see."

It seemed a lifetime ago that she had last seen him, though it could only have been five years. Because she had been eighteen, and so had he, and the last time they met—

He had taken her virginity.

And she had taken his.

THREE

T HE DAYS AFTER HUGO'S father's visit passed much like the ones that preceded it: in excruciating boredom.

He had even risked a visit to Amelia B-T that morning just to break the monotony. Tears, shouting, recriminations, possibly a slap around the face had all seemed preferable to another hour in his father's office going through estate reports and spreadsheets with Howell, his father's steward. But Amelia had *denied* him. And her smug butler Janson had clearly taken a huge amount of pleasure in doing it.

Denied by Amelia. Turned away with a smirk by fucking *Janson*, who had known Hugo for years, and who, therefore, certainly knew how he ought to treat the son of an Earl. But the Banberry-Thompsons had the unfortunate habit of treating their staff as though they were part of the family. It was no wonder they forgot their manners.

And now, to cap off a perfect day—a perfect week—he had a meeting with two lawyers to look forward to. Oh, the joy.

They had called yesterday, requesting a meeting to discuss "a matter of some delicacy," though they wouldn't say exactly what. He walked into his father's office, and the lawyers stood up from the chairs by the desk where they had been waiting for him.

They nodded. "Viscount Leighton."

"Take a seat," he said, gesturing to the comfier seats by the fire, where his father had recently eviscerated his character. Such fond memories this room held. And now he was seldom in any other room in the whole bloody house.

"Drink?" he asked them.

They both declined, but Hugo poured himself a scotch. It was gone noon, after all. Almost.

He joined them by the fireplace—still unlit—and stretched his legs out. He studied the lawyers for a moment. A man and a woman, both middle-aged, and both dressed extremely smartly in dark suits.

The male lawyer glanced towards the door. "Are you the sole representative of your family here today, my Lord Leighton?"

Hugo frowned in annoyance at the question. "I'm convinced I will suffice. Perhaps you could tell me what this is about?"

"Of course, Lord Leighton," said the woman, hastily retrieving some papers from her briefcase. "As you know, we're from the firm of Cole and Brook. We've recently been handling the estate of The Marchioness Banberry."

Hugo raised an eyebrow at the name. He'd met the woman once himself, at his friend Biffy Shilstone's birthday party. But despite the shared name, the Scottish Banberrys had very little to do with his neighbours at Redbridge Grange.

"There were many old documents in the archives of Castle Deveron, the property Lady Banberry inherited," continued the male lawyer. "It has taken us some time to go through them all, but we have discovered one that concerns both of your families—the Blacktons and the Banberry-Thompsons."

The female lawyer handed him a document. It seemed to be a photocopy of a very old will, written in an illegible looping script.

"This is a legal document written in 1812 by Baron Blackton, your direct ancestor, which would have been some years before the Earldom was granted."

Hugo nodded. Family history bored him.

"It seems that at the time, the Baron wished his daughter to marry into the neighbouring Banberry family. There was...um...a greater discrepancy in wealth and power between the two families then, with the Banberrys being the...more elevated, shall we say. It seems, however, that Lord Banberrys's son and heir, William, married a person of little means, a maid, in fact, by the name of Lucy Thompson."

"Old Billy Banberry knocked up a serving girl, did he?" said Hugo, taking a sip of whiskey. "Admittedly it seems more like something a Blackton would do. Though they probably wouldn't have married her."

The lawyers discretely made no comment to this.

"This marriage appears to have...um...infuriated Baron Blackton, judging from the few items of correspondence we have unearthed. His life-long wish was to unite the families. As a result, he had this document drawn up. And created the accompanying trust fund."

Hugo sat forward. "Trust fund, you say?"

The female lawyer paused before she spoke, her eyes, for some reason, flickering from Hugo to the window, which faced vaguely in the direction of Redbridge Grange.

"The document says that the money in the fund is to be released as a marriage settlement in the event of a marriage between a Blackton and a Banberry."

"Right," said Hugo. "But how much money are we talking about? Shilling and sixpence?"

"Not quite," said the lawyer. "The fund was invested and, with compound interest, is now worth...thirty-two million pounds."

Hugo stared at the lawyer for a moment, then looked down at the document he held. The scrawling words had been replaced by flashing pound signs. "Well. That's a…er…nice chunk of change."

Thirty-two million… Sixteen each if they split it. He was starting to have a vague vision of himself casually telling his father about the money, *fait accompli*. If he said, or at least strongly *insinuated*, that he got it through investing the Belgravia portfolio, then surely that would prove he had the skills to work at the company? Or at least, that he was wasted up here at Conyers, working as a glorified housekeeper.

And if his father didn't believe it… Well. He'd still be in possession of the money and have no need to beg for his allowance. And he would be free of Conyers.

"Marriage with a Banberry is the only way to release the funds?"

"As far as we can tell."

"The Lancashire Banberrys?" he confirmed, because that Scottish Marchioness was already halfway down the aisle with someone else, so Hugo didn't rate his chances there.

Not that his chances were much better next door.

"Yes. The family currently residing at Redbridge Grange. They are the direct descendants."

"Hm," said Hugo.

"Of course, we should advise that…um…marriage is an institution not to be taken lightly, and that financial considerations should play no part—"

"Yes, yes. But do they know? The Banberry-Thompsons? Have you met with them?"

"We met with Lady Banberry-Thompson earlier today."

That was Amelia's mother.

"And was anyone else present at the meeting?"

"No, my Lord."

"Did Caroline—Lady Banberry-Thompson—mention telling the family? Her daughters?"

"That is not information we possess."

Hugo sat back, deep in thought, only dimly aware of the look the lawyers exchanged.

"This is a layperson's summary of the legal document," the female lawyer said, putting some papers down on the small table next to his chair. "And a current financial statement of the fund."

Hugo picked it up, eyes drawn to the figure at the bottom of the column.

"How I love compound interest," he murmured, before looking up as the lawyers prepared to leave.

"We would recommend speaking to your own legal advisor," the male one said. "But we are happy to answer any questions you might have."

He handed Hugo a business card, and Hugo showed them to the door where the butler was hovering, waiting to escort them from the house.

He stood absently for a moment, looking blankly down the empty corridor long after they had left, then returned to his father's office. He finished his whiskey, looking out of the window in the direction of Redbridge.

Marry one of the B-T girls...

Was it possible? Would they ever say yes?

It would have to be Amelia, of course. Cassie wasn't in the country. And he doubted she would contemplate even a temporary sham marriage so soon after the breakdown of her engagement with David.

But Amelia... Amelia...

The last time he saw her, she had run crying from the room.

But a few moments before *that*...

She had kissed him. She might be persuadable.

The problem with Amelia B-T though was that she was Little Miss Good. She had *principles*. And how he hated principles.

Because he knew that even though Amelia's family needed the money, if he made this about *that*, Amelia would blanch and refuse, despite it being a perfectly sensible suggestion. Get married for a day or two, and both end up sixteen million pounds richer. Anyone else in the world would say yes. But Amelia...

He would have to go carefully. Win her over gradually. Get her forgiveness before he raised the idea of marriage.

Get her to like him again.

Because Amelia wasn't the sort of girl who would marry him for money.

But she might do it for love.

———◆———

"I just didn't connect the name at all," Amelia said dazedly as she shook Toby's warm hand.

He smiled again. "I wouldn't expect you to. Like I said, it's been a while. I admit though... I *may* have volunteered when this meeting was suggested."

He laughed and scratched a jaw that was, Amelia couldn't help but notice, much firmer than it had been the last time they met.

They'd been at sixth form college together, each a member of different friendship groups that overlapped. And in the summer after sixth form ended, those groups had more or less merged, and eventually, she and Toby had started a vaguely defined relationship. They'd both been shy about it, and so they didn't get together until August, meaning they lasted all of six weeks before university started. And those weeks had involved little more than some mild hand-holding, a few cinema dates, and some self-conscious kisses.

Until a house party the day before Amelia left for university, when, emboldened by drink, they revealed to each other that neither wanted to start university a virgin.

Toby had been nice. Convenient. Non-threatening. An extremely sensible choice for Little Miss Good to make. He was the son of a farmer and despite the hours he laboured on the farm, his face still retained a little puppy fat. He wore baggy, faded corduroy trousers and ugly jumpers with ragged cuffs, and his hair had been cut shorter, his fringe flattened to his head...

In short, he hadn't looked anything like he looked now. Because nonthreatening was not the word. *This* boy, this *man*... She would never have had the courage to date him.

"You're...erm...with the running club?" she asked stupidly.

"Yes. Actually, I founded it. This branch of it, anyway."

She started to gesture to some seats in front of her desk, but the thought of sitting almost knee-to-knee, eye-to-eye with him seemed a bit too much, so she gestured to the door instead.

"We may as well walk the grounds as we talk. Kill two birds with one stone."

Toby nodded amiably and followed her from the room.

"What made you take up running?" Amelia asked as they navigated the corridors to one of the house's many back doors. "I would have thought the farm work would be exercise enough. If you're still doing that?"

"I am. And still the same farm. I never actually made it to agricultural college."

She glanced at him. "Oh?"

"My father got sick. Cancer. He's OK now, in the clear, we think, but he had several surgeries and they left him unable to do a lot of the heavier work. So I stepped in. Never really stepped out." He shrugged slightly then looked up at the sky as they exited the house, seeming to give the coming weather a practised assessment. Or maybe he found that easier than meeting her eye.

"I'm sorry," she said. "I had no idea."

He looked back at her with an easy smile. "Don't be. The farm was always in my future. I just came to it a few years sooner than I expected. And I love the work." He scrubbed a hand through the short curls at the back of his head. "But it's tough. Not easy to make a living from it."

They were walking now through the somewhat neglected and weedy parterre—the formal garden on the terrace at the back of the house, with its once neat lines of box hedges now straggly and frost-bitten from the winter. The large fountain in the centre of it had broken last summer—in the middle of the heat wave, of course—and was now full of dead leaves floating thickly over stagnant water.

"But that's why I started running," Toby continued. "Mental health. If it's not too soon to get onto such a heavy topic. I needed a way to deal with the stress. And a time that was just for myself, away from the demands of the farm and everything."

Amelia nodded, fully able to empathise.

"Enough about me, anyway," he said. "Tell me about you. What have you been up to these last five years?"

"I did get away... To university. And now...well...I suppose I'm back." She shrugged and gave a small laugh.

"You're living here at Redbridge?"

"Yes."

He glanced back at the house. "Not a bad little pad, eh?"

"A very large and draughty pad."

"Mm. The old farmhouse isn't much better. Mum and Dad are in a little bungalow now. Dad says he hates it, but it's a damn sight warmer and more convenient."

"And you live at the farmhouse?" Which was the closest she could get to asking *"You live there alone?"*

But Toby clearly heard the question behind her words, or perhaps he just wanted to volunteer the information. "Yep. Just me and the dogs."

29

Amelia nodded, suddenly shy. Not that she was interested in Toby in that way. Not that she was looking to start a relationship with anyone right now. But it would always inevitably be awkward, she mused, to talk to a man who had once been...well...*inside* you.

"Erm..." she said, shaking away that unhelpful line of thought. "So, in terms of the run, I've been looking at the footpaths through our land, seeing how we can join them up into some kind of circuit..."

"I can do that, if you send me the maps. I'll come up with some routes, and you can tell me if they're feasible."

"Of course."

They stepped down from the parterre and onto the lawn. Amelia headed across the garden to a row of distant trees. Enormous old cedars grew along a tall brick wall, and even further along, was the start of a wood.

"While you're here, shall I show you the path through the oak wood? I'm not sure if it's going to be wide enough, but I thought it could be a nice section."

"Lead the way," said Toby with another easy smile.

But as they drew nearer to the brick wall, a tall, dark-haired figure stepped through the gate that was set into it. Amelia stopped dead, because it was Hugo, and she had no Janson to shut the door in his face, no door at all to hide behind.

"Hello, Amy."

FOUR

T HERE WAS A MAN with Amelia, which was a bloody in-
convenience. A young, fair-haired man, about her age or
his.

Amelia flushed, her cheeks turning almost the same dusky
shade of pink as her lips. As usual, her brown hair was scraped
back into a messy knot, and, as usual, she was wearing jeans and
a shapeless dark jumper. She was not, and never had been, a girly
girl. She stood regarding him with a grave, implacable coolness,
which was an improvement on the feared hysterics but didn't
bode well for a warm reception.

"Toby," she said to the man beside her, who was studying
Hugo with polite interest. "This is my neighbour Hugo from
next door."

She left off his titles to annoy him, he just knew it.

"And Hugo, this is my old friend Toby. He's captain of the
local running club."

The man stepped forward and shook his hand. "Viscount
Leighton," he said. "I know you by reputation. I know your father—well, I know his steward Howell better. We farm around
a thousand acres of your land, mostly just outside Kelleton."

"Ah," said Hugo, wondering if he was supposed to know
these sorts of things. Or care. "Pleasure."

He was more interested in what exactly being Amelia's "old

friend" involved. From a pedantic point of view, he could argue that *he* was her oldest friend, having known her since she was born. He had been about four years old, and he still had a hazy recollection of being brought over to Redbridge and told to sit down and be quiet while the grownups cooed over a red-faced creature wrapped in white blankets.

He smiled at the man. "What brings you to Redbridge, Toby?"

Toby looked briefly at Amelia with a fond smile that Hugo found intensely irritating. "Amelia's family are kindly considering hosting a running event here on the estate. We're just ironing out some plans."

"Yes, I was about to show Toby the oak wood path, so if you'll excuse us..." Amelia turned to go.

"A running event?" Hugo asked Toby before he could follow. Amelia paused with a barely suppressed sigh.

"Yes, a 10k."

"And there's enough room here at Redbridge for that?"

"If we do two or three circuits..."

"But perhaps...not the most exciting route...?"

"Are you volunteering the use of Conyers?" Amelia asked, head tilted sweetly. Because damn it, of course he wasn't.

"Erm..."

"I couldn't impose on Lord Leighton," began Toby.

"But it's for such a good cause," said Amelia. "I'm sure Hugo and his family wouldn't mind."

Given Conyers had never once been opened to the public in its three-hundred-year history, Amelia patently knew this was untrue.

"And with your lake," she continued, "you could even think about hosting a triathlon one day!"

Toby brightened. "You know, that *was* one of the original ideas—"

"I'll think about it," said Hugo shortly. "And now I'll let you get on with your walk. Before it rains."

Toby glanced sagely up at the sky. "Reckon it'll hold off till five, maybe six."

Hugo smiled thinly.

He stepped back through the gate as they walked away, but he stayed where he was, hand on the edge of the brick arch, looking over the manicured grass to the perfectly symmetrical mass of Conyers House in the distance.

Behind him was Redbridge, a little wilder, scruffier, older. He leant back against the brick with that feeling of being poised on the edge of two worlds, much as he always had as a boy.

The gate itself had once been painted blue, but so long ago that only flakes of colour remained on the warped and weathered wood. It was always open, it had been open his whole life, grass growing up around the gate's base, the soil under the archway worn into a hollow by the passing of so many feet. Though weeds were growing now.

As children, they had all—Hugo, Roscoe, Evelyn, Cassie, Amelia—crossed back and forth through the gate, roaming the grounds of Conyers and Redbridge as one scruffy, rather wild pack, climbing trees, stealing fruit from under the gardeners' noses, playing tennis, cricket, football, chase, hide and seek...

Or at least until he and his brother Roscoe had reached double-digits and realised playing with a bunch of girls was not cool.

Then he had been away at boarding school, followed by university, and then living in London, and he had hardly seen Amelia and Cassie at all, except at Christmases and birthdays and the other infrequent visits he made home.

He had to duck these days, to fit through the gate. The arch in the brick had been built two hundred years ago, presumably when people were shorter, because Hugo, at six-foot-two, was taller than the gate itself. And once it had seemed so big, so important...

The portal from Conyers to another world, a merrier one, where muddy footprints weren't quite so scolded, and the Banberry-Thompson's father, big and curly-haired, boomed his way around the ancient flagstoned hallways on his visits home, two giggling dark-haired girls clinging impishly to his legs.

Or so Hugo remembered it. Drinking lemonade in the Redbridge kitchen. Tennis racket in a sweaty hand. Roscoe begging the cook for biscuits, Evie humming as she stroked the fat ginger cat that slept in the sun on the kitchen doormat and thus got tripped over fifteen times a day. Cassie arguing with anyone who would listen, and Amelia, little Amy, quiet somewhere in the background, getting Roscoe his biscuits, handing Hugo a wet cloth for the graze on his knee from tripping over that damned cat...

Little Amy. Little Miss Good. It should have been easy to get her to go along with this wedding, just another scrape in a long line of stupid scrapes, Amy, his disapproving little shadow, always there to step in and rescue things before they went too far wrong...

If only he hadn't kissed her.

If only she didn't hate him.

He stepped back through the gate into Redbridge. Amelia and Toby were dots in the distance before the wood. Walking quickly, Hugo crossed the gardens and made his way to Redbridge Grange.

The paths she had walked with Toby were muddy, and Amelia's shoes and jeans were splattered with it by the time she returned home. She kicked her shoes off in the coat room, then walked tiredly upstairs to change and shower before dinner.

But she stopped dead in her doorway, because Hugo was sitting on her bed. All six-foot-something of his dark-haired arrogance leaning back against her headboard, navy blue eyes smiling at her.

"Hello," he said as she stood and stared. "Just who I was hoping to see."

"I don't know who else you were expecting to see in my bedroom."

Hugo lifted a corner of her duvet and peeped underneath. "Not much traffic in here, hm? Pity."

"Get out."

He lifted his hands. "Don't worry. I'm not here to ravish you. Unless you want...? No?"

She stared at him, her shock swiftly transmuting into rage. "How dare you come into my room—"

"It's hardly the first time I've been in here. You used to drag me here to play Barbies. I'm fairly sure I remember you giving me a very fetching make-over at that dressing table over there, complete with fake eyelashes and everything."

"Get. Out."

"Actually, weren't the lashes Cassie's? I seem to remember her being very angry about something..."

She stalked to her desk and grabbed the old-fashioned house phone, stabbing the number for the staff quarters. "Is Janson there—?"

"What? Wait—"

Hugo flew across the room and pulled the handset from her, dropping it back onto the cradle and cutting the call.

"Don't get me thrown out, Amy. I only want to talk to you."

He was right there, looming over her. This was the closest they had been since that disastrous night last year. Their chests were inches apart, and his navy eyes took possession of hers, holding her still, though her heart jack-hammered and her mind skittered crazily about like a mouse in a box seeking a way out. But instead, it got stuck on irrelevant things like the width of his shoulders and the strong line of his neck and the deep colour of his lips, which always looked as though they had just been kissed—

And she couldn't help but remember that moment before his mouth had come down to meet hers, the way her stomach had swooped and then flown—

His eyes dipped momentarily, as though he too remembered.

"I don't want to talk to you!" she said through gritted teeth. "Haven't I made that clear?"

"Admittedly, I've been getting a slight hint of reluctance—"

She made a noise, half-groan, half-shout, and turned away from him, flinging herself down into the chair by the small desk she kept in her room.

"Amy—"

"Don't call me that."

"It's sort of your name...?"

She crossed her arms, trying to still her body's ridiculous trembling. "Only my friends call me Amy."

"Come on, surely we're still friends? We've known each other our whole lives."

"And that didn't even give you a moment's pause, did it? Not when it might have interfered with your stupid prank."

"It was more of a wager..." He held up a conciliatory hand at her murderous expression. "OK, I admit, it perhaps wasn't my finest hour."

"Do you *have* any? Are there any *fine hours* in your life, Hugo? Moments that you look back on with pride?"

He laughed a little haltingly, looking away, and scratched his jaw.

For a second she thought perhaps she had hit her mark, but when he turned back he was smiling, those navy blue eyes smouldering with their familiar wicked heat. And she wished she hadn't sat down, because he seemed taller than ever as he looked down at her.

"Oh, dozens…" he said. "Dozens and dozens of extremely fine hours." He nodded carelessly towards the bed. "Most of them in places like that, come to think of it."

"You're vile."

He shrugged and sat back against the edge of her desk, his leg only inches from her knees. "Amy, I'm here to say sorry. What will it take?"

"Your head on a stake?"

"Perhaps something that doesn't require my dismemberment…?"

"Nope. Can't think of anything."

"You do realise you kissed me back? Quite enthusiastically, if I recall—"

Amy shot to her feet. "You filmed it on your phone!"

Oh God…

She stepped unseeing down her room, feeling that hot, humiliating sickness again, the moment she had realised—

Hugo's lips on hers, indecent and demanding, kissing her like she had always known he would, drawing the secret of her helpless desire from her with every touch of his tongue—

And then, they had broken apart, breathless, needing air.

Or so she thought. Until she realised with a disorientating lurch that he was not looking at her but was glancing at the phone he held aloft—

Checking they were centred in the video he had been taking of their kiss.

Though he didn't need the proof, because even as Amelia dazedly stepped back from him, still trying to make sense of what was going on, still feeling the burn of his lips on hers, she heard men laughing. Hugo's friends, poking their heads around the door, braying and sniggering and calling out, "No way! Blackton did it! He scored the B-T double!"

She had met Hugo's eyes for one horrified moment as comprehension dawned. And she had seen the grim triumph that gleamed there.

And she had run crying from the room.

"I didn't, actually," he said now.

She turned back to him, still reeling from the weight of that awful memory. "What?"

He shrugged one shoulder. "I meant to record it. But I didn't press the button."

"That's... As if that even matters!"

"I guess I was distracted," he said, looking her over, eyes lingering on her mouth, a smile tugging the corner of his. "You really are an *exceptionally* good kisser. Who would have thought it? Little Miss Good, and an absolutely filthy tongue."

Stupidly, she felt sudden tears prick her eyes. Because he was still laughing at her, even now, having kissed her. Even having stolen the secret of her hunger for him—had that decade-long secret amply, *enthusiastically,* demonstrated—she was still a joke.

"Go away, Hugo. Please. Just go away."

She was more of a joke than ever.

FIVE

H UGO WATCHED AMY AS she slumped down to sit on the edge of her bed, shoulders bowed. For a terrifying moment he thought she was going to cry. Her voice had cracked ever so slightly as she told him to go away.

Now though, she just looked glum and tired, staring fixedly at a spot on the floor. Looking sad rather than angry.

It wasn't an improvement.

"Amy... Amelia... It was just a kiss. It's not worth being this upset over. I don't think even Cassie cares as much as you do. You know it wasn't personal. I didn't set out to *hurt* you. It was only a bit of fun."

She didn't say anything, didn't react at all, just stared unmoving at that spot on the floor.

Hugo sighed, getting a little irritated, because he was starting to have the uncomfortable feeling that he needed to do *more*, but he was at a loss what exactly that ought to be. And Amelia was being no help at all.

Then she said in a flat, hollow voice, "Why did you say the things you said?"

"What? What things?"

"Before you kissed me. Why did you say those things?"

Hugo tried to think back to that rather blurry night. He'd been quite drunk, and besides, it was ages ago...

Redbridge Grange, the house full of people... Music, dim lights, bright lights, voices, laughter, booze, lots of booze, girls in short dresses, long legs everywhere, men in suits, in tuxes...

His hands on Cassie's hips, those silver sequins slipping like cold scales beneath his fingers... Boxing her into a corner, one hand on the wall by her head, the other hand on her waist, his mouth bent to her ear saying... What?

You look so sexy in this dress...

One last chance...

A goodbye kiss...

Some nonsense or other, whatever rubbish had come to mind, then his hand turning her jaw to him, his eyes on hers for a moment, the bright thrill he saw there, the slight wildness, the decision being made, and then lips meeting, mouths moving, all the mechanical aspects of a kiss, none of the heat.

And after that? He didn't really know. Laughter, his friends around him, celebratory shots being pressed into his hands, the burn of tequila—and he *hated* tequila—

And sometime later... Seeing Amelia across the dancefloor in a dark-blue dress, dancing with Evie, laughing at something, her dark eyes bright. And Hugo had smiled because it felt good to see her, such a familiar, friendly face, after so long away...

And someone, watching the direction of his gaze, had said, "Thinking about the double, huh? Both B-T girls in one night. Don't reckon even you could pull that one off..."

Hold my beer...

"What did I say?" he asked Amelia, suddenly wishing he could remember.

She folded her arms where she sat, eyes still on the floor. "You told me I was beautiful. You told me you'd wanted to kiss me for years."

"You *are* beautiful."

She shot him a look.

"You are," he said again, taking the opportunity to be truthful about at least one of the things he had supposedly said. Because the other one was too awkward to either admit or deny. "Cassie too. You both are."

Amelia snorted and rolled her eyes. "Of course. So you had to kiss us both. You just couldn't help yourself."

"I didn't exactly force myself on either of you, and you know it. And as for Cassie... Do you really think she should have married David? They'd only been together a few months. Did you actually see it lasting?"

"They never got the opportunity to find out, did they?"

"You think she loved him? And was going to live happily ever after with him when she stuck her tongue down my throat at the first opportunity?"

Amelia scoffed. "How are you managing to make it sound like you did her a *favour*?"

"She was marrying him for the money."

Amelia flashed him a look of outrage.

"It was obvious," he said before she could speak. "Everyone knows your family is broke. And his owns half of England."

"This isn't a Regency novel!"

"He'll be a Duke one day. I hear women still quite like that. They certainly like the heirs to Earls," he said with a grin, enjoying the rage on Amy's face. It was far better than seeing her sad.

"You're unbelievable. I don't know why I ever—"

"Ever what?"

"Nothing."

"Ever kissed me?"

"No."

"Because I might not remember what I said. But I do remember the kiss."

He couldn't help but look at her mouth as he said it. His mother always said the B-T girls were chocolate and peaches,

41

and he thought he knew what she meant. Their eyes and hair were dark—or Cassie's had been, before she went blonde—and their lips and cheeks were pink; Amelia's lips a rich, dusky pink, entirely natural. And he could remember the shocking pleasure of them, so perfectly warm and soft and seeking, and her tongue finding his, asking for more... And the sound she made when he gave it to her...

He cleared his throat, disorientated by the blood rushing to his cock and the sudden urge to taste her again.

"Do you know what I remember, Hugo? I remember the sound of your friends laughing. I remember looking up and finding your phone camera aimed at us. I remember the *humiliation*. That's what I remember." She stared at him, eyes bright with the sheen of unshed tears.

"Amy..."

He walked softly over to her. She flinched as he dropped to a crouch by the bed, and he had to admit, that flinch didn't make him feel particularly great. He stopped himself from taking hold of her hand, not wanting to have her recoil from him.

"I'm sorry. And I'm especially sorry that I made you cry."

"Did you just say...the *S-word*?"

"What? Sorry?"

She drew a theatrical breath and looked around in mock panic. "Do you feel that? I think the earth is shaking! The sky is falling!"

"Hah-hah. Very funny. But I mean it. I want to make things right. My father isn't happy about this breach between our families, and I—"

"*That's* what you care about? Your father?"

"That's not what I said."

"That's exactly what you said!"

"I meant that I agree with him. That I'd rather go back to how things were before."

Amy said nothing, and Hugo sighed. He felt a bit ridiculous crouched on the floor at her feet. She was resolutely not meeting his eyes, her arms still folded, face turned to the side. Her jeans, he couldn't help but notice, were absolutely filthy with mud around the hems.

He absently reached out to scratch a dried splatter of it from her knee, and then they both froze as they realised what he was doing. He dropped his hand.

"How do you know this Toby, anyway?"

"Your apology's over, is it?"

"No. But I'm clearly making a hash of it. I figure I'll try again when you're in a better mood."

"Well, thank goodness I have something to look forward to."

"Will you ever believe I'm sorry?"

"I believe you feel sorry for yourself. I believe you're sorry that people are angry with you and that life is a little uncomfortable for you right now. And I believe you're sorry that no one is bending over backwards to make things right for you. But that you're actually, genuinely *sorry*? No. I don't think you're capable of it."

Her brown eyes glittered as they met his, her chin tipped up resolutely.

He was used to Amy's disapproval. It was a constant companion of his life. But this merciless...disdain? This *contempt*? That was new. He didn't like it.

He got to his feet and moved a few steps away from the bed. For the first time, he started to feel unsure. The ultimate goal—getting the money, getting Amelia to agree to help him—seemed laughably distant.

And he didn't feel much like laughing.

He turned back towards her, catching her in the act of studying him. She bit her lip, looking down.

"Tell me what to do," he said.

"No."

"Amy... Just tell me how to fix this. Please."

"No." She stood up, and there was a dismissal in her tone, as though she was already relegating him to yesterday's news. To the past.

"I'm not telling you what to do, Hugo," she said, going to a chest of drawers and rummaging through it for some clothes. "Because unlike almost everything else in the world, it's not my responsibility. And because, quite honestly, there's nothing you *can* do. It was unforgivable, Hugo. So, no, I can't forgive you."

She closed her drawer, clean clothes in one hand, and looked at him without quite meeting his eyes.

"I really did mean it when I asked you to leave. The only thing you *can* do...? Go away. Leave me alone."

She walked into her en suite bathroom and turned the lock with a resolute snap.

SIX

A MELIA WOKE THE NEXT morning feeling drained. She had spent an embarrassing amount of time last night crying into her pillow. And she *hated* crying.

She hated Hugo. She hated herself for ever believing even for one moment that he might have meant the things he said. She hated that her whole life had been spent longing for him. And most of all she hated the fact that she couldn't hate him enough to get over him.

He had been right when he'd said they'd known each other their whole lives. And that entire time she had been in thrall to him. As a toddler, she called him Googo, and followed him everywhere, or as best she could, because he had been six, seven, eight years old and impossibly fast and long-legged. And he had known all the best hiding places. And he could climb all the tallest trees. And even then, he laughed at her, and called her Splat, because she had once dropped the whole top of her ice cream on the floor and cried for what seemed like forever.

And, of course, it was *Roscoe* who gave her half of his, while Hugo just snorted and rolled his blue eyes, and she wanted to kick him and pull his almost-black hair.

But he was their King. He was the eldest and the strongest. The quickest and the wildest. And he cared about nothing. He was tall and lean and mocking. His hair was dark and his eyes were the deepest sort of blue and his skin was a little pale, and he fascinated her—the way he moved, the way he spoke, the way blue and black and white all shifted and flashed as he ran and jumped and climbed.

And hung upside down from trees and threw mud on her teddy bear's picnic.

She yearned for him in the sexless way that small girls yearn for ponies, unicorns, dragons... Fantastic beasts that promise adventure. And danger.

Because he had always seemed dangerous. There was a feral, feline grace to his leanness. And as he grew older and harder, that promise of danger seemed to coalesce into something that whispered of secrets and shadows and seductive disgrace.

And Amelia began to yearn for him in a different way.

The problem with liking someone for so long was that they didn't just take up residence in one's brain—they shaped it around themselves. Like a tree growing up around an unyielding fence, until the tree enclosed it, and the fence ran right through its heart.

That was Hugo. A wormy, rotten sort of fence.

She'd always known he wasn't *good*. Anyone could see that. His personality was dreadful. Which had led her to the inescapable reason that she liked him purely for his looks—and that was a rather mortifying realisation for the sensible, level-headed Amelia.

It turned out that she was shallow. And had terrible taste in men.

These edifying thoughts were still heavy in her heart when she dragged herself out of bed and went downstairs for breakfast.

Despite her reputation for hard work, she wasn't much of a morning person, and she was extremely tired, so it was almost nine when she sat down at the table with some toast and a cup of tea. Her mother was out. She liked to go and feed the chickens before breakfast.

Janson came into the kitchen. "Morning. There's a...um...delivery for you. But I'm not sure if you'll want me to sign for it."

"Why? What is it?"

"I think you'd best see for yourself."

She followed him to the side door of the house, which was the one used for deliveries and general comings and goings—the rather grand front entrance really only used when the house was open to the public.

A delivery driver was just outside the door, and on the ground at his feet was the most enormous and elaborate bouquet of flowers Amelia had ever seen.

It was just as well she didn't want it, because she doubted it would have fit through the door.

"Hugo," she muttered darkly.

Janson nodded. "I saw it was his name on the consignment sheet when they asked me to sign for it. That's why I...um...wanted to check with you first."

"Can you return it to the sender?" she asked the driver, who was looking rather impatient and annoyed.

"Not really, miss, I only get paid for deliveries."

"I'll take it over," said Janson when the driver left. "Any message to give?"

"No." She shook her head. "No. Just take them away."

Amelia was spring-cleaning the drawing room when her mother came to find her—dusting inside the display cabinets, which was an irritatingly painstaking task, as all the fragile ornaments and things had to be removed and carefully dusted as well. She quite often had the urge to bin the whole lot. But given they were a priceless family collection, that probably wouldn't have been prudent.

"Did you see Cassie's email?" her mother asked as Amelia laboriously removed dust from the intricate carvings around the rim of a Wedgewood plate. How things got so dusty inside the cabinets, she had no idea.

"No, I've not had a chance to check my emails today."

"She's thinking of staying in Canada another week or two. Some friend or other is coming to stay and she doesn't want to miss them."

Amelia set the delicate plate down and slowly stretched the fingers of her suddenly rigid hand. "She's not coming back?"

"Not *yet*..."

"Right."

"It's just... As you know, I *had* been planning to stay until she came back, so I could get a chance to see her, but if I do that then there's not much point in me going to Peru at all. The film crew should have everything sorted in a few weeks and then they'll be back filming and I will have missed my chance."

Amelia turned back to the display cabinet and kept her eyes on the dusty dark corners of it as she took a deep breath and let it slowly out. "Of course. I understand. You can't miss this opportunity. And someone has to keep an eye on Dad, right? Because I'm sure he's going to go native one of these days and never return."

She turned back to her mother and managed a smile.

Her mother returned the smile gratefully. "Are you sure you don't mind? Cassie will be back in plenty of time to get up to speed before you leave for your Europe trip."

"Yes. I'm sure. So... When are you off?"

"I may as well go right away if I'm not waiting for Cassie. I need to check flights, but possibly tonight or tomorrow."

Amelia just nodded and reached back into the cabinet for another piece to dust. There was a sort of keening, whistling noise in her brain, a bit like tinnitus, or a kettle on the boil. And her chest felt a little tight. But she ignored those things as she always did, and extracted another plate. This one featured a bewigged and powdered fop in a long blue coat leaning over a blushing maiden. There was also a lamb frolicking nearby. She supposed it was symbolic.

He's an idiot, she silently told the blushing maiden. *Don't fall for his charms.*

"Why are you dusting, anyway?" her mother asked. "Where's Sarah? Or Eszter?"

"Eszter's daughter is off school sick, so she couldn't come in. And Sarah is trying to remove that mark on the floor from the leaking radiator."

Her mother looked around the room, frowning. "I'm sorry to leave you with all this. Should I not go? Say the word, Amelia, and I'll stay."

As if it was that easy.

"It's fine. There's still nearly two weeks until we open."

"I'm sure we must have money for another cleaner. Just a temporary one."

"But it's so hard to find ones with the experience to deal with antiques. You know that."

"I know, but... Surely we can find one to just dust and do general things?"

"Do you remember the one who sprayed furniture polish on the Chippendale writing desk and took the finish right off? Cost a fortune to get it restored."

Her mother grimaced. "Don't remind me." She sighed unhappily, looking around the room again, then absently picked up one of the plates Amelia had cleaned. "Well. I know I can trust you to do the right thing. If there's anyone who knows best how to look after Redbridge, it's you. I honestly think we'd be lost without you."

Amelia just nodded and tried to take that as a compliment. But it felt like a lead weight.

————◦————

Even though she had told her mother and informed the staff that she would be out for lunch, Amelia still felt she was doing something sneaky as she grabbed her car keys and bag and headed for the yard at the side of the house where the car she shared with her mother was parked.

But maybe that was due to the unfamiliarity of it. It had been...two...? Two whole weeks since she had last left the estate and gone into town, and even then she had only gone to drop off some dry cleaning for her mother and collect some wire from the hardware shop for Hodge, the Head Gardener. This time she was going for *lunch*.

With Toby.

He had suggested it so casually as they walked around the estate—just two old school friends catching up—that she had agreed without even thinking much about it. Until a few moments ago, when she found herself in her room, looking critically at herself in the mirror on her wardrobe and wondering if she ought to get changed, because she was still in the old jeans and jumper she had worn for dusting the drawing room. And perhaps... Perhaps she ought to maybe try and look a little nicer?

She had frowned at herself in the mirror at that thought. She hated thinking about her appearance. It led to all sorts of annoying questions like: When had she actually last had a haircut? And, should she start wearing gloves when working so that her fingernails weren't quite so battered and broken? And did she even *have* anything nice to wear at all?

And why should she care anyway?

It wasn't a date.

But she had put on some slim black jeans, and some ankle boots, and a newish jumper that she hadn't, to her knowledge, yet worn for stable duty or gardening or scrubbing the floor.

And she had brushed her hair. And put on some lip gloss. Then wiped it off, because it felt kind of gross and annoying.

The low heels of her boots made an unfamiliar clacking sound on the flagstone floor as she headed outside, and she had a twisty, excited feeling in her stomach, as though she was doing something daring and exciting. But when she got to the yard, she stopped dead.

Lee, the Stable Master, roared through the gate in one of the estate's old Land Rover pickups and jumped out, shouting at her, "Hurdles? Are they still in the barn? Call Chris in from the garden. We need his help."

Amelia hurried after Lee's enormous form as he practically ran into the old barn.

"What's going on? The sheep?"

She knew Lee and Hodge had been planning to move the estate's small flock of heritage sheep to a new field today. It seemed things were not going entirely well.

"Aye, the bloody sheep!" Lee flung over his shoulder, hauling some old metal sheep hurdles out from behind a heap of assorted junk. They looked a bit like metal gates or fence panels and were used for penning and directing sheep. "Flock broke up when we were halfway down the lane with them. Some idiot in a low-flying plane came over and startled them. They've scattered all over."

"Is it that annoying buzzy little plane I've been hearing all morning?" asked Amelia, grabbing some plastic buckets and looking around for sheep nuts. "I thought it was the gliding club, but they don't normally come this far."

Lee carried the hurdles out and threw them into the bed of the pickup. The Stable Master was a big, powerfully built man,

51

alarmingly gruff on first acquaintance, but incredibly gentle with any non-human living thing.

"Nope," growled Lee. "Not a glider."

"Let's drive the lodge route," said Amelia, clambering into the passenger side of the Land Rover. "We can pick Chris up on the way. He was meant to be up in the orchard today."

Lee nodded and set off. "Thought you was out today?"

"Meant to be," said Amelia ruefully, bracing herself on the door as the Land Rover took a pothole at speed. "Actually, I should probably..."

She got her phone out, biting her lip for a moment, then steeling herself with an in-breath. She dialled the number Toby had given her.

"Hi. I'm so sorry, I'm not going to be able to make it. The sheep have got out..."

Toby listened to her slightly garbled explanation, which was briefly interrupted by needing to get out and hail Chris. Amelia squeezed herself into the middle seat, a lanky gardener on one side, Lee's enormous bulk on the other.

"Maybe another day?" she said to Toby.

"Whereabouts are you? I'll come help out."

"Oh... But... No, that's very kind, but... Aren't you an arable farmer, anyway?"

Toby chuckled. "Yes, potatoes mainly. But I can hold a hurdle and shake a bucket or whatever else you need. Tell me where you are. I'm just in town, so I'll only be ten minutes or so."

So she told him. And then Lee was pulling up, and they were piling out, finding the crabby old gardener Hodge leaning on a fence and looking balefully at half a dozen rather hefty looking sheep that were very definitely not meant to be in the field of turnips they were currently in.

"Bloody Lonks," he grumbled, that being the name of this particular breed of sheep. "Mad, the lot of 'em."

Just then, the distant sound of the plane grew louder—and louder. Amelia looked up in disgust as a small red plane came into view over the top of a nearby copse of trees. It was extremely low and she scowled as the roaring sound sent the sheep fleeing across the field.

And then her scowl froze, because the plane was pulling a banner, and the banner said: *SORRY AMY*.

She found the others looking at her, Lee scratching his jaw awkwardly. "Ehh, yeah... Didn't want to say anything. Janson thought it best not to."

Amy looked back up at the plane, watching it sail over the trees and out of sight towards Redbridge.

"That. Bloody. Idiot."

Chris and Lee laughed. Hodge nodded sagely.

Furious, she pulled out her phone and took a few steps away. It barely had a chance to ring before Hugo answered.

"Amy," he purred. "I h—"

"Your plane is scaring my sheep! Get rid of it! Now!"

She hung up before he could speak. Then she redialled. "And stop being a bloody idiot!"

She shoved her phone into her pocket, quite literally trembling with rage.

Hodge spat on the ground and straightened up from the fence. "Well," he said slowly, nodding towards the field. "Reckon we've got some work to do."

SEVEN

AMELIA WAS EXHAUSTED, HOT, and filthy by the time all the sheep were in the correct field. Her black jeans and the ankle boots she had worn were wet and sticky with mud.

But, strangely...she'd had fun.

Toby had arrived just as they got to work. He'd worked well, and hard, as you'd expect from a seasoned farmer who had been helping his dad since he could toddle. And he'd developed an instant rapport with the other guys. Even Hodge and Lee seemed to like him, and they weren't the easiest men to impress.

He'd manned a hurdle, while Amelia had been on bucket-shaking duty, and together they had triumphed over their selected targets, falling about in helpless laughter when a rather ambitiously heroic lunge by Toby had him face-planting in the mud. He'd got to his feet, doubled over with laughter, wiping dirt from his face, blond hair curling impishly above his twinkling eyes as he grinned at her...

And her stomach had done a little flip.

The least she could do to thank him for his assistance was to make up for missing lunch. So she invited him back to Redbridge. She travelled with him in his car. And now they were all sitting around in the yard, eating the sandwiches and drinking the mugs of soup Sarah brought out to them. Amelia was sitting on the end of the pickup, the tailgate down. Toby was next to her.

She turned to face him, leaning against the side of the pick-up's bed, one knee up, one leg hanging down, her foot swaying slightly as she watched him. He took a bite of sandwich and looked at her, one eyebrow raised in silent query.

"I'm just thinking how sore I'm going to be tomorrow," she said, which wasn't quite what she had been thinking, but was the first thing that came to mind.

"Yeah?"

"I suspect it's all in a day's work for you."

"Potatoes aren't normally so flighty."

She laughed.

He gave her a smiling look that seemed to take all of her in, from her muddy boots to her messy hair—and seemed to approve.

"It's good to see you get your hands dirty," he said. "A surprise, like. But then I don't know why it'd be a surprise. You never did act like the lady of the manor. At college you was just one of us."

She quirked a brow. "Human?"

"You know what I mean."

"You own an enormous farm. I'm fairly sure the Patrick farming dynasty has roots going back even further than the Banberrys."

"But I like that you know how to work hard. That's what I'm saying." He nodded past her to the house. "It'd be easy to get...sort of spoilt by all this."

She turned, frowning, as though she needed to be reminded what the house looked like. As though it wasn't etched into her brain.

"It's hard for me to look at *'all this'* and see anything *other* than hard work."

"You say hard work like it's a bad thing."

"No, not bad, but... I do sometimes wonder what it's all *for*."

"My hard work puts food on people's plates."

"Exactly. But what does mine do?"

"Maintain a legacy? History? People like to come and look at beautiful places. Beautiful things."

Amelia snorted slightly, wrinkling her nose. Toby glanced away. Sandwich finished, he briskly brushed the crumbs from his lap and jumped down from the tailgate.

"Speaking of hard work... I've got some I ought to be getting back to."

"Oh, of course..."

She made to jump down, but he stopped her with a light hand on her knee. The touch sent a small flutter of excitement through her. Toby looked up from his hand and smiled slightly—and unapologetically. He gave her knee a squeeze, thumb brushing over the inside hem of her jeans.

"Stay. You've not finished your lunch. But maybe we can...catch up again sometime soon?"

"Yes. OK."

He nodded, letting go of her knee, and walked away to his car. Before he got in, he called out, "And I'll give you a shout if I have any runaway potatoes!"

———◈———

Janson turned Hugo away at the door, with the exact smug smile Hugo had expected. He returned one of his own and sauntered off around the side of the building as Janson closed the door.

Just as he had the day before, he was sure he could find an open side door. Or, if not, a window. He knew Redbridge Grange as well as he knew Conyers. He'd been ducking through its doors for decades.

But as he rounded a corner, where the driveway curved around the house to the back, he was passed by a car being driven by that blond farmer he'd met in Amelia's company. The driver saw Hugo and acknowledged him with a small wave Hugo could only interpret as *cocky*.

Hearing voices, Hugo followed the driveway to the yard, where he found Amelia sitting on the back of some kind of battered pickup-type vehicle.

She scowled as he strolled over. "You have a nerve coming here after that stunt with the plane. You do realise everyone here would quite like your head on a pike?"

Hugo spared a brief glance at some of the men in the yard—Hodge, the old gardener, and some others.

"There's a queue is there?" he said, coming to a stop in front of where she sat. Her seat on the truck made her slightly higher than him, allowing her to look down on him. Both literally and morally. "Don't worry, I'll get you a VIP pass to the front of it." He ran his eyes over her. "Why are you always covered in mud?"

"Because of work, Hugo. I know that's a strange concept to you."

"Mm. I came to see why you were getting hysterical at me about some sheep."

"Your stupid plane scattered the flock. It's taken us hours to round them up."

"But you love hard work, Amy. You know…fresh air, exercise. Rolling around in the mud with your farm boy."

"I don't know what Hallmark movies' list of grand gestures you're working from, but I swear to God, if you scorch the word 'sorry' into our lawn this close to opening I will scorch something far worse onto your head."

"Little Miss Bloodthirsty," he murmured, eyeing her appreciatively until he began to worry she was going to burst a blood vessel. "Fine, fine. I'll call off the mariachi band."

She scowled at him, eyes narrow slits. There were three tiny crumbs at the corner of her mouth from her lunch. He had the urge to brush them away with his thumb. He had the urge to slip his thumb into her mouth and let her bite it. He also had the urge to pull her hips towards him, her legs wrapped around his waist, grinding her core against him as he kissed—

Since when did he have fantasies about mud-splattered girls in the back of rusty pickup trucks? He had clearly been in the countryside for too long.

Christ, he wanted to go to a bar. But not alone like some sad weirdo on the prowl. He wanted to go out with his friends. He missed them, idiots that they were. He hadn't even seen Jay Orton in months, but the man had caught a bad case of monogamy, and Hugo and his friends were starting to fear it was terminal.

Jay in love and Hugo having farm girl fantasies?

The world was getting very strange.

Hugo was still staring at the crumbs on Amelia's lip when Janson the butler crossed the yard from the house.

"The roofing inspector has finished, Miss Amelia. He's waiting in your study."

"Thank you." Amelia flashed Janson a smile. It transformed her face, sent a rush of warmth and light to her eyes. Then she turned back to Hugo, still scowling, as though it had never been.

And the crumbs were still there.

"I have to go."

"Hm?" said Hugo, hand half-raised to those crumbs before he collected himself—realised Amelia was looking askance at his outstretched hand. He lowered it, put it in his pocket, and turned casually to Janson with one of his most infuriating grins.

"It seems you were wrong after all, Janson. Miss Amelia *was* at home."

58

"My mistake. How distressing," deadpanned the butler, before turning on his heel and going back to the house.

Amelia snorted softly, shaking her head and hopping down from the pickup. She started to follow Janson without so much as a backwards glance at Hugo.

"Wait!" He grabbed her hand.

Across the yard, Hugo was vaguely aware of one of the men, the big one from the stables, straightening and staring hard at them, arms crossed. But it was the cold anger in Amelia's eyes that made him let go.

"I just want to talk to you," he said. "Come on. Tell me what I need to do. I *miss* you. We've been friends forever and now you won't even talk to me."

"I think you told me everything I needed to know about you last year. What else is there to say?"

"Seriously, you're never going to forgive me?"

She glanced around, more concerned about their audience than he was. But she always had been one of those people who cared what people thought of her. She tried to please everyone. It sounded exhausting.

"Please," he said. "Look me in the eye and tell me that twenty years of friendship means nothing to you."

She did look at him. She seemed to look right through him, her eyes dark and merciless, so that they stripped him down. She looked through all the layers of him, his manhood, his self-belief, until he was just that boy with the grazed knee, trying not to cry even though it hurt like hell. But he was a *boy*, he was the eldest, and he could not, would not cry. Not even when Amy came to him with that damp cloth before he even had to ask and knelt before him, placing it gently on his torn flesh.

He trembled now a little as he had trembled then, feeling the doubt, the realisation, the dawning fear...

He was not worthy.

"That's exactly what you told me," she said, pinning him with her eyes so that he could not look away. "That's what you told me that night. Our friendship means nothing."

She turned, and again she walked away.

"Wait, wait!"

He ran a few steps to get in front of her, make her stop. The staff, he was dimly aware, had retreated, giving them some privacy. Though he was sure they were still gawking, staring from the privacy of windows and doorways. He didn't care.

"Amy... What can I do?"

She shook her head, tried to step around him. "I have work to do."

He took her hand again, held it in both of his.

"If you don't want my apology," he said, thinking wildly. "How about vengeance?"

"What?"

He glanced down at the dirty floor but pushed back his distaste and dropped to one knee. Amelia stared down at him in horrified confusion.

"Use me, abuse me," he said looking up at her, her hand held in both of his. "I'll be your slave. Humiliate me. I surrender myself to you. Nothing is off the table."

"What?" she said again.

"Get your revenge. If I made you feel stupid... If I tricked you, used you... Then do the same to me. Honestly, do anything you like to me. I'll crawl around on a leash... Actually, I'd probably quite like that..."

"Hugo, this is—"

"I need you to forgive me. I don't know how to make you believe I'm serious."

She looked down at him kneeling on the muddy floor. "I'm not sure this is the way."

Her voice was dry, an edge of amusement in it. He saw the

way her mouth twisted, fighting back a smile, and he felt a surge of hope as he got to his feet, Amy's hand still in his.

"Will you?" he said.

"Take my vengeance? I'm not that petty."

"But think how much fun it would be."

This time, her smile won free, mirroring his for a second before she managed to clear it away.

"You're impossible," she said.

"So punish me."

He deliberately let the suggestive tone lower his voice, made it a murmur, a caress that hinted at filth and flesh. She flushed slightly, pulling her hand away, and he felt another glimmer of hope.

"I have work to do. Go away. And leave my sheep alone."

He watched her walk back into the house feeling more hopeful than he had done in days.

One step closer to the money.

EIGHT

THE ROOFING EXPERT PUT the crumbling section of wood down on Amelia's desk where it promptly crumbled some more, shedding brown flakes and dust.

"Dry rot *and* woodworm," he said.

She stared at the ruined wood, heart beginning to race, though the rest of her body felt frozen. "Just..." She had to swallow, her throat was tight. "Just in that one area or...?"

Or the whole house. Was the whole house rotting away? Waiting to fall down and crush her?

"The woodworm was significant in that area. It looks like damp has been getting in for some time. You're familiar with woodworm? They need a certain level of moisture to survive."

Amelia nodded. Yes, she was familiar with woodworm. Beetle larvae pests that ate antique furniture, destroyed floorboards, riddled everything with holes until there was little left. They were a constant menace. But dry rot... Dry rot was a thing of nightmares.

"And the...the..." She couldn't bring herself to say it. She was circling a dizzying blackness, terrifying sums of money with too many zeroes dancing across her vision. Images of ceilings collapsing, plaster crumbling, tiles sinking, the whole house coming down and no one but her here to stop it. And what could she do, what could she do—?

"Are you OK, miss? You look very pale. I know it's not good news but—"

"Yes. Yes. Sorry. I'm fine."

She pulled herself together. *Breathe,* she told herself. *Take a breath, and then take another one. Push it all back down and keep your chin up...*

She looked up at the man, her fingers laced together on her desk, squeezed so tightly together it hurt.

"Go on. You were saying?"

"Um... Well, we need more time to make a proper survey. We couldn't access much of the crawl space. And we need scaffolding to take a proper look at the rest of the roof. It's the moisture that's the issue. If we can control that, get all the timbers dried out..."

"That will solve the problem?"

"It'll stop it getting worse. But a lot of your beams and roof joists are in that condition." He nodded at the crumbling wood on her desk. "I'd say maybe thirty or forty percent of what we saw up there is structurally unsound. It's a miracle that part of the roof is still standing, if I'm honest. It'll all need to come out, be replaced. We can treat the stuff that's not too bad, inject it with epoxy..."

He trailed off, and Amelia knew it was because she had gone white again and was sitting there nodding her head—nodding and nodding far too fast, but she didn't seem able to stop.

"I'll erm...put something in writing," said the man. "Send you an email."

"Yes," Amelia managed to say. "Please do."

———◦———

She stayed sitting at her desk for a long time. At first, she stared at nothing, then her eyes fell to the rotten wood on her desk. She opened her laptop and searched feverishly for dry rot treatment, case studies, estimated costs... But she didn't really take any of it in. There was a spinning sensation in her mind, a sort of vertigo. She kept feeling as though she was falling, but when she took a breath to steady herself, her chest was tight.

Dry rot can cause severe structural damage to buildings...

...has been known to travel through walls, behind plaster...

...treatment with chemicals, however these toxic compounds can diffuse into the wood...

...an extremely serious issue, especially in neglected buildings...

...requiring drastic remedies to correct...

...destruction of original timbers...

...significant...

...structural...

...collapse...

The words on the screen were a blur. There was a roaring, rushing sound drowning everything out. The sound of her blood, her heart. She couldn't breathe. And her mother was on a plane to the other side of the world. Her whole family was on the other side of the world. And there was no one here to—

She got up. She didn't know why. Just needed to be moving, moving... She walked out of the office, up the stairs, running for her childhood bedroom as though that was some sort of sanctuary. As if, if she curled up under the duvet and cried, someone might come eventually, her mother might come and soothe her, hold her, make everything OK.

But there was no one to come. No one in the whole house. Seventy-two rooms and no one but her to decide what to do about all of it.

She stood with her bedroom door closed behind her, getting her breathing under control. But the room seemed too large. Even here there was too much to do, the wallpaper in the corner was peeling and the tap in the en suite was dripping, and it all needed tidying, but when did she ever have the time?

She looked a little wildly around the familiar space, everything seeming to loom larger than life. Then she caught sight of the note on her pillow.

A note on her pillow?

She picked it up shakily and read:

You really ought to lock your downstairs doors and windows. I can't believe it's safe having the house wide open for anyone to walk in.

Anyway, you seemed busy, so I thought I would leave this note to remind you of my pledge:

I'll be your slave, Amy. I'm yours to use, abuse, humiliate. I'll do anything you want.

Make me pay.

You are worth the price.

And I know you don't believe me, but I am sorry. I hate that I made you cry.

Your humble servant,

Hugo.

She stared at the note, and not just because Hugo's handwriting was *terrible* and took some effort to decipher. She read it again. Then she started to laugh—hysterical rather than amused.

The idiot. The complete idiot. As if she even *cared* in the middle of this disaster of a day.

She sat down heavily on the edge of her bed, shaking her head. But she had to admit the note had served one purpose. Rather like a slap, or a bucket of cold water thrown at her face, it had distracted her from the panicked spiral she was in. She didn't really feel much better about things but at least she was no longer hyperventilating.

She looked at the note again.

I am sorry.

Was he really?

She found herself wondering if it really mattered. She was too tired to care. It all seemed so petty and juvenile now with the house literally rotting around her. That girl who had obsessed over Hugo with her every waking moment, who had watched him, dreamed of him, even loved him... That girl was just that: a stupid little girl.

Maybe this was what getting over Hugo really required. Simply not even caring enough to hate him.

She looked at the note again. He wasn't going to give up, was he? *Your humble servant...* But maybe that was it. If she put him to work around the estate, he could do some of the million things that needed doing, she could pretend to forgive him, and then maybe he would leave her alone and she could get on with the rest of her Hugo-free life.

She could expose herself to his presence, like letting sun and air reach the damp timbers of her heart, where her unhealthy obsession with him had secretly mouldered for years. She would never forgive him, or trust him. They could never really be friends again. But perhaps she could learn to be indifferent. One day Hugo might take up no more space in her mind than any other person. He would just be a man she knew. And her body wouldn't ache for him. And he wouldn't feature in every fantasy she had. He had finally managed to knock himself off the pedestal she had stupidly placed him on. Now she needed to keep him there.

And eradicate him from her heart like dry rot.

NINE

"**W**OULD IT BE WRONG to torture Hugo?"

"Never!" replied Evie with great certainty and alarming gusto.

Amelia twisted her chair from side to side, phone pressed to her ear. Evie Blackton was somewhere in Spain, saving wild goats or hand-weaving sun hats for donkeys. Something incredibly nice and worthwhile anyway. She always was. Although, for someone so altruistic, she could be surprisingly bloodthirsty.

"What's the special occasion?" Evie asked eagerly. "Or is this just a general response to his...Hugo-ness?"

"He's said he wants to help out at Redbridge." Amelia left out the more suggestively worded aspects of Hugo's proposal. "He seems determined to atone for what he did to Cassie and—and...um...David at the engagement party."

Amelia hadn't told Evie about kissing Hugo. She hadn't told anybody. It was too shameful to admit.

"Atone? That doesn't sound like Hugo."

"I know. I don't really believe him. But he's being weirdly persistent."

"I wonder if this is about Ross's promotion. I spoke to him the other day. Our father gave Ross a role at the company and Hugo got...erm...rather a drubbing. Apparently, father was going on at him about responsibility and maturity—you know, all those things Hugo is drastically allergic to."

"So you think getting my forgiveness—I mean, my family's forgiveness—is part of that? Like he's trying to prove a point to your father?"

"It could explain it."

Amelia nodded to herself, feeling stupidly deflated. For a moment she had almost thought he meant it. That he actually cared that *he* had hurt *her*. But she kept her voice level, nothing but dry amusement in it. "There's definitely something going on. He was basically grovelling."

Evie gave a snort of surprised laughter. "Hugo? No, I don't believe it!"

"Uh-huh. He said *sorry*."

Evie laughed again. "Oh my God. You have to film it next time. Promise? I would pay good money to see that."

Amelia laughed, but she was seeing that moment again in her mind's eye: Hugo glancing up at his phone while her lips still burnt for his...

"So I had this plan," she said quickly, forcing her thoughts onto a different track. "Accept his offer to work here and basically work him to the bone. God knows, we can always do with another pair of hands around the place. He said he wants me to make him pay. So I'm going to give him all the dirtiest, grubbiest jobs I can find."

Evie laughed. "He won't last a day."

———◇———

"These are the quarterly statements," Howell told Hugo. He pulled up yet another spreadsheet on the laptop in the Earl's office where they sat together at the desk. There was a painful sort of ringing sound in Hugo's ears, which he only got when he was literally about to die of boredom. "These coloured tabs along the bottom correlate to each of the expenditure streams I showed you in the accountancy package—"

Kill me, Hugo prayed to the universe. *Please kill me. I can't take a year of this.*

"Household expenses are compiled here. The Head House-keeper and the Butler are jointly responsible for—"

A whole morning looking at filing cabinets and spreadsheets. Hugo stared unseeing out of the window across the room, his eyes unfocused, colours blurring as he forced himself to sit still and fought the urge to run to the gun room. Or the drinks cabinet. Or maybe his bedroom. Some porn? A video game at least. There was that post-apocalyptic zombie one that Vik Singh had got him into—

"Salary budgets are allocated annually in agreement with the CFO, who is currently on secondment from—"

Bam! Hugo imagined, levelling an obscenely meaty-looking shotgun at a zombie in his mind's eye. *Bam, bam—* He wasn't altogether surprised that the zombies in his imagination happened to be dressed like accountants.

Maybe Roscoe was right and he wasn't cut out for life at an asset management firm.

But then...what *was* he cut out for?

"—which are adjusted annually in line with inflation—"

His phone beeped in his trouser pocket. He pulled it out and his heart skipped at the name on the screen.

"Excuse me," he interrupted Howell, fighting back a grin. "Duty calls. Urgent business. Apologies."

He practically ran from the room, Howell's disapproving glare palpable at his back.

———◆———

Hugo walked through the Conyers rose garden to the lawn

beyond, trying not to look too smug as he approached Amelia where she sat on the swing.

It was a large wooden bench swing that hung from the thick bough of an enormous walnut tree just at the edge of the lawn, near the entrance to the woodland walk. The swing was at least as old as he was and had been a favourite place to play as children, making an excellent boat, car, bus, aeroplane, pirate ship, or just somewhere to sit on hot days and drink squash or ginger beer.

And later, as a teenager, somewhere to bring girls and pretend to be romantic.

Amelia was sitting with her head tilted back, looking up through the branches of the walnut tree. The new leaves were fresh and green against the mild blue sky. She was dressed, as normal, in dark jeans and an unremarkable jumper, her brown hair gathered in a loose knot at the base of her neck.

Hugo couldn't help but contrast her appearance now with the girl he had kissed at the party. That deep blue dress that had hugged all of her normally hidden curves... And her expression, just for a moment as she looked up at him before they kissed... An expression of...wonder? No, even his ego couldn't quite believe that. But her look had been *something* anyway. Something nice.

Unlike the way she looked at him now.

He grinned and said in a sing-song voice as he approached, "Little Amy, sitting in a tree, K-I-S-S-I-N—"

"Shut up, Hugo. And stop calling me Amy."

He chuckled and sat down next to her, making the swing sway gently, one knee drawn up so that his body was turned towards her.

"You got my letter?"

"Yes."

"And? Am I to be your slave? You know it's an offer you can't refuse."

She let out a long breath, staring across the garden as she shook her head slightly, though he got the impression that for some reason she was more annoyed at herself than him. The fresh, yellow springtime sun brought out the mahogany tints in her hair and brushed with light the soft texture of her cheek.

She turned to look at him, some decision made.

"Have you heard of the labours of Hercules?"

"Of course," he lied smoothly, feeling rather like he was back in an Oxford seminar room, one of his professors about to sigh and look extremely disappointed.

"Hercules was set a series of tasks to atone for a terrible crime."

"I'm Hercules, am I? I suppose there *is* something rather godlike about me."

Amelia groaned and rubbed her forehead, muttering something about *Why was she even bothering?*

Hugo decided that perhaps he ought to be more sensible. Although, sitting here in the sun, Amelia one step closer to forgiving him, had put him in the best mood he had been in for months. The best mood he had been in since it happened, really.

It being the kiss. That damned, stupid kiss. Too much to drink and Amy looking pretty and it hadn't seemed like it could do any harm, could it? Just two friends chasing an idea that had surely occurred to each of them at one time or another.

A bit of fun. The biggest mistake of his life. And months later, he was still paying for it—perhaps to the tune of sixteen million pounds.

So, yes, if he wanted the money, perhaps he really ought to try and be more sensible and sober and serious and all those things that Amy probably wanted. But she was *here*, she was talking to him, the sun was shining, and anyway...

She was just too easy to wind up.

He had never been able to resist it. Teasing Little Miss Good, so earnest, so easy to read, so predictable it was almost a comfort. He could go away to university, to London, on wild holidays, and he could do wild, reckless, ruinous things, lose his head, perhaps lose a little of his soul... But he could always come back here, take a walk through the garden to Redbridge, and find Amy and make her scowl at him and huff and frown as though he was the same boy he'd always been, who'd never done anything worse than trip Roscoe while they played football or swap Evie's custard for salad cream.

Whatever he did, wherever he went, he had always been able to rely on Amy to bring him back to himself. Except now she sat there, worrying her lip with her teeth and looking very much like she regretted just about everything in the world.

He rested his elbow on the back of the bench seat, absently fiddling with a piece of flaking wood as he ran his eyes over her tense, unhappy figure. He attempted a more solemn expression. "A series of tasks?" he prompted.

"The thing is," she began slowly, looking out across the lawn. "If I'm being honest with you, I'm not sure I can ever forgive you. Not really."

Hugo frowned, and the piece of old wood he was fiddling with on the bench broke off under his thumb. He pulled the flaking fibres of it apart as he listened.

"But if you want to make amends, I suppose you can make them to the family, to all of us, to Redbridge. Because it wasn't just me that you hurt."

"Ah. You needed David's money, didn't you? For Redbridge?"

"No. I mean, yes, it would have helped. But that's not what I mean. It's not about *money*, Hugo. I mean there's a rift now, between our families. And no one really wants that, do they? Your sister is my best friend. Roscoe is a friend too. I know our parents don't exactly see eye-to-eye, but they've always been friendly towards each other. Our families have been friends for generations."

Hugo thought about the document in his room. The drama of two hundred years ago. Banberrys and Blacktons, mingling forever. But never merging.

"If you really mean it, about making amends, then I shouldn't get in the way of that," said Amelia. "But do you really mean it? Or is this just another game to you?"

Hugo brushed the flakes of wood from his fingers, adopting an easy smile and injecting it with warmth. "Of course I mean it."

"OK," she said, looking him in the eye for a moment. If she found his expression convincing, she didn't show it. "So if you want to repair this breach...you can work at Redbridge. God knows we need the help. There are a million tasks for you."

"It's *your* forgiveness I want."

She flushed slightly. "And Cassie's. And my parents'."

"I don't really care about what they think, so long as we're good again."

She frowned at that, but her colour deepened, and she looked away. The dappled shade of the walnut tree played over her face as the swing swayed, patches of sunlight alternately highlighting the warm chestnut of her hair, the smooth curve of her cheek, the dusky pink of her lips. And he couldn't help but remember that she hadn't kissed like Little Miss Good. She had kissed like...like her mouth was the pathway to the most perfect of sins.

It really was her forgiveness he wanted. The others would either come around with time or they wouldn't. But he needed Amy, if this marriage thing was ever going to happen. He needed Amy.

"If you help Redbridge," she began haltingly. "And I mean really help it. Not just turn up and mess around and get bored

73

after an hour. Then I... I will be grateful."

"And you'll forgive me?"

She didn't reply.

"That's what you care about, isn't it? Redbridge matters more to you than anything else."

It was a statement, not a question. But he thought she hesitated before nodding.

"Is it though?" he pressed, suddenly curious. "What is it that you really want? To live there forever? A glorified housekeeper?"

The question surprised her.

"I don't mind working there," she said, toeing the ground and setting the swing moving again. "I like to be useful."

"That's the epitaph you'd be happy to have on your grave, is it? *'Here lies Amelia Claire Banberry-Thompson. She liked to be useful.'*"

"And what would yours say? *'Here lies Hugo John Henry Croftwood Blackton, Earl of Carnford, wastrel and—'* Oh, I think they ran out of space after carving in all your names."

Hugo chuckled, glad to seize on the humour in her mocking response. When had she last smiled? When had he last seen her *laugh*?

He lifted an arm as though sketching out a grand vision. "Perhaps, *'He died as he lived, balls-deep in a fine—'*"

She made as though to smack him on the knee but held her hand back. "Ugh. Stop."

He grinned, then, more seriously, said, "You did...what? Geography at university? Not estate management, I'm sure."

"Not quite. I did International Relations."

"Countries and things. I was half-right."

"You were one hundred percent wrong."

"And what did you want to do with your *International Relations* degree?"

She looked away across the garden, hesitating, as though re-

74

vealing what she actually wanted to do with her life was somehow an embarrassing secret.

"I've always wanted to travel," she started quietly. "Like my father, but not in the wading through swamps and getting eaten by crocodiles sense. I mean... I've always wanted to see other countries and get to know them. Live and work in them. I guess I thought maybe I could work for the Foreign Office or the Diplomatic Service, be a diplomatic aide somewhere for a bit."

"Be useful to the whole world instead of just here?" he said, softening his teasing tone with a smile. "Is that why you're going travelling with Evie?"

"Maybe. We've been planning to go for ages. We were meant to go after university, but I couldn't find the time."

"Because you were stuck working here?"

"There was no one else."

"Not Cassie?"

"She was doing that journalism conversion course. And then last year, well...there was going to be the wedding, and then—"

"Me?"

"Yes. You happened."

"Do you honestly think, Amy, in your heart of hearts—and I'm persuaded you're good enough to have several person's worth of hearts—that Cassie would have kissed me if she truly wanted to marry David?"

"Is that how you get to sleep at night?"

"No. I normally just have a wank— Wait, don't go—"

She had stood up from the bench, giving a huff of disgust. He took hold of her wrist, aware of the warm skin beneath his fingers. Aware too of the urge he had to pull her closer, have her fall into his lap...

He *really* needed to get laid. Maybe he would call some of his friends. Organise a night out. In the meantime, he directed a winning smile up at Amelia's scowling face and said, "I was joking, Little A. I do *that* in the morning."

"You know, Hugo, the things you do with your penis aren't nearly as interesting as you think."

He gave her a slow smile. "I could make you beg to differ."

She gave a despairing groan and turned to go, pulling her hand free from his.

"Wait, wait! Tell me my tasks. Give me some clue. When do we start? Because we don't have much time before you go gallivanting with Evie—"

"Do you mean any of this, Hugo? Do you really?"

"Yes! Absolutely! Amelia, I promise I do. I swear on my...on my family name that I mean to win your forgiveness."

She looked at him for a moment, eyes narrowed.

"Fine. Tomorrow. Six AM. We'll start with one of Hercules' most famous tasks: cleaning the Augean Stables." She gave him a worryingly sharp kind of smile, amusement dark in her eyes, and said, "We only have four horses at Redbridge, but they certainly do produce a lot of—"

TEN

M ANURE.

Hugo was shovelling manure, and Amelia couldn't be more delighted.

She was also extremely surprised that he had turned up at all. *And* on time. But he was at the stable block even before she was.

She didn't normally get up quite so early, but she had dragged herself out of bed just to check Hugo kept his word.

And watch his humiliation, of course.

Except, being Hugo, he somehow still managed to look good, even ankle-deep in dirty straw and horse dung. He was wearing black jeans, with black Hunter wellies and a dark denim shirt that, together with the shovelling action, managed to show off the strong, lean lines of his shoulders and back. Amelia looked from the slice of slightly tanned skin visible between his shirt collar and the dark curl of hair at the nape of his neck to the flush of colour the exercise had brought to his cheeks despite the chill of the early morning air. The colour only served to highlight the disastrously exquisite bone structure of his face.

Not for the first time, she wondered just who he had sold his soul to. It wasn't *natural* to look like that.

He glanced up as he caught her watching from the stable door and rested one hand on the fork handle, pushing his hair back from his eyes with the other. He nodded at the insulated cup she held. "I don't suppose that coffee is for me?"

"No." She took a long, smug sip, eyeing him over the rim.

"Of course not," he muttered, and added another load of soiled straw to the wheelbarrow at his side.

The four horses at Redbridge Grange were mainly used during the summer, when the estate was open to visitors. There were two fat little ponies for children's pony rides, and two showy piebalds with sweeping manes and cloppy, feathered feet that pulled a carriage on tours of the grounds.

It was just over ten years since Redbridge had first opened itself up as a tourist attraction. At first, it was just the gardens. Then later, much of the house. Amelia had always been involved in the running of it, helping out at weekends and during school holidays, gradually taking on more and more responsibility—responsibility that was easy to claim, given no one else rushed to do so, and tasks were often left undone, waiting, begging, tripping everyone up and getting in the way until Amelia couldn't take it anymore and ended up taking on yet another job.

But she *was* good at it.

Most of what went on now during the open season—the pick-your-own fruits in the walled kitchen gardens, the farm-shop products made with their own hens' eggs, the pony rides and summer fete, and the Easter event she was currently busy planning—were all her own ideas.

And her own responsibility.

Because who else was there?

She glanced around as Lee, the man-mountain Stable Master, called her name and beckoned her over. She followed him into the tack room.

"I'm sorry to foist him on you," she said with an apologetic grimace. "I hope he's not too awful. But I give you full permission to haze him—send him to do all the dirtiest jobs you have."

Lee smiled but said, somewhat grudgingly, "Fair play to him. He turned up on time, and he got stuck in, even if he did look at me like I'd just asked him to lick Satan's arse."

Amelia laughed, nearly choking on her coffee. Lee scratched his stubbled jaw, looking speculatively through the open tack room doorway to the stable where Hugo was working. "I reckon though... Hmm. The gardeners could do with a few barrow-loads of manure, don't you think? And if you speak to Hodge, he could be persuaded the compost heaps need turning."

Amelia grinned and saluted Lee with her coffee mug. "Yes! Brilliant."

"But first..." Lee stepped out of the tack room and called across the yard. "Oi! Pence!"

"Pence?" asked Amelia in an undertone as Hugo poked his delightfully dishevelled head out of the stable.

"Short for pencil," Lee murmured back, "You know, Hugo Blackton. HB."

Amelia laughed. "Oh, I love it."

"Yes?" called Hugo, eyeing them warily—Amelia's grin in particular seemed to give him cause for concern. He narrowed his eyes at her, and she looked back innocently, sipping her coffee.

"Need you to fetch me a left-handed broom from the storeroom," said Lee. "And quick. I need it yesterday."

Hugo flushed darkly at being ordered about, the effort it took not to retort painfully obvious. Amelia smiled into her cup as he muttered, "Right," and propped his fork against the wall, setting off somewhat sulkily for the storeroom.

"Left-handed broom?" queried Amelia. "That's..."

"Yeah, no such thing," Lee said with a grin and a wink and left her laughing in the middle of the yard.

Hugo's lunch was a pathetic sandwich, tossed to him by Amelia's Stable Master, Lee, a despicable man who had trapped all of the vindictive arseholery of Harrow's worst physical education instructors in the body of a poorly-shaved mountain gorilla.

After sitting down to eat, Hugo could hardly move. His whole body ached. His muscles literally shook with fatigue. And yes, he had a personal trainer back in London who kept him aesthetically sculpted, but somehow those workouts didn't quite compare to the bone-breaking weariness of a day's physical labour.

OK, *half* a day's.

Amelia had him in the vegetable garden now, digging trenches for potatoes or something. There were rumours of a compost heap in his future, and he was starting to wonder if the significant sum in his trust fund might just be sufficient after all, and perhaps the thirty-six million could spend a bit longer locked away. Maybe he could propose to Amy in a decade or so, when she was in her thirties and desperate.

Except she might have married someone else by then.

Hugo started digging faster.

He was grateful when his phone rang, giving him an excuse to stop. He was even more grateful when he saw the name on the screen. *Roscoe.*

Jubilant after reaching an agreement with Amelia yesterday, Hugo had tried to phone his brother, needing someone to talk to about it. The call had gone to voicemail. He had tried again later that evening, and Roscoe had briefly answered, the unmistakable sounds of a bar loud in the background—music, laughter. Hugo had felt a tug in his chest at the familiar sound.

That was where he should be. In a dark bar, a dark corner, girls at his table, his thoughts nicely blurred by drink, talking nonsense, tracing idle circles on a bare shoulder... That was the kind of doing nothing he liked—the kind that stopped you from having to think. Not this nothingness at Conyers of the last week, echoing in an empty house, with nothing to do *but* think, ancestors staring down from every wall and asking *Just who did he think he was anyway?*

"Hugh," Roscoe had said somewhat indistinctly. "I love you, but I have someone far prettier sitting on my lap." Then he had hung up, and Hugo had been left smiling ruefully at his phone.

Fair play. He would have made the same choice.

Now his brother greeted him brightly and cheerfully, no trace of hangover in his voice. Of course not. He was a Blackton. They didn't do hangovers.

"Have you sprouted moss yet, Hugh? Do you find yourself leaning on gates chewing straw?"

Hugo looked down at his muddy boots, the spade in his blistered hand. "Close. But not quite. Actually, I'm doing something you'll approve of."

"Seems unlikely."

"I'm making amends with Amelia."

"Oh?" Roscoe's surprise was evident. "Cassie too?"

"Cassie isn't here."

"I thought she was due back from Canada?"

Hugo frowned. He wasn't quite sure he wanted Cassie on the scene. Talking to Amelia. Reminding her of exactly what he had done...

"Amelia hasn't mentioned it."

"You're talking then? She's actually tolerating your presence?"

"Sort of. I've worn her down."

"This sounds more believable."

"Anyway, it's all part of a bigger plan—"

"Oh God, I don't want to know. I want to be able to plead plausible deniability—"

"I'm going to marry her. For money."

There was a loud groan and muttered cursing. Hugo grinned. "Too late, Ross. You can't deny anything now."

"I hate you."

"Let me fill you in."

He told Roscoe about the lawyers, the document, the money. All of it.

Roscoe didn't speak for a moment. And when he did, the question wasn't one Hugo was expecting.

"Why are you really doing this, Hugh? If you want to apologise to her, just do it. You don't need to hide behind this...facade."

"That's not what this is."

"Really? Because you've been avoiding her ever since Cassie's party. You've been too scared to face her, haven't you?"

He twisted the spade he was leaning on a little further into the earth. "I want the money, Ross."

"Just learn to manage the bloody fund, Hugh. You don't need to do this."

How could he explain to the golden boy of BG, the investment wunderkind, that he didn't have a clue how to even begin doing that? It was easier to imagine marrying Amy than believe he'd suddenly be able to learn the work he'd spent his life avoiding.

"I want the money," he repeated. "Come on, that's basically the family motto: I didn't need it, but I wanted it."

Roscoe chuckled. "Mostly. But not wholly." He sighed. "But...marriage, Hugh? Really?"

"I don't actually want to get married. You know me. That's the last thing in the world I want. I'm going to put it in a legal agreement—we get divorced as soon as possible."

"And Amy's amenable to this, is she?"

"I haven't told her any of it yet."

Roscoe paused. A breeze blew through the vegetable garden, making the plants tremble.

"Um. OK... When are you going to tell her?"

"When she likes me again." Hugo stabbed the spade into the earth deep enough that it would stay standing. He rubbed his hand through his hair. "If I tell her about the money, she'll just think I'm apologising in order to get her to say yes."

"That's exactly what you are doing."

"Mostly," he said. "But not wholly."

Roscoe gave an amused snort at having his earlier words repeated back to him.

"I do want her to forgive me," Hugo continued. "We've been friends forever. It's not right, is it, to not be friends with the B-T girls? It doesn't feel right."

"No," agreed Roscoe. "They're basically family."

"They are *not* like sisters."

Roscoe laughed. "Not to you, clearly." Then he sighed and said, much more seriously, "But they are like sisters to me, Hugh. And I don't like the idea of you using Amy like this. She's going to get hurt."

"She'll get half the money. I'm having a lawyer put it in writing. It's not like I can force her to marry me. She'll only go through with it if she wants to."

"But you need to be honest with her."

"I will. When the time is right."

"No. Now. From the start."

"Look, I know Amy. She'd do anything for her friends. But I need to make sure she *is* my friend first."

He looked up at the sound of voices, and there was Amy herself, talking to Hodge, the gnarled and crabby head gardener.

"I have to go," he told Roscoe.

"Tell her the truth—"

He hung up and shoved his phone back into his pocket. Amelia glanced over but continued walking down the brick path that ran through the middle of the walled vegetable garden, deep in conversation with Hodge. She had a tablet and some papers in one hand. With the other hand, she patted Hodge lightly and affectionately on the shoulder, then finally turned and walked to Hugo.

"Working hard, I see," she said.

"That was Roscoe."

"And how is my favourite Blackton brother?"

"Insufferable."

"A family trait."

He laughed, and she almost smiled—more with her eyes than her mouth, which, with Amy, was always what counted. He pushed his hair back, hoping he didn't have soil on his face, and nodded at the documents in her hand.

"What's all that?"

He'd been catching glimpses of her around the estate all day, always walking briskly somewhere, or talking to one of her staff, or tapping away on her tablet. In short, looking incredibly busy and sort of...important.

"Oh, I'm just planning some of the cooking activities, seeing which vegetables and things Hodge thinks might be available to pick in a month or so." At Hugo's politely enquiring look, she elaborated: "We run classes here for school children. They come and pick vegetables from the gardens, then they get to learn how to cook them in the big kitchen. When we had the family kitchen installed in our private apartment, we reverted the old one back to how it would have been in about nineteen hundred. So it's like a history and cooking lesson all in one."

Hugo frowned slightly, waggling the tip of his spade into

the dark soil and resting both hands on its wooden handle. "Don't you mind having kids and tourists crawling all over your house?"

"No. I don't mind." Amelia managed to make her mild reply sound like a scold. "And even if I did mind, we don't have a choice."

Hugo watched a worm wriggle out of the earth he had been digging. It writhed around blindly, frantically trying to bury itself back in. He felt an odd swell of sympathy for the creature.

"This house and its gardens would be totally wasted on just my family," continued Amy. "It makes sense to share it—have it do some good rather than just crumbling away."

"Unlike Conyers, you mean?"

"Conyers isn't crumbling."

He scanned her face briefly although he already knew the answer. "You need money, don't you?"

"Of course we need money." She let out a breath, looking around the garden, then lifted the hand that held the documents in a sort of helpless shrug. "And even all this hardly helps. It's sometimes a miracle we break even at all."

"Maybe there's money out there with your name on it, just waiting to be claimed."

"Ah yes. The magical money tree. I'm sure your life is strewn with them, Hugo. The rest of us aren't so lucky."

"Maybe sometimes we can make our own luck."

She gave him a flat look, unimpressed. "I think what we need is fewer platitudes and more digging."

He smiled but stepped out of the trench he had made. The movement restored their usual height difference, and he much preferred it like this, looking down on her so she had to turn her face up to him.

Her brown eyes were frank, a little challenging, and he really must have been dazed with fatigue, because he had the sudden

85

urge to tell her everything and ask her to marry him. She raised an eyebrow as he looked at her, questioning his silent regard.

"I've been watching you run around all morning," he said quickly, before he did something stupid. "Quite honestly, it looks exhausting. Wouldn't you much rather not have to work like this? If there was a way?"

"I've already told you—I don't mind." Her eyes moved past his, and she looked for a moment at what he guessed was the top of his head. A small smile curled the corner of her lips.

"What?" he asked.

She reached out—towards his face. Instinctively, he went to stop her hand, his fingers wrapping around her wrist, but only gently, not enough to stop her. He felt the faintest touch in his hair, and then he drew her hand down between them. She was holding a small green leaf.

"It was in your hair," she said, but her smile had gone a bit crooked, and her cheeks were pink. Experimentally, or perhaps just because he couldn't help himself, he rubbed his thumb over the skin of her wrist where he still held her.

She froze. And now it was Hugo's turn to smile. With his free hand, he plucked the leaf from her fingers, examined it carelessly, and let it skip away on the breeze. "Thank you," he said, eyes on hers.

She pulled her wrist free. "I need to get back to work—" Her phone beeped. "Speaking of which..." She read a text message, her smile changing again, this time to something warm and amused. "Janson. Telling me Toby is here."

She shot Hugo a grin, nodding at the trench behind him. "Planting potatoes... It just occurred to me that you're doing what Toby does but on a teeny-tiny scale." And if the look in her eyes was innocent, the way she waggled her littlest finger left no doubt as to what she was insinuating.

Hugo scowled, fighting for a comeback. But she was already

walking away.

She gave him a careless wave over her shoulder. "Dig for Red-bridge, Hugh. Dig for victory!"

ELEVEN

A MELIA FOUND TOBY WAITING for her in the entrance
hall. It was a third the size of the one at Conyers, but it
was also twice the age. Truly gothic, having been built in the
mediaeval era, rather than the revival period of the eighteen
hundreds. Some plasterwork had been added to the stone walls
at one time or another, but the oak beams that curved up into
the ceiling arches had happily survived unscathed.

Toby was studying one of the somewhat grimy oil paintings
on the wall. He looked around at the sound of her feet on the
worn parquet floor and smiled. "I've been into town and had an
hour spare. I thought I'd risk seeing if you were free."

Amelia smiled back, despite being very much *not* free. And
despite having only seen Toby the other day, when he helped
with the sheep. True, he had suggested they meet again, but this
was somewhat sooner than she'd expected.

On the other hand, there was something nice about being
sought out and thought of. And also, she had to admit, there
was something nice about being smiled at by a well-built and
attractive man. He was wearing khaki work trousers today, with
a plaid shirt open over a white t-shirt. His dark blond hair tumbled low on his brow above his smiling blue eyes.

So, yes. She smiled back.

"I can spare a few minutes. Did you want to look at the

running route some more?"

"Sure. Let's say that."

He picked up on the slight hesitation in her laugh, because he said with a wince, "Sorry. I'm not playing this very cool, am I?"

"I'm not sure either of us have ever been cool, have we?"

"True. We were nerds in sixth form. Why change now?"

They both laughed, the allusion to their shared history easing some of the awkwardness.

"I'll make some tea, shall I? We can drink it while I show you around the house, if you like?"

"Sure, thank you. I've never really seen it before. Just what I saw the other day—your office, mostly."

Amelia led the way through the house. "You never visited before, did you? When we were...um..."

"Going out? No. Never got invited to the big house."

He said it with a grin, but Amelia felt he was being a little unfair. "I don't think I was ever invited to the farmhouse either."

"True. But I was embarrassed by it. I'm fairly sure I had a Beyoncé poster on my wall."

"Beyoncé? That's not what I would have guessed to be your musical taste."

"I don't think it's her music I was interested in."

Amelia grimaced, laughing.

"Anyway," said Toby, "we managed well enough, didn't we? Hanging around in town, going to the cinema. House parties."

He said the last with unnecessary emphasis. They had only been to one house party of significance. The one where they'd had sex. Amelia felt uncomfortable at Toby bringing it up so soon, but she just said lightly, "Lisa Cosgrove's, wasn't it? I wonder whatever happened to her."

"She trained as a dental hygienist."

"Oh? You stayed in touch?" Then, at the look on his face. "Ah, you dated her?"

"For a while. She didn't want to stay around here though. Too rural, she said. She moved to Manchester last year."

"Didn't fancy being a farmer's wife then?"

She said it jokingly, but Toby's slightly forced laugh suggested she had stumbled closer to the truth than she had intended. She began to suspect that possibly, just possibly, the farmer was in the market for a wife. Was that why he was here, trying to start things up again? No, no. That was a little presumptuous of her.

Luckily, they had reached the kitchen, and she was able to busy herself making the tea.

Toby looked around at the small, modern kitchen frowning curiously. "OK. This is *not* what I was expecting."

"It was put in two years ago. This used to be the gun room."

Toby leant against the counter, watching her fill the kettle. He frowned again in perplexed amusement. "My kitchen at the farmhouse is *bigger*. Bigger than the one at Redbridge Grange. How is that possible?"

"Size isn't everything," she said, then almost laughed, re-membering Hugo's face at her comment about his teeny-tiny potatoes. It felt so *good* to leave him spluttering and speechless. She pushed down the mirth before Toby asked her what was funny and flicked the kettle on.

"Don't worry," she told him, "I'll show you the old kitchen soon. It's big enough to roast five oxen."

———⊙———

"OK," said Toby about twenty minutes later, after she had briefly shown him the library and they had walked through the largest picture gallery en route to the old kitchen. "This is much more like I was imagining. Although..." He turned the handle of a spit roast in one of the two giant fireplaces. "I can see why it's maybe not quite so practical."

Amelia laughed in agreement, though she did love this old place. There were huge copper pans hanging from hooks in the ancient beams, the stones above the fireplaces were smoke-blackened from a thousand cooked meals. The stone floor along the vast oak kitchen table was worn away by the feet of generations of cooks who had stood exactly where she stood now. Kneading dough, making pastry, chopping vegetables... All the food that had nourished her ancestors for years and years.

It was impossible to escape the history of her family here, in this house, where her every view took in centuries. There was a weight to the very air. When had the oaks that made this table been cut down? When had the acorns they grew from been planted? Her family had been here then. And now the wood they had grown and felled was still here, two-hundred years old, the table still being used—albeit by school children these days.

But how much longer could it last? How long could it really expect to escape fire and flood and catastrophe? How long could anything last with the roof rotting and the rain coming in...?

The house had stood, in part, since the fifteen-hundreds. And there was an expectation that it would always stand—that it *must* stand. Because otherwise, whatever had it all been for? All the work of all those hands for year after year after year? Because it wasn't just her family that Amelia felt responsible for—her parents, her sister—it was everyone who had gone before. She didn't want the house to fail on her watch. To be the one who made all the struggle and trials of generations end in nothing.

It couldn't be her. She couldn't bear it.

"Amelia? Everything OK?"

"Hm?"

"You zoned out a bit there."

She looked up at Toby. He seemed to come into focus slowly. There was a rushing, roaring sound in her brain, like the sound of her heartbeat magnified by a million. She pushed it away, just as she always did. Now was not the time.

"Sorry," she said. "Just daydreaming."

But she frowned down at the table, running her fingers over the familiar notched surface as Toby crossed the kitchen and went to look out of one of the narrow, mullioned windows.

She *liked* this table. It was one of her favourite pieces in the whole house—better by far, in her opinion, than all the elegant antiques in the public rooms. But even as she smiled at something Toby said and crossed the room to answer his question, she felt the table at her back. She felt the sweat and the toil of generations. She heard the ring of pans and smelt the smoke of the fire...

The house had never felt bigger. Last night, she had slept in it alone. Janson and his wife Sarah, the housekeeper, lived in a cottage on the grounds. Lee, despite her family's many protestations about it barely being fit for habitation, insisted on living in the ancient grooms' quarters above the stables. The other staff lived in the village or nearby. Her mother was gone. Amelia had been completely alone in the house.

It wasn't quite the first time she had been alone at Redbridge, but for some reason, she felt it more keenly. All the rooms... All those empty rooms. And a mile away, wasn't Hugo just the same at Conyers? Except with even more rooms to crowd him out.

Two people and two hundred rooms between them... It made her feel small. Did Hugo ever feel like that? She couldn't imagine it. She couldn't imagine him lying awake in a bed older than himself, listening to the booming silence of a vast, empty house.

She was being ridiculous. She had nothing to complain about. She was lucky to live in a house like this.

And besides, she didn't have time to feel lonely.

———❖———

Amelia took Toby around the rest of the house. She kept expecting him to say he had to go, given he had already been there for longer than the hour he'd said he had to spare. But he didn't. And, though she was all too aware of the jobs that were piling up, she didn't want to seem rude, so she showed him room after room, until there were only the private upstairs quarters left, and she didn't really want to show him those.

"I think that's most of the house," she said at last, as they stood in the morning room. This had been her grandmother's favourite room and was still decorated as it had been when that lady used to sit at the desk by the window and compose her copious correspondence. The wallpaper was blue with hints of faded gold—oriental cranes and windswept grasses, a breaking sun on the horizon. Amelia had often sat here while her grandmother wrote, and she suspected that she could be anywhere in the world, close her eyes, and call to mind every single detail of the wallpaper here. Though that was true of much of Redbridge.

A climbing rose grew around the window. A stem tapped against the glass in the breeze. It needed tying back.

"Do you want to see the garden?" she asked Toby, because he still seemed in no hurry to leave.

"Sure."

They went into the sitting room next door and out through the patio doors there. The doors opened onto a terrace with a lichen-encrusted stone parapet that overlooked the formal garden—the parterre, with its gravel paths making geometric shapes through low box hedges.

"This part of the garden is one of the oldest," she told Toby. "Lots of these formal gardens got removed in the time of Capability Brown, when the vogue was for natural landscapes. But I don't think they could afford the work required here."

They stood for a moment looking down. The parterre wasn't

at its best. There were some pretty butter-yellow primroses strewn around, but there were weeds in the gravel, and the box hedges were untrimmed. At the centre was the large circular fountain—the basin nearly four metres across, a classical statue in the middle.

The statue was of a maiden, a basket on her shoulder. Amelia always felt sorry for her. The carved stone basket looked heavy, loaded with sheaves of wheat, and the maiden's stone dress had slipped down, revealing, of course, one extremely pert breast. The poor woman was too heavily laden to fix her dress, both hands holding the basket, so she was forever frozen like that—and now, to add to the indignity, she was stranded in a pool of stagnant water that was thickly covered by brown rotting leaves.

Yet another job to do. And who knew how much it would cost to get the fountain fixed?

Toby paused by the fountain as they passed through the parterre, looking up at the unfortunate statue in the middle.

"Demon taskmaster, there you are."

Amelia spun around at the sound of Hugo's voice. He walked down one of the gravel paths, his tall, dark figure cutting towards her rather like a shark moving through water. She tensed, like she always did anytime he was near. How he managed to move with such lethal self-possession while thoroughly muddy and work-stained, she had no idea.

Toby had turned too at the sound of Hugo's voice, taking a step closer to her as though staking a claim. She didn't quite like the way that felt.

Hugo looked from her to Toby and back again. "Working hard, I see," he commented, mocking her with her own words from earlier.

"Lord Leighton," Toby said, more deference in his words than his tone. "It looks like you're the one who's been working hard."

Hugo glanced down carelessly. Amelia suspected he knew full well that he wore his muddy clothes as though they were the latest Dior. "I've been helping Amy out around the estate."

"It's a sort of community outreach thing we're trying," Amelia told Toby, laughing at the dark look Hugo gave her. "A rehabilitation programme. You know. Making work for idle hands."

Hugo gave her a combative look, eyebrow raised. "Yes. Amelia's *very* good at coming up with things for my idle hands to do."

Amelia flushed, woefully unable to come up with a suitable retort. Toby looked between them. "Good with your hands, are you?" he said lightly to Hugo. "Maybe you could have a look at this fountain then? Or do you think plumbing is a bit outside your expertise?"

"No, that's—" began Amelia, but the men ignored her, Hugo raising his chin as he looked at Toby, arms folded.

"I'm sure I can find my way around."

"Great. Why not hop in and have a look? I think I saw some sort of blockage in the centre there..."

"Wait!" protested Amelia as Hugo strode confidently to the fountain and put his hand on the wall, ready to jump over. "It's not—"

He jumped. And fell into the stinking stagnant water with a startled yell as the leaf-covered surface he had taken for the dry bottom of the fountain turned out not to be that at all.

"—dry," finished Amelia lamely, then clapped a hand over her mouth as Hugo staggered to his feet, spluttering and dripping and plastered with rotten leaves.

"Mother fucking fuckity *fuck.*"

Amelia couldn't hold it back anymore. She burst out laughing, tears coming to her eyes. Toby laughed too. "Sorry," he said, unconvincingly. "I could have *sworn* it was dry."

Hugo glared at him, dirty brown water dripping from his face. He took a quick stride towards the edge of the fountain. But the floor of the basin must have been slippery with slimy leaves and algae, because he fell again, with an even more vicious curse.

"Be a gentleman," he said to the laughing Toby. "Give me a hand up."

Toby sobered and went to the edge, holding his hand out. Hugo was on his knees. He grasped Toby by the hand, then pulled, hard, in what looked like some sort of judo move, because it caught Toby totally off balance and pulled him face-first into the fountain.

"Oops," said Hugo as Toby floundered and cursed in the water, spitting leaves from his mouth.

A dark look crossed Toby's face, and he shoved Hugo hard on the shoulder. Both men toppled over, and for a moment, all Amelia could do was watch in fascinated horror as the men wrestled, a splashing tangle of large, masculine limbs and muffled grunts.

After a moment, they broke apart with a final vicious shove and both surged to their feet, soaked and filthy. They glared at each other, chests heaving. Their shirts were wet, semi-transparent and clinging to their bodies, Hugo all lean-chiselled angles, and Toby's bulk revealed as slabs of muscle, his biceps thicker than Amelia's thighs.

Amelia stared, biting her lip and fighting a ridiculous urge to giggle. She also had the urge to throw some jelly into the fountain, pull up a chair, and watch the show. She was only human, after all.

Instead, she said, "Erm..."

Hugo glanced at her, seeming to recall her existence. He laughed, breathless, and pushed his wet hair back with two hands, though there was a hard glitter to his dark blue eyes as he looked back at Toby. He was clearly resisting the urge to throw the burly farmer back in the water by a very fine thread. The sentiment seemed more than returned as Toby glared at Hugo, with no trace of his laughter.

"Maybe you should both get out of the fountain..." suggested Amelia. "Slowly," she added, as they slipped and slid their way to the side.

She held out her hand and helped Hugo out. He met her laughing look with a rueful grin. "Might be one for the professionals, Little A."

She laughed. "Noted."

Then she turned to help Toby out. He was still scowling and angry, but he forced a smile when he found her smiling at him.

"You can shower here," she said. "I can have your clothes washed and dried. Or find something of my father's."

"Thank you," he said stiffly, radiating embarrassment.

"Think you can fit me in your shower?" Hugo asked from behind her, tweaking a strand of hair that had come loose from her bun.

"You're welcome to use the staff facilities," she told him pleasantly. "Toby can use my en suite."

Hugo scowled at that, which was precisely why Amelia had said it. Though, as she led the sodden Toby back into the house, she wasn't entirely comfortable with the thought of him being imminently naked in her bedroom. She wished at least that he would cheer up and laugh it off as Hugo had done. Because for all his many, many faults, Hugo was always a good sport. Well—laughing things off was his entire attitude to life. And though he definitely could have done with taking things more seriously, at times like this it was preferable to sulky, wounded male pride.

Amelia stifled a sigh and got to work attempting to cheer

Toby up.

"I'm so sorry about that," she said as they started up the stairs, even though Toby had instigated the whole thing.

"Is he... That Leighton. Hugo. He seems to be here a lot. Is he just a neighbour or...are you...?"

"No. He's a neighbour. A childhood friend. Imagine the most annoying big brother in the world and multiply it by ten."

"Hm," grunted Toby, not seeming convinced. She couldn't blame him.

Then Hugo ran up the broad staircase behind them. "Just remembered I can use Cassie's shower. I'll take Daddy's finest suit, Little A."

"Like I told you," Amelia said as they watched Hugo disappear up the stairs. "Really, really annoying."

TWELVE

"THIS IS...ERM..." TOBY LOOKED around Amelia's small en suite bathroom much as he had looked around the new kitchen downstairs: sceptical, nonplussed, amused. "It's basically an antique."

"Yes, well, the whole house is an antique," said Amelia a little shortly. "These upstairs bathrooms were put in in the nineteen-fifties."

"And untouched since?"

"Yes."

Amelia glanced around it herself as she reached for the shower control, seeing it as it must look to new eyes. It was pink. Everywhere. The tiles were pink, the floor was pink, the bathtub, sink, and toilet were all pink. The frilly curtain around the window was pink and the cracked Bakelite toothbrush and soap holder below the pink framed mirror were also pink. About the only thing that wasn't pink was the grout between the tiles which had long since turned grey.

"The water takes a few minutes to warm up," she said, turning the shower wheel, which gave its usual groan and set the pipe rattling. "And I'm afraid that by the time it's been pumped all the way here from the boiler room, it's rather tepid. Leave your clothes on the floor. I'll have them washed and dried and sent over to your house when they're ready."

"Thank you."

She turned from the shower, tugging the pink plastic shower curtain into place. Toby was standing quite close. There wasn't room for anything else. He caught her eye briefly then looked away, half-smiling, half-frowning.

"I shouldn't have... I knew the fountain wasn't dry."

"Yes. I figured."

"I didn't like the way he talked to you."

"He always talks like that. You soon learn to ignore it."

He glanced back at her. There were bits of broken leaf in the damp curls of his hair, and some more stuck to his cheek.

"You looked like you minded."

Amelia turned away and began to quite unnecessarily re-fold one of the pink towels on the rail. "Hugo is a ridiculous man who takes up far more of everyone's attention than he's worth." She shoved the towel back into place. It was far less neat than it had been when she started. "I'll get you some of my father's clothes and leave them outside the bathroom door. Come downstairs when you're ready."

———❖———

Amelia found some clothes in her parents' bedroom. Her father was a big man, closer to Toby's rugged build than Hugo's athletic leanness. Hugo was also several inches taller than both of them, but if he had to walk home with her father's trousers showing his ankles, then it was far less humiliation than he deserved.

Falling in the fountain, however...

She laughed to herself at the memory as she rummaged through a drawer for socks. The look on his face, and that startled yelp! She laughed so hard she had to pause for breath. It had been a while since she had last laughed like that.

Toby had no reason to apologise. Her only regret was that she hadn't been the one to think of it. Well, that and the fact Toby had pranked Hugo on her behalf rather than just because he so richly deserved it. It made her uncomfortable that he thought she needed defending. And that he thought he ought to be the one to do it.

Arms full of clothes, she went back to her room, walking in cautiously, but reassured by the sound of the shower running. She left a set of clothes neatly folded by the bathroom door, then went back into the hallway and walked down a few doors to Cassie's room. She hurried to the bathroom door, practically flung the clothes down, and was ready to make her escape when the bathroom door opened and Hugo appeared with a cloud of steamy air, a green towel hanging perilously low on his sculpted hips.

"Ah, perfect timing," he said, grinning at her stricken expression and crossing his arms to lean against the bathroom doorway.

"Funny. I was just thinking the exact opposite."

"I forgot what these bathrooms were like." Cassie's was the sea-green version of hers. "I swear the ghost of your Great Aunt Petunia turned up to loofah my back."

In normal circumstances, when her brain wasn't short-circuiting, she would have laughed at that. Now, she started to back away, pausing reluctantly when Hugo said, "How's Farmer Giles? Has he forgiven me? Or am I going to find potatoes thrown through the windows of Conyers? I do have a lot of windows, but I hear he has a *lot* of potatoes..."

She couldn't help it. The sight of Hugo was impossible to avoid. Her eyes flicked down from his amused smile and his wet hair, water beading at the ends and dripping down his neck... Lean, hard, male, perfection. Those were the words her brain unhelpfully insisted on supplying. And the arrogance with which he stood there watching her helplessly watch him should have made him less attractive. But it didn't. Because it seemed to say that not only did he know his body looked good, but he also knew how to use it.

She only took a glance, but she saw it all. The shoulders, the collarbones, the muscled arms folded across his chest, and that dark trail of hair, the flat dip at the base of his abs, the undercut V of muscles, all of it pointing shamelessly *there*...

Hugo's mouth quirked. "You've seen it all before, Little A. You've been swimming at Conyers often enough."

"Not for a while," she said automatically, dragging her eyes away and fixing them on one of Cassie's bookcases. Not since they were sixteen, seventeen, eighteen... And he had looked almost as good back then. And she had been just as pathetically affected by it. Her decade-long crush had been built on extremely understandable foundations.

"You should come. Have a swim. Relax. My mother finally finished turning the old stable block into her dream spa... There's a gym, sauna. Massage room."

"Um."

"When did you last relax? Come tomorrow. Chill out there."

"Can we have this conversation when you have more clothes on?"

"I'd prefer to do it when you had less. No...?" He chuckled at her scowl and bent down to pick up a top from the pile of clothes at his feet. "As you wish."

He began to tug his towel free. Amelia ran from the room.

Hugo watched Amelia flee with a mixture of amusement and regret. He'd had no intention of really letting the towel fall. He wasn't that gross. And also, he had the unmistakable beginnings of a raging hard-on. Amelia might have been fully dressed, but *he* had been almost naked while in the same room as her, and his dick had leapt to certain conclusions.

Conclusions that were unfortunately unfounded. Although one thing was becoming hard to deny—excuse the pun. It seemed he had the horn for Little Miss Good.

He fancied Amy? That was...inconvenient. Because, difficult as it was to accept, he wasn't sure that sleeping with her would help his cause. If he was going to present this marriage thing as a mutually beneficial business deal between friends—one that would help her to help her beloved Redbridge—then sleeping with her would only muddy the waters. Especially when simply *kissing* her was what had caused this mess between them in the first place.

Not for the first time, he found himself regretting that kiss. Or not the actual kiss itself, because that had been sublime. But he regretted everything that led up to it, and everything that came after. And he also regretted it because if he hadn't kissed her then he wouldn't know what it was like, and he wouldn't be constantly tortured by the teasing memory of it.

His dick twitched. Fuck. But he wasn't going to rub one out in Cassie's bathroom. So he dressed quickly, gathered his wet clothes, and headed for home.

His own bathroom was larger than Cassie or Amelia's entire bedroom. It had been installed two years ago and was liberally tiled with Blue Bahia granite slabs. The giant walk-in shower was remote controlled, and he flicked it on, turning it up to scalding as he stripped off his borrowed clothes.

The lukewarm dribble of a shower at Redbridge really hadn't done the trick. He could still smell stagnant water on his skin, feel bits of leaf in his hair. So he showered properly. And thought of Amelia. Imagined what would have happened if she hadn't run but had stayed when he stripped his towel and looked at him with those dark eyes turning big and round, licking those pink lips as he stepped towards her and she got down on her knees...

He groaned as he leant forward, one hand braced on the shower wall, water sluicing off his back and neck as he gripped his cock, eyes closed, seeing Amelia's lips, imagining the wet heat of her mouth...

Fuck. Fuck—

He came so hard his knees buckled and he staggered sideways a step. He let out a huff of laughter, chest heaving, and rested his forehead against the granite wall as his breathing returned to normal.

After his shower, Hugo sat on his bed and flicked on his TV. He picked up his phone, ignoring the several messages from Howell, and sent a text to a few of his friends.

Stuck at Conyers. So bored. Come party here? This weekend?

The replies trickled in over the next hour.

Vik: Sounds lame. No.

Biffy: Soz, can't. In LA for the season.

Jay: Why stuck?

Hugo scowled at his phone, feeling more disappointed than he cared to admit. He messaged the kitchens to bring him some food, then called Jay, who seemed, as was often the case, to be the most promising of his friends.

"Can't do this weekend," said Jay by way of greeting. "I'm running a fundraising triathlon with Soph for the charity I volunteer at."

Hugo paused, digesting that. "I think you pronounced 'getting shit-faced in Antibes' wrong."

Jay laughed. "Seriously. I'm meant to be doing the swimming

section. I'm terrified I'm going to lose her lead."

"I don't know who you are," said Hugo slowly. "Can you put Jay on, please? Heir to Viscount Orton? Inexplicably successful with women? Total wanker?"

Jay laughed again. "I'm not going to let you rot alone at Conyers, don't worry. Tell me another date and I'll be there. Why can't you leave, anyway?"

Hugo muttered something about needing to do a job for his father, then said, "Did you hear Biffy's in LA?"

"Yeah. Gone there for the Oscar parties. Ever since his cousin Lansbury snagged an actress, he's determined to follow suit."

"I thought he was still hot for Fel Pennington?"

"I'm sure he is. But it's been years. I think he's beginning to accept that unless he can manage to turn into a horse, Felicity's not going to look at him twice."

"She's definitely one of the weirder Penningtons."

"She's not that bad. She's friends with my sister Jules. And cousins with Sophia. She's just...much more interested in animals than people."

"Not interested in Biff, anyway. Which is probably a point in her favour."

Jay made a noise of agreement.

"So," said Hugo after a moment. "This Sophia. Serious, is it?"

"Mm."

"Not like you to be shy, Jay."

"I'm not being shy. I just... If I start waxing lyrical about Sophia, you're going to laugh at me for it. And I refuse to be laughed at about that. Let me just say... I wake up in the mornings now and I don't hate myself. And I don't think I'm ever going to get bored of that feeling. That's all I'll say."

Hugo didn't speak for a moment. Partly because Jay's words gave him an uncomfortably hollow feeling in his chest, that sort of pinching ache you got when you'd been too busy to eat all day and hadn't realised how hungry you were. And partly because this was all extremely awkward. He might have known Jay since they were eighteen, but they had never really talked about Feelings-with-a-capital-F before.

"That's... I think that's saying plenty."

"Yeah," agreed Jay.

Hugo looked around his room, phone pressed to his ear, trying to think what to say next. His eyes fell on his little-used desk. "Don't suppose you know anything about investing money? My old man signed over a portfolio, and he's expecting me to do something with it."

"You're a Blackton. Isn't financial investment in your blood?"

"I think that's more Roscoe's line."

"Then ask him."

"Mm. Yeah. Though his ego's big enough as it is..." Hugo trailed off with a weak laugh.

"Anyway," said Jay, "don't ask me about making money. The last time I tried to earn some..."

And then he started laughing properly, and no matter how much Hugo tried to get him to say more, Jay resolutely refused.

"Best job I've ever had," was the only elaboration he would give. "Best job in the world."

Hugo said goodbye to Jay when one of the housekeeping staff arrived with his tray of food. He ate it watching TV but not really taking any of it in. He kept thinking instead about Amelia, all alone at Redbridge, and wondered how she was spending her evening.

He hoped the farmer had gone home.

And then he started to consider seriously how he could persuade her to come and use the Conyers spa. He'd seen enough at Redbridge to know how hard she worked. She really could do with a bit of real luxury and relaxation. Except that inevitably brought his thoughts to whether he could persuade her to make use of the massage room—in his company. And despite that being both extremely unlikely and unwise, he still spent a while dwelling on the idea, until he was achingly hard again.

For fuck's sake.

Little Miss Good. Little *Amy*. Of all the girls in all the world, why did he have to get the horn for her? His little sister's little friend. Always so scowling and uptight and lecturing, and right about bloody everything, and who could barely stand to be in the same room as him...

He really, really needed to get away from Conyers.

Or find a way to get some more girls here. Because he'd much rather be a chooser than a beggar.

THIRTEEN

A MELIA WAS EXTREMELY SURPRISED when Hugo turned up for work again the next morning—and on time.

She found him in the stable block, mucking out the stall of one of the piebalds. The mare was tied up outside the loosebox and snuffled at Amelia's pockets as she paused in the doorway, watching Hugo work.

He looked up as she slipped a pony nut from her pocket and the horse delicately took it from her palm. He nodded at the insulated cup of coffee in her other hand. "Don't suppose that's for me?"

"Nope."

"Of course not."

"But..." She turned and stooped, picking up the other cup she had brought. "This one is."

He raised his eyebrows, and the surprised smile he gave her was so genuinely pleased, so full of good-humoured warmth with no trace of his usual smirk, that she turned awkwardly away as he took the cup from her, feeling that she had done something far more intimate than she had intended.

He followed her to the stable door and leant against it, taking a sip of coffee. "I'm so bruised after that fracas yesterday, I was thinking about making use of the spa later. A sauna. Massage. You should come. Like I said—you could do with some relaxation. At least have a shower with hot water. It's revolutionary."

"I don't have time. Especially after wasting most of yesterday."

"I'm sure there's a phrase about pouring from an empty cup...?"

"I'm sure you also said something about wanting me in your spa with my clothes off, so it's a hard pass from me."

He coughed on his coffee. "I was joking. You know I don't mean the things I say."

"Yes," she said darkly, remembering the phrases he had breathed against her skin the night of the party. *You're so beautiful... I've wanted to do this for years... How have I never noticed you're perfect and you've been here all along...* "I know very well that you don't mean the things you say."

He straightened up, clearly getting her meaning. "I've said sorry so many times... I was drunk... My friends—"

"Don't pin it on your friends. It's on you and you alone."

"One stupid kiss—"

"That was the culmination of a two-decade career spent being a total *dick*. With no regard for anyone but yourself and your own amusement."

He scowled at that, and she stood there, heart pounding, heat rushing to her face, wondering where on earth that outburst had come from, but finding that she didn't regret it at all. Not until he said:

"Do you know what, Amelia? I think you wouldn't be so annoyed with me if you hadn't kissed me quite so enthusiastically back!"

She glared at him, and pathetically, the only words that came to mind were '*I hate you*', but she had too much self-respect to stoop to something so childish. So she turned on her heel and stormed away instead. Which wasn't much of an improvement. Especially when Hugo flung after her:

"Who are you really angry with, Amy? Me? Or you?"

———◇———

Hugo found her a few hours later in the estate office where she had been trying to get through the backlog of emails and arrangements for the Easter weekend event. It was only ten days away. And there was still no word from Cassie about when she would be back.

She looked up at the light knock on the door. It was open and Hugo stood there, looking unusually diffident, his head tilted as though considering how best to approach. But he walked into the room with his usual sangfroid when she snapped, "Yes? What?"

He sat on the front edge of her desk, fiddling casually with her stapler. There was a scratch on the back of one hand, probably from a plant, and a smudge of dirt on his thumb.

"I've done the stables. Helped Hodge in the garden. Tied up some raspberry canes and about a dozen other jobs I had no idea even existed until now."

"Great. Do you want a medal?"

"No. I want to know what to do next. You pitched this to me as the Labours of Hercules. I'm not sure raspberries seem very Herculean."

"Well, neither do you. But do let me know if you suddenly turn into a heroic demi-god."

"I confess, that normally only happens between the sheets. But if you'd like a demonstration...?"

"Why?" she said with a groan. "Why are you this person?"

He chuckled and put the stapler down, fixing her with a look under lowered brows. His mouth was playful, but there was something serious in his eyes. "It's who I am, Little A. I'm not sure I can change."

110

She rubbed her face and he laughed again. "Come on, give me a proper task. I need to win your forgiveness. Are you sure you don't have any puppies that need rescuing from burning buildings?

"Sadly not. And don't think about setting anything on fire just to give yourself the opportunity."

"As if I would."

"Hm.""

She leant back in her chair, twisting it from side to side as she considered his request. "There *is* the fencing in the east pasture." The ground there was notoriously rocky and hard to dig, which was probably why no real fence had ever been put up before. "It's one of the boundaries between our estates. Your father's steward asked us to install proper fencing a few months ago, but we haven't got around to it yet, partly because of the cost, but also because we're not entirely sure that boundary is our responsibility. But as we can't afford a solicitor to look into it, I suppose we might as well put the fence up. It's the cheaper option. This..." she said, looking away and clicking around on her laptop in an important manner because Hugo was frowning and watching her intently. "*This* is why the poor get poorer and the rich get richer."

"I'm sure I could speak to my father," said Hugo.

"Or," said Amelia, smiling sweetly as she imagined the back-breaking work. "You could put the fence up for us."

———⊗———

Hugo cursed as he dug the spade at the earth and, yet again, nothing bloody happened. What was the ground made of here? Concrete?

One of the gardeners had dropped him off at the edge of the grassy, weedy field, driving there cross-country in a rusty 4x4.

111

Hugo had been left with a load of wooden fence posts, some quick-set cement, and a few worn tools.

And a deepening sense of regret.

Give me a proper task...

What an idiot.

Only... Amy's little attack at the stables had shown him how far he still had to go. He had thought, with the coffee and everything, that she might be thawing. But it was clear the anger was still festering.

The anger and the hurt.

He swung the spade harder at the iron earth. It bounced off a stone with a metallic clang and nearly hit his foot.

He could be relaxing in the spa right now. Going for a swim. Calling one of the Swedish masseuses his mother kept on her books... And instead he was sweating and digging in the dirt, and all because Little Amy wanted a fence.

He would *pay* someone to build a damn fence. Now there was an idea...

He got out his phone and made some calls. It took a while, because he first had to figure out how one went about finding the sorts of people he needed to hire—tradesmen and the like—but, that done, he got back to work feeling much more cheerful. It would use up most of his available funds, but the payoff would be worth it.

There were few things that couldn't be fixed by throwing money at them.

Maybe even Amy.

———◆———

Several hours after Amelia had dispatched Hugo to the east pasture, Janson came to her office and said, "There's someone here about the fountain."

"What? A plumber? Did you call them, or did Hodge?"

"I assumed you did?"

Frowning, Amelia shook her head and followed Janson to the yard at the side of the house where a smart-looking plumber's van was parked.

"Miss Banberry-Thompson?" said the man. He was dressed in a monogrammed polo shirt and looked more like he should be serving drinks at a country club than crawling around looking at U-bends.

"Yes. That's me."

"I'm here to fix the fountain. I believe it's located in the terrace garden?" He looked down at a tablet, checking the job details.

"Yes. It's been broken since last year. But... I'm sorry, who asked you to come? I don't recall..."

He glanced down at the tablet again and gave her a slight smile. "It's been booked in by...erm...Hercules? I believe that's what it says. Possibly an error..."

"Hugo," she said grimly.

"Ah, is it? That's quite some typo. My apologies. I'll speak to the office."

"No, it's... Never mind. Come. The fountain is this way."

She led the man to the fountain in the parterre, her thoughts churning. She wasn't stupid enough to look a gift horse in the mouth—so long as Hugo really was going to foot the bill. But she was irritated. She was the one in charge at Redbridge. And him going behind her back like this was just another example of his high-handed, arrogant approach—

"Miss?" Sarah interrupted her on her way back to the house.

"Yes, Sarah?"

"This cleaning team that's turned up... I'm extremely glad of the help, of course, but I wasn't expecting... We hadn't discussed... I mean, honestly I'm surprised we have the budget for

113

it. There's five of them, and they say they've been booked for the next two weeks?"

Amelia stared blankly at her. "Cleaning team?"

"I'm not complaining. Their references are astonishing—they worked at Hardwick Hall! And they're all trained in antique care—all five of them! Soft furnishings and wood! Just think! We'll be sparkling by opening day, and we'll be able to get the green saloon opened up, and we never thought we'd have time for all that! But I'm... Are you *sure*, Miss Amelia? Can we afford it?"

"Erm. Can you stall them for a moment, Sarah? Make them some tea, show them around? I just need to check something first."

She practically ran the rest of the way to the yard, then flung herself into one of the Land Rovers and gunned it down to the east pasture, bumping and rocking over the uneven ground.

She came to a stop part-way down the field and stared at the sight before her.

There seemed to be an entire construction crew at work. There was a digger on caterpillar tracks, the deafening sound of a pneumatic drill, an enormous concrete mixer, and a dozen men in hi-vis jackets busy at work, erecting quite the most magnificent fence Amelia had ever seen in her life.

And, to her surprise, thick in the middle of the action, working alongside the builders, was a tall, dark-haired figure. He glanced up at the Land Rover and gave a casual wave. She was too far away to see his expression, but she imagined it involved an infuriating grin.

She eased the Land Rover closer, hands tight on the steering wheel. She parked it and got out, feeling ever so slightly swimmy and not one-hundred percent sure she wasn't, in fact, dreaming the whole thing.

Hugo broke away from the work group and sauntered over,

with, yes, an infuriating grin plastered to his face.

"Should be done in an hour or so," he said jauntily.

It was a hot day for Spring, and he had rolled up his shirt sleeves. And, for reasons pertaining purely to being Hugo, he had also undone all the buttons, so his shirt hung open, revealing a sweat-slicked chest and stomach.

"What...?" tried Amelia. "What is going on?"

"I'm building your fence, Little A. And I know you're going to get all moralistic and start lecturing me about how I'm meant to be doing it with my own fair hands, but look—" He gestured to his body, then held his dirty hands out for her inspection. "Sweat. Blisters."

She dragged her gaze away and looked past him to the workmen. One of them saluted her.

"And...the fountain? The cleaners?"

Hugo shrugged. "Things you needed help with."

"I can't... We can't pay you back..."

"I don't want paying back. I spend more than this on a night out. Well. Maybe a weekend away. But it's pocket change to me, Amy. I won't even notice it."

She didn't know what to say. She felt she ought to refuse. Because this felt like charity, and she didn't want to be obligated to him, not like this. And she definitely did not want his pity.

Hugo working at Redbridge... It was meant to show him how capable and competent she was. But he'd taken one look and seen she was fraying at the seams, barely keeping afloat.

She turned away, sudden tears in her eyes.

Hugo was studying her. She felt his attention the way she always did, like a physical brush against her skin.

"Amy... It's OK to do things the easy way sometimes. It's OK to accept help."

"I don't need help."

The thundering sound of the pneumatic drill started up

again, and Amelia winced, shoulders tense. Hugo stepped around in front of her. He put his hand lightly on her arm and bent down to speak in her ear but hesitated, as though changing his mind about what he was going to say. When he did speak, he said, "I'll get your tools and things, load them into your vehicle so they don't get mixed up with these guy's."

She nodded and followed him to help. They both picked up the rusty, bent old shovels and picks he had been left with and took them to her Land Rover. "The posts too?" Hugo asked as the drill finally stopped.

"Yes." After all, she couldn't afford to waste them.

"I'll carry them," he said. "They're heavy."

"It's fine. I'm strong enough."

He looked at her but said nothing. They walked together to the pile of wooden posts. Hugo picked the first one up, then winced and swore, dropping the post almost on his foot.

There was blood welling from a gash on his palm. Amelia stared stupidly.

"Must have been a nail or something," said Hugo, frowning at his hand.

"We need to get that cleaned," she said, coming back to life, her practical self taking over. She gripped the sleeve of his uninjured arm and led him to the Land Rover, dimly aware that he didn't need leading like an invalid but doing it anyway.

She opened the passenger door. "Sit there."

Her bag was in the footwell and she reached past him to pick it up, hunting for tissues. Fortunately, she had some. "Press that on it for now. Try not to bleed all over my car."

Hugo gave the filthy interior a pointed look. "Do you think you'd notice?"

She ignored him, and buckled the seatbelt for him, having to lean across him to do so and getting an eyeful of bare torso and a lungful of hot skin and whatever shower gel he used. It was

116

undoubtedly ludicrously expensive and seemed purposefully designed to trigger a flood of interest in every single one of her erogenous zones.

She slammed his door shut, got in, and drove.

"You've had your tetanus shot?" she said as they bumped back over the field to the track.

"I presume so." Then he laughed, amused at some thought or other.

Amelia glanced at him. "What?"

"I was just thinking. You've had my sweat, and now my blood. All you need is my tears."

"Are they on offer?"

"If you make me put up any more fence posts, I'll cry you a river."

"You make it sound so tempting."

He chuckled at that. There was a pause, and then he said, "Have I made it worse? With the contractors and cleaners and everything? Shall I send them away?"

"I wish I could afford the luxury of telling you to."

She felt his gaze on the side of her face. She kept hers fixed on the track. The house was in sight now and she took a left onto the driveway to the yard.

"You're annoyed though. Upset. That wasn't my intention."

"No. But you didn't—" She cut herself off, aware that anything she said would be ungrateful.

"I didn't what? Tell me."

"You didn't stop to ask. You never do. Your whole life you've just done and said exactly what you wanted without stopping to think about anyone else."

He didn't answer straight away, and she risked a glance at him. He was looking out of the window, unusually pensive, a frown creasing his forehead. He still held the tissue against his palm. It was soaked red.

"That's...probably true," he said.

Amelia said nothing more. They were at the yard now, and she focused on parking, pulling the handbrake on and then looking up at a strange van parked near the stables. Lee was talking animatedly to a man Amelia assumed was the driver. And on the ground between them was a large wire crate full of—

"What the hell?" said Amelia.

Hugo gave her a sheepish grin. "Um...I may have bought you some peacocks."

FOURTEEN

P ERHAPS, HUGO HAD TO admit, Amelia wasn't one of those problems that could be solved with money. She seemed more annoyed with him than ever, and, for a sickening moment back there by the fence, he thought he had almost made her *cry*.

Things hadn't gone quite to plan.

But she wasn't shouting at him, and she was now leading him through the house with the apparent intention of ministering to his wound. So he was hopeful things could be salvaged. He would have quite happily bled a bit more if it led to her forgiveness.

She took him to the kitchen and started rooting around in a cupboard, presumably for the first aid box.

"I miss the old kitchen," he said, looking around at the modern space. And normally he was sick to death of grand, old buildings. "What happened to that fat ginger cat? It was always asleep in the doorway."

"Colonel Mustard? He died years ago."

"Pity."

"I never knew you were a cat lover."

He almost made a joke about being extremely keen on pussies but manfully resisted the urge and said instead, "I have fond memories of that kitchen. Don't you? Raiding it for lemonade and jam sandwiches? Roscoe always managing to find wherever Cook hid the biscuits?"

"Of course I remember."

She pulled out a large green box with a white cross on it and opened it on the kitchen counter. "Wash your hand." She nodded towards the sink.

Hugo did as he was told, concealing his wince as he pulled the sodden tissue away. It was his right hand, which was annoying. Because that was the hand he used for...well...everything. And it hurt like hell, but he wasn't going to admit that to Amelia. He threw the tissue away and washed the cut, watching dolefully as the pink-tinged water swirled down the plug hole.

"Is it clean?"

"I think so."

He turned the tap off and leant back against the sink. Amelia held his wrist and looked at his palm, tilting his hand this way and that. Her fingers were warm on his skin and he was tall enough that he was looking down on the top of her bent head, which let him notice the way the mahogany strands of her hair threw off tiny glints of gold as the light caught them.

"I don't think it needs stitches," she said doubtfully. "But I think the nail went in quite deep, then tore through your skin a bit when you dropped the pole."

"Just a scratch," he said, ignoring the throbbing pain.

She glanced up and gave him a sceptical frown. "Maybe you should get it looked at properly. I don't want to be blamed if Carnford's heir dies of sepsis."

"Don't worry. My father's more than happy with his spare."

Her eyes widened, and her mouth opened to form some protest or question or other. Hugo winced internally, regretting saying anything, and poked her foot lightly with the toe of his. "Come on, Nurse Amy. Bandage me up before I get blood on your shiny new kitchen."

She dried around the cut with cotton wool, and Hugo gritted his teeth, because she was more thorough than tender. Then she got some antiseptic spray and said, "This might sting a bit."

He hissed, then tried to cover it up by drily commenting, "Just how badly do you want those tears?"

"Sorry."

"It's fine. I'm surprised you didn't just leave me in the field to bleed out, to be honest."

"It was tempting," she said, rummaging through the first aid kit for a bandage. She flashed him a grin. "But, you know...Insurance claims and things."

He chuckled, then had to grit his teeth again as she pressed a gauze pad over the cut. She started to wrap a bandage around his hand, and he looked down, watching her fingers work.

Neither of them spoke. The kitchen suddenly seemed very still and quiet. There was a clock ticking. Behind him, the tap dripped once or twice. Distant voices came from the outside. But it all only seemed to highlight the weight of the air between them, the way it was warmed and stirred by Amelia's breath. His shirt was still open, and he swore he could feel the air she breathed out touch his skin.

Amelia snipped the bandage and put the little scissors down with what seemed to be a very loud clatter. She tucked the end of the bandage in, and then, not looking up, she began to button up his shirt.

Hugo had been still, but now he froze. He was aware of his heart beating, but mostly he was aware of Amelia—of her bent head, of her fingers brushing against him as she fastened button after button, the light pressure against his chest, then his stomach, then lower, to the level of his belt—

He wrapped his fingers lightly around her wrists, ignoring the twinge in his hand. Amelia took a breath, and now it was her turn to freeze. She didn't look up at him.

He wasn't sure why he had stopped her. Or no—it was because he was rock hard, straining against his fly, and if she had happened to brush against him and felt it, then...

Well. That could have been awkward.

But he also touched her because...because he needed to touch her. Except now he didn't know what to do.

Amelia was the first to break the silence. "Why do you care so much? About getting me to forgive you?"

"Because I miss you."

She glanced up, both doubt and surprise clear in her dark eyes. She looked quickly away.

"But we've hardly seen each other these last few years."

"I miss knowing that you're my friend. And...and I wake up in the morning, and I feel this twinge of shame. And I don't want that."

"What *do* you want?" she asked.

"What I want is..." He moved his hands down her wrists slightly, absently rubbing her skin with the thumb of his good hand. "What I want is...if I'm talking to someone and they ask where I'm from, and I say 'Lancashire' and they say 'Oh, do you know the Banberry-Thompsons?' I want to be able to say 'Yes, I do. They're great friends of mine.' I don't want to have to say, 'I used to know them. Until I cocked everything up for a drunken dare.'"

"But...that's exactly what you did do."

"I know. And I regret it all. Except..."

"Except what?"

"No. Nothing."

"You were going to say something. I think I have a right to know. Except what?"

"Except I find it hard to regret kissing you."

He knew he shouldn't have said it the moment it passed his lips. But the way she looked at him confirmed it. It felt a little like being cut all over again. There was pain in her eyes. Dismay. Fear.

"Sorry," he said, letting go of her wrists with an apologetic squeeze. Hadn't he just resolved last night that he was not going to sleep with her? That this couldn't be about that?

He gave a small laugh. "You were right earlier. Why *am* I this person? Always thinking with my other brain. Saying stupid things. I'm going to stop it. It was a good kiss, that's all. And I can't stop thinking about it. But I know you don't want any more of...that sort of thing from me. So. Enough. No more innuendos. I just want to be your friend again, Amy. Can I please be that?"

She had moved away during his idiotic, rambling speech and was rather haphazardly flinging things back into the first aid box.

"Friends," she repeated, somewhat bitterly. "Were we ever really friends?"

"I used to think so."

She shoved the first aid box into the cupboard and looked back at him. For the second time that day, there was the alarming glitter of tears in her eyes.

"The thing about friends, Hugo, is that they need to trust each other. And I don't know if I can ever trust you."

"Then I'll work on that, too."

She met his look, and he knew she didn't believe him, that she wanted to fight it, and tell him not to bother, that she never would trust him, that she never would forgive him, and that all this that he was doing, was for nothing.

Was she right? He suddenly saw a version of that future, in which things were never put right between them. In which he didn't visit Redbridge, never saw Amy, only heard about her from things Evie let slip...

He didn't want that. He didn't want to wake up in the mornings and feel the way that hollow, pinching vision made him feel.

"Amy..."

Janson knocked on the open door and stepped into the kitchen.

Amelia turned toward the butler with a polite smile, and Hugo closed his mouth, not sure what it was that he had been planning to say.

"Sarah caught me just now," Janson said to Amelia. "She forgot to mention in all the surprise over the cleaners that Toby Patrick's clothes are ready. Should I drive them over now?"

"That's OK, Janson, thank you. I'll do it."

The butler nodded, then looked at Hugo, taking in the bandage on his hand. "Everything OK here?"

"Hugo cut his hand open on a nail."

The butler failed to look sympathetic. Instead, he tilted his head and smiled faintly. "On a nail, hmm? Puts one in mind of the crucifixion. One wonders whose sins you were dying for, my Lord Leighton?"

"Oh, I'm sure I have plenty of my own," said Hugo, too used to Janson to rise to his bait.

The butler just chuckled, nodded to Amelia, and withdrew.

Hugo looked at Amelia for a moment. "Toby Patrick," he said, because apparently this was bait he was unable to resist snapping at.

"Yes. What of it?"

"I never quite got around to asking... How do you two kids know each other?"

"Sixth form college. And we dated."

Hugo's eyebrows shot up. "He's your ex?"

"Yes." She coloured slightly, but met his look squarely.

"And...is he going to stay an ex?"

"What's it got to do with you?"

"I just think you could do better."

"Given what happened the last time I kissed someone, I suspect Toby is a vast improvement."

Hugo clenched his jaw, pitifully unable to come up with any reply that wasn't an incoherent string of swear words.

"I'll go and return his clothes then," said Amelia, picking up some car keys from a dish on the windowsill. "I'm sure you can see yourself out."

And she left him in the kitchen, with his jaw still clenched, his hand hurting like damnation, and the dawning realisation that he, Hugo John Henry Croftwood Blackton, Viscount Leighton, heir to the Sixth Earl of Carnford, was jealous of a potato farmer.

FIFTEEN

A MELIA DROVE SHAKILY OUT of the yard. She got as far as the lane beyond the border of the estate, then pulled onto the verge by a gate and put her head on the steering wheel with a groan.

Oh God.

Just... She couldn't even...

I find it hard to regret kissing you.

Why did he have to say that?

And: *I miss you.*

And: *It was a good kiss.*

And: *I can't stop thinking about it.*

Stupid, impossible man.

And now all she could call to mind was the heat of him standing bare-chested before her, and the scent of him, and the feel of his fingers wrapping around her wrists and gently holding her still, while her heart pounded and she didn't dare meet his eyes.

Why had she buttoned up his shirt? She had no idea. Her fingers had moved of their own accord while her rational mind looked on in horror. She knew better than to touch him. It had been one of the first rules she established when she realised the horrendous depths of her infatuation. *Don't touch him.* Because even the briefest, most accidental touch left her craving more.

And the one thing she had promised herself was that Hugo could never know how she felt. He was the sort of man to use it against her. To take her helpless devotion and play with it like a cheap toy. And he had, hadn't he?

She knew him far too well.

Except, then he had said, *"I just want to be your friend again, Amy. Can I please be that?"* And he had sounded so sincere. So little-boy-lost that her heart had ached. And she despised herself for that. She could feel herself beginning to weaken, beginning to consider forgiving him. Why did he have to start being nice and saying nice things? It had been so much easier to simply hate him. To know he was one-hundred-percent irredeemably bad.

It had been a relief, after ten years, to finally have a rock-solid reason to put her crush firmly behind her. But now it was slipping back into place, slithering those seductive chains around her heart.

Would she ever be free of Hugo Blackton?

She sat up, staring fixedly through the windscreen, fingers flexing on the steering wheel as she breathed determinedly in and out. She was sensible. She was competent. She was wise beyond her years. And she would conquer this.

Putting the car into gear, she drove on towards Toby's house.

———◦———

Amelia hadn't been expecting a hovel, but she also hadn't been expecting Toby's place to be as big as it was. The farmhouse was a long rectangular building, simple and sturdy, made of the local grey limestone. She counted two windows to the left of the attractive front porch and five to the right. There was the same number of windows on the floor above, and four small dormers in the slate roof. Probably six or seven bedrooms...? Small, true, compared to Redbridge, or the colossal overstatement of

Conyers, but no average house.

The broad, gravelled drive was tidy, with a few outbuildings at the edges and a sweep of lawn between it and the fence that ran along the road. There were a few plant pots along the front of the house and what looked like bay trees either side of the porch.

Amelia parked her car, feeling more nervous than she had expected. Really, she hadn't given much thought to seeing Toby again at all, her thoughts too full of Hugo and the need to flee. But now, she sat in her car, the engine clicking as it cooled, the neatly tissue-wrapped parcel of clothes on the passenger seat by her, and tried to work out how to act.

He probably wouldn't be in anyway.

She felt distinctly relieved at this idea, enough that she got out of the car. She was turning back to pick up the parcel of clothes when an older man's voice said in a strong Lancastrian accent, "Hello, and who might you be? You here on farm business?"

She turned to see a man of about fifty years dressed in well-worn clothes walking towards her from one of the out-buildings.

"I'm here to see Mr Toby Patrick. Is he in?"

The man paused, seeming surprised by either her face or her accent, which always sounded wincingly cut-glass to her ears whenever talking to someone with a country burr.

"He's up in the north field or thereabouts, but I'll let him know you're here." He pulled an ancient mobile phone from a pocket.

"I don't want to interrupt if he's busy—"

But the man had already made the call. He took the phone from his ear and asked, "What's your name, miss?"

"Amelia Banberry-Thompson."

The man's eyes widened, seemingly recognising the name. Redbridge and its family were well known in the area. He conveyed this detail over the phone, then ended the call. "He'll be ten minutes. Said I was to take you into the house and make you some tea."

"Oh, I don't want to be a bother—"

"Come. You'll get me in trouble if you say no."

So Amelia followed him into the farmhouse.

The stone-flagged hallway led directly to a large kitchen at the back of the house. Copper pots hung from wooden beams in the ceiling, a new-ish looking dark-blue Aga was set against one wall, the rest of the walls being given over to pine work counters and a large Belfast sink opposite a huge fireplace, now stacked with logs. Amelia looked around at the blend of old and new with a degree of envy. This was how she would have done the kitchen at Redbridge if they had been able to keep it for their own instead of giving it over to the public.

The man, who turned out to be one of Toby's employees, bid her to sit at the large pine kitchen table and busied himself making tea, chatting inconsequentially about the weather, and giving her little to do but make noises of agreement and look around the room. In doing so, she came to a better understanding of Toby's surprised amusement at Redbridge's facilities. But he didn't live in a museum. There would always be compromises to make in a house that could never truly be a home. Not while it had to earn its keep, at least.

The man left her as Toby came in, his cheeks ruddy, his hair looking tousled and windswept, and his eyes bright. He smiled at her and she felt guilty for her earlier reluctance at seeing him again.

"Hello. This is unexpected but welcome. How are you?"

There was a trace of that same country burr in his voice. A warmth to the edges of his words.

"I'm on errand duty," she said with a smile, nodding at the parcel on the table. "Your clothes."

129

He looked momentarily disappointed but covered it with a laugh and opened the parcel, giving the crisply ironed clothes a brief glance. "Thank you."

"Thank Sarah, really. My housekeeper."

He smiled at her, and she got the impression that he had been about to say something about appreciating the fact she had personally delivered them but had changed his mind. He looked uncertain for a moment, and shy, much more like the boy she had known at eighteen. He was only twenty-three, the same age as her, and he had this whole house on his shoulders, the whole weight of his family's farming empire, and none of it seemed to bother him at all. He was one of those sturdy, dependable people who just got on with things. Unlike her, sleepless at night, choking with pressure during the day, demands flailing around her mind like mad leaves in the wind.

It was all very well for Hugo to tell her to take the easy option, to let him help with haphazard gifts of workmen and peacocks—as if they were any help at all—but that wasn't reality. That wasn't what kept the show on the road, day after day, year after year. It was work and graft and dedication. Turning up and getting on with things and never giving in.

How could she sit around in his spa…? How could she waste time daydreaming about dark blue eyes and that mocking, knowing mouth…

"While you're here, I could show you around the farm, if you've got time?" said Toby. "You showed me your place, I'll show you mine."

She laughed because he did, wondering how he would interpret her saying 'Yes' while knowing she couldn't bring herself to be rude and say 'No.'

So she finished her tea, and they went out into the yard. There was a 4x4 parked there, newer than the ones at Redbridge but just about as muddy. Toby drove them down the lane, then turned onto a track, and they bumped their way to the top of a low hill where he turned off the engine. "This is about the best place to see it all. Almost everything to the horizon that way and to that line of trees to the east…that's all mine. There's more elsewhere, but it's disconnected."

"You lease this from the Blacktons, don't you?"

She said it without thinking, her mind dwelling on the thought that though she knew Hugo's family owned most of the land around here, she had never really thought what that would actually look like. The vast scope of it all. Her own family's land began and ended with Redbridge. Everything else had long been sold off.

"Technically, we lease it," said Toby shortly. "But that's in name only. It's let in perpetuity."

"So they can't kick you off?"

He gave her a sharp look. "Do you think they would?"

"What? No. Not at all. They're probably just glad someone is doing the work for them."

"I don't work *for* them. It's my farm."

"Sorry. Of course. I'm talking without thinking. My mind is wandering today." She smiled apologetically. "Possibly I could do with getting some more sleep."

But Toby just gave a thin smile and turned the 4x4 around, heading back the way they had come. Amelia looked out at the passing fields, chastened and guilty. But despite the awkward atmosphere, she couldn't help asking, "Does it ever feel too big? The land, the farm? Does it ever feel like too much to do?"

Toby took his eyes off the farm track and gave her a thoughtful look, his expression softening. "Sometimes. That's why I took up running, remember? To help with the stress. But I try to remember that, like running, I just have to keep putting one foot in front of the other. Keep going and I'll get there."

Amelia nodded, though she didn't feel much comforted. It

seemed to her as though it was impossible to get *there*, wherever 'there' was. The finish line? It felt like it was always being moved further and further out of reach.

"You're the same though, aren't you?" Toby said.

"The same as what?"

"As me. I mean... You don't mind hard work. It seems like you're looking after Redbridge pretty much single-handedly, and I respect that. I think we're quite similar. We both have a connection to a place, and we're willing to work hard. Life here, on the farm... You'd understand that. You're willing to put the graft in. You understand your duty."

The word settled around her like a yoke around her shoulders. She frowned out of the window. "Is it wrong that I sometimes wish I didn't understand it?"

"I'm not sure it's something we have a choice about."

But Hugo had said: *It's OK to do things the easy way sometimes.*

And she wondered if her run-in with Hugo hadn't left her trembling just because he had stood so close, talking of kisses, fingers caging the pulse point of her wrists... But rather because, for an instant, seeing Hugo at work in the field, she had caught a glimpse of what life could be like with an ally—with someone who went out of their way to ease her burden rather than adding to it. Someone who took control—however ill-thought-out and grandiose—and took on jobs without even being asked. And gave her gifts, however stupid. And told her to relax, have a spa day, even when she couldn't possibly... A tall, dark-haired, blue-eyed boy who stood at the door and asked her out to play.

And kissed her when he shouldn't have. And told her he didn't regret it even when he should have been apologising.

A man who hinted at sin instead of duty. Who sought and promised pleasure with every fibre of his being. Who sometimes didn't make her feel like being Little Miss Good at all, but someone else entirely…

She inhaled sharply, pushing down an ill-timed rush of heat, and nodded towards the softly undulating fields that seemed to stretch on forever. "I suppose you could have your running event here. You've plenty of room."

"I don't really want people trampling my crops. Besides, it doesn't hold the same cachet as hosting it at Redbridge."

"Is that why your club approached us? For the cachet?"

"Partly." And then, keeping his eyes firmly fixed ahead, he added, "And I wanted a chance to see you again."

She had no idea what to say to that, even though it was what she had begun to suspect. The farmer wanted a wife. And she was a hard worker. She'd have his dinner waiting on the table and clean the mud off his boots…

The silence thickened until Toby turned into the yard outside his house. He switched off the engine. She found herself blushing, embarrassed by the awkwardness of it all.

"I liked you, you know?" he said quietly, still looking through the front windscreen. "Back at college. I think I liked you a lot more than you liked me. And I never really stopped."

"Toby… I…"

"I know. You don't need to say it. This is humiliating enough."

"I'm so sorry. I'm just not in a good place for this. There's too much… Too much going on in my head."

He gave a humourless laugh, rubbing a hand down his face to his jaw. "Not sure why I ever thought I stood a chance against a viscount."

"It's not like that, Toby."

"Let me believe it is, hm, Amelia?" He smiled, but it was brittle and full of hurt. More wounded male pride. She was glad when he got out of the car and she could follow suit.

"I'm sorry, Toby," she said again. He didn't answer, just

watched her walk to her car and drive away.

SIXTEEN

H UGO COULD INDEED SHOW himself out of the house just as Amelia had suggested, however loath he was to leave it. He was also loath to imagine her driving off to the potato farmer's house and all the things that might possibly happen next, but he still ended up envisioning them all as he walked back to Conyers, his aching hand clenched at his side.

He crossed the entrance hall, indulging in an exceptionally petty but satisfying fantasy of kicking the potato farmer off his land when a familiar figure emerged from one of the side doors.

Hugo stopped in surprise. "Roscoe?"

"The one and only." He nodded at Hugo's bandaged hand. "What have you been up to? Strained your wrist? I get it. It's lonely up here..."

Hugo rolled his eyes and continued across the hall, heading for the stairs. He could really use a shower. And some painkillers. Roscoe fell into step beside him.

"I see you took my advice and got a haircut," commented Hugo.

Roscoe ran a hand over his short brown hair. "Turns out Poppy doesn't like me no matter what my hair is like."

Hugo frowned. "Poppy? Is that the same girl you mentioned last time? Who is she?"

"No one. Girl at work."

Hugo examined his brother's slightly awkward shrug as they reached the top of the stairs and headed down the landing. He didn't bother to suppress his smirk. "Having girl trouble, Ross? That's not like you. Should I give you a few tips?"

"As I'd quite like her to still be speaking to me afterwards, I think I'll pass."

"Hm, funny," said Hugo, pushing Roscoe on the shoulder so that he staggered sideways into the wall and nearly destroyed a priceless oil painting. Several *objet d'art* had met their end in this manner over the years.

His brother cursed him and regained his balance. "It's not like you to not be able to take a joke. I take it you haven't won Amelia over yet?"

"I'm working on it."

"There's this word you've probably not heard of. Starts with 'S' and ends with 'orry'. It's tricky to say, but you soon get the hang of it." Laughing, he ducked out of the way before Hugo could shove him again.

"Did you come here just to be annoying?"

"No, I came because I thought you might like my brotherly support at dinner tomorrow, though I'm starting to regret that generous impulse."

"Dinner? What dinner?"

"The parents are arriving tomorrow. And given it's one of those rare planetary alignments with both mother *and* father under the same roof at the same time, it's bound to be black tie and at least five courses. And an invitation to the vicar, or whoever else they think is deserving of the Blackton beneficence."

Hugo stopped walking. "Why did no one tell me they're coming?"

"Well, when I saw Howell just now, I believe his words were 'Have you seen your brother? I've been trying to contact him all day.'"

"Oh," said Hugo, recalling the text messages and missed calls on his phone that he had been busily ignoring.

"So just what *have* you been up to? I'm scared to ask, given you seem to be covered in mud and smell rather like Aunt Mabel. Taken a fancy to horsey girls?"

"Not quite."

"Going to elaborate?"

"No."

When they reached the door to his room, Roscoe gave him a serious look, scanning his face before saying, "I came up a day early because I thought you might want to talk one-on-one before the parents get here."

"About what?"

Roscoe gave an exaggerated shrug. "Oh, I don't know... Your plans to trick our lifelong friend into marrying you for money?"

Hugo flashed a look up the corridor, but there were no staff in sight.

"We already spoke about it on the phone. And it's not a trick. It's a...multi-stage plan."

Roscoe let out a long breath. "The thing is, Hugh...and don't fly off on one...but this all started after that conversation with Dad."

"Oh? You mean the one where he promoted you over me and basically condemned me to purgatory?"

"Yep. That one."

"It's shit and unfair and I hate it. I'm not sure there's much more to say."

"But this thing with Amelia...don't you think it might be some sort of... I don't know...emotional redirection? A way of distracting yourself from the real issue?"

Hugo gave him a narrow look. "What's with the therapist speak, Ross?"

Roscoe gave a dismissive shrug. "I'm a very modern man."

"Hm. Well, I'm not. So, if it will make you leave me alone, I'll tell you the truth. And the truth is... I really, really want to sleep with Amy. That's it. That's the story. I want to sleep with her and I can't seem to stay away because I'm like a dog with a really fucking persistent bone. OK?"

Surely that would shut Roscoe up. Because Hugo really didn't want to be questioned on exactly why he was so desperate for Amelia's forgiveness. The money, of course—and his need for it, given his total ignorance of how to develop the Belgravia portfolio.

But having admitted out loud his attraction to Amy, Hugo, for some ridiculous reason, found himself blushing.

Roscoe grimaced. "Ah, that's a bit awkward, given the whole her loathing your existence thing."

"Thanks for the reminder, Ross."

"Weren't you meant to be proposing this marriage thing as a mutually beneficial agreement between friends?"

"Yes. Exactly. Just as soon as she *is* my friend again."

"So... You can't really sleep with her, can you? Unless you're proposing a different kind of mutually beneficial agreement."

"I thought you studied Economics, not Stating the Bloody Obvious."

Roscoe just grinned, enjoying his brother's torment. Because that's what brothers do. "And how's the *friendship* coming along? Any signs of forgiveness? Wait... Did she stab you? Is that what the bandage is about?"

But Hugo didn't want to talk about it. About the tiny glimmers that had started to mean so much to him. How desperately he watched for them, and the relief, the gratitude he felt when they happened. Being handed a coffee. A smiling look. The way she had tied his bandage so neatly and with such care...

Roscoe wouldn't understand. So Hugo just rolled his eyes and closed his bedroom door on his brother's unsympathetic face. Then he had a long, hot shower. Because he really did smell like Aunt Mabel.

<hr />

Hugo woke up early the next day. He had breakfast in his room and nearly managed to escape the house without seeing anyone but was caught at the door by Howell.

"Good morning, my Lord. I thought we could go over some of the estate planning today."

"Perhaps this evening. I'm at Redbridge today."

"Again, my Lord?"

It never ceased to amaze Hugo just how much scorn his family's loyal retainers could squeeze into his courtesy title, all while being excruciatingly polite. It was quite the skill. He couldn't help but contrast it with the warmth with which Amelia's staff spoke to her.

"Yes. Again."

"If I might remind you, your father will be expecting a report on your progress. And his Lordship is due here later today."

"Don't worry. You have permission to pin my ignorance on me rather than on your own efforts. My father will have no trouble believing it."

Howell regarded him gravely, then stepped aside. "As you wish."

The cool morning air felt refreshingly crisp after that exchange, and Hugo took a deep breath of it as he hurried down the short set of steps and strode away across the garden towards the gate in the distant wall.

Of course, Howell was right, damn the man. And the depths of his father's disappointment would no doubt reach new lows. But his father's disappointment was infinite in scope. Almost too big for Hugo to bother worrying about. And besides, they didn't understand—Howell, Roscoe, his father—none of them understood the importance of him being at Redbridge.

The morning dew soaked the toes of Hugo's leather boots. His hand ached and itched under the fresh bandage he had rather inexpertly applied after his shower—the one Amelia had put on being soaked and ruined. He had felt a bizarre pang at throwing it away. And as he stalked, frowning, across the lawn, breakfasting birds fluttering up chirping, he felt suddenly that maybe he also didn't understand...

"Why do you care so much? About getting me to forgive you?"

"Because I miss you."

The mammoth looming bulk of Conyers House was silent behind him as he walked away from it, the morning sun stretching its cold shadow out across the lawn even to here, halfway to Redbridge. It was waiting for its master, the servants no doubt already scurrying, dusting all the gleaming things so that they glittered even more harshly, making the perfect more perfect.

And here he was, heading away from it all, towards that blue gate, the sun on the old brick wall, and the messy, imperfect chaos beyond. And if he truly cared what his father thought, he wouldn't do it. He would be in that overlarge office, looking at numbers with Howell, working out how to make money make more money. And Amelia... Amelia would be just under a mile distant, doing everything alone, and hating him forever.

His duty was clear. His duty was to Conyers. His duty was to be his father's son.

When had he ever cared for duty?

Hadn't he always done just what he wanted? Amelia had told him so.

And what he wanted lay ahead of him, past that sun-warmed wall glowing orange in the morning light, the immense cedars that grew on the other side, dusky, lush, and green, sentinels to a great secret...

He put his father from his mind and crossed through the gate.

———⊷———

"Miss Amelia said you was to go up to the house today. If you turned up," Lee told Hugo when he arrived at the stable block. The man nodded at Hugo's bandaged hand. "No stablework, she said."

Hugo thanked him, and the big man nodded. They had reached a sort of truce over the last couple of days. He was certain Lee still loathed him and would quite happily bury him in the muck heap, but he seemed to have a grudging respect for the way Hugo had shrugged off his hazing on that first day.

Lee had sent him to find a left-handed broom, and when he failed to find that, he had asked for a glass hammer. Hugo had been idiot enough to fall for it momentarily. But he had soon twigged. Or rather—he had when he ducked into an empty stable and looked up glass hammers on his phone, unsure whether he was supposed to be finding a hammer *made* of glass, or one designed for use *on* glass. Both had seemed like ridiculous options.

Which of course, they were. Because there was no such thing, and neither were there left-handed brooms.

Hah bloody hah.

But he had smiled it off. Been a good sport. If there was one thing he prided himself on, it was his ability to take a joke. Besides, the Stable Master's hazing was tame compared to the things that happened at boarding school—and the far worse things he'd done in university societies. That pig for example...

Hugo shuddered.

He entered the house through the side door and looked in the kitchen first, but Amelia wasn't there. The house was quiet, too early for even the cleaning staff to have arrived. Janson frowned at him when he found Hugo crossing the hall on the way to the bedroom stairs.

"Amelia?" Hugo asked.

The man's reply was reluctant. "Normally in her office, first thing."

Hugo thanked him, but the office was empty. He looked at her empty chair for a moment.

I find it hard to regret kissing you...

Good lord, had he really said that? Obviously, he *meant* it. But he didn't normally *say* the things he meant. Nothing good ever came of that. And he'd been rightly punished. That look of horror in her eyes...

He turned on his heel and headed once more for the stairs. There would be no more of that emotional stuff today. He would be sensible, and hard-working, and grown-up—

She was coming down the stairs. They both froze.

"You look..." He scanned her pale face, the shadows under her eyes. "I'm not sure what the polite way of saying this to a woman is, but you look...tired?"

Amelia coloured slightly and swept past him. He turned and followed her.

"I didn't get much sleep last night."

"Oh," he said, unhelpfully. Then his step faltered as he followed her brisk stride back through the house towards the kitchen, because he remembered that the last time he had seen her she had been on her way to see the potato farmer, and now he couldn't help but imagine all the possible things that could have kept her up at night.

The pain in his clenched hand made him wince, and he straightened the fingers slowly as he walked into the kitchen, two steps behind Amelia. He leant against the counter and watched her fill the kettle.

"And how was Farmer Giles?"

"Fine," she said, without looking at him, seemingly absorbed by the task of putting the kettle back on its base. Then she flashed him a glance, her lips quirking into a smile. "He wanted to show me the size of his...erm...land."

"I bet he did."

He failed to match her playful tone, and her smile turned into a frown. She busied herself getting cups out. "Coffee?"

"Please."

Hugo tried to rally his good humour, finding it harder than usual. "So... Lee said no stablework. What's on the agenda for today, demon taskmaster?"

"I thought your hand could do with a rest. So I thought we could do some admin."

"Admin?"

"Office work."

He couldn't suppress his grimace.

"Would you rather muck out stables?" Amelia asked pointedly.

"You know, I think I might."

"Well, I don't think it would be a good idea. You need to keep that cut clean."

Hugo said nothing, too busy basking in her show of concern. It was a very nice feeling. And he liked it too when she handed him a coffee.

"Thank you," he said. And he meant it most sincerely.

SEVENTEEN

"You know," said Amelia, about twenty minutes after they had started work in her office. "I really do think you would rather be working outside than in here."

She had to say something. Because it was far too quiet. Far too...*the two of them*, alone, in a rather small room.

The last ten minutes had been silent, except for the sound of paper on paper. The creak of the old office chair Amelia sat on. The too-loud metallic rolling, grating sound of the filing cabinet drawers Hugo had just closed somewhere behind her.

And the sound of Amelia's heart beating, of Amelia breathing, barely. The hairs on the back of her neck lifting as she shivered for some reason, though the room was warm and there was no breeze. The sound of silence from behind her. Hugo there, motionless, listening. Looking at her? Hugo Blackton at her back, and all the weight of his presence.

I find it hard to regret kissing you...

She forced herself to turn her chair and look at him. He was leaning against one of the tall filing cabinets, regarding her with a mixture of amusement and curiosity as he twisted a paperclip in his fingers. "Oh?" he prompted.

"Any time you get in an office, you get all twitchy. You start to fidget."

They both looked at the paperclip in his hand. It was bent

completely out of shape.

"Perhaps," he conceded with a smile.

"But you were always like that," she continued thoughtfully. "That's how I always remember you as a boy. Outside, running around, climbing trees. You like to be active."

She saw him fight the urge to turn that into a smutty pun. The effort it took was clearly visible, and she bit back a smile as he realised she had sussed his struggle. He crossed the room with a rueful look and dropped the ruined paperclip in the bin by her desk.

"You might be right."

"I'm always right."

"Not much of a career though in running around outside. Unless I suddenly decided to take up football. Possibly too late for that."

"A career? I thought you were dedicated to a life of bacchanalian excess?"

He smiled drily, then sat on the edge of the desk near her seat. Her heart rate picked up. He looked down at her, his lips still quirked in that dry smile, but his eyes held a challenge, as though what he was about to say held something of a dare.

"Not quite. I planned to work at my father's company. There was supposed to be a job waiting for me. It went to Roscoe instead."

Then he looked down, fiddling now with some imaginary imperfection on the knee of his trousers. He looked away, as though he regretted taking that dare.

The truth, she realised. That was what he had dared himself. To tell her something true about himself.

"Is that what you really wanted though? To be a...financial analyst? Fund manager? To be in London, in an office, for twelve hours a day?"

He smiled flatly. "You know me. I hadn't actually given it that much thought."

"The last time I saw Roscoe, he was still doing the internship there. He told me he was up here for a break. That he hadn't slept more than an hour or two at his desk in days."

Hugo frowned, and she wondered what it was that these brothers, so close in so many ways, actually talked about.

Beer, probably. Sport. Women.

Did men actually talk about women? She was a woman, and she hardly ever talked about men. But then, her best friend was the sister of the man she had spent the last ten years obsessively fantasising about. It had been a topic she'd been keen to avoid.

Her little secret. Until Hugo literally stole it from her lips.

She was looking at his lips now, she realised with a guilty start. Her eyes lingering on that firm, seductive line. Luckily he hadn't noticed. He was lost in thought, frowning down at his hands. He reached absently to the side and picked up her stapler. Started fiddling with it.

"The truth is," he said at last, with a bitter breath of laughter. "I'm not even any good at maths. I *hate* numbers."

Amelia eyed her poor, abused stapler. It looked close to breaking point.

"So... Find something you are good at."

He shot her a look. "What though?"

She smiled mischievously. "Mucking out stables?"

He let out another breath of laughter, less bitter this time. "Right. I'd better buy some horses."

"Oh, you're welcome to muck out mine."

He gave her a slightly wicked look—trust him to find the innuendo in that statement—but put the stapler down with a light chuckle. "Right. Thank you."

There was a pause. But a comfortable one. Or it was until Hugo looked at her, and they stayed looking at each several heartbeats too long.

Hugo was the first to look away. He let out a long breath and stood up briskly. "You're right. I hate office work. Find me something else to do. I beg you."

―――――◦――――――

Amelia led him to the east turret.

Like many large houses that had been added to over the generations by various hubristic ancestors, Redbridge Grange had a complicated roof structure. There were lots of odd angles and small flat bits and random turrets. It was no wonder it was prone to leaking. To rotting… But she pushed that flare of anxiety firmly down and turned to Hugo, who was regarding her quizzically as she paused at the base of the turret stairs.

"The perfect Herculean task," she said. "Opening the un-openable door."

He lifted his eyebrows but followed her gamely up the narrow stone spiral staircase. It was only a short flight, and the landing at the top was cramped. Hugo had to duck his head against the ceiling. Her shoulder brushed his chest as she turned towards him, and his head was bent to hers, his blue eyes glinting sea-dark in the shadowy space.

Silence, just for a moment, in which her heart beat too hard and her mind veered uncontrollably towards him, towards the line of his jaw, his lips so close to hers…

"Erm." She turned her back on him, aware now of his breath on her neck. "The trapdoor." She gestured to a wooden door in the ceiling, reached by a short metal runged ladder set into the stone wall. "We need to open it to get to the flagpole to raise the flag for the summer season. But it's completely jammed stuck."

Hugo squeezed past her. He climbed the ladder and slid back the bolt on the trapdoor with a rusty squeak. He pushed on the door. Put his shoulder to it and heaved. It didn't budge.

147

He climbed back down. Looked at her. "OK," he said slowly. "Any ideas?"

She led the way back down from the turret, needing air, space. "There's the other turret," she said quickly, heading that way without looking back at him. "We might be able to see more from there. It's probably just swollen with water from the winter, but I suppose it's worth taking a look."

A few moments later, they stood in another identical cramped landing, an even older-looking runged ladder leading up. Hugo climbed it, drew back the bolt, and with a slight "Hah!" of triumph, managed to get the heavy wooden door open. He climbed up and disappeared through the gap. Amelia followed him, climbing out onto the little round roof.

There was a low crenellated wall, about knee height, running around the edge. But it didn't do much to put her nerves at ease—she was not a fan of heights. The breeze was stronger up here, picking up her hair and tugging it over her face. She pushed it back and stood next to Hugo who was looking across the roof to the other tower. The white flagpole was there, the empty rope flapping slightly in the breeze.

Hugo looked at it for a moment, then down at the slate-tiled roof ridge about a metre below the turret roof.

"If you can't go up," said Hugo. "How about across?"

"What?"

But Hugo was already moving, swinging one leg over the low wall and climbing down onto the steeply pitched roof line.

"No! Stop!" She nearly grabbed for his sleeve to haul him back, but she was scared of making him slip. And he was already almost out of reach, skirting his way precariously along the narrow ridge of the pitched roof.

Amelia's heart stopped, then raced, panic flooding her. "Hugo! Stop! You'll get yourself killed. This is stupid!"

He carried on. He was halfway across now, arms held out on

either side of him, the ground three stories below, and oh God, oh God, he was going to die—

His foot slipped—

His arms flailed, seeking balance—

He was in leather boots designed for poncing around Chelsea eating brunch, not climbing roofs—

If he lived, she was going to *kill* him—

He steadied himself, arms out, and carried on. Amelia watched in terror. How dare he do something so stupid...

He reached the other tower. He climbed over the wall. There was a stomping sound, a wooden groan, a loud creak... And then he was giving her a cheery wave. "It's open! Come on up, Little A!"

Hugo meant to wait for Amelia to join him, but he was too full of adrenaline to stay still. He took one last smug look up at the flagpole then climbed down from the turret. His heart was beating like crazy, his hands tingling, a grin splitting his face.

She thought she had given him an impossible task, did she? Hah.

He headed towards the other turret, expecting to see her coming his way. But he didn't find her until he was almost all the way there. She was leaning against the wall.

"That was definitely more fun than office work," he said laughingly before he realised something was wrong.

She was crying, though apparently trying desperately not to, scrubbing her face as though she could rub the tears away.

"Hey... Amy... What...?"

He went to her and put a hand tentatively on her shoulder. She pushed it away.

"How...c-could you?" She sniffed, her breathing jagged.

"What? You said you wanted the door open...?"

"But not...not like that!" She let out a strangled sob and hit him on the chest with both hands, pushing him back a step.

He grabbed her wrists. "Hey, hey, come on..."

"You could have died! You could have died! I hate you, and you could have died."

Then she was crying in earnest, and Hugo, slightly horrified and not knowing what to do, let go of her wrists and wrapped his arms around her, pulling her in tighter as he said stupid things like, "There, there... Shush, shush... It's alright..."

He honestly had no idea what he was doing. He started to stroke her hair, her face buried against his chest as she sobbed, shoulders shaking.

He'd never held her before, not once. Never given more than the briefest of hugs in all the years he had known her. She felt surprisingly small, trembling in his arms. He had a sudden furious need to keep her there, where he could keep her safe.

Except...he was the one who had made her cry. Again. Though he didn't really understand why she was so upset. He was fine. Nothing had happened.

Eventually her sobs died down and her shoulders were still. She sniffed against his chest, reaching up into the narrow gap to rub her face. Hugo could just see the curve of one tear-stained cheek, the fingers that scrubbed across it. He gave her a squeeze and leant his cheek against the cool strands of her hair. "It's OK. It's OK."

"You could have died," she said in a small, broken voice, muffled against his chest.

"I'm fine."

"I'm going to kill you."

He laughed gently at that, and the movement forced him to acknowledge what he hadn't until now. Her body, pressed against his. The softness of her down the length of his front.

Now was very much not the right time, but a wave of desire shuddered through him, tightening his arms around her. He thought she became aware of their closeness almost at the same moment as him. She went very still, a hitch in her ragged breathing.

"Amy…"

He whispered her name. He wasn't sure why. But his face turned so that it was his lips pressed to her hair instead of his cheek. She smelt so good…

And this was stupid, stupid, but he felt far dizzier than he had up on the roof, far more like he was falling… All he could think of was that kiss. That one stolen, terrible, wonderful kiss that had changed everything. He remembered it all, the mingled breaths they had taken, his mouth hovering above hers, the strangeness and the rightness of this being *Amy*. Amy whose mouth opened to him, Amy who moaned as his tongue found hers. Amy, Little Amy, who he needed to taste again…

Even if it cost him everything.

He brushed his nose and mouth across her temple, and then he was seeking the sweet breath he felt damp against his chest, finding her lips… And the hand that had been stroking her hair now curled into it at the back of her head, tilting her face up, his mouth skating across the tears on her cheek, tasting the salt of her.

A gasp. "No. No." Then she pulled away. "I'm not kissing you. I can't…"

She spoke dazedly, more to herself than him, and he was too foggy with need to question himself, to do anything but reach for her again and try to bring her back to him…

"I can't, I can't…"

She ran.

EIGHTEEN

I F THE ROOF INCIDENT had taught Amelia anything it was that Hugo wasn't going to give up easily. So it wasn't much of a surprise when he burst into her bedroom a few moments after she did.

"Why?" he demanded, his eyes dark and wild. She could still feel him against her mouth.

"Why what?"

It was an effort to speak. Her mind and body were still flailing from the terror of watching him cross the roof, from sobbing like an idiot against his chest, from his mouth seeking out hers and instantly tearing through every resolution she had ever made.

"You said we can't. Why can't we?"

She shook her head and turned shakily back to the window, as though there was some escape to be had. But Hugo walked towards her. Stopped right behind her.

"I know you think you should hate me. And you probably should. But you don't."

It was daylight, and she could barely see any reflection in the glass, but she knew him well enough to imagine exactly how he looked standing behind her, dark hair falling across his brow, deep blue eyes fastened to the line of her neck, his gaze grazing the curve of her cheek. The hand coming up claim her, make her turn towards him...

She sucked in a breath as his fingers brushed up her arm and tightened around her shoulder. He drew her around, and she went. He tilted her chin up, and she met his eyes.

"I've already said it, but you don't believe me. I am *sorry*, Amy. I am so sorry. And I even almost regret kissing you, because then I wouldn't be tortured by knowing what it's like. But maybe I'm not as sorry as I should be, because on some level, I think you wanted me to kiss you. And I think you still want that. Don't you?"

She stared at him.

"Deny it," he said.

"I..."

His hand was on her chin. He moved it, cupping her cheek, finding her bottom lip with his thumb.

She closed her eyes.

"What is this?" she said, little more than a whisper. "What are we doing?"

"What we want."

She opened her eyes again, her breath catching as Hugo's gaze dropped to her lips and back up, his blue eyes nearly black. She wanted to make him promise— Promise to catch her, because she was about to fall. Promise to be there, when it was over. But she knew he wouldn't. He would barely look back at the mess he left behind.

"I can't trust you," she said. One last plea.

"Amy..." He brushed his thumb along her lip, and she was helpless, weak... "Trust me. I want this. I want you."

"But..." she murmured, his thumb dragging her lip down, his breathing rough as he traced the pad of his thumb over her bottom teeth.

And he drew her to him like that—with his thumb hooking her jaw, as though she was a fish on the line. And he didn't kiss her gently. There was too much heat for that. He had already opened her to him with his thumb, and now he moved his hand, found her tongue with his, and growled as he stepped closer, one hand on the back of her head, pulling her hard against him.

She let him. She let him do whatever he wanted, already falling apart. She was dizzy, sinking, letting him undress her, his hands ripping at the button of her jeans, tugging them down her thighs just far enough that he could reach her.

He groaned at finding her wet, and she broke the kiss, gasping against his shoulder, biting his shirt as he drove his finger inside her, adding another, impatient and rough... Until he suddenly wasn't—he pulled out, held her head between his hands and breathed her name as he kissed her slowly.

"Amy..." he sounded half-delirious. "Fuck...you're so..."

He kissed her again, pulling her top off as she tugged at his. They undressed between kisses, until finally the hot length of his lean body was pressed against hers and her hands at last got to explore the hard muscle of his back, his hips...

"I want you so much," he murmured, walking her backwards to the bed, lips hardly leaving her mouth, her neck. "You have no idea."

Something inside her almost laughed at that. Because if there was one thing she did know, it was wanting someone. And now it was happening... Hugo, this, them...

It was a mistake. She didn't trust him. This was all another game to him. Not a prank or a wager this time, but still a game, seeing if he could win over the woman who hated him, get her into bed with him. That must be what this was, because he was still Hugo, and he was never serious about anything.

He breathed *I like you so much*, and he didn't mean it.

He whispered *You're so beautiful* against her neck, and he didn't mean it.

He kissed her like he would die if he didn't, but he didn't, couldn't, mean it...

And she let it all happen. She kissed him back, dazed and dizzy and drunk from his touch, because it was just as good as she had ever imagined. And she craved him, needed him, wanted to be filthy for him...

She sat naked on the edge of her bed, and he stood before her, six foot of arrogance and lean muscle, his hard cock as big and thick and beautiful as she had always known it would be.

He saw where her gaze had fallen. "That's what you want, is it?"

He stepped closer, knees touching hers. "Go on then. With that pretty mouth."

Oh God. His words flooded her with heat. She trembled with need, and she wanted him so badly, wanted the feel of him so thick and hard...

"But don't...don't come in my mouth. I don't enjoy that." She looked away, furiously embarrassed. Why had she said that? She should have kept quiet—

Hugo cupped her jaw and brought her face back to his. "Of course," he said, his eyes intent, dark with heat, but completely steady. "I'm your slave, remember? We do what you want."

He held her look until she nodded.

"Is this what you want?"

"Yes."

"Then open your mouth, Amy."

His thumb found her lower lip, hooked her jaw once again, pulling it down. Her mouth opened, and he held himself there, hot against her bottom lip, the smell of him raw and heady.

She moved forward, replacing his hand with hers, wrapping her fingers around the thick base as she took him into her mouth, as deep as was comfortable. She closed her lips around him, traced the underside of his shaft with her tongue, her eyes closed. She moaned at the hot salt taste of his flesh, the weight

155

of him thick against her kiss-swollen lips.

She heard his breathless grunt of pleasure and moved her mouth along his length, savouring the friction, the violent pulse of him as he throbbed and swelled harder still.

Hugo Blackton, so arrogant and cocksure, and now he was weak with pleasure, trembling at the feel of her, his groans coming harder and faster, tortured and wanting—

"Amy... Amy..." His hands were in her hair. His fingers tightened their grip. "We need to stop, or I'm going to..."

She looked up at him, his cheeks flushed, his eyes glazed, a beautiful, beautiful mess. But his look sharpened with predatory heat at the sight of her satisfied smile. "Little Miss Good," he growled, half-praise, half-admonishment. Then he was pressing her backwards as he leant down and kissed her neck, forcing her up the bed so that he could kneel over her.

He bent his head to her breasts, torturing her the way she had tortured him, teasing and sucking her nipples until she was writhing, hands digging into the muscles of his back. He reached down between them and grunted, giving a muffled curse at finding her so wet.

"Tell me what you want, Amy. Is it this?"

He stroked her slick flesh, circling her entrance lightly until she was arching against him, seeking more.

"Or is this what you want?" He slid his finger in.

"Yes," she panted. But he stroked her with slow, languid movements, watching her frustration in amusement, before kissing his way down her body.

"Or is this what you want?" he said, his breath warm against her wetness, his finger sliding out and leaving her wanting.

"Yes," she gasped, as he took a teasing lick. "Yes."

"As you wish."

He settled himself more comfortably between her legs, hands on her thighs to spread her open and hold her down as he explored her slowly with his tongue.

Oh God, oh God, he knew exactly what he was doing, giving her almost too much, but never quite enough, keeping her just on the brink, until she was panting with frustration, moaning, "Please... Please..." with her fingers in his hair as she tried helplessly to grind against him. But he held her down, hands tight on her thighs, implacable, teasing, teasing...

"Hugo, I can't... Please, I need..."

He chuckled and pushed himself up, arms braced either side of her shoulders, looking down in amusement at the desperate, panting wreck he had made of her. He took her hand and wrapped it around his cock. "Or is this what you want, Amy? Do you want me to fuck you properly?"

"Yes."

"Then we need protection."

"In the bathroom. Above the sink."

She waited, heart pounding, and Hugo returned a moment later. He knelt between her legs and leant over her, the beautiful angles of his face so familiar, but now so strange, with the fierce heat in his eyes focused on her, like the dream she'd had a million times but only just remembered...

He shifted position slightly, putting his weight on one arm so that he could run his other hand down her body, skating his palm over her breast, smiling as she gasped and squirmed. Then he reached between her legs and laid his palm flat against her pussy.

He made a noise of appreciation. "Soaking. So fucking wet. You feel like heaven."

Slowly, watching her face, he ground the palm of his hand against her until she was writhing again, practically whimpering.

"Please..."

"What?"

"Fuck me, Hugo, please."

Instead, he sat up, kneeling, and said, "Fuck me yourself."

NINETEEN

S HE STARED AT HIM, confused, so he made himself clear by sitting back on his heels and lifting her onto his lap. He held her hips so that she was just above him, the tip of his cock barely brushing her.

"Hands on my shoulders," he told her. "Look me in the eyes as you sink yourself down on me. I want to watch you take me. I want us both to know you're the one putting my cock inside you."

Her eyes widened, but they were glazed with heat, and he felt the shudder of arousal his words sent through her. But he wasn't just bossing her around because it was hot—although, *fuck*, it was hot—he meant what he said. He wanted this to be her decision. There was something in the back of her eyes that made him sure that, as much as she was into this moment right now, she would regret it afterwards. And a better man, a stronger man, would have walked away.

But...fuck. He was not that man. And he barely cared that this was probably going to cost him sixteen million. What he wanted was for her to admit that this was as much her decision as his. Just like that kiss had been.

"Your choice, Amy," he said, fighting to hold her still when every impulse was urging him to bring her down onto him.

He let go of her hips. She took her weight on her knees, her fingers tight on his shoulders. Biting her lip, meeting his stare, she began to move...

And she moved down. She lowered herself onto him, and he was so fucking grateful he could have cried—if that wouldn't have ruined everything. But anyway, it felt too good for him to do anything but grit his jaw and groan, because she was tight and wet and she made such an outrageously hot little noise of shocked pleasure as she took the full size of him into her that it was all he could do to hold still and not flip her over and fuck her senseless.

He groaned, heart racing. "Little Amy... So fucking good... Taking me so deep..."

She went down all the way, pausing, feeling the stretch, letting them both enjoy it for a moment before she started to move.

Hugo groaned again. They fitted together so well. His hands were braced behind him, his fingers knotted into the bed covers. Amy was riding his cock, fucking him, because she wanted him just as badly as he wanted her.

And it was heaven. And it felt like home.

She groaned, gasping his name as he fought not to come, wanting this to last and last... But she was tensing around him, her head on his shoulder, her hips rocking, so close... He kissed her. He had to. He kissed her as she came, and she moaned into his mouth and he savoured every breath, his chest heaving too.

He lay her down on the bed. She was spent, flushed, lips red. But she pulled his head down and kissed him dreamily, her mouth so warm and soft.

He ran his hand up her side, caressing every curve, cupping her breast. He hadn't come, was still hard and aching. She moved her thigh, making room for him.

"Are you sure?" he said, exploring her with his fingers, finding her slick and swollen. "You're not too sore?"

"No. I want you. I like you inside me."

He groaned at that, pushing his finger inside, kissing her before he removed his hand and entered her again, savouring the bliss of it.

She whimpered in pleasure, her muscles tightening around him, and he held himself still, looking down at her with a smile. "Let's slow things down," he said, "I think you can come again..."

He kissed her slowly, then kissed her breasts, working her up again, holding himself still inside her until she was squirming against him, her hips moving in a frustrated rhythm as he refused to move...

And God it was *torture*...

But it was also great fun.

He had found his new favourite way to wind up Amy.

And when he finally moved, the noise she made was reward enough for his restraint. He rocked into her slowly, slowly, giving her slow kisses, giving her time to reach that peak again...

Then he pinned her wrists by her head and said, "Now *I'm* going to fuck *you*, OK?"

She nodded, eyes wide. And he drove them both over the edge.

Hugo: How do you know when you're in love?
   Jay: Is this the start of a rude joke?
   Hugo: I'm not that much of a twat.
   Jay: Debatable.
   Hugo: Please.
   Jay: OK. I think it's when...
   Jay: When that person becomes the reason for your very being.
   Jay: And you'd break yourself just to make them smile.
   Jay: And you know you'll never get tired of just looking at them.

161

Hugo: ...
Hugo: Right. OK.
Hugo: Asking for a friend.
Jay: Sure. Good luck.
Jay: It's worth it, btw. The hell to get there, it's worth it in the end.

Hugo put his phone away as he reached the steps to the side door of Conyers. He'd left Amy in bed. Which had been an excruciatingly difficult thing to do, but she had insisted. And there had been something about the way she didn't quite meet his eye which made him sure that staying would have only annoyed her. And he didn't want to do that.

You'd break yourself just to make them smile.

What did that even mean? Was it this? Walking away when everything cried out to do otherwise? He had thought love might be more like that hot, sharp feeling in his chest when Amy had shown she wanted him. A feeling that felt far too big, as though it wasn't designed to be held inside just one person but to be shared... But maybe this sort of glow he was feeling now wasn't love. Maybe it was just the after-effects of good sex.

Great sex. The best of his life. Because Amy was... Well. She was hot as hell. But it wasn't just that. It was that...she was *Amy*. He liked her, cared about her, wanted to please her.

Wanted to do the things they had done again, and forever.

And you know you'll never get tired of just looking at them.

Maybe that part was true. He never normally wanted to hang around after sex, unless there was a second round on offer. But there wasn't anywhere he would rather be than back there, with Amy, even if they did nothing but talk, or sleep.

But she had work to do.

And so he was back at Conyers, crossing the entrance hall, heading for the stairs to his room and hoping that his parents hadn't yet arrived. Somehow, despite everything that had happened, it was still only the morning. And the house didn't quite have that heavy, brittle feeling. So maybe his parents weren't here and he was safe for now and could hold onto this feeling for a while longer.

And figure out what the hell this meant for their friendship. And the money.

Roscoe met him on the stairs, heading down, hair wet from the shower. He stopped and gave Hugo a look—then another, eyes narrowing.

"Oh God," he said.

"What?"

"It's happened, hasn't it?"

"What?" said Hugo irritably, although he knew what Roscoe had somehow managed to guess.

"Is she still speaking to you?"

"Of course she is. And she's coming to dinner."

Roscoe's eyes widened in surprise. But instead of congratulating Hugo on his diplomatic success, he said, "Are you trying to punish the girl?"

"Fuck off, Ross."

He made to carry on up the stairs, but Roscoe frowned after him. "Wait. Are there... Are there *feelings* happening, Hugh?"

Hugo shrugged.

"Does she know about the money thing?"

"No."

"Jesus, Hugh. You really need to tell her the truth if you're screwing her."

"Don't say it like that."

"Ah. So there *are* feelings."

Hugo said nothing, wishing very much that this entire conversation wasn't happening.

"You need to tell her," insisted Roscoe.

"I will. When the time is right."

"And when will that be?"

"I don't know," he said and carried on up the stairs. But surely it wasn't five minutes after sleeping with her.

"You should have told her before!" Roscoe called after him, annoyingly telepathic as always.

Hugo gave him the finger over his shoulder without looking back.

After showering, Hugo went into his father's empty office and sat at the desk. Amelia had said she needed to work, so maybe Hugo ought to work too. He couldn't think of anything else to do except hang out with his brother, and Roscoe would just ask lots of annoying questions Hugo didn't have the answers to.

Maybe he should study the Belgravia fund. All the workmen and peacocks and what-not had wiped out his ready money. And he had no idea what this morning meant for the marriage plan. Was she more or less likely to say yes if they were sleeping together...? Probably less, if he knew Amelia. Kissing her with ulterior motives playing out in the background had been one thing, but sleeping with her?

He thought about it properly for the first time. Imagined her finding out...

Oh, *fuck*.

It would destroy her. It would destroy what was left of their friendship if she thought he was playing her. And *that* would destroy him.

OK. So... He just wouldn't ever tell her.

Except they both needed the money.

Fuck, fuck, fuck.

He dropped his head into his hands, wishing he could have just stayed in that moment forever, in bed with Amelia, where everything had been right and easy. But she wanted space—needed space—as loath as he was to give it to her. And now she was no doubt using that space to start regretting what had happened and think up a hundred reasons why it shouldn't happen again.

And *he* was stuck having to regret one of the best moments of his life. This was why he hated consequences. They ruined all the fun.

The housekeeper knocked on the door. "Parcel for you, Lord Leighton."

Hugo frowned at the green and gold gift box in her hands. It was unmistakably from Harrods. "Are you sure it's not for my mother?"

"It has your name on it."

The housekeeper put it down on the desk and left. Curious, Hugo pulled off the ribbon and opened the box. There was a gardening set inside—one designed for children: a tiny bright orange trowel and hand fork, and a packet of seeds.

Bemused, Hugo read the note.

For your new life in the country, Jx

Jay Orton. That dick.

FUJ, Hugo texted him, a phrase so commonly used in their friendship group it had acquired its own acronym. *You won't be laughing when I grow the world's tallest sunflower.*

Jay: Yes I will.

Hugo shook his head, laughing despite himself. He toyed with the packet of seeds, listening to their dry rattle. Magic beans. That's what he needed. A goose that laid golden eggs.

Maybe he could *earn* the money they both needed. Develop the fund. Discover whatever Roscoe's secret was to making money magically multiply itself. And then Amy would never need to know about the marriage thing. Or not for years, until their friendship was rock solid and she trusted him. And in the meantime, they could keep on sleeping together, because he really, really wanted to keep on sleeping with her. Possibly forever.

He shook his head, clearing away memories of Amelia, of the feel of her, the sound, the taste, and resolutely pulled the laptop towards him, finally ready to get to grips with the family vocation.

Except... Shit. What was the bloody password?

TWENTY

A MELIA SAT AT HER dressing table and took a long, hard look at herself.

So. This is what an idiot looks like.

An idiot who had been walking around in a daze all day with sore lips, an ache between her legs, faint bruises on her thighs, and a disconcerting sense that her whole life until that morning had been a sort of watery, shadow thing only half-lived.

She had a bruise on her knee too from when she had walked into a bench while remembering how Hugo had—

Shifting in her seat, she forced the memory from her mind and picked up her hairbrush, eyeing her makeup critically. It felt like clown paint, despite being so subtle that most people would hardly regard it as makeup at all. But dinner at Conyers required a lot more effort than…well, dinner almost anywhere else. The Earl and his wife were the sort that still insisted on *dressing* for dinner. So Amelia had a dark-grey satin sheath dress hanging from her wardrobe door. And she had dug out some heels that were only a *little* bit scuffed.

It would have to do.

Of course, she would far rather not go anywhere near Conyers at all. She felt stupidly nervous about seeing Hugo again, and to see him like this, in company with his whole family—barring Evie, her one true ally—was slightly terrifying. But he had asked her that morning while she was still coming to terms with what had happened, embarrassed and exhausted and weak and wanting him to stay even as she pushed him out of the door.

She'd said yes just to shut him up and get rid of him. And then she had stood alone in the middle of her room and, stupidly, she had *cried*. And then she had a long shower, and, stupidly, she had *laughed*. And she was still caught somewhere between those two extremes even as she sat calmly at her dressing table and twisted her hair up into something far more elegant than her usual messy bun.

Her phone rang just as she was about to stand up and change into her dress. She felt a surge of...fear? Excitement? But it wasn't Hugo. It was Cassie, her sister.

"Hi, Cass, how are you?"

"Good, yeah."

Cassie's voice had that faint, tinny sound of a long-distance call. It wasn't helped by the fact there was noise in the background. It sounded like she was walking down a busy road. Cassie was generally trying to do five things at once.

"Do you have a date yet for your flight back?" Amelia asked. "Because Mum says she might be staying in Peru a bit longer than she planned. So there might be a day or two when you're here by yourself. Sorry."

"Yeah, you see... That's what I'm calling about..."

Amelia's hand tightened on the phone, a nasty premonition sending a spike of unpleasant heat through her stomach. "Oh?"

"It's that internship... At David's uncle's paper, you know? I thought it was a total bust after what happened, but it seems they still want me. And they want me to start next week. So I was kinda gonna fly straight to London, find somewhere to stay... I just mean... I don't think I'm going to be able to come home. You see?"

"But..." said Amelia as the unpleasant feeling in her stomach worsened to a writhing sort of nausea. The air in her lungs felt solid and sore.

"I'm sorry, Amy, but you can just delay your trip with Evie by a few days, can't you? Stay a bit longer until Mum comes back? You have to see, I *can't* mess them around. It's a miracle they're still taking me on at all. David must have pulled some strings or something, bless him. Put in a good word. He is *such* a nice guy, and if it wasn't... Anyway. The thing is, if I start asking for favours, like for them to put my starting date back by a few weeks, I'm going to look so ungrateful. And I *need* this internship, Amy. It's *The Globe*. It's a national paper. When am I going to get another chance like it?"

"I've already delayed my trip eighteen months. All the flights are booked. The whole itinerary..."

"So? Just skip the first stage. It's only Spain, right?"

"I've never been."

"Really? It's pretty cool... But, you can always see it another time. Spain's not going anywhere. Unlike this internship. This is a once-in-a-lifetime opportunity."

Amy frowned, fidgeting with the edge of her dressing table, pressing her thumbnail so hard against the edge it started to hurt. The pain was keeping the tightness in her chest at bay, letting her breathe, letting her speak. Just about.

Spain wasn't going anywhere. And she had a hopeless feeling that neither was she.

"I slept with Hugo," she said.

Why? Why did she say that? Maybe because her barriers were worn down. Maybe to annoy Cassie. Maybe because she *had* to tell someone.

"Urgh. I thought you had more sense."

"So did I."

The background noise wherever Cassie was suddenly dulled, the traffic replaced by faint, relaxing music.

"Where are you?"

"Spa. Just getting a wax. Maybe a massage. I'm feeling tense about this internship thing."

"Mm," said Amelia, feeling the whole weight of Redbridge's rotten roof on her shoulders. Maybe she should tell Cassie. But what would be the point? "Are you annoyed about Hugo?" she asked instead.

"More disappointed that there's now almost no one I know who *hasn't* slept with him. You know he slept with Jess Orton last year? And Cessy Pennington. They sort of...overlapped. Neither was particularly happy about it. And then he slept with Emma D'Arby at Biffy's—"

"OK, OK, I get it," Amelia cut her off, hot and sick at the thought of it. "I know what he's like. You don't need to tell me. I just... I thought you might be angry. Given he's your arch-enemy right now."

Cassie made a scoffing noise. "He's not even worth enemy status. I was angry. Obviously I was. But then I realised, he's not worth the mental effort of hating. He's an idiot, completely inconsequential. A pretty husk with absolutely no substance. But you know that, right?"

"Yes," said Amelia, though she felt oddly guilty for saying it. But Cassie was right. Two decades of Hugo's acquaintance had shown her that. And Amelia knew that while Hugo would quite happily sleep with her as long as he was stuck at Conyers with no other women around, he would soon go back to London without a backward glance.

It was just...she couldn't help but remember him sitting in her office, playing with that damned stapler, admitting that he had no idea what he wanted to do with his life. And she couldn't help but remember him that morning, both so demanding and solicitous, determined to give her even more pleasure than he took. As if he liked her. As if he cared.

He had kissed her after they had sex again, and for a moment, he had looked down at her, and he had seemed so incredibly serious... For a moment, she'd had the strangest feeling that she was seeing him for the first time. The real him.

Not *just* a husk... Not *entirely* without substance...

"He's sort of...been a friend this last week. An annoying one. But a friend."

Cassie grunted. "Friends with benefits?"

Is that what they were now?

"Maybe."

"Well. You're an idiot. But make sure he keeps it wrapped, because you never know where he's been sticking it. And make sure *you* keep your heart in a box."

"Don't look so worried, Janson. It's only dinner with the Blacktons. I don't think the Earl is planning to chain me to a stone table and sacrifice me to whatever demon they worship at Conyers."

Janson smiled at her in the rearview mirror as he pulled up in front of Conyer's imposing entranceway. She had opted to be driven over, given she was wearing heels.

"It's not the Earl I'm worried about," said Janson as he got out to open her door.

Amelia gave him a grateful smile as she stepped out of the car—attempting to do so with an elegance she doubted she achieved. She looked up at the stone stairs to the enormous front entrance at their top and tried to beat down her butterflies.

"Send a message when you want picking up," said Janson. "And I hope you have fun. Because you do deserve it, miss."

"Thank you."

She headed for the stairs as Janson got back into the car. He made no move to drive off, but waited, watching her into the house, rather like a father dropping her off at a house party. Or so she imagined. Her own father hadn't been around enough to perform such duties for the few parties she had ever attended as a teenager.

The door opened, and one of the Blackton's smartly attired staff ushered her graciously into the cavernous entrance hall. The domed ceiling was lavishly painted with classical scenes, embellished with gilt and plaster scrollwork. She looked up, as she always did, because it was a spectacular sight. Also because she had the habit whenever she came to Conyers of searching for her favourite little cherub down near one of the walls and wishing on it for luck.

Perhaps it failed her this time, because after she found it and looked back down, Hugo was walking towards her looking alarmingly attractive in a black tuxedo. He smiled at her, and something fragile fluttered inside.

Help.

"Oh, I see how it is," came another voice. "I'm away for a bit and you only have eyes for my brother."

She looked away from Hugo as Roscoe stepped forward, doing little to ease her flustered embarrassment by squeezing her hand and stooping to kiss her cheek. Why were they both so absurdly tall? And good-looking? It really wasn't fair.

"Ross!" she said with a smile, pretending she wasn't blushing and her hand wasn't sweating. "How are you?"

"All the better for seeing you."

"Alright, creep," said Hugo, shouldering him out of the way and tucking Amelia's hand into his elbow as though he had suddenly decided they might as well match their surroundings and go full Regency. Although, Amelia was sure a true Regency gentleman wouldn't be holding her hand quite so firmly against the muscled edge of his ribcage. And a true Regency miss probably wouldn't be having trouble walking straight due to the vivid memory of said gentleman's head between her legs.

"You look beautiful, by the way," said Hugo.

"Smooth," commented Roscoe, who was walking at her other side, grinning at them like he was having the absolute best time of his life. And making Amelia woefully sure he was fully aware of how things stood between her and Hugo.

"I will kill you," Hugo told his brother cheerily.

Roscoe laughed and made small talk in his usual friendly way until they reached the drawing room where the Earl and Countess were waiting. It had been almost a year since Amelia had last seen either of them. Their combined appraisal was somewhat unnerving.

"I see my sons can at least act like gentlemen occasionally," said the Earl with a smile that didn't quite remove the sting of his words. Or not for Hugo at least, Amelia thought, given the flash of annoyance on his face as he removed his arm from hers and turned towards the drinks cabinet.

"They certainly look the part," said the Countess, laying a fond hand briefly on Roscoe's lapel before gliding closer to Amelia. Even in her mid-fifties, she was still an astonishingly beautiful woman, her dark hair coiled atop a long, graceful neck, her eyes a disconcertingly similar shade of blue to Hugo's but starkly highlighted by heavy kohl.

"Little Amelia!" She put her cold hands on Amelia's shoulders and smiled down at her. "So pretty now!"

Amelia smiled awkwardly.

"I did invite the vicar to join us," said the Earl. "But he was engaged. He did tell me however to pass on his thanks to you, Amelia, for Redbridge's donation of flowers to the church's Easter decorations. I trust we also sent ours as usual?" he asked Hugo.

Hugo looked up from mixing drinks. "Um. I'm not..."

"I'm sure Howell would have included it in the notes he prepared for you."

"Yes. Quite. Possibly I overlooked it."

The Earl frowned at his eldest son, and Roscoe loudly launched into an anecdote to cover the awkward moment. Hugo crossed the room, handed Amelia a stiff drink, and downed his own.

———⋅◦⋅———

Dinner proceeded as it often did at Conyers—with an awkward mix of theatrical aesthetics and stultifying boredom.

Most of the leaves had been removed from the table, in an attempt at making a cosier family setting. The Earl sat at the table's head, his wife at the other end. Roscoe sat at the Earl's right elbow, and Amelia and Hugo sat on his left.

The food looked pretty and tasted as good as you would expect with a world-class chef in the kitchen. But Amelia couldn't help but compare it to the simpler but flavorful food Sarah prepared with their home-grown vegetables, the eggs from their own hens.

The Earl spoke mostly to Roscoe about work. Amelia noticed Hugo often turn towards the conversation, as though looking for an entrance into it. But mostly he spoke to his mother about mutual acquaintances. About life in London. Things she knew nothing about.

As the fourth course was removed for dessert, Hugo leant down and breathed, "Sorry," in her ear. She knew he was apologising for all of it, the tense atmosphere, the boredom, the whole evening. But although Amelia wasn't exactly having fun, she was also aware of a refreshing sort of feeling. Of being somewhere else, doing something different. A change of scenery.

174

Even if the scenery wasn't much to her liking.

It wasn't exactly Spain. But beggars couldn't be choosers.

She drank more wine than she probably should have. So did Hugo. He leant a little closer to her when dessert was served, and she was heart-stoppingly aware of his eyes on the side of her face. For once, the others were all involved in conversation together and Hugo's hand dropped down under the table and came to rest on the silken fabric covering her thigh.

She took a sharp breath, hiding it with a sip of wine, and kept her eyes fixed on her plate. Then Hugo's foot hooked around her ankle and slowly dragged her foot to the side, spreading her legs.

She was sure her face was burning, and she was sure this was a completely stupid thing to be doing. But her pulse was racing, and the throbbing between her legs was painfully strong and insistent.

Hugo's hand slid down her thigh to the hem of her dress at her knee. He never looked up from his plate, his other hand casually carving off pieces of cheesecake with the edge of his fork while his fingers slipped ever further up her bare inner thigh and he kept his foot around her ankle, holding her legs apart.

Oh God, oh God, she had to stop this. She couldn't let him touch her there, not now, not here. But she seemed to be frozen. Common sense had deserted her. All she was aware of was the inching progress of his hand, slipping up her thigh to brush against the already-soaked fabric—

She gasped. Heads turned. She stood up clumsily, bumping against the table before hastily excusing herself. "Sorry, bathroom..."

Cheeks burning, she walked unsteadily from the room.

Damn, Hugo!

She found her way to the nearest bathroom and locked the door, running the cold tap, not wanting to look at her flushed face in the mirror. A rap at the door made her jump.

"It's me."

Hugo.

"Let me in."

Why did she unlock the door? Why did she just look wordlessly at him instead of hissing that he was an irresponsible idiot?

Maybe it was because of the way he looked at her as he stepped inside and locked the door behind him.

"Amy…" he said, as though that was all the explanation he needed. Then he kissed her, walking her backwards to bump against the basin before dropping to his knees and pushing up her skirt.

He looked up at her, eyes hot and wicked as he dragged her underwear down, the scrape of it on her thigh indecently wet. He touched her, watching her face, and gave a hum of approval at what he found. And she made no protest—even though this was not a good idea, even though they shouldn't, *couldn't*, be doing this here, now—she did nothing but grip the sink behind her and widen her stance a little. Then his mouth was on her, and her head was tipping back with a soundless moan, every word driven from her mind.

She came embarrassingly quickly, shuddering against him, fingers gripping the edge of the sink behind her. He sat back on his heels and smirked up at her. "I always did like dessert."

———◦———

Hugo left the bathroom first, pressing a soft kiss to her mouth before leaving her to get her breath back—her breath and her sanity. Or maybe it was too late for that.

She cleaned herself up, then finally met her reflection in the mirror. Her eyes were large, pupils dilated. Her cheeks were flushed. Her hair somehow tousled even though Hugo hadn't touched it.

In short, she looked exactly like someone who'd received an illicit and mind-shattering orgasm in the middle of family dinner at Conyers.

A mess.

She left the bathroom and found the others had already withdrawn from the dining room. She headed towards the sitting room she thought they most often used but caught sight of Hugo standing in the doorway to the library.

He had his back to her, leaning against the door frame, only one shoulder and part of his back visible. Her heart gave a skip as she walked towards him, but she stopped at the sound of voices.

His father was speaking from somewhere inside the library.

"—disappointed that you haven't seen fit to develop the Belgravia portfolio. When I handed it over to you—"

"I'm trying, but you gave me no instructions," Hugo interrupted. His voice was irritated, and Amelia noticed that the line of back and shoulder visible to her were tense.

"Instructions?" laughed his father without humour. "What instructions do you need? It's the most straightforward portfolio I had with the most obvious investment opportunities. A child could manage it. Why do you think I chose it for you?"

Amelia winced at that.

"Thank you," said Hugo darkly, "for your solicitude."

"Don't sulk. I'm just at a loss to see exactly what it is you've been doing since I last saw you. Howell says you've done nothing around the estate. I thought I made my expectations clear."

"Did you not notice Amelia at your table? You told me to fix my reputation. Show you that I can be trusted to manage clients. Isn't me getting her here proof of that?"

Amelia went cold. She heard the Earl scoff.

"No one doubts your ability to flirt your way out of a problem. So *that's* what you've been doing, is it? I don't know why I expected anything more."

"It was hardly easy to convince her to trust me."

Amelia backed away, feeling sick.

She had known... She had *known*... Even Evie had told her Hugo had something to prove to his father. And that's all it was. Just a different type of game. A confidence trick. Some high-level schmoozing to prove a point.

She had known... So why was she crying? Angrily, she wiped tears from her cheeks. What was it Cassie had said? He was inconsequential. Not worth the effort of hating.

So. She wouldn't hate him. She would refuse to even care.

Blindly, she headed towards the back exit of the house, thinking only of getting home. Getting away. She was almost there when she heard Roscoe calling her name.

"Amelia! There you are. Just as I guessed, you got lost in this ridiculous pile. I'm here to escort you back to civilisation. Or what counts for it round here."

Then he saw her face.

"What's wrong? You're so pale."

"Just a headache, Ross. I thought I'd try some fresh air, but I think I might just go home. Would you please make my good-byes?"

He glanced up the corridor, towards the door at the end that led to the garden. "You were planning to walk? Let me get a car to take you."

"No. Thank you. I think the fresh air will do me good. Perhaps I had too much wine."

"Well... I can't let you walk home alone in the dark. Wait here. I'll get your coat."

He dashed off, and Amelia was tempted to leave without him. But she didn't want to draw more attention to her erratic behaviour. So she waited, attempting to think of nothing. To push it all down, the way she always did when things tried to choke her.

Roscoe came hurrying back, her coat and bag over his arm. Fortunately, he was alone.

"Father and Hugh are having *contretemps* in the library. I didn't want to interrupt. Best leave them to it."

Amelia managed a wan smile. Roscoe helped her into her coat. He held the door open for her. She paused on the stone steps down to the lawn, removing her heels so they wouldn't sink into the grass. Roscoe silently took them from her. She didn't have the heart to protest his gallantry.

"Sorry about your head," he said as they set off. "I'm not surprised though. An evening at Conyers would give anyone a headache. Anyway, we're down to the heavy drinking and character assassination part of the evening, so it's probably a good time to leave. I might just hide out at Redbridge with you."

Amelia managed a smile. There was a sort of large, wobbly ache in her chest, and she knew if she looked at it too closely, she would be in tears. So she fixed her eyes on the dark garden ahead of them and resolutely tried not to think.

After a pause, Roscoe said, "I couldn't help but notice you and Hugh are...er...closer than you used to be."

It took Amelia a moment to master her voice. Rather robotically, she said, "He's been helping me at Redbridge."

"Yes. He said."

There was a pause. Amelia prayed Roscoe wouldn't speak. But he was Roscoe, so of course he did.

"I just... I feel I need to say... Hugo is—I mean, don't get me wrong, I love him, in fact, I love him *almost* like a brother—but he's not always the most straightforward man. He has a bad tendency to not mean what he says, and not say what he means."

"I happen to have noticed."

"And he often doesn't think things through. Or think at all, come to think of it."

Despite everything, Amelia breathed a laugh at that. "You don't say?"

"I'm just saying that despite his childlike air of innocence—"

Amelia laughed again.

"—he's not quite as simple as he might seem."

"How do they cope with your humour down in London, Ross? I always imagine everyone at your office wearing grey suits and being completely straitlaced and humourless."

"Oh, yes, even their skin is grey. And greyest of all is their souls. But I'm very straitlaced too in London. Can you believe visiting here is the closest I come to relaxing?"

She made a noise of mournful sympathy at that. But the change of subject had done the trick, and Roscoe didn't mention his brother again until they reached the door of Redbridge.

"Are you sure you're OK, Amelia?"

"Yes. I'll take some paracetamol. Go to bed. Thank you for the...company."

"Forgive me for stepping completely outside my place, but I can't help but suspect your headache was caused by too much Hugo, not too much wine. Has he done anything? Because like I said, I love him like a brother, but I consider you almost as much a sister as I do Evie."

Roscoe's handsome, good-natured face regarded her gravely, lit warmly by the orange glow of the porchlight. He really would make a very fine brother.

"No. He hasn't done anything except be himself. But..." She lifted her hands in a sudden shrug of helpless despair. "He gave me *peacocks*, Ross. What does that mean?"

Roscoe frowned, troubled. "I have absolutely no idea."

TWENTY-ONE

H UGO WAS STALKING THE downstairs rooms hunting
for Amelia when Roscoe came in through the back saloon. He smelt of cold night air.

"Where have you been? Have you seen Amelia?"

"I just walked her home."

Hugo stared. "What? Why?"

"She had a headache."

"And you didn't think to come and get me?"

"I told Mother."

"Why not me?"

Roscoe fixed him with a look. "Because she had been crying,
Hugo."

Hugo went cold. "Why? What happened? Wait... You think
I had something to do with it?"

"Didn't you?"

Hugo took an angry step towards him. "That's what you
think of me? Believe me, the last time I saw her, she was perfectly...happy."

"OK," said Roscoe with a tired shrug, clearly unconvinced.
"But something happened to upset her."

"Then why didn't she come to me?"

Roscoe looked at him. "Why would she? What exactly are you
to her? Her boyfriend? Her fuckbuddy? Or the man trying to

181

trick her into marrying him for money?"

"Oh fuck off, Roscoe."

"No. You need to stop and *think* for once. Amelia doesn't deserve to be caught up in another one of your games."

"It's not a game!"

"Then what is it? Because I don't know. And I don't think she does either."

"What did she say to you?"

"She said you'd been yourself."

Hugo let out an angry breath. "Myself? And clearly that's terrible, right? That's what you're insinuating here?"

Roscoe shrugged one shoulder.

"Some opinion my family has of me! I thought you, at least, were on my side. But I'm clearly just a feckless idiot to all of you."

"Well, you do keep acting like one."

Hugo bristled, anger surging hot and thick in his chest. But there was the sharp pang of hurt too. He didn't normally argue with Roscoe. Not like this.

"When did you become such a sanctimonious prick, Ross? Was it when Father made you his heir in all but name? Or was it before that, when you decided to become his obedient little clone?"

Roscoe flushed. "Why does everyone think things just fall at my feet? I've not been given anything I didn't earn. And you have no idea how hard I've had to work to earn it."

"Clearly I have no idea about anything."

"Amelia aside, if you want to know why I'm angry, Hugh, it's because you're better than this. And we're all sick and tired of waiting for you to prove it. I'm tired full-stop, Hugh. I'm fucking exhausted. Of here. London. Everything." He flung his hands out in a despairing gesture, the startling glitter of tears in his eyes. "I'm tired of your pointless drama. I'm tired of watching you cock up, yet again." He shook his head. "I'm going to bed. I'm leaving early tomorrow."

He left the room, leaving Hugo alone, recriminations ringing in his ears.

———◆———

It was nearly midnight when Hugo crossed the gardens to Redbridge. He had spent a while trying to do as Roscoe told him—stop and think—but the only conclusion he could come to was that if Amelia was sad, he needed to go and find out why. And fix it.

There were still a few lights on in the old house, its shape so familiar even in the dark. He rang the bell at the kitchen door, but no one came. He rang it again, and was about to do so a third time, when he saw movement behind the glass, and Amelia's housekeeper, Sarah, opened it, looking tired and annoyed.

"What?" she barked.

She was married to Janson, the butler, and shared his low opinion of Hugo.

"I came to check on Amelia."

"She's in bed. With a migraine."

"Can I see her?"

"No."

Hugo knew a bit about migraines. His mother got them. Or claimed to.

"I'd like to check she's OK," he said, trying to keep the annoyance from his tone. "She might be sick."

"I'm looking after her. Just like I've done for years."

Sarah started to close the door. Hugo stopped it with his palm. "Sarah. It's Amelia's decision whether she sees me or not."

"She needs peace and quiet."

"Even so."

She held his implacable gaze for a moment, then submitted. "Wait here."

She was gone for what seemed like ages. When she finally returned, Hugo straightened from where he had been leaning against the doorway and went to step into the kitchen. But Sarah shook her head.

"She said no."

She shut the door in his face.

<hr />

Shit.

It seemed Roscoe was right and Hugo had done something. He just had no idea what.

Maybe it was what happened during dessert... But she had seemed as into it as him. After all, she'd come bruisingly hard all over his face, which Hugo had, up until this moment in his life, always taken to be a good sign.

But maybe she regretted it. Maybe she regretted everything they had done. Regretted *him*.

He felt sick at the thought.

"Roscoe?" He knocked heavily on his brother's bedroom door. "Roscoe?"

He heard a muffled curse and then Roscoe opened the door, wearing nothing but boxers, hair tousled, face scowling and puffy with sleep.

"I'm sorry I'm such a twat. Oh, and, erm, I'm sorry for waking you up."

Roscoe glanced down at the glass of whiskey in Hugo's hand. "It's two in the morning," he said weakly. "I'm leaving in three hours."

"Hardly any point going back to sleep then."

Roscoe didn't return his grin.

"Sorry," said Hugo again, more seriously this time. "But I needed to tell you before you left... I didn't mean what I said. I know you deserve the job. And that I don't. You were right. You're right about everything." He swallowed, an unaccountable ache in his throat. "Including Amelia."

Roscoe looked at him, then held the door open and stepped aside. "Come in, Hugh," he said tiredly. "Come in and talk to Uncle Ross."

Roscoe went back to his bed and sat against the headboard. Hugo walked to an armchair, but before he sat down, he turned and paced abstractly up the room.

"I went over, and she wouldn't see me. She had Sarah turn me away at the door."

Roscoe grimaced and rubbed his eyes, suppressing a yawn. "And you can't think of anything you've done to upset her?"

"No. We..." He wasn't about to tell his brother about *that*. "We, um, parted on good terms."

"You followed her to the bathroom."

"And we parted on good terms," Hugo repeated through gritted teeth.

Roscoe grunted. He blinked blearily, thinking. "She said something about peacocks."

"Peacocks?"

"You bought her peacocks."

Hugo shrugged. "She likes peacocks. Don't you remember we used to have that old one in the grounds when we were growing up? She used to collect the feathers. She's still got them in a vase in her room."

Roscoe eyed him thoughtfully. "Hmm."

"Hmm what?"

"Nothing. Just getting a sense of the bigger picture. She seemed...perplexed about the peacocks."

"It was something of a whim." He sat down heavily in the

armchair and sipped his drink. "I'm fairly sure this has nothing to do with peacocks though."

"They are annoyingly noisy creatures," commented Roscoe. "Remind me of someone, actually."

"Hah. Funny."

"Going back to the bigger picture... You slept with her, yes?"

"Yes," admitted Hugo reluctantly.

"You invited her to dinner. You...erm...followed her into the bathroom..."

"Where are you going with this, Ross?"

"No idea. It's just amusing watching you blush. I didn't realise you could."

Hugo reached behind him for a cushion and threw it at Roscoe's head. Roscoe caught it easily and tucked it behind his head with a grin. He always had been annoyingly good at sport.

"Why did she kiss you?" Roscoe said suddenly.

"What?"

"At Cassie's party. You know what she's like. She takes everything seriously. Unlike you, she says what she means and she means what she says. And when she means something, she *really* means it."

Hugo frowned in confusion. "What does... What does that, um, mean?"

"What I mean is... No. Never mind. I'm not about to accuse her of having feelings when she's not here to defend herself."

"Feelings? You think she... Back then, you think she *liked* me?"

"You're right. It's preposterous. I'm tired and talking nonsense."

Hugo frowned and drank his drink.

"I don't get why you haven't told her the truth yet," said Roscoe.

"Because it's never the right moment."

"What are you waiting for?"

"I need her to trust me. To know that I'm not...using her."

"Aren't you?"

"No! Not... It's not that simple. I want her to genuinely forgive me. And if I start talking about the money—and us getting *married*—she's never going to believe that I've honestly been trying to make amends with no ulterior motive."

"Ulterior motive like sleeping with her?"

Hugo rubbed his forehead. "That wasn't...the goal."

"You should have just told her the truth right from the start."

"She wouldn't even talk to me at the start."

"OK. So tell her now."

"I can't. She'll think everything that's happened between us was another trick. It's like the boy who cried wolf, don't you see? I fooled her once, and now she won't believe any of this was real."

"We all know how things stand at Redbridge. Her family needs the money. And Amelia would do anything for Redbridge. She might hate you when you tell her, but she'd probably go through with it for the settlement."

"But I don't want her to hate me! And I don't want her to marry me for the money. I want her to *want* to marry me." He heard the echo of his words. "Oh, shit. What does that mean?"

Roscoe was staring at him, eyes wide. "You know what it means," he said slowly.

"I do?"

"It means either you're a narcissistic prick who needs everyone to like them. Or...you're in love with her. Which one is it, Hugh?"

TWENTY-TWO

A S THOUGH SHE HAD summoned it by the headache excuse she had given Roscoe, Amelia came down with a
terrible migraine. The feeling of tension and pressure that had
been in her head all day—or perhaps all week—turned into
the dreaded pain around her right eye just as she was saying
goodnight to Hugo's brother.

She walked upstairs, squinting at the light. As always, the
migraine hit her stomach, which knotted and roiled, protesting
against the wine, the rich food, everything. And the pain in her
head seemed like a protest against the whole day. The fear of
watching Hugo cross the roof. The breathless excitement of
Hugo in her room. All the work she had done that day, wool-
ly-headed and abstracted. Cassie's inevitable abandonment and
the new weight of anxiety that it had twisted into her chest.

And then Conyers. And Hugo. And Hugo saying those
things...

She staggered into her en suite and threw up.

Sarah put her to bed and brought her some painkillers, but
she couldn't keep them down. The pain was a crushing beast,
a giant clawed foot gripping her skull. She whimpered, tears in
her eyes, drifting in and out of sleep all night, aware of Sarah
pressing a cold flannel against her head, Sarah helping her to the
bathroom and back into bed.

And then morning came, and the beast released its grip, but Amelia was exhausted and weak and her skull felt as fragile as glass.

She was too tired to lift her head or even open her eyes when Sarah came into the room and sat down on the edge of her bed. There was the touch of a gentle hand on her shoulder, and a voice said, "How are you?"

But it wasn't Sarah.

"Hugo?" Amelia croaked, turning to look at him and wincing at the movement. She was pathetic and bleary-eyed and probably smelt like vomit. "Why...? Please go away."

His dark blue eyes held the velvet of a night sky, and he looked unfairly fresh and healthy and beautiful as he looked down at her. He touched her forehead softly. "Has your migraine gone?"

"More or less." Her voice was dry. Hugo reached for a glass of water on her bedside table. She tried to sit up, but he put an arm around her shoulders and held the glass to her lips instead.

"Um. Thank you," she said awkwardly as he settled her back against the pillows. "Why are you here?"

"To check you're OK."

"I'll be fine in an hour or two."

He looked as though he was going to say something, but instead moved up the bed to lean against the headboard, pulling his shoes off. He stroked the hair back from her face and then kept stroking her forehead, his fingers warm and gentle. "You should sleep. You need to rest."

She frowned up at him from the pillow, then caught his hand in hers and took it from her face. She had been so angry with him last night. Now, she hardly had the energy. But she was still hurt.

"Go, Hugo. See your family before they leave."

"Roscoe's already gone. Mother's in bed. Father's in his office." He shrugged lightly. "Besides, I'd rather be here with

189

you."

"I don't even know what the time is. I need to get up. I have so much to do."

She tried to sit up, but Hugo pressed her back with a hand on her shoulder. "No. You need to rest. And get some sleep. Rest and relaxation. Doctor's orders."

"Don't be ridiculous. I have too much to do. Especially now—"

She stopped, embarrassed for some reason to admit that her family, yet again, had decided to abandon her to Redbridge.

"Especially now what?"

"No, nothing. Just Cassie isn't coming back quite when I expected, so I have even more to do."

Hugo's face took on an unusually hard expression. "She's leaving you here alone to do everything? When's your mother back?"

"I'm not sure. She keeps changing her mind."

Hugo's expression turned even darker, and he scowled across the room as though the far wall had personally offended him.

Her tired eyes dropped from his face, and she looked instead at his chest, at his arm, the soft navy of his brushed cotton shirt only serving to highlight the hard muscle it covered. She looked down at his legs stretched out on her bed, crossed casually at the ankle, and she became freshly aware of the sheer physical weight of his presence, the way he made the mattress dip, the faint scent of clean clothes and clean skin.

She felt so gross and grubby and small. And she desperately needed to brush her teeth.

"It isn't fair for them to leave you here alone to cope with everything. Tell me what you need and I'll help you with it. Anything at all." He smiled. "Add them to Hercules' list."

But the mention of his tasks, the efforts he had made to atone, reminded her of his conversation with his father last night. Her chest ached, like pressing on a bruise.

"You've done what you set out to do," she said quietly. "No need to carry on."

He turned sharply to look at her. "What do you mean?"

She looked down at the duvet, toying with the top edge of it. There was an embarrassing wobble in her throat. She swallowed and forced it away.

"You wanted to show your father that you could repair the bridge between our families. That's what this was all about, wasn't it?"

"No—"

"It's fine. I knew it wasn't really genuine. That you weren't really sorry."

"Amelia, no..." He sat up from the headboard, his large frame tense. "It wasn't for my father. It was... It's because I..." He pushed a hand through his hair, dark waves awry. "I do care. I am genuine. I thought you were starting to believe that?"

"Because of yesterday?"

It came out bitterly, and she almost said something to soothe it over, especially when Hugo flushed as though hurt.

"Partly. But not just because of that. I thought we... I thought we were friends again, at least."

"Like I said, you need trust for that. And I still don't think I can trust you."

He paused, seemingly thinking hard. His mouth opened to say something, then he cleared it away, seemed to give himself a mental shake. "Then I will earn your trust, Amy."

———⊙———

Amelia looked up at him, doubtful, hesitant. So pale and fragile that his heart ached to do something, anything, to bring her back to health.

"Rest now, though," he said. "You should be asleep. Or do you want some breakfast? I can fetch you some toast?"

"Sarah can—"

"Please. I want to."

She finally let him. And he hurried downstairs, not wanting to leave her alone for long. He ran into Sarah in the kitchen. She wasn't pleased at finding him in the house.

He had woken early in the morning, determined, after his talk with Roscoe, upon a fresh new course. It would involve openness and honesty. And grovelling.

He would start with the grovelling. It seemed easier.

And the openness and the honesty would come soon. When she felt better. When she liked him a little more and he wasn't so scared that one wrong word would undo the fragile thing he had managed to build between them.

Because if last night had taught him anything, it was that he couldn't stand it when Amelia was angry with him. It had physically *hurt* when Sarah closed the door in his face. He didn't ever want to feel like that again.

Amelia was leaving the en suite when he returned with a breakfast tray. She was in white cotton pyjama bottoms with a pale candy-pink stripe and a white cotton vest top with a print of pale-pink roses.

Perhaps it shouldn't have been, but it was alarmingly hot, and he put the tray down somewhat clumsily on her bedside table as his body rapidly switched control to his stupider brain.

"Erm. There's tea, and orange juice too. And toast. And some porridge, which Sarah insisted on, but..."

He trailed off, sitting down again on the bed and trying not to notice the way the thin fabric of her pyjama top skimmed her breasts.

Amelia sat back against the headboard, hands wrapped around a cup of tea. "You don't need to stay."

"But if I don't, you're going to get out of bed and do something stupid, like try to work."

She smiled faintly. "I *have* to work."

"Do you even stop at weekends? I haven't seen any evidence of it."

She wrinkled her nose, unable to deny it. "But if I don't work—"

"If you don't *rest*, then this happens." He gestured towards where she lay in bed.

"I get migraines every couple of months. It wasn't triggered by work. It was..."

"What?"

He had the suspicion she'd been about to say, "You." Instead, she said vaguely, "There's just a lot going on." She put her tea down. "I need to get up. And I ought to...um...shower."

She coloured faintly at that. Hugo opted not to notice—or to make any of the suggestions that were currently crowding his mind with images of soap-slicked skin.

He hopped off the bed. "I'll run you a bath. A long, hot soak and then..." He ran his eyes lightly over where she sat on the edge of the bed, a faint blush on her cheeks. "And then...a nap."

———◦———

Other than the nauseating abundance of pink, Amelia's bathroom was about as austere as you'd expect from someone who had probably never uttered the word "pampering". Unless it was preceded by "I don't have time for—"

Which was almost word for word what she was saying now as he searched her bathroom for bubble bath, or bath salts, or anything vaguely indulgent. *He* had more products in his bathroom than this.

He poured out a generous slug of lavender-coloured shower

gel in lieu of any better options and swirled it around with his hand as the tepid water slowly coughed its way into the bath from the ancient tap. He hoped it was going to get hotter than this.

"You are *so* having a spa day," he muttered to himself.

"What?" asked Amelia, from where she hovered in the bathroom doorway, frowning at his preparations as though he was planning to boil her alive.

No chance. Not in this water.

"Nothing," he said, pouring in another dollop of shower gel for good measure. At least it was starting to foam. "Does it get hotter?"

"Eventually."

"Come and eat something while you wait."

To his surprise, she did as he said, sitting down on the edge of the bed and nibbling at the corner of a piece of toast while he leant in the bathroom doorway, checking the water's progress over his shoulder every now and then.

Steam. Hallelujah.

He stole a moment to study her while she was occupied with pouring more tea from the teapot. The teapot had a hand-knitted tea cosy on it, which was somehow so very *Redbridge* it hurt his chest.

There was a tiny bit more colour in Amelia's cheeks, though her eyes were still shadowed. Her lips were bitten dry. Or maybe kissed dry, from yesterday. Her hair was down, messy strands falling across her cheek, brushing the skin of her shoulder. She looked so fresh and soft.

"You're incredibly pretty in the morning."

She shot him a look. "What?"

He shrugged one shoulder, looking back into the bathroom to cover his embarrassment. He hadn't meant to say that out loud. "Just an observation. Anyway. I think this is ready."

He left her to it and sat down to wait.

TWENTY-THREE

AMELIA SAT IN THE bath feeling self-conscious until the hot water worked its magic and she relaxed a little, letting her head fall back, her eyes closed.

But she couldn't forget that Hugo was waiting in the next room. On her bed.

An involuntary clench of desire made her toes curl. She forced them straight and let out a long breath.

Migraines always left her feeling tired and hollowed out, but they also strangely refreshed her, as though they washed her clean of all the built-up anxiety and stress she had hardly allowed herself to acknowledge. Her head felt spacey and drowsy, and at the same time, her thoughts felt slightly brighter.

Hugo was here. And for some reason, he was being impossibly nice to her, albeit in his usual high-handed way. What was his new game? Still trying to prove something to his father? Perhaps to himself? She had no doubt that whatever his game was, she was merely a pawn in it. Hugo's true concern would always begin and end with himself.

That was just how he was. It was like Cassie had said. There was no point expecting anything more from him. And so it was ridiculous, really, how upset she had got last night when she overheard him with his father. After all, he had just been proving that he was exactly who she had always known he was.

But the other thing he had also proved yesterday was that his smug arrogance was extremely well-founded. He had good reason to be cocky. To prowl around the place oozing sexual confidence. Because he was…

Well. She felt another rush of arousal at the memory of his touch, her nipples tingling as tension gathered between her thighs.

She'd always known it. Her body was a slave to his.

She got out of the bath and dried herself before her mind could run away from her. But when she emerged from the bathroom in her ratty old dressing gown and saw him sitting on her bed, she came to a decision. Or rather, she gave in to one.

Hugo dragged his eyes from the still-damp skin of her legs to her face. She hoped he would attribute the flush of her skin to the heat of the bath.

"The only redeeming feature of that dressing gown," he said, head tilted, navy blue eyes holding her fixed in place, "is its length. Or lack thereof."

Cassie said he was a joke. But to Amelia, he had always been a fantasy. Whatever he was, he definitely wasn't serious. And so that was how she ought to treat him. A bit of fun. And if she went into it eyes open, she wouldn't get hurt.

Friends with benefits. Fuck buddies. Casual, dirty, fun.

Maybe the best way to get Hugo out of her head was to give in to him.

He shifted over on the bed and pulled her duvet aside. "Nap time."

"Hugo, honestly, I can't spend the day in bed." She fidgeted with the frayed cord of her dressing gown, stopping when she found his eyes tracking the movement. Making bold resolutions in the bath was one thing. Breaking the habits of a lifetime in order to act on them was another. "I'm feeling fine now, really."

"You look like a mild breeze would knock you over."

She scowled, annoyed at clearly looking pathetic just when she had made up her mind to succumb to his seduction. Maybe he really did want her to have a nap?

That would be as embarrassing as it was disappointing.

"An hour," he insisted. "I'll set an alarm and wake you up."

"You're planning to...to stay? And watch me sleep? Because that's..."

"I'll nap too. I stayed up far too late last night talking to Roscoe."

"I'm never going to get to sleep with you here."

"Why not?"

"Because...because you make me tense."

He smiled slightly. "How about I do something to relax you?"

Her flush deepened and her heart started pounding painfully against her chest. Hugo seemed to misinterpret the way she stood there frozen.

"Not like that. I mean a massage."

He got up, taking control of the situation, which was just as well, because her mingled arousal and embarrassment had rendered her temporarily stupid. Or maybe she was chronically stupid to even be considering going ahead with this. It was *Hugo*. She ought to be ordering him from her room and getting on with the millions of things she had to do that day.

"Lie on the bed," Hugo said, walking past her towards the bathroom. "You can keep yourself covered with the dressing gown. I'm sure I saw some lotion or something in one of your cabinets. If I can't get you to the Conyers spa, I'm going to bring the spa to you, Little A."

She walked towards the bed, refusing to think. "Do you even know how to give a massage?"

"I've had enough to know the basics," he said from the bathroom.

Amelia hurriedly took advantage of his absence from the

room and undid her dressing gown, removing her arms but holding it around herself as she lay down on her front. She pushed it down from her shoulders and back but left it covering the rest of her.

Hugo returned. With her face turned to the side, she could just see his legs as he stood near the bed. But she could feel his eyes on her skin.

The mattress dipped as he knelt on the bed, his weight coming over her, his knees on either side of her as he straddled her legs. "This needs to come down a little further," he said, tugging gently on the dressing gown. "Unless you just want a neck rub."

How did he sound so calm? She had never been more tense in her life, and she flinched when his hands touched her shoulders. So much for relaxation.

"Sorry, it's probably cold," he said. "It'll soon warm up."

His fingers were firm on her shoulders, rubbing and kneading with an insistent pressure that did almost feel professional. Except her body was not interpreting it that way. Waves of heat rushed through her with every circle or squeeze of his hands. She was agonisingly aware of being more or less naked, of the pressure of him sitting astride the backs of her thighs, pressing her into the mattress. Her breasts were so sensitive she felt every movement that pressed her against the bed, and heat pooled, liquid and needy, between her thighs until she was trembling with tension.

Hugo worked in silence, though occasionally she felt his breath on her too-hot skin. He massaged her shoulders, the base of her neck, then he worked his way down her back, thumbs pressing into the muscle either side of her spine as his fingers fanned out across the back of her rib cage. His hands were big enough that the length of his fingers almost brushed the sensitive skin of the side of her breasts where they were flattened against the bed. But they didn't quite reach, just teased and teased until she had to bite back a whimper.

His hands moved down to her lower back, to the almost ticklish skin of her waist, and then his weight shifted backwards, pulling the dressing gown down a fraction as he shuffled further down her body, letting him reach the base of her spine, the inch of skin just above her backside.

She bit the sheet, throbbing with need, but his hands moved back up the way they had come, back to her shoulders, and she had the sinking realisation that maybe this was just going to be a massage after all.

Until Hugo leant down, mouth against her shoulder and whispered, "Let me make you come."

———⋅⊙⋅———

Amy tensed beneath his hands, shoulder blades drawing together with the sharp breath she took. "What?"

"It'll relax you. Get rid of any tension left."

Her voice was tight with embarrassment, as though she spoke through gritted teeth. Her face was hidden in the pillow, hands pulling the edges of it up around her as though she quite wanted to smother herself with it. "You said this was just a massage."

Hugo smiled to himself, hands sliding down her back to the lovely little dip at the base of her spine. "I think we both know that became a lie the minute I touched you."

The dressing gown was only just covering her. He left it in place as he slipped one hand underneath and swept it over the curve of her backside to the damp heat gathered between her thighs.

She sucked in a shaky breath. Hugo slid one finger into the gap. Her legs were pressed together with him sitting aside the back of them, but he could reach the heat that pooled there. She breathed in sharply as he dipped his finger into her wetness, just tracing his fingertip along her opening.

She moaned.

"It doesn't have to be a sexual thing," he said, as he slowly rubbed his finger back and forth. "Like I said, just a release. Something to relax you. You can keep this dressing gown on if you want."

She didn't answer, but he felt the new rush of heat that slicked his finger.

"Roll onto your back," he said, moving so that she could do so.

She did, and he bit back a laugh at the arm she kept across her eyes, the way one hand clutched the dressing gown, holding it across her chest.

"That's OK," he said, as he knelt between her legs. "Stay covered. Keep warm. It's this I need." He touched her clit as he spoke, and she twitched, biting her lip as he circled it slowly. It was already pink and swollen, a little wet with her own arousal. He ran his hands down her thighs, spreading them wide.

"I'm going to go down on you," he said. "I'm going to fuck your pussy with my tongue."

"Hugo..." she protested feebly, her voice breathless.

"I'm going to taste you and smell you, and you're going to come all over my face. Really fucking hard." He leant down and kissed the inside of her knee. "Doctor's orders," he murmured, kissing his way up to the sensitive skin of her inside thigh.

Fuck, he was so hard. His dick was throbbing. Her pussy lay exposed, inches from his face, pink and dripping wet, and he ached to plunge himself inside it, to have her tight warmth holding his shaft—

He groaned to himself, and then his mouth was hovering over her, the hot, tangy smell of her filling his lungs. He licked her, savouring that first heady taste. And oh God, she was so fucking perfect and ripe and tight... He made a noise that could only be described as a growl and licked her again, running his tongue along her until he came to her clit. He licked it, sucked it, grazed it with his teeth, and she cried out, hips writhing. He held them tight, brought his hands up to grip her thighs and hold her in place, keeping her wide open to him. He worked her slow and fast, slow and fast, bringing her almost to the peak and then climbing back down over and over until she was trembling, begging him—

"Please, Hugh, please, oh God—"

So he took her back to the peak, his lips on her clit, one finger sliding deep inside her, and he pushed her over the edge.

"Fuck, fuck, fuck—"

She came just like he had promised. Really fucking hard, fluttering and quivering against him, her thighs tight around his head. Then she lay back gasping.

He sat up, smiling, but she groaned and turned her head away from him, arm still hiding her eyes. He thought about pulling that arm free, making her look at him. He wanted to kiss her. He wanted that quite badly. To kiss her, and have smiling eyes meet his. But he wasn't sure she would smile, and he hated the thought of seeing regret in her eyes.

So instead he moved to lie behind her, tucking the duvet up to cover her bare skin.

He lay with his head propped on one hand and looked at the dark hair that was all he could see of her head, the rest being hidden by the pillow she seemed to be silently screaming into.

"Why are you so embarrassed?"

She made a muffled incoherent reply.

"I never feel embarrassed," he said. "It's a completely point-less emotion."

He thought he heard something along the lines of, "It's not something you can *choose!*"

"It is. You can simply choose to...let go. Let go of whatever the conflict is that you're feeling between what you think you *ought* to have done and what you actually did do. Because it seems to me, that the thing you just did was something you enjoyed, and that I enjoyed, and that hurt absolutely no one, and so how can that be wrong?"

She made no reply, but there seemed to be a thoughtful, listening silence emanating from the pillow, which encouraged him to continue. Because he did feel this was important—that Amelia learnt to put herself first, to value her own needs, her own pleasure.

"What good does feeling embarrassed serve? You've already done the thing, so it doesn't help you. And it doesn't help anyone else either, except maybe make them feel a bit awkward or guilty. Instead of feeling bad right now you could be doing something else. Like having a nap, or ordering something to eat or drink, or talking to me. Or...doing it again."

He couldn't help but look down the length of her body as he said those last words, his unspent desire tightening. The duvet hid most of her shape, but he could see a small area of bare shoulder, the skin firm and smooth with a silky sheen he longed to touch. And he could imagine the rest. Could still taste her on his tongue.

"Is that how you feel?" she said quietly. "Awkward and guilty?"

He looked back up and found she had let go of the pillow, though her face was still turned away from him, looking blankly across the room.

"No. Not at all. I feel..." How did he feel? His feelings weren't something he often tried to put into words. "I feel...happy, I suppose, that your headache is gone. Relieved. And I feel warm and comfortable lying here with you. And I feel...glad? Privileged? That you let me make you come. And mostly I feel that I'd really, really like to do it again."

"You didn't come, did you?" She turned her head and looked at him, something ridiculously like guilt in her brown eyes. "I guess you're...um..."

"Horny?"

"Frustrated."

"I'm not frustrated, Amy. I just got to do something I loved doing. And I can sort myself out later. You don't have to worry about us being...even. I'm not keeping score." He chuckled. "And anyway, I'll be using this memory, so you've already done your part."

She didn't return his smile. In fact, she looked very serious, and the words she spoke seemed to slip out without her realising she was about to say them. "I want to watch you come."

He stared at her, eyes wide as she flushed and bit her lip. But she didn't look away.

"OK," he said slowly, trying to keep his wits about him as his heart started pounding and blood rushed straight to his cock. "Tell me what you want."

She blushed deeper. He was sure her heart was racing as hard as his, could feel the tense excitement in the breath she took.

"I want to watch you come. Here. With your...with your top off and your...your jeans still on, but undone, low on your hips... You kneeling over me, looking at me..."

He nodded, forgetting for a moment how to speak. His pulse was raging, his skin burning. He was so turned on he couldn't think straight, but Amelia was looking at him not quite as though she trusted him, but as though she *wanted* to, as though he might be someone she could learn to trust, if only he did not fuck this up. And the thought of being that man...it gave him an ache in his chest that went far beyond the ache in his balls. It seemed to cut right through him, expose an entirely new level of himself. And it also seemed to wrap all the hot, urgent physical things he was feeling in something that made them both enormous and yet unbearably fragile.

He needed this so badly. He needed her. He needed to not fuck this up. But he couldn't overthink it. He had to trust in their bodies, in their mutual desire, in the things he knew how to do.

"Lie on your back," he said, his voice as gentle as he could make it with the rough edge of need closing his throat. "And take the dressing gown off. I want to see all of you."

She nodded and did as he said as he pulled his shirt off and unbuttoned his jeans. He moved to kneel between her legs and looked down at her naked body, the swelling curves, the hard, dusky pink nipples.

"Amy... You're so beautiful."

He kissed her, because he had to, then pushed his jeans down and freed his cock, wrapping his fingers around it. It felt so hard and heavy in his hand, so sensitive he knew he was only moments away. He rubbed his hand along his length, eyes flickering shut at the sensation, his balls tight and hard, every muscle clenching.

"Is this what you want, Amy?"

"Yes."

He looked down her body, at the little pink pussy. He really wanted to fuck her. His cock cried out for that warmth and heat. He stroked himself again, harder, finding a rhythm that had his dick singing with pleasure.

"I want to come on your pussy. I want you dripping with my cum. Are you on the pill?"

It was an effort to talk. He hardly recognised his own voice.

Amy watched him, eyes wide, biting her lip, her chest rising and falling deeply with her excited breaths. "Yes."

"So I can? I'm safe, I assure you."

"Yes."

"You want that?"

"I want that. Come on me."

"Fuck, Amy, you're so fucking hot—"

He leant forward, closing his lips around her nipple. She moaned, and that was all it took, he came hard, spilling himself between her legs, the pumping pleasure dragging a tortured groan from his throat.

He stroked himself slowly, looking down, watching the last of his cum spill out. Then he sat back and admired his handy work, the cum streaking her thighs, tangling in her dark hair, dripping over her core.

"Such a beautiful mess," he murmured. He reached out and ran his hand over the mess, mingling them together on her skin. She moaned, but when he looked up, her arm was again over her eyes. He pulled it gently away with his sticky fingers.

"Hey, look at me."

She met his eyes reluctantly.

"I wanted that. You wanted that. Say it."

"Say it?"

"Yes."

"I...I wanted that."

"Now smell us." He lifted his hand to her face. "Taste us. Go on."

He licked his finger to demonstrate, then held it out to her. She opened her mouth and sucked.

"That's it. Good girl. No shame, OK? No embarrassment. I loved that you asked for what you wanted. Always tell me what you want. I meant it: I'm your slave."

He held her eyes until she nodded.

"Be greedy, Amy. Tell me what you want."

"Make me come again."

He reached down between them, bent his head to her breasts, and did as he was told.

TWENTY-FOUR

A MELIA FELL ASLEEP IN Hugo's arms, which was not
something she had ever imagined she would do, not even
in any of her most involved and detailed fantasies. But after
they had cleaned themselves up, he tugged her back to the bed,
insisting on that nap after all. And then he wrapped his arms
around her, her face on his chest. And he was strong and warm
and smelt so good... She heard his heartbeat—for the first time
in all the years she had known him. She heard the beat of his
heart. And she slept.

When she woke, he still had an arm draped over her, but
they had moved onto their sides, her back against his front. His
arm tightened around her, and she realised what it was that had
woken them.

Sarah, the housekeeper, standing by her bed and looking
down with pursed lips and averted eyes.

"I knocked, miss. But there was no answer. I thought you
would want to know that it's noon and the volunteer guides will
be here in an hour."

"Erm," croaked Amy, her voice muggy with sleep and rigid
with embarrassment. "Yes... Thank you..."

"And the roofing survey people are here, and Hodge wanted
to know if it was still quince trees you wanted planted in the—"

"Thank you, Sarah," Hugo cut her off. His voice was somewhat sleep-roughened too, but it still held a note of firm command. Different to the arrogant assurance she was used to, though no less confident. "Give Amelia time to wake up. She will be down when she's ready."

Sarah nodded, cheeks tinged pink with what Amelia guessed was as much annoyance at being told what to do by Hugo as embarrassment at finding him here.

"And last I checked," he said as Sarah moved to the door, "this was Miss Amelia's private suite."

Sarah's shoulders stiffened, but she made no reply, just left the room and shut the door with more force than was strictly necessary.

Amelia sat up, holding the duvet to her chest, all her drowsy warmth gone. "Please don't boss her around."

Hugo sat up too, his chest bare, and scrubbed a hand through his mussed-up hair. His eyes were soft with sleep, but they sharpened at her tone.

"I'm just standing up for you, Amy. Given you won't do it yourself. She's staff. She shouldn't be coming into your room without permission. You need to have some boundaries. Say no to people."

"She knocked! She was right to wake me. And I don't need to 'stand up to her'. She's almost like family."

Hugo grunted. "Like *your* family perhaps. Just as ready to put you to work."

Heat flared in her chest, as much humiliation as anger, because she hated that he was right. She hated that he saw her inability to say no. Just as she hadn't said no to him.

"And what would you know about work, Hugo?"

"Not much. Clearly." He shrugged as though he wasn't bothered by her scathing tone, but the tension in his back and the way he didn't look at her as he got out of bed and started hunting for his clothes told a different story. She dragged her eyes from his naked body, the muscles that flexed as he moved.

"She was right to wake me," she said again. "I have to train the volunteer guides today. They give up their free time all summer. I can't just not turn up."

"OK," Hugo agreed carelessly, buttoning up his jeans.

"And the roof…" Her stomach clenched with anxiety. "The roof is important."

Hugo nodded as he pulled on his shirt and started to button that too. It hung off his lean frame in a way that made him look hardly more dressed than he had been before. He pushed a hand through his hair and then sighed, softening slightly as he finally met her eyes where she still sat on the bed, duvet clutched to her chest like the prim and awkward girl she really was.

"I just hate that everyone takes advantage of you."

Like you? A spiteful, but probably quite intelligent voice said inside her head. But she didn't let the thought show on her face. Because he was…he was looking at her like he meant it. Like he cared.

She looked away, before she started to believe it. "They're not taking advantage of me, Hugo. It's my job. I have responsibilities. Working hard all day isn't some kind of…unjust cruelty. It's what people do. Normal people, anyway."

"And I'm not normal?"

"No. You're not. Because you don't have to work."

"Maybe I want to."

Her disbelief was clearly evident, because he smiled slightly in acknowledgement of it, even as his eyes took on a serious look. He sat on the bed next to her. She felt oddly wary, even after everything they had just done. Because serious Hugo was new, and that look, directed at her with those navy blue eyes…it was intense.

"I want to work hard if it helps you," he amended, taking her hand and playing with her fingers almost nervously. "I meant what I said earlier, I'll help with this Easter event now Cassie isn't coming. Let me shoulder some of the work for you."

"Why?"

He looked up in confusion. "To make life easier, of course. You don't have to struggle on alone. It's not wrong to let people help you."

"No, I mean...why do you want to help me?"

"Because I..." He took a sharp breath that seemed involuntary, then let it out slowly. "Because I care about you. Deeply. And I still have a lot to make up for."

"Before you go back to London."

She wasn't quite sure why she said that. Hadn't been aware that it was a thing she was even thinking about saying.

He gave her a frowning look, eyes searching her face. "I'm not planning on going any time soon."

Why not? But she didn't dare ask. She drew her hand from his. "You should worry about looking after Conyers, not here."

"Conyers doesn't need me."

"Neither does Redbridge."

Hurt flickered in his eyes at that, and she regretted saying it. But it was true. She would cope without him. She would cope without anyone's help, the way she always did. But she hadn't meant to sound so harsh.

Hugo stood up. He turned for the door, then paused. "This running race... Do they still want to use my lake?"

"Oh." To her annoyance, she blushed. "I think they've...they've decided to go with a different venue."

Hugo nodded. He said nothing, but when he left the room she felt sure he was almost smiling.

———◇———

How was it that they had done all of the wonderful things

they had just done, but the things preoccupying his mind as he walked back to Conyers were the relative merits of *'Redbridge doesn't need you'* versus *'Farm boy has gone with a different venue.'*

He needed to speak to Roscoe. Or, if he was really desperate, Jay. Because, a month ago, if a girl had begged him to come on her, he would have been fairly certain she was into him. But this was Amy. And it wasn't a question of whether she fancied him, it was a question of...

The heart?

Love?

Either way, he had absolutely no idea how she felt.

Redbridge doesn't need you...

That certainly felt like a rejection. Rather like being stabbed in the chest, if he was honest.

But if he interpreted her slightly embarrassed response correctly, the farm boy was no longer sniffing around, and she didn't seem sad about it.

That was positive. Right?

And she had made that comment about him going back to London... Did that mean she wanted him to stay around? Did that mean she was considering this thing between them in the light of a possible relationship...?

Because he was.

Which should have been terrifying. His longest relationship had been five days, and that was only because they were stuck on a small Caribbean island together and there had been no escape.

But the idea of a relationship with Amy *wasn't* terrifying. Which is what was scary. He wanted Amy. He wanted to be with Amy. All the time. Every day. Every minute.

And she...she might not want that. She might not want him.

And if that was the case...what the hell could he do about it?

His pace quickened as a panicky feeling tightened his chest.

211

There were too many thoughts and questions swirling around in his head. Too many questions he didn't have answers to. And he didn't control the answers—they depended on Amy. And though, as the son of a somewhat authoritarian father, he was used to not always being in control of his life, his usual tactic of simply choosing not to care wasn't an option here.

He cared. He was in love. His happiness no longer belonged to himself.

It belonged to someone better than him. Someone who could take his happiness and double it, quadruple it, make it something bigger and brighter than he had ever conceived.

And that was as terrifying as it was wonderful.

———◇———

The house was dim and quiet when Hugo returned to it. The weather was playing its usual April tricks of sunshine one minute and black clouds the next. The sun had gone in just as he was going up the stone steps to the back door by the patio garden. A sudden heavy shower of rain hit the enormous windows as he crossed the drawing room, making him feel as though he was underwater. A fish in a tank in a forgotten shadowy corner, going about its pointless back-and-forth existence in its artificial world. Real life a blur outside the glass.

Amy would be hard at work by now. Meeting her volunteers. All those people who gave up their time merely to help her. Retired old ladies following her around the crooked ancient rooms of Redbridge while she taught them its history, as she probably had done year after year. Then what next on her agenda? The roof? The garden? Hodge and Lee and Sarah and Janson and all the others, waiting for her instructions, loyal and trusting and all happy to be there.

That was one thing he had learnt in his time helping at Redbridge. The staff loved their jobs. He wasn't sure if it was quite a family, like Amy had put it, but they all enjoyed working there. They felt at home.

Redbridge doesn't need you.

Where had his sudden desire to be *needed* come from? He had been content his whole life to be popular instead of needed. To have friends, to have fun. To make himself...not quite the class clown, but school had taught him he wasn't academic. And though he was good at sport, he didn't have the dedication or discipline to get up early or spend his evenings in a muddy field. So what else had been left except making himself popular by being the one who was game for anything? The fun one. The one who never said no to any kind of jape or caper, no matter how ridiculous or ill-advised.

But what did that leave when there was no one around to laugh along with him?

Did Amy ever feel like this? Did she wander around her home wondering what on earth she was doing with her life or who she really was?

Maybe she was too busy for that. Maybe Redbridge was the answer to those questions for her. Perhaps everyone needed to be needed, and Redbridge was what needed her.

And now *he* needed her too. But who needed him?

He paused at the foot of the west stairs, the idea of going to his room and playing video games with the rain pissing grey against his window no longer appealing. And the thought of studying investment options appealed even less. Because he was beginning to suspect that he abhorred every facet of market analysis. Which was unfortunate, given the respect of his father and his freedom from Conyers depended on it.

Although...Amy was here. So did he really want to be free? Where else would he rather be? And as for his father's respect... He'd lived without it for nearly twenty-seven years. He was used to its absence.

Amy's respect though... He quite wanted that. And, perhaps...he wanted his own.

He wandered over to the arched window at the end of the hall with its stained-glass sunray in the semi-circular pane at the top. It was a rare splash of colour in the otherwise cream and taupe decor scheme here. Even the gilt on the frames and furniture looked brown in the dull light.

But there was a hint of colour coming through the yellows and blues of the stained glass, and as he looked out of the clear section below it at the rivulets obscuring the view, he thought the sky brightened, his inexpert eye finding a streak of bright white above the horizon beyond the garden.

Maybe there would be a rainbow.

When had he last scanned the sky for a rainbow? Probably as a child, running through the garden, patting Amy on her bony little shoulder and saying, "Look, Splat, up there. Race you to the end?"

Where, presumably, if they *had* found a pot of gold, he would have claimed it for his own and pushed her in the mud. Because he was a Blackton. And that's the sort of thing they did.

Although Roscoe wouldn't, would he? Or Evie. So perhaps the whole Blackton thing was an excuse.

He turned at the sound of footsteps and saw his father's steward, Howell, crossing the hallway. He was wearing a green waxed jacket and wellington boots, but they were currently dry.

"Off out?" Hugo asked.

Howell stopped, surprised to see him there. Or surprised at the question. He gave a curt nod. "Got to see one of the farmers."

"Not Toby Patrick?"

Howell looked surprised again. Maybe at the simple fact that Hugo knew a farmer's name.

"No. Andrew Thomas, out Longmorton way."

"I'll come with you," said Hugo, this time surprising them both.

He hurried off to the boot room before Howell could ask any questions and changed into the wellingtons he had been borrowing from Roscoe the whole time he had been at Conyers—without Roscoe's knowledge of course. Hugo did not have his own pair. Though, he reflected ruefully as he helped himself to Roscoe's waterproof jacket too, perhaps it was time he outfitted himself like a country gent, if he really was going to stick around.

Wellies and waterproofs. If only his friends could see him now.

Howell was waiting for him near the side door in a large Range Rover. Not one of Redbridge's battered ancient green things, but a large, sleek black one, probably only a year or two old. It was more or less pristine except for some splashes of mud around the wheel rims.

As they drove, Hugo said, "I've had an idea. Tell me about the estate and our land as we drive through it. I think I'll learn better if I'm out and about in it, seeing things with my own eyes rather than looking at a computer."

Howell glanced at him, nodded once, then began.

Because Amy was right. He wasn't very good at sitting still in an office. But the thing that Amy didn't know—that very few people knew, and which Hugo seldom ever thought about—was that he wasn't very good at reading. The words all just danced around and wouldn't go into his head. 'Dyslexic' was the word a tutor at Harrow had once used in a meeting with Hugo and his father. But his father had said coldly but firmly, "I don't think so." And that had been that. Hugo wasn't dyslexic because his father didn't want him to be.

But he could look out of the window as Howell explained the

215

land they drove through, and he could see it all in his mind's eye like an enormous three-dimensional map, colour-coded to match the colours he vaguely remembered from the spread-sheet. And all the half-familiar names he'd grown up hearing but not really heeding finally started to click together: the Holm Oak avenue being that dark line of trees in the distance, and the water meadow being that swathe of green at its foot, and the Lady Mary hollow being that dip over there, and the border of Farridge's farm being that line of telegraph poles near where the old railway line had once run...

And so on, for the forty-minute drive, and then back again via a different route so that Howell could show him even more.

It really was rather a lot, Hugo reflected, looking out on the rolling fields and feeling more humble than proud. And this was barely a third of their land. And there were two other, smaller estates belonging to his father, one in Derbyshire and one in Dorset, both occupied by ageing great aunts. Not to mention the other holdings of land and forest, and, he was fairly sure, a small castle in Northern Ireland, and a few houses dotted about the country, and their main residence in London, and his own London house, and Roscoe's flats, and the things they owned purely as investments. And the chateau in France.

And hadn't he bought a flat in Switzerland a few years ago? Just because it had ended up being quicker than renting it, for some reason he didn't understand at the time and had even less chance of understanding now. He'd only stayed there for a weekend, and had, until this precise moment on a muddy and rain-slicked country road in deepest darkest Lancashire, forgotten all about it.

No wonder his family despaired.

He sat back against the seat, head lolling against the headrest as the car dipped and lurched through a series of potholes. He was staring rather dazedly at nothing until the sight of a familiar-looking green Land Rover made him sit up.

It was one of the Redbridge ones, he was sure of it. And it was at an angle across the road, leaning to one side, a back wheel half in the ditch.

He swore, unbuckling his seat belt as Howell stopped their own car just behind it. He flung himself out and rushed over, chest tight, hoping, praying that it wasn't Amy, that she had come to no harm—

It *was* Amy. But she was standing next to Lee, and they were both looking rather grimly down at the stuck wheel which was half-buried in mud.

"You're not hurt," he breathed in relief.

She looked up, surprised at the sight of him, then smiled, looking for all the world as though she was actually glad to see him. "No. Just stuck."

Lee grinned. "Well met, Pence. You can push."

Hugo eyed the mud with distaste. It had just about stopped raining, and in that maddening April way, the sun was now bursting joyfully from the clouds as though it had never stopped shining. Soon the road would be steaming.

"Or we can tow you out," he said flatly.

Lee laughed, then turned to Howell and started to discuss what to do. Howell carefully inched the Conyers vehicle past the stuck Land Rover, careful not to strand it in the other ditch, then attached a tow rope.

Hugo and Amelia watched from the sidelines. Mud sprayed in a dirty plume as the wheel spun. It missed Hugo by a few inches, and he stepped hastily to the side, bumping into Amelia. She laughed up at him and he opened his mouth to make some smug statement about escaping without a splash of mud—just as Lee stuck his head out of the window and said, "No use, Pence. You're going to have to push after all."

So he rolled his sleeves up, Amelia watching half-aghast,

half-gleeful as he pushed with all his strength, feet slipping in the mud, and getting liberally sprayed from head to foot. He spat mud from his mouth, heaved again, and the Land Rover came free with a lurch that sent him sprawling to the ground.

Fuck. But he didn't care. Because Amelia was laughing, and he liked that sound. And anyway, there was something in the sky that made him smile.

"Look, Splat," he said. "Up there."

She glanced up, smiling in delight at the rainbow. But he only had eyes for her.

TWENTY-FIVE

H UGO WAS HAND-PAINTING WOODEN Easter eggs and
Amelia couldn't be more...surprised.

Or maybe *happy* was the real word. But that seemed too
strange. Too much like an invitation for heartache.

They were sitting on straw bales, a sheet of old plywood
between them as their makeshift table, and they were working
in companionable near-silence. The sun warmed their backs as
they worked together to decorate the twenty large wooden eggs
that would be hidden around the gardens for the Easter egg
hunt.

That's what they were supposed to be doing anyway. But
Amelia's attention kept drifting from the egg she was working
on—purple with green spots—to the man sitting across from
her who was frowning down at his own creation with such intense concentration she couldn't help but smile. He was painting thin blue zig-zag lines on a cheerful yellow background. The
blue looked familiar, and she realised it was almost the same
shade as the remaining flakes on the old gate between their estates. Artistic wasn't a word Amelia would have ever associated
with Hugo, but he was doing an impressively neat job of it. He
had always been skilled when it came to physical tasks.

Something made him glance up, and he crooked an eyebrow
at finding her watching him. She coloured slightly and removed

the wooden tip of the paintbrush she had been chewing from her mouth.

"What?" he asked, warm amusement in his eyes.

"Nothing. Just...the last time I saw you concentrate this hard on anything was when you were determined to beat Roscoe at Mario Kart."

Hugo laughed softly and picked up more paint on the tip of his brush. "And I did, didn't I?"

"Only because you elbowed him in the ribs at a vital moment."

Hugo chuckled, beginning another neat zig-zag line. "All's fair in Mario Kart wars."

"Not sure Ross saw it that way."

"Sore loser."

"Mm. Literally."

Hugo laughed, though managed not to let the action interfere with his steady hand. A lock of dark hair fell across his brow as he bent his head over his work. She had the urge to brush it out of his eyes. She had the urge to cup his face in her hands, her fingers cradling the hard angle of his jaw, and pull him down to her mouth and marvel, as she always did, at how soft his lips could be when the rest of him was all firm muscle and sharp angles and ready strength.

But instead, she turned back to her own work and looked ruefully at the purple splotches and messy drips.

Three days ago, he had come back to Redbridge with her and Lee, being too muddy, he said, to get into Howell's immaculate vehicle. And just like after the incident with the fountain, he had showered at Redbridge. But this time in her en suite, not Cassie's, despite complaining loudly that his own shower was far superior. And then, inevitably, he had ended up in her bed.

And stayed the night.

Sleeping with Hugo seemed like a far riskier idea than, well, sleeping with Hugo, as far as her sanity and her heart were concerned. But he had made no move to go home. And for some reason, she hadn't really wanted him to. It had been nice, having someone in her room to talk to, laugh with. They had watched a film, even though Amelia had a thousand admin tasks she should have been doing, and they had eaten dinner from trays on her bed even though Redbridge had ample rooms for dining in. And then they had watched more TV, and talked more and laughed more.

It was like...like they really were friends again. Better friends than they had been even before Cassie's engagement party.

Except then they'd had sex again. Which wasn't really what one generally did with a friend. But she had still felt that same caring warmth from him both during, and after, and then they had curled up together and gone to sleep.

Curled up with *Hugo Blackton* and gone to sleep.

And now he was still here, after three days of proving himself surprisingly helpful with all the Easter event and opening day preparations. And after spending every night in her bed.

Almost as though they were...*together* somehow. As though Hugo Blackton was the sort of man who had girlfriends and stuck around.

But he wasn't. And she needed to remember that.

He was a man of wild nights out, of luxury bars, of casual sex, of girl after girl after girl, of bad choices and excess. She was fairly sure his usual idea of a good time involved bar tabs with three too many zeroes, girls whose names he didn't know, and quite possibly recreational drugs.

Whatever he normally did for fun, it wasn't sitting on a straw bale painting a wooden Easter egg.

"When *are* you going back to London?" she said suddenly.

Hugo looked up, startled—quite understandably—by the abrupt question, then glanced back at his egg, grimacing at the line which had gone crooked.

"That question again," he said.

"Which you haven't answered."

He tried, not very successfully, to repair his crooked blue line, then gave up the attempt and lay down his brush with a sigh. "Anyone would think you can't wait to get rid of me, Little A."

"I'm just... I'm confused."

"Confused."

"About what this is."

"About what this is."

"Why are you repeating me?"

"I don't really know. Maybe I don't want to say the wrong thing?"

Amelia said nothing, fervently wishing she hadn't said anything at all, because all the happy companionship of the last half hour—the last three days—was now strained and awkward. She shivered, despite the sun on her back.

Hugo absently picked up his brush again and rolled the long wooden handle between his fingers, looking at that, rather than her. "Have you forgiven me yet?"

"Is that what you're waiting for? I forgive you and then you leave?"

"No."

"So what then? Why are you still here? You hate the country-side."

"Maybe I want to be here. Maybe I like helping you. Maybe...you *need* me here."

Amelia scoffed at that, though it was a half-hearted attempt, almost drowned by the horrible fear that he was right. She couldn't possibly be stupid enough to have started relying on the most unreliable man in England?

"Cassie isn't coming back," Hugo said gently. "You can't get hold of your mother. You don't really want to do this whole

Easter weekend by yourself, do you?"

I have my staff, she nearly said. And she didn't need anyone else. Honestly, she didn't. As hard as it would be to run the whole opening season solo, she knew that she was capable of doing it. And she hated the thought that Hugo didn't believe that of her.

She looked up, eyes snagging on the ugly scaffolding the roofing surveyors had erected. It was just visible at the back of the house from where they sat in the yard at its side. The yard was where the Easter petting zoo would be—that's what the straw bales were for—and the scaffolding wasn't visible from the front of the house, but it was horrible having it there at all, marring the house's beauty just when she wanted it to look it's best.

The surveyors had erected it three days ago. They were still up there now, investigating the extent of the work required—she spied a yellow-jacketed man examining one of the flat leaded roofs. Even the survey was costing thousands. But it had to be done.

The sun dimmed, white clouds flooding the sky, blown in by the merry skipping breeze that was twirling loose strands of straw around the yard. Amelia shivered again and started to pack up the paints.

"Be honest though, Hugo," she said as he too glanced up at the sky and joined her in packing away their things. "You don't want to be doing this Easter thing really, do you? You'd rather be back enjoying your normal life, doing whatever it is that you do with your friends in London. Don't..." She forced herself to say it, even though the words gave her a ridiculous urge to cry. "Don't stick around just because you feel sorry for me."

"That isn't why."

He met her eyes. His were dark and serious, a light burning within them that was half heat, half...something she didn't understand, but which was perhaps a little bit like fear.

Whatever it was, it cleared, and he retreated from the intensity of the moment into a familiar grin. "Don't worry about me wasting away up here anyway, Little A. I'm planning the mother of all parties at Conyers the moment this Easter thing is done. You're coming, of course."

"Me?" she said warily, with a strong presentiment of doom. As much as she knew Hugo didn't belong here among the mud and straw of Redbridge's yard, she didn't really want to see him in his natural environment either. She didn't really like that Hugo. Just look what had happened at the last party.

He seemed to see something of her worries in her eyes because he grinned and said, "I'll only kiss you this time, Scout's honour."

She punched him in the arm hard enough to make Roscoe proud.

———◦———

"I finally got through to my mum," Amelia told Evie over the phone. "And she's not going to get back in time for the Easter opening weekend."

She held the phone away from her ear, expecting a loud wail. But the disappointed sigh Evie gave was worse. As though she had always known Amelia would let her down. And Amelia really, really didn't like to be the person who let people down.

"She's somewhere so remote that it would take her three or four days just to get to the airport. Then there's the flight, the jet lag... She wouldn't get here until it's over, and even when she arrived, she'd be no real help. I'm sorry, Evie."

"Sure. Yeah."

"Please, Evie. You know this isn't what I wanted."

"I know. It's just... Why do you find it so hard to say no to everyone except me?"

Ouch. Amelia literally winced. And the sharp sting of Evie's words was followed by the prickling of tears behind her eyes. Since when had she been such a weepy mess? She forced the feeling down, along with the tightness in her throat.

"It's not like that. They're family. This is Redbridge. I can't just abandon it."

"Mm. I heard Hugo is still there."

"Erm, yes. What does that have to do with anything?"

"I don't know. You tell me."

"I'm not staying because of him."

"Roscoe said he thought there was something going on. And you said you were going to torture him, but when I called him the other day he sounded bizarrely *happy*."

"Well. We're friends again. I thought you'd be glad about that. Deep down. Deep, deep down?"

"Mm," said Evie again, but without the sharpness this time. "Maybe very deep down on some idiot level, I'm happy that my best friend doesn't hate my brother, even if he does deserve it. But Amy!" Now came the wail that Amelia had been expecting. "I can't believe you're doing this again!"

"I know. I'm so sorry. But I'll be there in two weeks. I promise."

She tried not to think what that would mean for this thing that was happening with Hugo. It would mean nothing. He would be back in London by then. And this last week would be nothing but a weird fever dream.

"If you go ahead, see Barcelona without me—"

"The thing is Amy," Evie cut her off apologetically, "it's not going to be much fun doing all that without you. I've already seen most of the places on our itinerary. The fun part was going to be showing them to you. And if you're not coming... Well, I met these cool people the other day. They're planning to walk the Camino de Santiago—it's an old pilgrimage route through

Spain and France. Goes to some tomb, St James or someone. You know I'm not really religious, but it sounds like such a good way of seeing the country. Seeing it properly. Everyone's doing it nowadays. It's like the new Interrailing. And these people seem really good fun. So I kind of thought...if you're not coming...maybe I'd go with them. We could see where we are in a couple of weeks and meet somewhere?"

"Right," said Amelia, nodding even though Evie couldn't see her. "Sure. Yeah. That makes sense."

She swallowed the lump in her throat. She had no right to feel disappointed. Abandoned. Not when she was the one abandoning Evie. But how nice it would be to join them. Walk from village to village along old, half-forgotten roads. That was exactly how *she* wanted to see the country.

"It sounds fun," she managed to say.

"I'm sure it'll be nothing but blisters and getting lost. But I'll send you some photos, yeah?"

———◦———

After her call with Evie, Amelia stood still for a long time at her bedroom window, looking out over the garden. She hugged her arms around herself, phone forgotten in one hand as she stared at the darkening view.

It was only just gone six, but the evenings were still short in April, and there was another bank of thick grey cloud on the horizon. There had been a brief hailstorm earlier. It had only lasted five minutes, but it had been enough to shred the delicate petals of the flower arrangements that festooned every stall laid out ready and waiting on the lawn at the front of the house.

Her room looked out over the back. She could just see the corner of the fountain in the parterre and hear it splashing merrily—now fixed, thanks to Hugo. Away to the east was the long line of the brick wall that separated the estates. The dark green brush strokes of the huge cedars that flanked the gate in the wall were almost black against the lowering sky. She couldn't see the gate itself from here. It was open anyway. It had always been open. An absence in the wall, a breach in the defences through which two small boys had come running, day after day.

Had Redbridge been a sanctuary for them? A place to escape a strict father and a vacuous mother who cared only about what they wore and how they looked, her children just another kind of accessory?

Not that her own parents had been much better. Her father was always away. And Amelia had slowly come to realise that her mother, though loving, was absent in mind as often as her father was absent in person—always dreaming of a younger, more exciting life. A time before two children came along to claim her every moment.

So if the Blackton boys had come seeking sanctuary in Redbridge, they hadn't found it in her parents. Perhaps they hadn't even found it in Redbridge's scruffier grounds, where trees could be climbed and football was allowed on the far from immaculate lawn. Perhaps they had come for her and Cassie. For friendship and laughter.

Was that why they still came? A retreat from the grown-up demands of life? Roscoe had said as much on his last visit. Being here was as close as he got to relaxation.

And maybe it was the same for Hugo. This time here, with her, messing about in the garden, laughing as she teased him for the care with which he was arranging daffodils and tulips around the raffle stall... Maybe it was just a holiday for him. A break from whatever extremely *adult* kind of life he had been leading before.

Which was exactly how she had decided to use him that day he ran her bath. A fantasy to be indulged in, knowing none of it was real. And that none of it would last.

It wasn't love.

It was a boy running through an open gate, playing football with *girls*, because they were the only other children for miles, then returning home, back to reality, to be packed off to Harrow and his real friends.

And she would be stupid to miss him when he inevitably left. Just as she had been stupid to miss him all those years ago when he really had gone off to school and her days had gotten so much smaller.

She turned at the sound of the door opening. Hugo walked into her room, smiling at seeing her. His cheeks were reddened from being outside. There was mud on his knees and a splash of paint on his shirt.

"There you are," he said. "You know, *some* of us are downstairs working hard..."

She gave a guilty start. "Sorry. I'm coming."

But he came up to her and held her still, his hands on her shoulders as he smiled down at her. "I'm only joking."

Of course he was. Hugo was always only ever joking.

He looked past her to the window. "Do you remember? This is the first place I kissed you. Properly, I mean."

His voice was soft and as full of secrets as the twilight shadows outside.

"I wonder where the last place will be?" she said.

He frowned. "Last? Never. I want to kiss you always and forever."

And when he bent his head to hers, it didn't feel like he was joking at all.

TWENTY-SIX

H UGO WAS A BLOODY coward. He couldn't possibly deny it any more.

But how *did* one go about telling a girl that you loved them?

It probably wasn't now, when she was running around on a very hot bank holiday Monday afternoon, after having been up since five AM—actually, up since five AM for the last four days running. And working sixteen hours straight each of those days.

And, yes, he had also been up since five and working alongside her for all of those hours, but it hadn't been him making the decisions, it wasn't him that every useless person constantly turned to for advice, it wasn't his grit and determination and insanely impressive ingenuity that kept the whole show on the road.

She was...awe-inspiring. Like a reverse hurricane, leaving order in her wake. And he could barely keep up.

"Can you take these tickets to Anne?" Amelia hurried over to him, cheeks flushed from the heat. She was wearing a short cotton summer dress he approved of very much, and her hair was coming loose from the casual bun she had wrangled it into that morning as he watched, while trying to appear as though he wasn't from the bathroom doorway. "I need to speak to Lee about getting some more shade in the yard. I'm worried about the lambs in this heat."

Then she was off again, disappearing into the crowd.

Hugo made his way across the trampled lawn and through the bustling visitors to Anne at the raffle stall, stopping to direct two people to the toilets, one young family to the pony rides, and once to comfort a small boy who was in tears about not being able to find the final Easter egg. Perhaps Hugo *had* been a bit too enthusiastic about hiding them, but honestly, kids these days had it too easy.

"Find the yew tree that looks like a dragon," he told the boy, "and climb inside. Just don't...er...fall off," he added in an undertone the boy's parents couldn't hear. "Because we don't want to be sued."

Once the raffle tickets had been safely delivered, Hugo looked around for the next thing to do. He decided to go and see if he could help Amy in the yard, because apparently he was also one of those useless people who needed her to tell him what to do. But halfway there, he did a double-take as a familiar face passed him in the crowd.

"Toby Patrick." The name came out more like an accusation than a greeting.

Judging from the way Toby was looking at him, he was equally unhappy at the meeting. "Lord Leighton. Is Amelia around?"

"She's busy."

Toby seemed inclined to point out that this wasn't actually an answer to his question, so Hugo crossed his arms and looked down at the man. Hugo was three inches taller and exceptionally pleased about it. To his height and crossed arms he added an arched brow and a good dose of the aristocratic hauteur that Amy pretended to hate but which Hugo was convinced she secretly found pretty hot. If he hadn't been wearing bunny ears, the effect might have been more impressive.

Toby's eyes wandered questioningly to the headgear. Hugo snatched the bunny ears off and resumed his glower. "Why are you here? Isn't your race being held elsewhere?"

"I saw the sign for the Easter event and thought I'd drop in and say hello. Amelia is a friend."

"Friend."

"Yes. A good friend. I've known her for years."

"Not as long as I have."

"Is this a competition, Lord Leighton?"

No. Yes. God dammit.

Why was this man here, with his bloody ruddy cheeks and farm boy curls? Hugo had a strong urge to try and drown him in the fountain again.

"Well..." said Toby after a moment. "If you don't know where she is, I'll carry on looking."

"She went that way." Hugo pointed over his shoulder, the opposite direction to the yard. He watched Toby disappear into the crowd, then set off to find Amy at a jog.

———✦———

Amelia stretched a little further, trying to hook the end of the rope holding up the tarpaulin over the edge of the old iron hook on the wall. But the tarpaulin was heavy, the rope was already stretched as tight as she could pull it, and she just couldn't quite reach. She stretched further, on tiptoes on the stacked straw bales she was balancing on. Almost, almost—

She lost her balance, started to fall—

But two strong hands found her waist and steadied her. She looked down at Hugo, heart hammering from her near accident. Then she decided that given he was there, she might as well make use of him.

"Hold me while I reach."

"Yes, ma'am."

She hooked the rope over, and Hugo lifted her down, leaving

his hands on her waist.

"Thank you," she said, then twisted out of his grip, because he looked very much like he was about to kiss her, but they were in public, Lee was on the other side of the yard, and she had a million things she needed to be doing, and Hugo absolutely was not one of them.

But as she turned away, she found herself glancing back with a grin and saying, "Where are the bunny ears? I miss them."

He pulled them from his back pocket and put them on her head, smiling down at her as he touched her lightly on the nose. "They look much better on you." He ran his eyes down her with a considering smile. "I think maybe these later...and nothing else."

She pretended to scowl, although she couldn't help laughing. She picked up an empty bucket and headed for the tap, squeezing past a group of young mothers who were eyeing Hugo with far more interest than their children were eyeing the lambs.

Mine, she thought smugly. And then quickly quashed the thought, because he wasn't. Not in any permanent sense of the word.

She set the bucket under the outside tap and watched the cold water filling it as Hugo came to lean against the wall beside her.

"I just bumped into your ex," he said faux-casually.

She shot him a surprised look, her thoughts immediately conjuring Franklin, the only serious boyfriend she'd ever had. An uninspiring eighteen months at university during which she had slowly come to the inescapable conclusion that her perfectly nice, pleasant boyfriend was the most boring person alive and so utterly passive that he wouldn't realise he was on fire unless she pointed it out first. *I say, Franklin, have you noticed you're being engulfed by flames?*

And then he would have asked her what he should do about it.

"I mean Farmer Giles," Hugo pressed, clearly fishing.

She shot him a look, genuinely surprised this time. "Toby's here?"

Hugo studied his nails. "Yeah. The potato guy."

She belatedly realised the bucket was overflowing and hurriedly turned off the tap, frowning in thought. Toby here? The last time she saw him he had been so angry and hurt she had assumed he never wanted to see her again. Which had been something of a relief. Although, on later reflection, it also made her feel a bit sad. They had been good friends once. And she didn't have many of those. Perhaps if he had come to his senses, decided to be mature about things... Maybe they could really be friends again. She thought she might like that.

Especially when Hugo left, and she was here alone again.

She tried to pick up the heavy bucket and slopped half of it over her shoes. Hugo took it from her and carried it back to the lamb's enclosure. She watched one of the little creatures frisk around and nose at the straw as he refilled their trough.

"Did Toby say... Was he here for the event or...?"

"He was looking for you."

She nodded, feeling Hugo study her as she watched the lambs.

"Amelia?" She turned at Lee's voice. "I think it's time I got these ducklings out of here. Could you fetch the cages? I put them in the barn. And maybe get some more feed for the pigs."

She nodded and went into the barn, Hugo at her side.

It was shadowy and cool inside, the air always smelling for some reason of old hay and paraffin, though neither were stored here. Dust motes flickered in the shafts of light that filtered in through gaps in the old wooden walls.

Amelia let out a breath, glad to be out of the sun and away from the bustle just for a moment.

The cages were stacked neatly by the door, but the bags of

feed were at the back of the barn. She skirted the broken down tractor that took up most of the space in the middle of the floor, and Hugo followed, as he seemed to constantly these days.

She didn't mind at all.

Because she liked him being around. So much so that it scared her. There was something infectious about his carefree attitude. Something about him that eased the tension in her chest. Even at his most infuriating, he was a distraction from the buzz of anxiety in her mind. She began to see just how seductive it might be to live life as though it was a game, a joke, taking nothing seriously. Things didn't matter as much. They couldn't hurt you in the same way.

But she also knew that it wasn't sustainable. Life was real, whether you wanted it to be or not. And jobs had to be done. Money had to be made. Roofs rotted and had to be fixed. And you couldn't just laugh that off. Still. It was nice to have him there beside her with his easy grin and his blithe assurance. And the way just one touch could take her mind off almost anything...

The only problem was how much she would miss him when he was gone.

"What's wrong?"

She glanced back at him. "Hm? What?"

"You seem sad all of a sudden."

"I'm just tired."

He took her wrist and pulled her gently around to face him. His knuckles brushed her cheek as he looked at her with quiet concern. "Tell me."

"There's nothing to tell."

"I don't think that's true."

He seemed to debate something inside himself. And she wanted to squirm away from the probing way he looked at her. She wanted to run away from this whole moment before she revealed just how vulnerable she was. How much she cared.

"Your mood changed when I mentioned Toby," he said at last, an awkward question hiding behind the statement. "You've both told me you're friends, but is there...? There's more to it, isn't there?"

She shook her head, relieved this was a topic she could at least be honest about. "No, not much more to it. We dated, briefly, in sixth form college. Then he turned up the other week and I thought maybe we could be friends. But he wanted more. And when I...didn't, he was hurt. If he's here now though, perhaps he wants to move past that and really be friends?"

Hugo looked sceptical, lips pressed together as he studied her hand in his and brushed the skin of her wrist with his thumb.

"That's what you want? To be friends with him?"

"Yes. If we can be. It's not like I have many friends around here. And when you go..."

He shot her a burning look. "When I go you'll move on to him, is that it?"

"No! Not like that! I'm not...I'm not *you*."

"What does that mean?"

"Nothing."

"I sleep around, is that what you mean?"

"It's hardly a secret."

He let out a sharp breath, angry, frustrated. And again Amelia wished she could unsay everything that had just been said, roll back time to ten minutes ago when he was putting bunny ears on her head and looking at her so warmly she almost...

Almost believed it.

But it was all a mirage.

"I'm not sleeping around now, am I?" he said.

"I'm the only girl for miles."

"You think I couldn't go to a bar in town? Call up a friend or two?"

"I'm sure you will. When you go home. Back to London. Your old life. And this..." She gestured between them. "It won't be there anymore."

He gave her a searching look. "Do you *want* me to stay here? With you?"

She looked away, not wanting to be put on the spot like that, the pathetic one, begging the other for something he had never even hinted at.

"You won't. You'll get bored. I know what you're like, Hugo. A different girl every night. We're all just interchangeable to you. No—" She cut off his protest. "It's true! You just...go through them. Cassie said you slept with Jess, then Cessy, then Emma D'Arby—and they're all your friends too. Or were. It's not like I'm different just because we know each other so well. You kissed me and Cassie on the same night! The only reason you're sticking around here with me is because... Well. I'm not sure why. But I suppose there's no one else around, and any port in a storm, right?"

Even in the dim light of the barn, she could see the vivid flush on his cheeks. The angry glitter in his eyes. "That's what you think of me?"

"It's what your behaviour has proven. Time and time again."

"This is different!"

"How so?"

"Because you're not like those other girls."

"Why not? What makes me special?"

"Everything!"

She scoffed, trying to turn away and escape this ridiculous argument. But he would not let go of her hand.

"It's different," he said, "because I wasn't in love with any of them. And I'm in love with you."

TWENTY-SEVEN

S HIT.

Judging from the horrified look on Amy's face, declaring one's love on a hot bank holiday on a Monday afternoon in a decrepit barn while looking for pig feed was *not* the way to go about it.

But honestly, what choice did he have? He had been backed into a corner that was, admittedly, of his own slutty making, and he refused to have Amy think even for one minute that all this between them meant nothing to him.

"You...love me?" She seemed to choke slightly on the word.

"Yes. Pathetically, stupidly—well, not stupidly. I don't mean it's stupid to love you. I mean... Well. What I *seem* to mean is that it has quite clearly rendered me stupid because I can't form a coherent sentence."

She started to laugh, and he felt his own lips twitch irresistibly too, even though he was fairly sure that being laughed at while telling someone you loved them was not a good sign.

"You can't love me," she said incredulously when she had got her breath back. "You're *Hugo Blackton*. You don't go around...*falling in love* with people."

"No. Only with you."

Something about the way he said that rendered her speechless. Maybe it was the way the words felt dredged from his very

237

soul. She stared at him wide-eyed.

"Only you," he said, stepping closer and taking hold of her hands. "I've only ever fallen in love with you. And I only ever want to be in love with you. Always you."

She looked so comically shocked, the bunny ears lopsided on her hair, her brown eyes wide, that he wanted to smile. And she looked so beautiful that he wanted to cry. What he did instead was try to kiss her, but she was saying something, so he grazed his mouth along her jaw as she spluttered, "But...but... I don't believe it. I can't."

He kissed her neck, nuzzling the soft skin and breathing her in with his eyes closed. "I hardly believe it myself," he said, his voice too soft with emotion to carry the dryness he had intended. He cleared his throat slightly as he moved his head back up to look down at her. "But it seems inescapable. I do apologise."

Her dark eyes were wide, a question in them, or perhaps a plea. A little of the fear he still felt: *please, please don't reject me.*

She reached up to touch his cheek, the brush of her fingertips fragile, as though she feared he would turn to smoke. "Hugo...?"

His name a whispered question. And he answered it with a kiss. *It's real, it's real...*

He kissed her deeply, savouring the softness of her mouth and the flood of warmth as he found her tongue with his. And she kissed him back just as needily, as though to say: *Show me. Prove it.*

Gut-clenching desire made him groan, and he walked her backwards to bump gently against the side of the old tractor. But they kissed slowly, lost in the heady rush of what had been revealed, mingling their breath, and Hugo felt maybe he could convey the weight of the searing bond he felt like that. Press his love into the softness of her, somehow melt the two of them together...

She kissed him back almost as desperately as he kissed her. Her hands tangled in his hair, running over his shoulders, pulling him hard against her. She moaned as his thigh fitted between hers, and he finally ran his fingers over the bare skin of her legs just the way he had been wanting to do ever since she got dressed that morning.

He ran his hand up her thigh, teasing the edge of her underwear with his finger as she ground against his leg.

He broke the kiss, resting his forehead against hers, her arms around his neck. He wanted to hear the breath she took when he touched her. He treasured them all, stored them up, because it still felt like a miracle every time she let him.

He moved his hand to the seam of her underwear, rubbing the damp fabric until she moaned. "I love you," he said, which really wasn't fair of him, given the breathless way she trembled with need at his touch. But he wanted her to say it back. He wanted that badly.

What she said instead was, "Please."

He slipped his hand under the wet cloth, ran his fingers over the slick skin, and it was his turn to be breathless with need. He grunted with pleasure at the way she moved to meet his touch, and he gave her his fingers—one deep inside while his thumb teased her clit.

She hid her head against his shoulder, muffling her cries into his shirt.

And then... Then there was a knock on the open door of the barn.

"Amelia?"

The fucking potato farmer. Hugo growled with anger rather than desire this time.

Amelia's head snapped upright, staring at him wide-eyed. Hugo stilled his fingers. But he didn't remove them. Something darkly possessive inside him made him want to stay exactly where he was.

"Amelia?" called Toby again. "Lee said you were in the barn. Hello?"

He couldn't see them where they were hidden behind the tractor. With his eyes locked on Amelia's, Hugo moved his fingers slowly, resumed the circles his thumb had been making. Her eyes went even wider, and she bit her lip, suppressing a moan.

"Amelia?" called Toby.

Fuck. He really didn't want to stop. And she was so close...

But she was Little Miss Good. So she shook her head, pushed slightly on his arm. With a sigh of reluctance and fervent hatred for all blond-haired potato farmers the world over, he gave up and stepped back.

Amelia took half a second to straighten herself, then put a smile on her face and stepped out from behind the tractor.

"Toby! What a surprise!"

He heard the man say, "A welcome one, I hope?" And, more to the point, he heard the smarmy smile that accompanied the words.

It was simple. The potato farmer had to die.

Hugo stepped out from behind the tractor too, and the dismal way Toby's face fell was almost—*almost*—worth the interruption.

"Leighton," he stated flatly.

"In the flesh!" said Hugo brightly, the double entendre earning him a warning look from Amelia.

"How have you been?" she asked Toby cheerfully, as though this was a chance meeting with a casual acquaintance in the street and not a three-way sexual Mexican stand-off. Given the flicker of fury with which Toby had greeted Hugo's appearance, he wouldn't be hugely surprised if the man really did pull out a gun. Probably a shotgun.

Run, wabbit, run.

Hugo stood beside Amelia. He wasn't going anywhere.

It was as though Amelia heard him. As though the universe heard him. Because she smiled up at him and took his hand, stepping close against his side before turning back to Toby and waiting for the answer to her question.

Had she seen the anger with which Toby looked at him? Had she come to the same conclusion as Hugo? Friendship was not what Toby was after.

"Well. I came to see how you were," Toby said, voice dulled and sulky. "But I suppose there's not much point."

"I'm always happy to see a friend," replied Amelia with far more courtesy than Hugo could have mustered.

Toby flinched at that last word, and an ugly sort of smile crossed his face as he nodded. "Right. Of course." He tipped his head towards Hugo. "So. You chose the toff. No surprise, I suppose. I guess the likes of me are only good enough for the practice run."

Regrettably, Hugo got a much clearer insight into the exact nature of their history together. But he didn't care about that, only the way that Amelia stiffened at his side.

"I think you should leave," he told Toby.

Toby laughed slightly. "For once, Leighton, this isn't your land to kick me off of."

"No," said Amelia. "It's mine. And I do think you should leave. Because I won't be spoken to like that."

Polite. But so much command in her steady voice. He looked down at her, awash once again with awe. He wanted to whoop and lift her up and spin her around. But he kept the harsh glower on his face directed at Toby until the man turned and left.

"I really do love you," he said.

———•———

Hugo put his arm around her shoulders as she stared at the doorway through which Toby had just disappeared. His arm felt good, especially given she was trembling.

Mostly, she was shaken from that confrontation with Toby, but it was also from the words still echoing in the air.

"I really do love you."

She just...

She couldn't take it in. Not only because it was too hard to believe, but because she was scared. If she let it into her heart, if she let herself *feel* it...

I only ever want to be in love with you...

Hugo was saying something about talking to Lee, Janson, the other staff, making sure Toby really did leave the grounds. She nodded numbly and turned towards the cages for the ducklings.

"I need to get these to Lee."

Hugo paused, watching her pick up a cage, aware that there was something off in her tone. She hoped he thought it was just because of Toby. His interruption had been useful at least as something to hide behind.

"I'll take those to Lee," said Hugo, taking the cage she held and picking up the other. His voice held the tender note she had often heard these last few days. And she knew if she looked at him, she would see the warmth in his eyes that she now realised meant, *"I love you."*

His words, his voice, his look, his actions... *I love you. Always you.* It was there, a promise held out to her. A patch of golden sunlight just one step away. And if she let herself step into it, let that warm glow bathe her, she knew exactly how it would suffuse her with joy...

But she had believed him once before, hadn't she? At a party, nearly a year ago. She had believed for a moment all the words he whispered to her, and it had been a lie. One false kiss had almost broken her heart. If she submitted to the happiness he now promised her and that turned out to be false too...?

It would destroy her.

"Sit down in the shade," Hugo said. "Watch the lambs for a bit. I'll get you a cup of tea."

So she sat feebly on a straw bale while he went off to do half a dozen things she ought to be doing herself. She would much rather have been doing them than sitting and thinking.

But her limbs felt oddly weak, and her mind kept skipping from thing to thing: the bright flash of sunlight on a phone screen, the little sounds of the ducklings as Lee stowed them safely in their cages, the babble of children's voices, the ugly look in Toby's eyes, the feel of Hugo's hands, the warmth of Hugo's lips, the sound of Hugo's words...

I love you.

What if he didn't? What if he was just confused because they were friends sleeping together and having a good time? What if he was just trying it out like a new fashion, like yet another game to pass the time?

She shivered and glanced up, realising she needn't have bothered finding a seat in the shade. The fierce heat of the sun had been swamped by a barrage of thick grey cloud. In a few minutes there would be yet another of the short, sharp showers that had plagued them over the last few days, sending the Easter visitors scurrying for shelter, jackets pulled over their heads.

Amelia stood up, cold in her light summer dress. She had left a coat somewhere, maybe by the information kiosk?

She set off to find it, but got caught up on her way in half a dozen issues: there was a problem with the portaloos (there was always a problem with the portaloos), the generator for the bouncy castle was making a funny noise, someone had lost their car keys, another car was blocking the access road to the yard, and so on and so on...

The rest of the afternoon passed. The promised rain came,

but the clouds didn't go. They built in the sky, turning heavy and black, until, as the last of the guests left and Amelia and the staff and volunteers set to work clearing up, there was a rumble of thunder from the sky.

Hugo glanced up. He had a black bin liner in one hand and a litter picker in the other, and Amelia couldn't help but smile at the thought that Viscount Leighton, heir to the Earl of Carnford, was collecting rubbish.

For her?

Maybe he really did—

No.

He shot her a smile as he turned back from surveying the sky. "I think we're in for trouble."

TWENTY-EIGHT

I T TURNED OUT HUGO was right about the weather. Halfway through the clean-up, there was a stinging shower of hail followed by a furious downpour.

The rain was so thick Amelia could hardly see through it. She blinked water out of her eyes, looking grimly across the sodden grass at the hunched figures still manfully litter-picking and disassembling stalls.

"I feel so guilty for making them carry on," she told Hugo for what was probably the third or fourth time. "But we're open from tomorrow. Everything needs to be put away."

"We'll get it done." His dark hair was plastered to his head, rivulets of water running down his jaw. Yet somehow, there was still a glow of warm good humour in his eyes. "Stop feeling guilty. You smashed your income target, didn't you? Be proud, Amy. Everyone who's here is here because they want to be." He grinned at her woeful expression and bumped her shoulder with his. "Come on. Buck up. Stop fretting and just get on with it."

She had the urge to stick her tongue out and say that was rich, coming from the man who up until now had never done a day's work in his life. But instead, she just smiled slightly to herself as she shook her head and forced her numb fingers to move.

Hugo was right. She *had* done well. Maybe she was allowed to stop worrying for a few minutes and simply...bask.

When finally, *finally* it was done—or as done as was humanly possible in the circumstances—they walked wearily up the stairs towards her room.

"I'm dying for a hot bath," she said.

"In this house? You must be joking."

She stopped at the top of the stairs, a retort frozen on her tongue. There was a puddle on the floor. And coming from the ceiling was the persistent drip-drip of water.

"Oh, fuck."

Hugo met her despairing look with a grimace. "I'll get a bucket?"

"Please. There should be one in the cleaning cupboard at the end of the hall."

Amelia walked on, eyes scanning the ceiling, opening the door of each bedroom in turn. She found another leak in one of the spare rooms, then she opened her own door and let out a pathetic wail.

"What?" Hugo hurried over, then saw the answer for himself. A huge leak, right above her bed, water coming down in more of a steady stream than a drip. Her bedding was soaked.

"Right," said Hugo. "You are coming to Conyers."

He took charge after that, telling her to pack a bag while he directed Sarah and Janson to bring buckets and search the rest of the house for leaks. Then he dragged her half-protesting by the hand out of the house and into the rain.

"Run! It'll warm you up!"

So they ran hand-in-hand across the gardens and through the gate. It was a breathless, stupid dash through the choking rain. And maybe she was really just running away from the holes in the roof, from all the worries and jobs that loomed at her back, but when had they last run laughing through the gardens? And as Hugo said, they couldn't get any wetter.

They clattered gasping into the deathly stillness of Conyers

House. Amelia sagged back against the wall before straightening and looking guiltily at the wet mark she had left on the silk wallpaper.

"Never mind that," said Hugo. He took her hand again and towed her up the stairs.

"You know I could have just stayed in a different room at Redbridge. There are plenty to choose from."

They had reached his bedroom. She stood still for a moment, looking around. She had only been in here once or twice before, and not for over a decade. She didn't really remember it, and it had probably all changed anyway. The dark, luxurious decor was fresh and new. She could see no traces of boyhood anywhere.

But she could see traces of Hugo. The decadent quality of the fixtures and fittings, the large bed made for sin. But also... The smell of him, so familiar. The very feel of him all around. The dirty jeans from yesterday still hanging over the back of a chair, as though he didn't always want housekeeping coming into his room, as though he held this place private—part of his secret, inner life. A secret life she now knew held far more depth than she—or Cassie, or anyone—had ever suspected.

I'm in love with you.

Hugo Blackton didn't fall in love. She'd just told him so. But Hugo Blackton also didn't work tirelessly in the rain, didn't charm old ladies into buying raffle tickets, didn't laughingly help small boys find hand-painted Easter eggs hidden in trees. He didn't sacrifice time and energy and comfort merely to help her. He didn't care. He couldn't possibly, really, *care...* But maybe she had never really known who Hugo Blackton was. And maybe he hadn't, either.

Now, he put her overnight bag down by his bed and peeled off his dripping coat. Then, smiling at the way she stood there dazedly, he came to unzip the front of hers—chiding her for

247

staying in wet things. And she realised that the sensation she had felt on walking into his room, the feeling that had made her stop and stay stupidly still was...relief.

She was here, and she was warm, and she was safe. A weight on her shoulders lifted, and she felt her chest ease. This was sanctuary. And it was because she was here. Not at Conyers—but *here*, with Hugo. It was Hugo that made her feel safe. Cared for. Loved.

Could she really keep pretending she didn't believe it?

"You're freezing," he said, taking off her wet coat for her as though she was a child. "Let's get you warmed up."

He hung her coat next to his, then crossed to the en suite, picking up a remote control from a sideboard on the way. He pressed a few buttons on it, glancing into the bathroom, and Amelia laughed as the shower came on remotely.

She looked into the expansive space, taking in the marble, the sleek black fittings. "You are *such* a spoiled little rich boy."

"I know. Disgusting isn't it?" said Hugo with a grin. "But this is why you are here." He waved a hand to the shower. "Hot running water that is actually hot. You need to get warm. Then you need to be fed. And then have a long sleep in a warm, dry bed. Amy... You need a break from Redbridge. From worrying about Redbridge. Plus..." His grin tilted as he stepped closer. "I think I owe you an orgasm from earlier."

She pretended to deliberate. "Well... I *suppose* it's a compelling argument..."

Hugo laughed. Then she squealed as he suddenly picked her up and carried her fully clothed into the shower.

———◦———

In the shower, they picked up where they had left off in the barn. Then he insisted Amelia sit in a bubble bath until she protested she was getting wrinkly. And then he wrapped her in a big, snuggly dressing gown and stowed her safely in his bed.

Possibly he was being a bit much. But she was here, in his bedroom, and he felt a bit like an over-excited child at Christmas. And that awful chill that had crept into her eyes after Toby appeared—after Hugo had told her he loved her—was finally starting to fade.

Which was good.

But she still hadn't said it back.

Which was fine. Obviously. It didn't really matter. It was just that it felt like his heart was swinging on a pendulum over a pit in hell and one wrong word might plunge him down into its fiery depths forever.

Jesus.

He had totally lost his cool.

"Why does this dressing gown have the name of a tile company embroidered on it?" Amelia asked, sitting against his headboard and peering down at the small, embroidered logo on her chest.

"They send me gifts at Christmas. They were very expensive bathroom tiles," he elaborated at her puzzled look.

"Of course."

"What would you like to eat?"

"Anything really. I don't mind."

He phoned the kitchen and put in a slightly absurd order.

"TV?" he asked, coming to sit next to her on the bed.

"Sure."

He put the TV on. They sat and looked at it. He wanted to crawl out of his skin. But maybe only he felt the tension, because Amelia just sat and watched the TV, seeming totally relaxed—until her lips twitched.

"Why are you staring at me, Hugh?"

"I'm not."

She turned to look at him. He looked resolutely at the TV.

A second or two went past, then she reached out and took hold of his hand, wrapping her fingers through his. "Thank you," she said softly. "For your help today. The last few days. All of it."

"That's OK." He didn't know why he was blushing, but he was.

She turned on her side so she could look at him better, then reached up and touched his cheek, turning his face to hers. "Hugh...?"

His heart pounded. She was looking at him like maybe she was about to say...

"Yes?"

But she leant up and kissed him, and if he felt the tightness of tears in his throat, that was his problem, not hers.

She deepened the kiss, then moved to straddle his lap, holding his face in her hands as she kissed him. She undid the cord of the dressing gown—an invitation he was happy to accept—and he pushed it from her shoulders, revealing nothing but skin underneath.

He ran his fingers up her arms, down her chest, palming her breasts then breaking the kiss to move his mouth to her nipples as she gasped and shifted on his lap.

He kissed her again, dragging the dressing gown the rest of the way off and throwing it to the floor. Amy, naked on his lap and he—

"Fuck," he said.

"What?"

"I don't have any condoms here."

She gave a laugh of disbelief.

"I don't bring girls here," he protested. "I had some in my wallet, but we used those at yours."

Amy bit her lip, hands on his chest. She moved them down,

toying with the waistband of the jogging pants he had put on after their shower.

"I know you said before that you're...um...clean... Are you definitely? Because I'm on the pill."

"I don't... I mean... I've never done it bare. So yes. I'm safe. I get tested sometimes, anyway."

She shot him a look of surprise. "Never?"

"Too risky. Not just the erm...health reasons. But with money, and a title, there's always someone who thinks a baby might be the way to get both."

She stared at him. "Seriously?"

He shrugged slightly. "I've heard the stories. Been more or less told it to my face once or twice."

She resumed toying with the hem of his trousers, running the tips of her fingers distractingly under the elastic.

"So if we did this," she said cautiously, "it would be your first time...?"

Amy. Bare. The thought of it sent such a rush of blood to his cock he almost winced.

"Yes."

Then he realised she was smiling. Almost laughing.

"What? Is that funny?"

"Just the thought of Hugo Blackton still having a first anything to lose."

He hooked his finger under her chin, smiling too but completely serious when he said, "Only with you."

"You trust me then?"

"That you're not trying to trap me into marriage? Yes. I trust you. And do you trust me? That I'm safe, I mean."

In answer, she raised herself up and freed him from his trousers. He sucked in a breath at the touch of her fingers and then the world went still. There was nothing but his heart beating, and her eyes on his, and the need he had, not just for her body, but for everything she could give him.

She lowered herself, pushed him deep inside.

"This is me trusting you. And I know you've been waiting to hear it. I do love you, Hugh. I've never been able to do anything else."

TWENTY-NINE

A MELIA SUPPOSED THIS WAS what it really meant to make love. The first time for both of them. With absolutely nothing between them, no barriers now, no mistrust, no suspicion, no resentment. Holding back nothing and giving all.

She surrendered herself entirely. And so did he, something in his eyes when she said those words—*I love you too*—that cut to a place far deeper inside her than touch could reach; something passing between them that rearranged her heart and changed it forever. A look she could never unsee: Hugo's very soul.

Him. Him. The man she loved.

He moved her onto her back and entered her again, watching her face, as though he couldn't get enough of that feeling, the press of his heat against her slick warmth. Holding her thigh, he angled her so he could move deeper still, and she willed him inside in a haze of love and lust, wanting them to merge, to never break apart.

Afterwards, she lay in his arms, their legs tangled, skin-to-skin as though anything else would be strange. She was so tired after the last few days, but part of her didn't want to let go of this moment. Eyes half-open, she trailed a finger sleepily over the dips of muscle on his shoulder. His chest was hot beneath her cheek, his heartbeat loud.

"I think we probably missed them knocking at the door with our dinner," said Hugo, his voice a rumble beneath her ear.

She laughed lightly, because it was such a mundane, unromantic thing to say after everything that had just passed. But she liked that. She wanted this with him: to be normal and everyday and utterly human.

"I'm more tired than hungry," she said.

"You should eat though. You barely even had lunch. I'll call the kitchen again."

He leant over and picked up his phone from the bedside table. She played with the ridges along the edge of his ribcage as he spoke to the chef. He lay back down, head on the pillow close to hers so they were eye to eye.

"Food, then sleep. And tomorrow, a long lie-in. Spend the day relaxing here, then the party in the evening."

"It's tomorrow?" she asked. He had mentioned arranging something with his friends, but she hadn't realised it was so soon.

"Yes. Just a dozen friends or so. Nothing too crazy. But it'll be fun to let loose after all this."

Amelia kept her doubts from her face. She wasn't really sure a party with Hugo's friends would be anything other than crazy.

"I can't spend the day here," she said instead. "We're open for the summer now. That Easter event was just the beginning of the hard work, not the end of it."

"I do think you ought to have a day off though. When did you last have one?"

"I can't Hugo. There's only me."

"When does your mother come back?"

"She said two weeks."

"And then you're off to Europe with Evie?"

She hesitated, torn. Because of course, now that she was so close to finally being able to go, there was a part of her that didn't

254

want to leave.

"You should go," Hugo said before she could answer. "I'm not going to ask you not to. I know how much you've been looking forward to it. I'd come with you, but Evie wouldn't want that. And maybe... I don't know. Maybe this is something you think you need to do by yourself? See," he said with a crooked grin as he reached out and curled a strand of her hair around his finger, "I love you enough to want you to choose *you,* not me. I'm basically a saint. Although...I might have to pop over to wherever you are for a day or two. I might die otherwise. There's a limit to my asceticism."

She smiled. "I'd like that—you to join us for a bit."

"I suppose that means telling Evie," he said with an exaggerated grimace. "Or does she already know?"

"Not yet."

"Which of us do you think she'll hate more?" Then he answered his own question. "Me, of course."

"Obviously," Amelia agreed with a smile.

There was a knock at the door. Hugo pulled on some jogging bottoms and went to answer it, returning with a heavily-laden tray in his hands. "Suspiciously quick," he muttered. "Probably microwaved the last lot."

Amelia just laughed to herself because he was, despite everything, still odiously spoiled and didn't even realise it.

As they ate, the wind rattled the windows, and another fierce downpour made itself heard over the television. Amelia's thoughts inevitably turned to Redbridge. She put down her fork, chest suddenly too tight to swallow.

The roof was failing. And other than fire, nothing destroyed buildings faster than water.

"What is it?" Hugo asked, sensing the turn in her mood.

She wanted to say, "Nothing," and get on with their evening, safe in this pristine, luxurious bubble where everything was delivered at the press of a button. But as she kept trying to remind herself, real life was inescapable.

"It's just...I'm worried about the roof at Redbridge. They found dry rot, and now the leaks, and even the money raised by the Easter event will barely cover the cost of the survey. How can we ever afford the repairs?" Ridiculous tears suddenly stung her eyes as the weight of it all came rushing back. "I don't know what to do, I don't know how to save it..."

Oh God, she really was crying now. And she *hated* to cry.

"Hey," said Hugo gently, moving to sit next to her on the bed. He wrapped her in his arms, her face to his chest. "It'll be alright. There's always a way."

"But it's millions of pounds," she said with an agonised gasp. "Redbridge needs *millions*. And we simply don't have it."

"Maybe you do," said Hugo.

She drew back and looked up at him. There was an odd look in his eyes, half-fear, half-hope.

"I know a way you can get the money. If you...if you trust me."

"I can't accept a loan or anything like that."

"No. It's not a loan. It's your money. Our money, really. The only thing is... To get it...you have to marry me."

THIRTY

A S PROPOSALS WENT, IT probably wasn't the best.

Amy stared at him with a sort of stunned suspicion that was precisely why he hadn't brought it up before. Well, actually, he had genuinely forgotten all about it over the last couple of days, deliriously happy in the busy idyll of Redbridge and life with Amy. Meeting the lawyers seemed like a lifetime ago. And that man who had thought he was apologising to Amelia purely to bring this marriage about and get hold of that money...? That man had been an idiot.

But he was terrified—petrified—that even now, after all they had shared, that man was who she would see.

"Married?" she repeated incredulously. "What...? What on earth do you mean?"

"There's a fund," he explained, moving the tray off the bed and onto the floor before sitting down to face her properly. "Some lawyers discovered it when looking through an archive of legal documents."

He explained it all as best he could. Amelia listened mostly in silence, her brow creased in confusion and doubt.

"They've looked into it, and they're fairly certain it's ironclad. The fund can only be released by marriage."

"Between us?"

"Between the Blackton heir and a member of your family."

257

"Me or Cassie, you mean?"

"I'd really far rather it was you," he said, attempting a smile. She didn't return it. Didn't seem to even notice it. Her thoughts were all turned inward.

"How long have you known about this?"

Shit. This was the sticking point.

"Um. Not long."

"You didn't think it was worth mentioning?"

"Well... Honestly, the idea that you'd ever marry me, even for this, seemed pretty far-fetched."

"Until now," she said—far too flatly for comfort.

He tried another smile. "Would you? Consider it now?"

She shook her head slightly, but more—he hoped—as a way to clear her thoughts than to indicate *no*.

"I'm just... Why didn't the lawyers speak to me? When did they come?"

"They came...erm...two days ago." Hugo winced internally at the lie, regretting it the minute it was out of his mouth.

"During the Easter event?"

"Well... I erm... I met them briefly. You were busy."

Ouch. Ouch. Each lie felt like a brand upon his soul. What was he doing...? What the *fuck* was he doing? But she already seemed so sceptical. And every question she asked confirmed the suspicious direction her thoughts were taking. He couldn't bear to have her mistrust everything they had just built together. It was real. And if he had to lie to protect it, then he would.

Amelia let out a breath, shaking her head again. "And it's really worth *sixteen million pounds?*"

"Thirty-two. But yes, that would be sixteen each."

"That's... Well. It's crazy."

Hugo nodded, beginning to feel more hopeful. Was she considering it...?

"And we really have to get married?"

258

"Yes."

She looked at him, then started laughing. "This is crazy! We can't! Can we? No! Of course we can't."

"Can't we?" he said, taking hold of her hand. "Is it really so crazy?"

"Us getting *married?*"

"It doesn't have to be forever," he said, though his heart ached at the thought of that. "If you want to...to get it annulled the next day, then we can do that. Whatever it takes to get you the money you need, I'm happy to do it."

Her expression softened with gratitude, and she turned thoughtful, then frowned. "It doesn't seem right though, treating marriage like this. I guess I'm old fashioned, but it doesn't feel right to say those words if we don't mean them."

"I would mean them."

Her eyes went wide, and he squeezed her hand, then found he had to look away. He swallowed around the lump in his throat—his heart. "I would marry you for real, Amy."

"But..." The word was the merest breath.

"We've known each other forever. It's not like we need to get to know each other. And I love you."

It all seemed quite simple. He looked ahead to the future, and he saw her. There was nothing else he wanted.

"We've been together for *days...*"

"We've known each other forever."

"You've never even had a serious girlfriend."

"Because none of them were you."

He touched her cheek, and she leant into his palm. He wanted to kiss her, but she turned her head slightly and sighed.

"I need to tell you something."

He tensed, suddenly fearful, but she laughed softly and said, "It's going to be extremely embarrassing for me, so please don't laugh."

"OK..."

"I've always, always had the biggest crush on you." Her cheeks flamed and she grimaced slightly, looking down and toying with the bed cover. "Since forever. And I'm talking all-consuming, obsession-level infatuation. I *told* you this was embarrassing."

But he wasn't laughing. He was only smiling, because he felt suddenly warm all over, a giddy sort of joy rushing through him. He felt like a schoolboy. She liked him, she really, really *liked* him...

"You're laughing," she protested.

"I'm not! I'm not. I just... I always assumed you'd have better taste, to be honest. I could have understood if it was Roscoe you liked, but me...?"

"I know," she said laughingly. "It makes no sense."

"As much as my ego appreciates hearing it..." he trailed off as her face turned sombre.

"I'm telling you now because it explains why what happened at Cassie's party hurt me so much."

Oh. Guilt cinched his insides with cold, sharp fingers. What an *idiot*... What a *total idiot* he had been.

"You said things that were like all my dreams coming true. It was like you knew somehow exactly what to say... I figured you had guessed how I felt and were using it to win your bet or game or whatever it was you were playing at. I was so embarrassed. I was... Honestly? It broke my heart a bit, Hugh, when I realised it was just a trick."

He had never felt so wretched. He took her hand again, tears in his eyes as well as hers. "I'm sorry. I'm so sorry..."

She shook her head slightly, not finished yet. "I'm telling you this because it has been so hard for me to trust you again. And now, this... Everything that has happened today, all the things you're saying... It's like it's happening again. All the things I never dared hope for are coming true. And I don't know how to trust that it's real. That you mean them. Do you? Do you really?"

"I do. Amy. I really do."

She looked at him. He brushed a tear from her cheek.

"You're being honest with me?" she asked. "Everything you're saying is true?"

He nodded, uncomfortably aware of the small lie he had told her about the lawyers. But it didn't matter, surely, not when all the important things were true?

"I know I've been stupid. And thoughtless. But I've never meant to be cruel. I've never once meant to hurt you."

"But..."

"I know. I know it's hard. But trust me, please? I love you. I love you so much. And I will marry you for real today, tomorrow, whenever you want. Or I will marry you temporarily just so you can get this money, if that's what you want. You decide, Amy. But even if we get divorced the next day, I will wait a year, or however long I can bear it, and then I will ask you again. Because you're the one, the only one."

She sniffed, tears falling more freely now. He brushed them away with his thumbs as best he could, his own eyes far from dry. "Can I tell you something?"

She nodded.

"Whenever I've been away from here and I think of home...it's your face that I see. Scowling at me normally, true. But it's you. Little A. Amy. For years and years, I hardly knew it, but you have meant home to me."

THIRTY-ONE

A MY WALKED BACK TO Redbridge the next morning feeling a little dazed. And tired. They had, yet again, not got much sleep.

For a lot of the night, they had just been talking. Making plans. *Wedding* plans.

Tomorrow, they were getting married.

"Here," Hugo had suggested. "The Conyers chapel. I can find a minister. We can have Roscoe and some of the guests as witnesses—he's coming to the party. It's perfect timing. It can be a joint hen-stag do."

So Hugo stayed behind at Conyers to make both party and wedding arrangements, while Amelia walked across the gardens to do a day's work at Redbridge.

The rain had stopped at some point in the night, but the grass was sodden, and the cedars by the wall dripped, a strong, cold breeze shaking a shower from their branches as she passed under.

The day was overcast, more dark clouds on the horizon, and the breeze tugged crazily at her hair as she crossed the Redbridge grounds, sudden gusts sending leaves and stray litter from yesterday whipping across her path. She looked grimly at the sky as she passed the fountain and climbed the steps to the back terrace. It seemed they might be in for a small storm.

What a perfect start to the summer open season.

But it was the scaffolding at the back of the house that really gave her pause. The wind was whistling past the metal struts, lashing a stray dangling rope back and forth. She pushed back the familiar tide of anxiety. She didn't need to worry anymore. She could save Redbridge. Save Redbridge and marry the man she loved.

It seemed too good to be true.

One of Hugo's peacocks made her jump as it came fluttering out from behind a large plant pot, ruffling its wings irritably as the wind tugged at its feathers. She remembered the day he gave them to her. How he had told her that it was OK to accept help and do things the easy way.

Perhaps he was right. But it was still so hard to trust that things would turn out as perfectly as he had spent most of last night envisioning them.

"A small wedding here, and then later, we can do the big society thing, with our families and everyone there. But I like the idea of it being just us. A small, private ceremony. No fuss or stress. Anyway, it's what everyone does now. Even Harry and Meghan did it."

She had laughed at that. At the thought of little Amelia B-T being in any way fashionable, even though, deep down, she felt uneasy at the idea of getting married without her parents knowing.

"Let's not tell them," Hugo had said. "They'll only want to interfere and make us worry about things that aren't worth worrying about. I sort of like the idea of being married in secret, no one but us knowing."

"And Roscoe. And whoever else is there."

"Yes, but he can keep a secret. Not that I want to keep you a secret. I want the whole world to know that I've chosen you, and, more to the point, by some miracle, you've deigned to choose me. But let's save Redbridge first."

Then he had kissed her, made love to her...

Save Redbridge. Marry Hugo. Maybe the real reason it was so hard to believe was because she wasn't used to getting what she wanted. And here it all was, on a platter. Laid out like the meal in a fairy palace. All too perfect.

She shook her head as the bird made its regal way down the terrace steps, dragging its lavish tail behind it.

Good things can happen, she told herself firmly. Even to her.

It was time to stop looking a gift peacock in the mouth.

———◆———

It was raining again and almost dark when Amelia crossed back over the grounds to Conyers. The wind hadn't let up all day, and the cedars were groaning as they swayed in the darkening sky above the gate.

But Conyers was a beacon across the lawn. For once, almost every window was lit, and the wind brought with it the faint sounds of music.

Had the party started already? It was only just after seven—later than she had intended to return, but she'd had all of yesterday's unfinished tasks to complete as well as opening day to contend with. She had a garment bag over one arm and another bag on her shoulder. There had seemed no point getting dressed and doing her hair at Redbridge when the wind, rain, and mud would just spoil it all before she arrived. But some small vanity shrank away from the thought of walking into Hugo's party dressed as she was in old jeans, her hair in even worse disarray than normal.

Oh well. There wasn't much she could do about it other than hope to navigate her way up to Hugo's room unseen.

The music grew louder as she approached the house, coming

from somewhere deep inside. The large windows of the back drawing room revealed it was full of people, so Amelia changed course, heading for the side door that would take her past the library and down to one of the old servants' stairs.

But as she passed the library, a familiar voice called her name. Roscoe was inside, talking to a handsome brown-haired man—one of Hugo's closest friends, Jay Orton.

"Amelia!" Roscoe greeted her with a smile. He stood up, and so did Jay. Roscoe crossed the room and kissed her cheek. He took hold of her bags and helped her out of her wet coat. "You know Jay?"

"We've met once or twice," she said, smiling politely. She had never quite warmed to Jay, no matter how handsome he was. There had always been something remote in his cool grey eyes, as though he was watching life from a distance, and not terribly impressed by any of it. And he was a bad influence on Hugo. Or so everyone said. Because where Hugo's dissolution had always seemed borne of a desire for fun, Jay's commitment to sin seemed like his very reason for being—or so everyone said.

Now though, he was smiling at her with a warm sort of curiosity in his eyes. "Nice to see you again."

Roscoe put her bags down by a chair as though he was expecting her to stay. They were drinking whiskey, a decanter of the amber liquid on a low rosewood table between two leather armchairs. Roscoe tugged a third chair over.

"Where's Hugo?" she asked.

"Being the hostess with the mostess," said Roscoe. "We just ducked in here to escape the gabble for a bit. And...well...to discuss Best Man and usher duties. I hear congratulations are in order."

Her cheeks flamed. "Erm. Yes," she mumbled as Jay poured her a glass and handed it to her.

"Sorry it's not champagne," he said.

The men sat back down, and she sat too, looking at the amber liquid in her glass with no intention of drinking it. It was far easier to look at her drink than Roscoe's face. His knowing smile.

"Did Hugo...um...explain the situation?" she asked awkwardly.

"I know a little of it," said Roscoe.

"Redbridge needs a new roof."

"Of course," he said smoothly, and when she glanced up, she saw the exact smug grin she had known she would. If only she had a cushion to throw at his face.

"Honestly, Amelia," said Roscoe, turning more serious. "I don't quite know what's going on, but I'm glad of anything that makes you my sister. And I'm glad my brother has finally, finally made a sensible choice for once in his life."

Jay laughed lightly. "Who would have thought that being sentenced to a year at Conyers was the best thing that could ever happen to him?"

"Sentenced?" repeated Amy just as Jay caught sight of Roscoe's warning glare, the smile abruptly dropping from his face.

"What do you mean sentenced?" she asked again.

Jay looked wide-eyed at Roscoe for help. "Was that...a secret?"

"No, no, of course not," said Roscoe hastily.

"Well, it clearly was to me," said Amelia. "What's going on, Roscoe?"

He let out a breath, then said in a rush, "Our father told Hugo he had to stay at Conyers for a year and learn to manage the estate as a way of proving he was mature and responsible enough to get a job at BlacktonGold—our company. It was his punishment, I suppose, for what happened at Cassie's party."

"But I thought..." She stopped, because it was too embarrassing to admit. *I thought he stayed for me.* Judging from the sympathetic glance the men exchanged, they had figured out her mistake already.

"I didn't know he hadn't told you," said Jay. "I'm sorry."

"He's hardly told anyone," said Roscoe. "I think he was...ashamed of it, Amelia."

She didn't speak for a moment, too busy thinking hurriedly back over all their past conversations. He had never exactly said why he was at Conyers, had never exactly *lied* about it... But he hadn't told her the truth either. Not even when she had told him hers.

Was a lie by omission still a lie?

"Amelia, if he didn't mention it, it's only because he was too embarrassed. And it's got nothing to do with... I mean... He's a grown man. He wouldn't have stayed here if he didn't want to, no matter what our father said. You know Hugo. He does what he wants." Roscoe said the last with a slightly desperate sort of smile.

Amelia returned it, out of politeness, then took a sip of her whiskey, wincing at the taste.

Maybe Roscoe was right. Hugo really wasn't the sort of man to do something he didn't want to. But it felt...embarrassing, disconcerting, to know that he had only been here because he had been *ordered* to be. And no wonder he had been so determined to make things right between them if his father had been driven to punish him over it. She took another sip of whiskey, reliving the conversation she had overheard between them the night of that dinner. It all made much more sense.

She was vaguely aware of the awkward glance Roscoe and Jay exchanged, and she tried to pull herself together.

"Talk to him," suggested Jay kindly. "Things are always better if you talk about them."

She nodded and put her glass down as she stood up. "I need to go and shower and change anyway." She forced herself to smile as she picked up her bags. "I'm cold and muddy and not fit for a party. See you in a bit."

She left the room, too deep in thought to remember quite where she was going, and ended up following the corridor all the way to the great hall. She passed several guests on the way, recognising none of them, eyeing the gorgeous, gleaming girls with a sort of helpless envy.

Somehow, Hugo had contrived to decorate most of the main areas of the house. Probably he had called in an event company. There were tiny, sparking lights everywhere, balloon arches around the doors, streamers hanging from the ceilings, all of it in tones of gold and silver. There was a champagne fountain in the hall, a gaggle of people posing in front of it, phones in hand.

One phone call and *poof*, instant party.

How different from the laborious prep for that long Easter weekend...

She shook the thought away, stepping around a couple making out on the stairs as she headed to Hugo's room.

He wasn't there, but she hadn't expected him to be. She put her bags down and looked on the sideboard for the remote control that operated his shower. There were documents strewn across it—letters and legal things to do with the fund their wedding tomorrow would release. He had shown her some of them last night: the old legal document drawn up hundreds of years ago. She wondered what the old Baron would make of her.

The remote control was peeking out from under a letter. Her eyes snagged on a familiar name as she picked the letter up to put aside.

Lady Caroline Banberry-Thompson.

That was her mother. But why...?

She started to read. It was from the lawyers.

Lord Leighton,

Further to our meetings with both Lady Caroline Banber-

ry-Thompson, representing the Banberry-Thompson family, and subsequently yourself, representing the Blackton family, here follows a summary of our discussion with both parties...

Her mother knew? But why hadn't she said anything? She had spoken with her only that morning. And how had the lawyers met with her when she was in Peru?

She glanced at the date on the letter.

March. Not two days ago as Hugo had told her. But back in March—just before her mother left. Hugo had known about the money all this time. And that date...

She sat down limply on the bed, feverishly trying to count back.

That was the day he had first come to see her, to try to apologise.

The lawyers had come, told him about the money, and then he had come to apologise.

She pressed a hand to her mouth, holding back she didn't quite know what. A sob? A scream? Some awful sort of bleak hysteria...

This wasn't just a lie by omission. He had told her—he had *told* her the lawyers came during the Easter event. He had lied to her face and then promised he was telling the truth.

And how much else had he lied about?

Had any of it, any of it been real?

Oh God, oh God... It was all about the money.

A quick wedding here, keep it secret, don't tell her parents—*of course* don't tell her parents, because her mother would know instantly what was going on—and then get divorced in a day or two... That's what he had offered her, making it sound like a sacrifice so she wouldn't suspect that was what he was hoping for all along. And of course he didn't mind if she went off with Evie afterwards. He probably couldn't wait to get rid of her.

But why... *Why?* He didn't even need the money. Why do this to her?

Greed? Another stupid game?

She got blindly to her feet and headed for the stairs. She couldn't stay here. She needed to go, go...

But he was there, at the foot of the stairs, laughing at something someone said as they snagged a glass from the champagne fountain. He turned and broke into a grin at the sight of her, holding his arms out, saying something, she didn't know what. And for some reason he was wet, dripping from head to foot.

"Some idiots got into the spa," he told her, half-laughing as she stood frozen before him on the bottom step. "Then Em pulled me into the swimming pool."

"Emma D'Arby?" she repeated stupidly. The girl he had slept with a few months ago. Of course she was here. Why wouldn't she be? He had probably slept with every girl she had seen tonight.

"What's wrong?" he said, the smile falling from his face. "You look pale. Are you OK?"

He reached for her, but she moved back, stepped around him. "A headache. Sorry. I'm going home."

"Oh no. Not another migraine? Wait, I'll come with you—"

"No, no. You stay. It's your party. Bad luck to see the bride the night before anyway." She could hardly get the words out. They were sharp and staccato, sticking in her throat.

"I'll get you a car. You can't walk in this weather..."

She shook her head, moving away, stepping aside as someone ran up to them. Roscoe.

"Hugh. Shit. Have you seen?"

"Seen what?"

"Belgravia. It's tanked."

Roscoe had his phone in his hand. Passed it to Hugo, whose face paled. "I knew it had dipped, but fuck..."

Money. Money. Of *course* they were talking about money. They were Blacktons. It's what they did. But at least it answered her question. Now she knew why he wanted this marriage.

"Amy," he called after her. "Wait in the foyer. I'll call the car around…"

She made no answer as she left Conyers forever.

THIRTY-TWO

A MY LEFT, AND EVERYTHING started to go wrong.

"It's gone, Hugh," Roscoe said.

Hugo dragged his eyes away from Amy's retreating figure. She looked so pale. He hated to let her leave, but she seemed determined to go. He would call her, text her, see that she was home safe, that Sarah was looking after her.

"What?" he said distractedly, trying to make sense of the charts on Roscoe's phone.

"The whole portfolio has been wiped out. What did you do?"

"Erm. Invested it?"

The spirals of anxiety that had started to swirl around his gut at Roscoe's first words grew thick and heavy, forcing their way sharply between his ribs. All the numbers on the phone were red. All the lines on the charts plummeted down.

Shit, shit, shit, shit...

Roscoe grabbed the phone back, jabbed at the screen, pulling up more charts, things Hugo didn't understand. "It was hedged," Roscoe was saying. "It was all hedged, but you pulled it out and put it in Courtwell? What the fuck? They've just collapsed. They were under investigation by the European regulators. Why on earth would you invest there?"

Hugo flushed hot, then cold. "I don't know! I just recognised the name. I went to university with a Courtwell—"

Roscoe gave a horrified bark of laughter. "This was a multi-million-pound portfolio! You can't just invest it on a whim! It's not like choosing a horse at the Grand National just because you like the name. For fuck's sake, Hugo. Why didn't you analyse the market, do some bloody research—?"

"Because I don't know how! I don't know anything about it!"

"But that's the job, Hugh! What do you think I do all day? Swan around in a suit having liquid lunches? No! I'm analysing, researching—"

"I'm not that sort of person."

"So why the bloody hell do you want to work at the company?"

"I don't!"

Roscoe stared at him. Hugo repeated the words, hearing them as though for the first time. "I don't want to work at the company. I want... I think I want to work here." He looked around the hall, not seeing the party lights or the people—most of whom were staring at his and Roscoe's heated conversation—but instead seeing what lay beyond the walls. The grounds and gardens. The fields and farms. And Redbridge, just a walk away. "I want to stay here. I want to manage the estate. I think...I think I could be good at it."

Roscoe was wide-eyed. For a moment he looked as though he doubted Hugo could ever be good at anything, but he nodded shortly and put his phone back in his pocket. "OK," he said. "Maybe that's...best."

"Father's going to kill me, isn't he?" said Hugo grimly. "When he finds out about Belgravia?"

"Quite probably," said Roscoe with a small smile.

Hugo let out a long sigh, then laughed slightly. "At least I have some money coming my way. I can pay him back." He winked, turned to grab a glass of champagne, and was just in time to see a drunk party guest lose their balance and send the whole stack of glasses crashing to the floor.

—⋄—

For weeks, Hugo had been desperate to see his friends, party, have some fun. And now it was here, all he wanted to do was find Amelia, confess about Belgravia, have her scowl and scold him, and then find a way through it together.

She had left several hours ago and he *missed* her. The text he had sent had gone unanswered, but he didn't want to phone in case she was sleeping. He had called Sarah on the Redbridge kitchen number and been told, extremely curtly, that Amelia was safe and in her room.

So really, there was nothing to do but count down the hours until tomorrow—and have fun while he did it. Except fun was proving difficult to find.

The event company he had hired had installed a mini casino in the saloon. He was at the blackjack table when Tristan, one of his more irritating friends, lumbered over drunkenly, complaining about the lack of food. There had been catering staff serving finger food, but they had finished an hour ago, and Hugo had put the kitchen on alert, telling them to provide whatever guests asked for.

"Is it your phone that's broken or the ovens, perhaps?" asked Tristan, waving one of the house phones around in a drunken hand. "I called hours ago, and no one has brought anything." With an exaggerated squint at the phone, he hit the buttons and droned idiotically, "Helloooo... Earth to kitchen. Come in, kitchen..."

Hugo snatched the phone off him. It was probably just as well Amelia wasn't here. She would hate Tristan. She would probably hate the whole party, come to think of it.

He told Tristan he'd speak to the kitchen and left the room, frowning in thought. Was that why she had looked upset? She didn't like the party? But she had been having a good time at Cassie's party, before he—

In all honesty, he hadn't actually *asked* her, had he? He hadn't considered if tonight was what she would want. And true, he had organised it all a while ago, before they were really together, but still...

He should have asked.

Leaving the saloon, he put the phone back on its holder on a side table, then turned to find himself face-to-face with Emma D'Arby. Her blue eyes were wide, a little unfocused, and she swayed as she grinned up at him, hooking her arms around the back of his neck.

There was a strand of blonde hair sticking to her lip gloss. On instinct, he brushed it aside, and she smiled, stepping close to him, body pressing up against his as he hastily tried to retreat, bumping backwards into the side table.

"No, Em..."

Shit—he had told Amy that Em had pulled him into the swimming pool. He got a sudden flash of memory, Amy repeating, "Emma D'Arby?" in a slightly shocked voice.

Because she knew they had slept together. Cassie had told her...

Was *that* why she was upset?

But it had been months ago. Hugo hardly remembered it himself, and he and Em were old friends, they'd had a few hookups over the years. But it wasn't...it wasn't anything that meant anything, Amy had no need to feel *jealous*...

Em shimmied closer, pushing a hand into the hair at the back of his neck as he stared down at her without seeing her, his thoughts far distant.

He hadn't even thought about it when he'd sent out the invitation to Em. She was one of his oldest friends, he had invited her as a matter of course. He hadn't thought about how it would look to Amy...

Because he didn't think, did he?

"Em," Hugo said again, gently pushing her back from him. "I'm not single. I'm with someone now."

She pouted. "Boo. I did hear rumours. Is it true?"

"Yes. Very much so."

Her eyebrows lifted in surprise, then she patted him on the chest, laughing slightly. "First Jay. Now you. Where have all the good men gone, hm?"

He laughed. "You'll find someone." He winked. "You always do."

She laughed at that. "True. But you getting all serious with someone... This is end of the world stuff, Hugh. I think I need a drink."

"Are we still friends, Em?"

"Always. But I'm not in the mood for a friend tonight." She stroked his cheek in farewell and went off into the crowd.

Hugo watched her go, rather enjoying the novel experience of having turned down sex. And it hadn't even been difficult. He had no desire for Em. For anyone here tonight. Only Amy. He just needed to make sure she believed that so that his past didn't get in the way of his future.

———◦———

There was chaos in the kitchen when Hugo arrived, although there was only one person there. Or perhaps the chaos was *because* there was only one person: a middle-aged woman he recognised as the day cook who did most of their general day-to-day cooking, his father's chef only coming up from London when there was a dinner or guests in residence.

The woman was rushing from station-to-station, face red,

damp hair escaping the white cap she wore.

"What's going on?" asked Hugo. "I heard there was a delay sending food up."

The cook shot him a venomous look that took him by surprise. Staff did not normally look at him like that.

"What does it look like is going on? I'm single-handedly catering to eighty people with no bloody notice—"

"I did leave a message to expect guests—"

She cut him off, talking over him, as she tipped something into a hissing pan. "This morning! And you said a dozen!"

"Admittedly, more people have turned up than I anticipated—"

"So I get dragged in to do a bloody double shift—"

"I don't appreciate the language, Mrs...erm..."

"And I shouldn't even bloody be here, I should be at home with Alfie—"

"Who's Alfie?"

"My son!" She turned hotly from the pan and glared at him. "And who am I, hm? Who the hell am I, *Lord Leighton*? I'm sure as shit that you don't even know my bloody name."

He flushed, annoyed at being spoken to in such a way. Annoyed at himself, really, because she was right. He didn't know her name.

"Seven years I've worked here!" She snatched the cap off her head, pulled off her chef's whites. "But not anymore. Weeks you've been staying here now, taking us all for granted, putting in ridiculous orders at all times of the day. Seven years and you don't know my name. I quit. Cook for your own party guests."

She tossed the white overall onto the loaded counter while Hugo stood there stupidly, an all too familiar sense of dismal regret swamping his chest.

"I'm sorry." He knew the staff at Redbridge. Why the fuck didn't he know his own?

The woman just scoffed and made to storm past him, but paused, catching sight of something, or someone, behind him.

"Apologies, Lord Carnford," she said, "but I'm handing in my notice. I've given my reasons to your son."

Hugo's stomach lurched, and he turned to see his father in the doorway, the man's face as stern as he'd ever seen it.

"I'm sorry to hear that, Emily. Maybe we can speak another day? Because we really would be sorry to lose you."

The woman—Emily—gave an unenthusiastic grunt. "Maybe. I'm not sure. I'm going now, anyway."

Hugo's father nodded heavily. "Well, I hope we can speak soon. But give my regards to Alfie. I hope he is feeling better."

Hugo listened to the exchange, wishing the ground would open up. Why, why, *why* did he always get things so wrong...? And now here was his father, turning the full weight of his disapproval on him.

The Earl gestured angrily to the door through which Emily had just left. "*This* is what happens when you don't think. There are consequences, Hugo, of every action, or inaction. I thought being here, in the heart of this household, with staff to manage, people depending on you, might make you realise that actions have consequences. That you have responsibilities. Not just as my heir, but as a *man*."

Hugo stood silent, choked with mingled shame and irritation. But if he could just speak, try to explain—

"I've had report after report from Howell of you doing nothing. You've spent all your days flirting with Amelia Banberry-Thompson while neglecting Conyers. I asked you to look after one safe, simple portfolio, and you lost it in days. I came up here to see for myself what the hell is going on, and I find the house full of your idiot friends, and my loyal staff feeling they can't stand to work here anymore. Are parties really all you know how to do? Do you have any idea of how lucky you are to have all this?"

He swept his arm out, encompassing not just the room, but all of it: the money, the title, the land.

"I made myself clear last time that my patience was running out. My patience is...exhausted." He took a sharp breath, face red, rage barely contained. "I've moved past disappointed, Hugo. I'm disgusted. You are...nothing...but a...waste...of space—"

Hugo flinched. His father took another sharp breath, face now turning white with anger as he struggled to find the words to deliver whatever blow was coming next.

Except...it didn't come. The Earl's hand flew to his chest, and with an incoherent groan of pain, he collapsed to the floor.

THIRTY-THREE

G IVING HIS FATHER A heart attack was probably one of the lower points of Hugo's existence.

He sat in a hospital corridor, elbows on his knees, head in his hands, Roscoe silent beside him.

"I want to speak to Amy," he said, voice muffled against his palms.

"It's two in the morning," said Roscoe tiredly.

Hugo lifted his head slightly, staring unseeing at the pale green wall opposite. "I know. And she's asleep in bed with a headache. But I just...really, really want to talk to her."

She was the first person he had thought of as his father collapsed. She was the person he wanted beside him as they waited for the air ambulance. She was the person whose hand he wanted to hold as a doctor told them the tests that would need to be run.

Even in the middle of his concern for his father, she was the start and end of every thought.

"You can't tell her anyway," said Roscoe. "We can't tell anyone."

Hugo sat up. "What?"

"It'll crash the company share price if it gets out that he's ill."

"How are you even thinking about stuff like that at a time like this?"

Roscoe gave a hollow laugh. "Oh, I'm never allowed to think about anything else. But it's not my rule anyway. It's his."

Hugo leant his head back against the wall. "That's...fucked up."

"Mm."

Hospital staff passed up and down the corridor. No one seemed in a particular hurry.

"Should we ask someone what's going on?"

Just as he finished speaking, a male nurse approached them, clipboard in hand. "Family of Mr...er...Earl Blackton?"

In any other circumstances, he would have laughed at his father's misnaming. Now he just said, "Yes."

"You can see him now. This way."

The room was as horribly uncomforting as hospital rooms always were, but the man in the bed looked far better than Hugo had dared hope.

Their father was sitting half-upright, looking haggard, but a steadily beeping machine by the bed was the only real sign of what had just happened.

"Mild," he said with a wry twist of his lips. "I'll live."

Roscoe clasped his father's hand and received a warm smile. Hugo stood on the other side of the bed and watched the exchange.

"How are you?" he asked.

"As I said, I'll live. Sit down, both of you."

They did so, and their father explained what the doctors had told him: that it was a mild heart attack—as far as these things went—and had left little damage. "More of a warning. A shot across the bow."

"You work too hard," said Roscoe. "Don't pretend you don't. I've seen it with my own eyes."

He grunted. "Well. If I do need to take a step back, at least I have every faith in my replacement." He squeezed Roscoe's hand, which was still clasping his on the bed cover.

Roscoe darted a look at Hugo, something like an apology in his eyes. But Hugo didn't need it. He had no jealousy anymore about Roscoe's role at the company. In fact, although he was only human and couldn't completely avoid feeling the sting of his father's words, he was more concerned about how strained Roscoe's answering smile had been. For the first time, Hugo realised the enormity of the responsibility on Roscoe's shoulders.

Perhaps it was easier to be the disappointment than the protégé.

They talked for a while about the company, about how to manage things for now, about who would tell their mother. Hugo volunteered himself for that role. Then he said to his father:

"I need to tell you something. Several things, really. No, you stay, Roscoe, because you should hear them too. First: I'm sorry. I've spent almost twenty-seven years being selfish, thoughtless, and thinking only of myself. And I'm sorry to everyone who has been on the receiving end of that."

Roscoe made a noise of protest, and Hugo loved him for it but cut him off. "No, let me finish. The second thing I need to say is that I'm going to step up and manage Conyers. Permanently. I want my life to be up here. Thirdly: I've been doing some online tests and things recently and I'm fairly sure I'm dyslexic, and possibly have dyscalculia too—which is a bit like dyslexia but with numbers. I'm going to get it assessed properly. And fourth," he continued firmly, ignoring his father's frown at that last point, "I'm going to marry Amelia. That's why I've spent so much time at Redbridge, Dad. Not because I was wasting time, but because I was learning what's been right in front of me my whole life. She's wonderful, and I love her."

There was a pause in which Hugo caught Roscoe wiping a hand across his eyes before clearing his throat. Hugo winked at him and grinned, and Roscoe grinned back.

"Oh, and fifth, I'll pay you back what I lost on Belgravia."

Then Hugo jumped, because his father had taken his hand in his.

"Maybe your stay at Conyers hasn't been a complete waste of time. And if you really mean it...then...I'm glad I'll still be here to see it."

The next day—the day of the wedding—dawned with a weak blue sky, the stormy weather of yesterday having mostly blown itself out. Hugo buttoned his shirt, looking out of the window at the wispy clouds, the wind-torn leaves scattered across the lawn.

He should have felt exhausted. He'd had about three hours' sleep since leaving the hospital. Almost everything that could possibly go wrong had gone wrong, and yet... Today he would marry Amelia, and the whole world would be right again.

Now that he knew his father was going to be OK, nothing else mattered. To use that clichéd old phrase: Today was the start of the rest of his life. And he could not wait.

Downstairs, he joined Roscoe in the drawing room, where they waited for Jay who had stayed on after the party due to his role today as groomsman—and who had in fact proved surprisingly helpful in wrapping up the party and looking after everything while Hugo and Roscoe were at the hospital. Hugo had expected to return to chaos, but had instead found a mostly empty house, already well on its way to being restored to order.

Roscoe smiled at Hugo, but neither man spoke. After last night, it felt as though enough had been said to last them both a lifetime, and now the morning was heavy with expectation. Hugo paced before the window, something far closer to excitement than nerves sparking feverishly through his bones.

"Don't we all look lovely," said Jay, entering the room with one of his casually wicked smiles as he took in Hugo and Roscoe in their suits. He tugged the cuffs of his own. "I feel like I'm in a photo shoot for GQ magazine. I should be draped over a chaise longue, holding a fat cigar." Spying that exact item of furniture, Jay threw himself backwards onto it and said, "Do we *have* any cigars?"

Hugo smiled slightly, Jay's entrance breaking some of the tension he was feeling. "Probably. Somewhere. But I'm not about to get married smelling of cigar smoke."

Jay sat up on the chaise longue with a grin. "Why does getting married after a one-week relationship seem like the most Hugo move ever?"

Roscoe laughed. Hugo narrowly resisted the urge to clip Jay around the head.

"Because it's bold. Confident. Something you two women aren't man enough to do."

Jay laughed. "Sure. That's it."

"Don't you think you'll marry Sophia? You should just ask her. Why wait?"

"Because I've spent the last six months trying to prove I'm not an immature idiot. Besides, Sophia doesn't like surprises. I'll ask...when it's right."

"Speak of the devil," murmured Roscoe as Jay's phone beeped with a message.

"Angel," Jay corrected him, albeit somewhat absently, his attention focused on the screen. He smiled a secret sort of smile as he read the message, a glow in his eyes as he slipped the phone back in his pocket. Hugo felt as though he understood. He would probably look just as soppy if Amy texted him.

Not that she had.

"You two are disgusting," said Roscoe with a roll of his eyes.

Hugo laughed. "Your turn next, Ross."

"Unlikely."

"No? What about this Phoebe? Poppy? Penny?"

"No. Nope. Not going there." He made a decisive 'X' in the air with his hands. "Change of topic, please."

Hugo and Jay exchanged a look which clearly communicated the imminent need to get Roscoe drunk enough to spill the beans. Roscoe changed the topic himself, looking at his watch. "Is Amelia meeting us here?"

"At the chapel."

He nodded. "Well then. I think it's time for you to go and get married, brother."

———◆———

The Conyers chapel was admittedly not a part of the house Hugo often visited.

It was designed to look like a small church, but bright on the inside with pale pink and yellow plaster on the walls and pews made of white oak.

The housekeeper had hastily decorated it with flowers from the gardens. He could smell their perfume in the otherwise stuffy air. The sight and the scent of them reminded him of Amelia, and he wondered if he would always associate the first flowers of spring with her, the first fresh warmth of the year's sun...

He stood near the pulpit, the minister standing stiffly behind it, somehow managing to radiate mild disapproval as he toyed with the corner of a Bible, eyes fixed beyond Hugo on the chapel door.

Hugo kept looking that way too. They all did: Roscoe, who was standing nearby, and Jay, who sat on one of the pews, ankle on his knee, elbows on the pew's back. He looked back over his shoulder for the dozenth time then met Hugo's eye with the lift of a brow.

"She definitely knew it was here, right?"

"Of course she did," snapped Hugo.

Roscoe glanced at him, then at his watch. "She's only twenty minutes late…"

"She's probably got held up at Redbridge. The roof's leaking. Or there's a disaster with the chickens. God knows!" He glanced at the minister and mumbled sorry for the blasphemy. "But there's always something going on that they can't possibly do without her."

Jay nodded reassuringly. And unconvincingly.

Hugo stared at the door again.

"Have you called her today?" asked Roscoe. "Didn't she have a headache last night? Maybe she's poorly."

"No… Not yet…"

He was too embarrassed to admit that he had wanted the first words he spoke to her today to be here, at the ceremony. That he wanted the first glimpse he got of her to be as she appeared through that door, walking towards him to become his wife…

He pulled his phone out and mumbled, "I'll try her now."

The phone rang. And rang.

"No answer."

Roscoe and Jay exchanged a look. "Um…" said Roscoe. "Maybe try the house? Sarah or Janson? Maybe she really is poorly and still asleep?"

So Hugo tried calling again, a flush crawling up his neck as he held the ringing phone to his ear, all too aware of Roscoe, Jay, and the minister watching him. Watching and wondering…

She had to come. Surely she was OK. Surely she wasn't going to stand him up at his own wedding…

She wouldn't. Why would she? Everything was fine. Everything was fine—

Except he remembered how pale she had looked last night. The way she hadn't quite met his eyes... But then Roscoe had come, and she had left, and the night had gone the way it had...

But Amy had to be OK. And things were OK between them, surely they were. Why wouldn't they be? What could possibly have gone wrong...?

"Hugo?" prompted Roscoe.

He dropped the phone from his ear. "No answer."

Roscoe and Jay exchanged another look. "I could walk over...?" suggested Roscoe.

But Hugo was already heading for the door.

He was running by the time he left the house, the smooth soles of his dress shoes slipping on the wet grass. He was dimly aware that Roscoe and Jay were following him, but all his attention was focused forward—on Redbridge, on Amy, on whatever the hell was happening there.

Then he came to a sudden stop, skidding almost to his knees, chest heaving from the run while he gazed in horror at the sight before him.

The wall, the gate... The section of old brick wall with the gate was smashed. The wind last night had brought down one of the huge cedar branches and it had smashed right through the crumbling brick arch and the ancient gate.

Hugo walked over, staring mutely at the cracked red bricks tumbled across the grass, the broken pieces of gate half-hidden under the massive branch and its battered green fronds. He looked to the house beyond, fearing some terrible disaster, but it seemed undamaged. Shaking his head, he scrambled over the ruined wall, heedless of the dust and dirt that marred his suit, and sprinted through the gardens to Redbridge.

The back door was locked, the side door too. He knocked and knocked, but no one came. He ran to the front of the house, rang the bell, beat the door with his fist.

No answer.

He turned wildly, thinking to try the yard next, the stables... Roscoe and Jay were there, faces tight with concern.

"Where...? What...?" Hugo could hardly talk, he was out of breath, panic clogging his thoughts. She had to be here somewhere. What the hell was going on?

They all turned at the sound of footsteps. Janson appeared around the corner, car keys in his hands. He stopped at the sight of them, his expression grave.

"She's gone," he said.

Hugo felt a shot of horror. "What?"

"She left this morning," said Janson.

"But... Why? Where? I don't...I don't understand what's going on."

Janson reached inside his coat and pulled out an envelope. He handed it to Hugo reluctantly. "She instructed me to give you this."

Hugo tore the envelope open with shaking hands. He could barely read what it said, his thoughts were too chaotic, panic and horror buzzing too loudly in his mind.

Hugo

I must be a coward, because I can't face the thought of seeing you to say this in person. Maybe one day I will be angry enough to feel strong, but for now I am only destroyed. And weak, and stupid, as you've known all along I must be. Because I did believe your lies.

You won, I suppose. If that's what the game was: my heart. I gave it to you, and you broke it. I don't even care what you do with the pieces—pin them to your wall as a trophy if you want. I don't want them back. I don't want anything you've ever touched.

I don't know why you did it. Was money really enough of a

reason? But I will go mad if I try to work out why. The inexcusable doesn't need a reason anyway.

If you have any trace of decency, you will let me go the rest of my life without seeing you again. I hate to ask anything of you, but I have to ask you that. Never try to speak to me again.

Amelia

Hugo was trembling. He couldn't see, and then he realised that he was crying. He was saying something too—something like, *No, no, no, oh god oh god oh god—*

What—?

Why—?

He couldn't bear it. His breath stuck in his throat, his chest heaving as he turned blindly, head in his hands, leaning on the rough stone of Redbridge's wall for support.

Someone took the letter from him. Roscoe. Jay. They both must have read it. He heard them speaking, mumbled words that partly echoed the ones storming through his mind.

"Oh shit—"

"What the fuck...?"

"Why does she think...?"

"Hugh? Hugo?" A hand on his shoulder. Roscoe shaking him. "Hugh! Listen. We'll sort this out, OK? But you have to tell us what this is about."

"I don't know!"

"But what does she think you're lying about?"

Hugo scrubbed a hand across his eyes. Jay was frowning down at the letter. That damned, fucking letter—

"That I love her. That's what she thinks I'm lying about."

"But you *do* love her."

"I know!"

"So why would she...? Oh."

Roscoe broke off as Jay communicated something to him with a meaningful look.

"What?" asked Hugo. "What is it?"

"Just...um... We found out last night that you hadn't told Amelia the reason for you being at Conyers."

"The reason? Because *she's* here. Why else?"

"I mean the original reason. Father ordering you to stay here for a year. She didn't seem to know about that."

Hugo paused, ice sweeping down his spine. "But that's... I mean... That's why I *came*, but it's not why I *stayed*."

The others said nothing.

"I didn't lie to her!" Hugo protested. "I just... It didn't seem...relevant."

Roscoe bit his lip. Jay pretended to study the letter again. Hugo fought the urge to howl.

"But what...what did she say? Was she upset? Upset enough for *that*?" He pointed at the letter.

"No. I don't think so. She just went a bit quiet, then said she needed to go upstairs to change."

Hugo tried to think back to last night, retracing her steps like a forensic scientist. What had happened in between her leaving the others and her bumping into him on her way out of the house? Had she met one of his friends, had one of them said something to her?

She went upstairs...

She went to get changed...

Presumably she would have gone into his room...

...where the lawyer's paperwork was.

Hugo ran all the way back to Conyers.

And that's when he saw it: the letter she must have seen, with the date of the lawyer's visit long before the date he had told her.

He stared at it breathlessly as the others joined him.

"I lied to her," he said as though only just realising it himself. "I lied to her. And she found out."

Roscoe looked at him sadly, but he didn't need to say it, Hugo heard it loud and clear.

I told you to tell her the truth.

And just as loud, he heard his father's voice from last night.

Actions have consequences.

He sank down limply onto the bed.

"Evie," he said. "I bet she's gone to Evie in Spain. But which airport?"

"Janson told us," said Roscoe, "when you ran off. He'd just come back from dropping her off. He said to tell you... Well, um, his exact words were, 'I still think he's awful, but I believe that he loves her and that she loves him. And so, for everything he's done for her recently, I'll tell you where she's gone.' It's Manchester airport. But her flight leaves in an hour. We'll never make it."

"Yes we will," said Jay. "Because I'll drive."

THIRTY-FOUR

A MELIA CHECKED IN AT the airport, then abruptly ran out of energy, the awful weight in her chest too much for her to bear. She sat down weakly in a corner half-hidden by a large metal strut and looked numbly at the passing crowd.

She hadn't slept last night. Had spent most of it choking on her own sobbing breaths. All she had known was that she had to get away, because that's what you do when things hurt—recoil from the pain, get as far away from it as you can. So she had packed this morning before the sun even rose and booked a seat on the first plane to Spain that she could find with space. There hadn't been many at such short notice, and it was the Easter holidays, the airport full of families with children clutching colourful backpacks.

Parents and mums and dads and husbands and wives...

She swallowed the tearing ache in her throat. She felt too raw to be here, in this vast glassy space, the light bright, the noise discordant chaos. The only wish she really had was to curl up and hide, somewhere dark and alone, where no one could see the ridiculous, stupid mistake she had made.

"Yes, the lawyers came to visit me," her mother had confirmed when Amelia had called her, shaking and sick in the car that drove her back from the party. The lawyers had come, just like the letter said—and on the day the letter said. There was no doubt that Hugo had lied.

"Why didn't you tell me?" Amelia had asked.

Her mother had drawn a breath, her voice soft with apology—and something else. Pity. "Because I know how you feel about Redbridge, and I thought that you might be tempted to go through with it just to get the money we needed. I didn't want to put you in that position. And I didn't want you to consider marrying that boy, not even for a moment."

And when Amelia had said nothing, her mother's voice had grown softer still.

"I've spent years watching you watching him. And I still don't know quite what happened at Cassie's party, but I saw your face afterwards. Cassie was the one who lost her fiancé, and yet somehow *you* were the one who looked like they'd had their heart broken. He has a power over you that I don't trust."

Which was when Amelia had given in to tears before confessing all to her mother.

"Yes, go to Evie in Spain," her mother had agreed. "I don't think any good can come from seeing him. Don't worry about the estate. Sarah and Janson can manage for a day or two until I can get home. I'll make Cassie come back too if I need the help. But Redbridge will be fine. Don't worry."

So Amelia was finally given permission to leave. And it had only taken being destroyed to achieve it.

There was an announcement over the airport tannoy. Last call to board her flight. She stood up, then froze as she heard a familiar voice nearby. Roscoe.

"I forgot you drove like a maniac, Jay."

Amelia glanced around the corner and saw the two of them. Roscoe looked pale, and they were both breathing heavily as though they had been running.

"I don't know what you mean. I happen to be a very careful driver. These days, anyway."

Roscoe shook his head. "Now I remember why I don't normally hang around with you two. I don't have the constitution for it."

Jay just grinned and slapped him on the shoulder, then stepped forward to join—

Hugo.

He was scanning the departure boards. She could only see his back, his side. His hair was mussed and disordered, his body tensed as he strained his neck to scan the departing flights. She felt an agonising pang at the sight of him, more familiar to her than her own reflection.

There was a little bit of mud on the trousers of his suit—

The suit he had put on for their wedding.

Her heart gave a painful kick, and she drew in a sharp breath just as Hugo turned towards Jay. But he looked straight past his friend and found her instead.

She couldn't stand the look of bright relief that crossed over his face. She retreated a step, bumping up against her suitcase. She picked it up, the handle heavy and hard in her palm. Gripped it until it hurt.

"Amy!"

"No."

She stepped away as he strode towards her. He put out a hand to touch her arm, but she shrank back from it. Pain replaced the relief in his eyes. Pain—and a pleading sort of sorrow.

"Amy," he said again. "Please, please listen to me."

"No. I told you not to come. I asked one thing of you—to stay away—and you couldn't even do that."

She spoke quickly, feeling as though she would soon lose the ability to do so. She tried to step around him, but he moved in front of her, his head bent earnestly, trying to look in her eyes.

"Please listen. It wasn't a lie—I mean, it was, about the lawyers—shit—sorry—but what I mean is that the rest wasn't.

It was real. How I feel is real."

"You tricked me and lied. And then tricked me and lied again when I begged you for honesty, and I—" Her voice broke. "I think I'm going mad, Hugo. I don't think anything is real. You're not real. I don't trust you, I don't trust myself..."

Tears came. She scrubbed them angrily away, trying once more to get past him.

"I'm so sorry, please—"

He touched her arm and she jerked away, aware that everyone was staring—Roscoe, Jay, and countless strangers. But she barely had room to care about the humiliation of such a public scene. Everything was disordered and jumbled and far too hot, and she had to get away, away, away—

"Amy, I'm so sorry I hurt you."

He dogged her steps, walking backwards, trying to keep looking at her as she turned toward what she hoped was the departure area.

"Uh-oh," she heard Jay say. "Airport security are looking our way."

Amelia stopped. She spotted the men in uniform.

"You have to go," she told Hugo. "I told you not to come. There's no point."

"I stayed at Conyers for you. It's always been about you. I don't care about the money—I don't want the money. I want you."

"The very day you first came to see me was the day the lawyers came to speak to you! Look at me, Hugo, and tell me honestly that it had nothing to do with your apology?"

He stared at her, eyes burning, jaw clenched.

"You can't, can you?" she said.

"No." He closed his eyes briefly, looking so wretched that even now, a stupid part of her ached to comfort him. "I did think about the money. I did plan to get your forgiveness so that I might one day access that fund. And... You're right to hate me for that. But then it did become real. I fell in love with you. I *do* love you."

The words stung, thudding into her chest like bullets.

"You can't love someone you don't respect. And you can't respect me if you lie to me. I deserve better than that. For once in my life, I'm going to stick up for what I want. Just like you told me to. And what I want is someone better than you."

He inhaled in pain. She turned to go.

"Amy, no... Don't do this. Please. Don't end it like this."

She carried on walking. Behind her, she heard him swear, turn to his friends.

"Shit, shit. I need a ticket on that plane—"

"Hugo, it's already boarding."

"Then I'll charter my own fucking plane. Call Biffy. He has a jet, doesn't he?"

"I think it's his uncle's..."

"I'm not giving up! Call him! Hang on... Amy!"

He ran, was once more in front of her, tears in his eyes. "Please, please, please, I'm begging you. Give me another chance, I'll do anything, say anything—"

"That's the problem. You always do just say anything. You'll do anything to get what you want. For once in your life, forget about what *you* want, and give someone else what they want. And what I want is for you to go away and leave me alone."

"I came in the morning, before the lawyers—I came to see you in the morning, but Janson turned me away—"

"The damage is done. It's done. There's nothing you can say or do. I can't trust you, even if I wanted to. I can't like you, I can't... I can't love you."

He slumped in defeat, head in his hands. He was crying, and God, she hadn't thought her heart could break any more, but it tore even deeper as she left him there and walked away.

It took hours to get from the airport in Madrid to the village near Seville where Evie was staying. Amelia had told her nothing other than that she needed to get away, but from the careful way Evie avoided all mention of Hugo, she suspected that Roscoe, or perhaps Hugo himself, had already given her the story.

Amy couldn't really remember arriving at the bright little apartment, or what she ate or did, but Evie soon packed her off to bed, and when Amy woke the next morning it felt as though she was seeing the place for the first time.

Long white curtains moved hazily across an open window, the weathered black paint of a small Juliet balcony visible through the gaps. The bed was small and slightly hard, but the cushions were plump and fresh. Amelia lay on her back, listening to the unfamiliar sounds of foreign voices in the street below, the occasional passing car, the clunking of a pipe in the wall behind her head. The bathroom, she supposed. Evie getting up.

A floorboard creaked, and Evie knocked gently on the door, poking her head around it without waiting for Amy's reply. In that sense, she was very much a Blackton. And her hair, cut pixie short, was as dark as Hugo's, her blue eyes almost as arresting—though closer to Roscoe's shade than Hugo's deep navy.

Amelia swallowed and looked away as she sat up in bed. She would just have to get used to the fact that absolutely everything would remind her of him.

"Sleep OK?" Evie asked.

"Yes. Surprisingly. Think I more or less passed out, to be honest."

"You did look exhausted."

"It's been a busy week."

"Mm," said Evie with a small nod, seeming to deliberate whether to allow this conversation to proceed along its determinedly Hugo-free path. Clearly, she was feeling kind, or perhaps Amelia looked too pathetic, because she just said brightly, "Breakfast? There's a nice cafe down the street."

And the day followed that pattern, with Amelia pretending everything was OK, and Evie making cheerful conversation, showing her around the town.

"Are you still up for walking this pilgrimage route? The Camino de Santiago? It's probably best to fly north a bit. The route from here is really long."

"I don't mind that," said Amelia. She was sitting on a low, stone wall, looking out over the dusty countryside, the shadows of mountains in the hazy distance. The air was as warm as dragon's breath and idly stirred the dusty, dried leaves of an olive tree around the worn stone at her feet. "I don't want to get on another plane. I just want to...walk."

"It's getting close to summer. It'll be hot."

"We can walk in the mornings. Only go a little bit each day, find a new village or town every night... Even stop for a few days to rest if we find a place we like the look of. You're in no rush to go home, are you?"

What she really meant by that was: I don't want to go back to Redbridge.

Evie, of course, realised this. She shrugged slightly. "No. I'm in no rush."

"What about the others though? The friends you wanted to go with. What are they doing?"

"Oh." Evie frowned and looked away with another small shrug. "I don't think those people were quite as cool as I hoped they were going to be. Well, OK... There was a guy, and now he's with a girl, and that girl's not me, so...*pfft*. Fuck 'em. Let's walk

298

this route ourselves. Who even needs men, anyway?"

Amelia managed a crooked sort of smile. "Exactly."

After a couple of days of planning and buying supplies, they set off, just the two of them, to walk across most of Spain.

Amelia didn't really think about it in those terms. Evie studied the maps, and Amelia just concentrated on putting one foot in front of the other. That's how she would get through this. One step at a time. One breath after another. Until the pain in her chest eased.

Because it had to, one day, surely?

A week went by. A week of sunshine and easy conversation and new sights and sounds. A week under an endless sky, the plains of Spain eternal and humbling. A week of heat and sweat and blisters upon blisters. But neither of them complained.

The second week went by, and they passed through low mountains, the Sierra Morena, bird song and the scent of pine now accompanying their slow march.

A third week, and it began to feel to Amelia as though perhaps she could get away with never talking about it at all. And then it would be like it had never happened. And if she noticed Evie frowning sometimes at her phone, or walking away to make a call, she pretended not to. And if Amelia did sometimes feel as though she was made only of paper, a thin sort of nothing person wrapped precariously around a deep black chasm, then no one else needed to know that. And if she did sometimes wake up in the night with a desperate sob lodged in her throat, then did that really matter? So long as she could stay in this bubble pretending everything was fine and normal?

Until one day they set their packs down on a ridge of stone that looked over a valley. They stretched their backs, they drank some water, they sat down together to have lunch, and Evie said, "I'm upset with you, you know."

"What?" asked Amelia, cold fingers trailing warningly down her spine.

"You didn't tell me anything. I had to hear it all from Hugo. And he might be my brother, but you're supposed to be my best friend. I always thought we were closer even than sisters would be. So you should have told me. Years ago. When you first fell in love with him."

Amelia swallowed. She scraped a finger over the rough rock on which she sat, looking at that, at every tiny grain in the stone, while she fought the sudden swell of emotion that was threatening to tear through her paper-self.

"He called you?" she said, her voice sounding weirdly distant.

"On the day you arrived, when you were on the plane. He said he had hurt you badly, and asked me to look after you—as if I wouldn't anyway. Then what he said became largely incoherent. I don't want to embarrass the boy, but it wasn't pretty. And he's called me a few times since, to check how you are." Evie picked at the dry tufty grass that grew at the edge of the rock she sat on, snapping the tawny-coloured stems. "He's a wreck, Ames. And you look... You look like you've been staring into the eye of hell and it's been inviting you in. And I still don't quite know what's really been going on between you two."

"I'm OK," she lied.

"Really? You're still not going to talk to me about it?"

"If I talk..." Her voice was already beginning to crack. "If I talk about it, I'll break."

"So do it. It'll do you good. And then we can put you back together again. Like Humpty Dumpty."

Amelia let out a gasp of laughter, and then she was crying. Eventually—largely incoherently—she confessed the whole to Evie—and it wasn't pretty.

"Fuck," was Evie's conclusion. "And fuck you for not telling me any of this sooner—for not telling me about Cassie's party. Why didn't you tell me what he did to you?"

"Because...I was embarrassed. And I...I didn't want you to hate him."

"Seriously? You were protecting him after he did that?"

"I told you it was embarrassing."

Evie shook her head, looking out over the valley. "He really is the worst."

Amelia said nothing, trying to force herself to agree. Her rational mind knew it, but even now, after everything, her heart shrank back from acknowledging it.

This would all be so much easier if she could hate him.

They were silent for a while. Some kind of bird wheeled high above them, hanging on the thermal currents, a black speck against the unrelenting blue sky. The grass was loud with insects, and the warm breeze stirred the trees at their back, making the branches sigh.

Amelia's thoughts turned homewards. She had heard about the fallen branch that had brought the gate down. Every few days, she phoned her parents, or they phoned her. They were both at Redbridge now, her mother and her father. And they always told her the same thing: that everything was fine, everything was under control, she didn't need to worry.

Enjoy yourself. Forget about this place for a while.

As if it was that easy.

As if she didn't spend every moment wondering what *he* was doing.

He haunted her. She kept seeing his face just before she walked away at the airport—the way that irrepressible good-humoured light in his eyes—that irresistible essence of him—had shuddered and died at her words.

I'm sorry, I'm sorry, she wanted to tell him.

I hate you, I hate you—

But the words fell flat, without conviction.

I hurt.

That was the only thing she knew. *I hurt. This hurts. It all hurts so much.*

Beside her, Evie let out a long breath.

"He's the worst," she repeated. "But for what it's worth, I think he does love you."

Amelia went very still.

"I don't know if that hurts you or comforts you," Evie continued, "but it's the truth. And you seem pretty keen on being told the truth."

"I..." began Amelia helplessly, the sound more a gasp than a word. "I..."

"I'm not saying it because I think you should forgive him. You know I believe in hos before bros—especially in this particular bro's case—but if it's truth you want, then I believe he really does love you."

"But...but I can't...I can't spend my whole life with someone wondering if they really mean a word they tell me. It would drive me mad."

Evie nodded at that. "I know. I understand. But I need to say something—and this is more about us than him. I don't want to lose your friendship, but I feel like if I don't say this, it's going to eat away at me and ruin it anyway." She took a breath, looked fixedly out over the valley and said, "You're a hypocrite, Amelia."

Amelia flinched. "What?"

"You're angry with Hugo for lying—and I get that. You're right to be angry. But you lied to me about him. You've been lying for years—possibly lying to yourself, too. But I trusted you, and it hurts that you've been keeping things from me. And then on the phone a few weeks ago, I straight out asked you if there was anything going on. And you said no."

Heat crawled up Amelia's neck. "I... It's not like that. I meant that we weren't *together* together, because we weren't. Not at the time."

"Well. It feels like a lie to me. It feels like you didn't trust me. It *feels* like...like I've been an idiot—thinking we were closer than we really are."

"Eve... I'm sorry. We are close, I do trust you. You're my best friend."

"But you kept things from me because...? Because you didn't think I would understand?"

"He's your *brother*."

"And? I'm probably one of the few people in the world capable of understanding why you like him. I know I joke around and pretend to hate him, but of course I don't. He's thoughtless and selfish and immature, but he's... He's a good person, under it all. Or I thought he was. Until all this."

"I think he might still be," Amelia admitted quietly. "Parts of him, at least. But I can't... How am I meant to forgive him?"

"The same way I forgive you?"

Evie looked at her for a moment, as though checking the truth of her own words. "I forgive you for lying to me because...because I can understand why you did it. And because I know that you're only human and we all do things we shouldn't. And because some things are worth fighting for—fighting *yourself* for. I know the boys always called you by that stupid nickname, Little Miss Good, just because you didn't always go along with their idiotic schemes. But I do think you have a way of drawing quite hard lines between what's good and bad. You draw lines around yourself. You put yourself in a box: Amelia, the saviour of Redbridge, who can never say no. And maybe that's what you've needed to do to cope with your family taking advantage of your good nature—don't try to defend them; we all know it's

303

true that they never put your wishes first. But the thing about drawing those lines in the sand is that they can keep people out. You didn't tell me about Hugo because you didn't want me to think less of you. Little Miss Good would never be stupid enough to fall for an idiot like my brother, right? But maybe consider that Hugo lied about the lawyers because he didn't want you to think less of him. Maybe he lied out of fear, because he couldn't bear the thought of you retreating back behind those lines."

Amelia tried to process Evie's speech, her thoughts dipping and turning like the bird in the sky above them as new ideas, new perspectives, came into view.

"Anyway," said Evie with a shrug. "Just something to think about while we walk the next 700 miles."

THIRTY-FIVE

H UGO HAD NEVER STAYED in one place long enough
before to watch the seasons change. But it was now July,
and he had spent the days since Amelia left walking the grounds
of Conyers and Redbridge—working, exploring, needing to
stay busy so that he didn't go mad—and he'd had ample opportunity to watch the daffodils give way to tulips, the tulips give
way to roses, to see tall umbellifers grow white and frothy along
every bank and hedgerow, and the leaves on the trees suddenly
expand and clothe the world in their dappled green.

He would have appreciated some shady trees at this particular
moment. But the shade of the cedars was all on the Redbridge
side of the wall. Here, where he knelt on the grass in the midday
sun, the brick wall cast nothing but a thin line of shadow at its
base. The sun beat down on his already tanned neck and the
smell of the paint he was using was heady in the still air.

He knelt, brush in hand, and ignored the discomfort as he
inspected his handiwork, wanting to make it perfect.

"You found the same blue."

He dropped his brush and kicked over the tin of paint as he
got hastily to his feet, dizzy from standing too quickly. Dizzy
because, unbelievably, impossibly, Amelia was there.

She stood on the Redbridge side in shorts and a vest top,
looking incredibly tanned and lean and strong. And effortless,

and fresh. And like heaven.

"Amelia."

She smiled slightly, not quite meeting his eyes, as though she couldn't. Not yet. She looked at the spilt paint instead, the splashes on the base of the brickwork. He had the strange thought, his mind still spinning, that maybe future generations would look at those streaks of blue and wonder how they came to be there. Maybe he would be the one to tell them.

"It's…" He cleared his throat. "It's good to see you."

Seriously? That's what he said? Good lord, he was an idiot. But his heart was hammering, his pulse was racing, his mind still reeling—

"You too," she said, and finally met his eye.

It stole his breath, that look. Those familiar dark eyes searching his soul with a glance.

Yes, he wanted to say. *Yes.* Whatever you need to ask of me: *Yes.*

Yes, I love you—

Yes, I'm sorry—

Yes, I've learned my lesson—

Yes, you can trust me—

Yes, I want you—

Yes, I'm yours—

"I heard you've been helping out at Redbridge while I was away."

"Yes."

He cleared his throat again, stooped down, and picked up the paintbrush, soil and grass clinging to its wet bristles. He righted the pot and dumped the brush in it. There was paint on his shoes. On his fingers. He barely even recalled what he was wearing but he was sure it was old and terrible. He scrubbed a hand over the back of his sweaty neck and probably got paint there too.

"Thank you," she said, "for doing that."

"It's the least I could do."

"The gate looks good."

She stepped a little closer, and his heart damn near stopped beating. But when she reached out, it was to trail her fingers over the fresh new bricks and mortar of the archway. A bright scar in the weathered old wall.

"I had a carpenter recreate the old gate. From photographs and things."

"It looks good," she said again.

"Amelia—"

She tensed, as though the inevitable words he was about to speak were a blow.

"I'm so sorry," he said. "I'm so, so sorry."

She looked down, and then up. When her eyes met his, she let out a shaky breath. "I know."

"I'm not asking for anything. You told me to leave you alone. And I will." Even if it killed him—and God it was killing him. "But I want you to know how sorry I am that I lied to you."

She nodded, then looked away as though steeling herself.

Hugo tensed, afraid of what her next words would be. Perhaps that she understood, but it didn't change things. Perhaps that she was leaving Redbridge forever. Perhaps... Perhaps that she had met someone—and how he had tortured himself all the months she had been away, imagining legions of handsome, charming Spanish men...

"I lied too," she said. "I said I can't love you. But the truth is, I can't *stop* loving you."

Hugo's chest expanded as he inhaled sharply. He took a step forward, met her under the arch of the gate. "Amelia?" he breathed, her name a question.

Once more, she nodded, and the motion brushed his chest. Because she was in his arms, face buried against him. He held her

307

tightly, too tight probably, his body trembling, feeling as though holding her was the only thing keeping him upright.

"I love you," she said, her voice muffled, the warmth of her breath against his shirt. "I love you. But...it might take some time to...to..."

"To trust me again. I know."

He pressed his face to her hair. The dark strands had been bleached lighter by the Spanish sun, and she smelt different, her shampoo new. But she was so agonisingly familiar, he didn't know how he had coped without her.

"I love you."

It was the truest thing he had ever said.

Hugo said, "I love you," and it sounded like a promise. She let herself sink deeper into his arms, savouring the feel of him after so long apart.

He was warm and strong. She heard his heart beating, breathed in the scent of his shirt and heated skin. It seemed so strange that she could touch him, that he was still here, still real, still waiting, still loving, still hers...

Desire stirred within her, hot, heavy and low, the feel of him pressed against her swamping her senses. But it was far too soon for that. She hadn't even been sure what she was going to say to him until she saw him kneeling on the grass, focused so intently on painting the wooden gate. Then the answer had been obvious. She loved him. She always would.

Now though, she forced herself to step back. "Show me the estate," she said, clinging to the idea like a life raft. "Show me what you've been doing. I heard you've been busy."

About halfway along the Camino de Santiago, a week or so after that difficult conversation with Evie, she had allowed

308

herself to think of possibilities that had previously been too painful. She had allowed herself to mention his name—during a phone call with her mother.

"And is...? Have you seen...? Is Hugo still at Conyers?"

That seemed to be the signal her family and friends had been waiting for, because after that, they began to mention his name to her.

She learnt that, yes, he was still at Conyers. She learnt that he was taking an active interest in the estate. She learnt that he was often at Redbridge, that he had rescued a peacock from the stable roof, that he had lent Lee a vehicle when the Redbridge Land Rover wouldn't start, that he had helped move the flock of sheep to a new field, that he had called out a plumber when the fountain broke again on a hot day and wouldn't hear of being reimbursed, that he had studied the roof survey report in great detail, then consulted Roscoe and helped draw up a financial plan—

In short, he featured in every phone call she made home. And though she listened mainly in silence, her heart swelled. *"Diligent,"* her father called him once. *"Hard-working. And so much energy. So many good ideas. And he's not afraid to get his hands dirty. He's out there working from dawn 'til dusk. Honestly, I'm not sure what we would do without him. And I never thought that's something I would be saying about Hugo Blackton."*

"Start with Conyers?" Hugo suggested now, and she followed him through the gate and out onto the wide bright green lawn.

"Not much has changed here," he told her as they crossed the lawn at an angle, not heading to the house, but to a path that ran through borders of bright red azaleas. "It's more of a care-taking role. Less interesting, really, than Redbridge, which is more of a working estate."

Amelia smiled at his lecturing tone. He caught her look and laughed. "Sorry. I'm boring now."

She shook her head. "No. Never to me."

He actually blushed slightly and didn't seem to know quite where to look. But she was intensely aware of him at her side as they walked among the flowers, the warm air thick with the pleasant drone of bees. His hand brushed hers as the path narrowed, and the humming sound, the heated air, it all seemed to be inside her, honey fire under her skin.

They emerged from the path onto another lawn, a smaller one, that led down to the swing on the walnut tree. She took a deep breath, trying to clear the intensity of his presence from her mind, then caught sight of a boy, about ten years old, playing football on the grass.

"That's Alfie," explained Hugo. "He's Emily's—the cook's son. He has bad asthma, and they were living in a flat in town right on the main road, which was making it worse, so I gave them a cottage on the grounds. It makes her commute much shorter too, which I think she appreciates. What?" he asked at the way she was looking at him.

She shook her head slightly, smiling as she bit her lip. "Nothing. It's just...very nice."

"I am nice."

He met her eyes, and there was something of the old Hugo in his grin as he added, "Sometimes."

And sometimes I'm naughty, his eyes and his smile said, and her body, which hadn't forgotten a single touch, lit up like paper to a flame.

He knew it. She was sure he knew it. But he just took her hand and led her after him. "Come on. We've got a lot of ground to cover."

And they did cover it, until her feet ached and she was thirsty from the heat—and from talking. They talked and talked, just like old friends. Which is exactly what they were. Friends, and much more than that. And she realised that she had missed his company as much as anything else.

They returned to Redbridge through the gate, having had a very late lunch on the terrace of Conyers. The shadows were starting to soften and stretch themselves out over the grass, and the last of Redbridge's visitors were packing up their picnics and heading towards the car park.

"Shall we?" said Hugo, nodding to an ice cream van in the car park. "Before it goes?"

Amelia smiled. "Why not. It *is* a very hot day."

Hugo bought them both soft whippy ice creams, coiled high on their cones, each with a flake. And sprinkles. And sauce. Because he was Hugo, and had to make everything decadent and sinful.

"Thank you," she said, laughing slightly as he handed her the absurd concoction.

"You're very welcome."

They turned back to the garden just as an excited young dog dashed their way. It leapt up at Amelia and knocked the cone from her hand. She stared mournfully at the mess on the ground as the dog enthusiastically started to lick it up and its embarrassed owner struggled to get it back on the lead.

"It's quite alright," Amelia told the poor woman, gratefully leaving the chaos behind her and joining a laughing Hugo in the garden.

"Don't cry, Splat," he said, "but the ice cream van's just left."

Amelia gave an exaggerated pout. "I have no luck with ice cream."

"Here." Hugo passed her his. "Have mine."

She took it with a smile. "How about we share it?"

"If you don't mind my boy germs, Amy?"

"I don't mind your boy germs, Hugh." She gave the ice cream a slow lick, eyes fixed mischievously on his. He followed the motion, eyes wide and growing dark.

"Oh Jesus," he muttered. Then he grabbed her hand and towed her after him through the garden.

———◦———

The evening grew gold and pink with the setting sun as they wandered the familiar grounds. Amelia's hand was in his. She was here, and she still loved him, and he didn't really feel like he deserved any of it. But he was damned well going to try to.

"I hope you don't mind," said Hugo as they walked towards the ancient old house. He was reluctant to go inside because he suspected then she would say goodnight and the evening would end. And there were still so many things he needed to tell her. "But I ordered a new flag for you. The old one got battered in the storms, and it looked a little drab and pathetic up there." He nodded to the flag pole high above them. "The new one arrived this morning. Shall we put it up now the visitors are gone?"

They climbed the stone staircase, Hugo holding the heavy flag folded over one arm. They didn't speak until Hugo opened the wooden trapdoor to the roof, flashing Amelia a smile when it opened easily. "Had it fixed. Not even a squeak."

He climbed out, then turned back and held out his hand to help her up.

"You know, I'm not that keen on heights," she said, standing back from the roof edge, her arms folded.

"You're safe. Trust me. The trick is to just look at the view."

She did as he said, turning a slow circle, arms still crossed warily. The whole of Redbridge was visible from up here, and Conyers too, in the distance.

"I really am grateful," she said quietly. "You've taken such good care of Redbridge. It's never looked so good."

"It's the money more than anything I've done."

She looked at him almost shyly. "I heard about the Redbridge

Restoration Fund. You've been applying for charitable grants. And Roscoe's been managing my family's finances. Making everything much more efficient."

"That man loves numbers," Hugo said lightly. He didn't want Amelia's thanks. That wasn't why he had done any of this. He had done it because...because it was the right thing to do.

"I heard too," Amelia began awkwardly, "about the legal document you had drawn up before our— Before I left. Roscoe told me. You were going to sign over all of the marriage fund to me. To Redbridge."

He shrugged, uncomfortable. "It wasn't about the money. Not by then."

Amelia looked away, out over the fields. Hugo began to winch down the old flag. It would take time, she had said. And he wanted to give her that, not press her before she was ready.

He started to unhook the old flag. Amelia came over and silently helped him, their hands brushing as they worked the old fabric free and attached the new.

Just those brief touches sent sparks through him, clouding his mind with need. When she had licked that ice cream... Christ. He'd almost gone feral with lust. But it would take time...

They hoisted the new flag together, watching it unfurl and catch the breeze.

"It was never about the money, was it?" she asked quietly.

"No. It was always about you."

She stayed looking up at the flag, arms tightly crossed.

"Sit down," he suggested. "Sit with me here, with your back against the wall. You won't mind the height so much, and I...I need to speak to you."

So they sat down together, side by side. The low wall still held the sun's warmth, and they could see nothing now except sky. It was just the two of them, alone, Redbridge and Conyers out of sight.

"You know how Roscoe is annoyingly right about most things?" Hugo began with a slight smile. Amelia laughed a little. "Well, he said I was using the lawyer's visit as an excuse. And I really do think he was right about that. I've been thinking about it all a lot over the last few months. And I think I was scared of seeing you. Of seeing you hate me. I think...I think I spent all those months after Cassie's party trying to forget. I did really stupid things that year, acted like an even bigger dick than usual. I spent most of it drunk, or on drugs, or sleeping around—you know the thing with Cessy Pennington and Jess Orton. I'm not exactly proud of that. But I was a mess. And I think I was trying to be bad enough that what I'd done to you would seem less bad in comparison. Stupid, right?"

"Quite stupid, yes." But she said it smiling, and he laughed.

"Do you remember the labours of Hercules?" he asked.

"I remember you risking your neck like an idiot."

He smiled. "It was worth it."

She flushed as pink as the sunset. "I wish..." She stopped.

"What do you wish?"

"I wish our first kiss had been real."

Hugo's heart ached at that. But he thought carefully for a moment and said, "I think in some ways it was."

She shot him a sceptical look.

"No one forced me to take that stupid wager. It was just an excuse. Like the lawyer's visit. Something that gave me the courage to do what I wanted to do anyway."

"You had your phone!"

He took her hand. "I know. I know. I'm not excusing myself. But I never pressed record. When I broke away from you, it was to check that I *hadn't* pressed the button."

Amelia shook her head.

"I don't know why I'm bringing this up now," Hugo said, as much to himself as to her. "But I'm trying to be honest with you about everything. I'm an idiot. That's the truth. But I love you. And that's also the truth."

"Why did you lie about the lawyers?"

"Because I'm a coward. There—another truth. I'm a coward. I thought you wouldn't believe any of it was real if you knew I'd known about the money all along. And I was scared of losing you. I let my fear get in the way. I should have trusted *you*. I should have trusted what we had."

She shook her head again and he was scared that by bringing it all up he had taken them right back to that terrible moment. She would remember why she had left him and leave again.

But she said, "I'm to blame too. I didn't give you a chance to explain. I listened to fear as well, instead of trusting you."

"I hadn't given you much reason *to* trust me."

"I know. But I loved you. And I should have stayed long enough to listen. It just... It hurt so much, Hugh. The thought that it wasn't real..."

Her voice cracked. There were tears on her cheeks.

"Amy..." He put his arms around her and held her close. "I'm so sorry for what I put you through. I'm so sorry."

She sniffed, already getting her tears under control, wiping them away roughly, as though annoyed with herself.

"It is real," he told her firmly. "It is real. I love you. Look at me."

He cupped her cheek with his hand and turned her face to his. Her eyes were dark and wide and sore, and he sought to bring the brightness back to them.

"You can punish me again," he said with a tilted grin. "Make me pay. I'm still your slave."

She gave a soft laugh. "I don't want revenge, Hugh."

"What do you want? Tell me and it's yours."

"I want... I just want you."

His breath caught. "You have me. Always and forever."

He stroked his thumb over her cheek, smudging the dampness of her tears. But she wasn't crying anymore, and her dark eyes held a different sort of look.

"Tell me what you want, Amy," he said, his voice low.

"I want you to kiss me," she breathed. "Kiss me. And mean it."

"I always meant it." He cupped her face in both hands, eyes locked on hers, forcing her to see the truth in his. "I'll always mean it. Every day, for the rest of our lives. Trust me."

He lowered his mouth to hers, and paused, the merest brush of his lips against hers as he whispered again, "Trust me."

"I do."

He tasted the promise on her lips, and gave her back his own.

Epilogue

ONE YEAR LATER

A MELIA DISENTANGLED A SMALL ginger kitten from the long hem of her dress. Despite the best efforts of her mother, sister, Evie, a dressmaker, hairdresser, and makeup artist, she didn't feel like a particularly elegant bride.

She frowned ruefully at the snags Marmalade's claws had made in the delicate white fabric of her train. "Hugo really needs to teach you better manners," she told the unapologetic kitten. She set it down on a padded chair in the Conyer's hallway where it proceeded to test its claws on the antique upholstery instead.

Oops.

Oh well. Hugo could deal with that. The kitten had been his idea. It turned out he was something of a cat person and got pathetically gooey around the animals. When no one was watching.

"This place needs some more life," he had told her when he announced the idea. They lived together at Conyers, Amelia appreciating the mental break she got from her busy days at Redbridge. It was nice to be able to walk away from it after a solid day's work, head through the gate, and enter a slightly different world.

A world with excellent plumbing and endless hot water.

She even used the spa. Sometimes.

Although, as Hugo normally joined her on those occasions, it often turned into more of a...um...aerobic session.

She blushed as a few choice memories chose that moment to invade her mind—timing made worse when her father walked into the hallway.

"I think I heard the carriage on the driveway," he said.

He was a big bear of a man with unruly greying-brown hair, and he looked both odd and handsome in the dove-grey morning suit he was wearing. She smiled at him with a sudden wash of fondness, daft tears pricking her eyes. Her emotions were all dialled up to eleven today.

"OK?" he asked her kindly, noticing her rather wobbly smile.

"Yes, yes." She flapped a hand uselessly at her face with a slight laugh. "Just feeling...all the feelings."

He smiled, taking her hands in his big, rough grip. "You look beautiful. I have no idea how you're old enough to be getting married, yet here we are." He gave her a more serious sort of smile. "I think I missed a lot of watching you grow up. I'm sorry for that. I was away so often... I always thought: one more film, one more trip, then next year, next year I'll stay... But there was always work coming my way. And I've been incredibly lucky in that regard, but I can't help but wish..."

"It's OK. I understand."

"I missed all three of you. You and Cassie and your mother. Having her there with me on that Peru trip...it made me realise just how much I did miss her. That's what made me decide to make that trip my last."

"Erm, Italy?" queried Amelia with a smile.

"Well, apart from that little film I made in Turin last autumn. But Peru was the last big trip. I can't be away from you all for that long again. And, not to be depressing, but I'm fifty-six now.

318

I've been married to your mother for nearly thirty years, and I've barely spent half that time with her. I don't want to miss the time we do have left."

"Dad..."

"No, I'm not being depressing, honestly. What I'm trying to say in my terribly clumsy way is... My marriage has been an incredibly happy one. One with a woman who has allowed me to rather selfishly live the life I needed to. She gave me the freedom to follow my dreams. And I want that for you. I want your marriage to be one that lifts you up, that supports you, that gives you both freedom and strength. And hopefully you can improve on the example I've set you by finding a way to do all that *together*. Because two people working together can achieve so much more than one person alone."

Amelia nodded, eyes brimming again. "You're going to make me ruin my makeup," she said laughingly.

Her father barked his usual gruff laugh. "I think that's my cue to stop emoting at you. Or your mother will kill me."

"Thank you, though." She swallowed around the lump in her throat. "That's what we do have. Hugo and me. We...we complement each other. And he always has my back. And... Oh God." She sniffed. "I really *am* going to ruin my makeup."

"Right, right, let's get back to being British. Stiff upper lip, yes?"

She nodded, laughing.

Her father put his hand on her shoulder. "But I'm glad. I couldn't let you go to anyone who didn't deserve you. And of all the strange and unusual things I've seen on my travels, the fact that Hugo Blackton is that man might rate as one of the very strangest."

She punched him lightly in the arm. "Dad!"

"What? You think that's bad? Wait until you hear the speech I have prepared..."

"I dread to think," she muttered just as the enormous front door swung open. Lee stood there, also looking bizarrely smart in a black suit. Down the steps, on the driveway behind him, were the two Redbridge horses, flowers plaited into their manes, the open-top carriage gleaming behind them, with more flowers from the gardens in garlands along its sides.

Fit for a princess. Which Amelia very definitely was not—managing to trip over her dress on the way down the steps, only her father's strong grip on her arm stopping her from falling.

"Steady there," said Lee with a grin, seating himself in the carriage driver's seat. "It's probably not worth breaking your neck just to get out of marrying him. Even if it *is* Pence."

"Hah-hah." She stuck her tongue out in a very un-Princess-like way.

Lee chuckled. "You know, he still never got me that left-handed broom..."

Then he clucked at the horses, and the carriage pulled out and away from Conyers.

Hugo stood sweating at the front of the village church. Outside, it was a gloriously hot summer's day. Inside the church, it was much cooler. But he was still sweating.

He took a deep breath and tugged on the front of his already perfectly straight waistcoat. Where was she?

It was one minute past eleven, and she was meant to be here at eleven...

Hugo glanced back at the church entrance, aware of Roscoe and Jay—and eighty other people—watching his every move. He tried to smile, but his jaw was too tight. He stared instead at his shoes, trying to control his breathing.

They had chosen the village church because the Conyers chapel didn't fit enough people, not even for the small wedding that they had planned—small compared to the weddings of most people in their social circle, anyway.

The guests were family, close friends—and, of course, Amelia had invited the staff of both Conyers and Redbridge.

Janson and Sarah sat with Hodge on a pew near the back. They were still barely more than civil to him, but it was a vast improvement on how things had used to be. Besides, he rather enjoyed their slight discourtesy too much to wish it gone entirely.

The Conyers staff occupied a few pews on the other side of the church. Emily the cook was there with her son Alfie, who had already been heard to comment loudly that, "This is *sooooo* boring!" Hugo had smiled at that, because even just a year or two ago, he would have been of the same opinion.

Amelia's mother sat on the front row on the Banberry-Thompson side of the church. Caroline still eyed him sceptically at times, but he was sure he was gradually winning her around. And Cassie, who was waiting with the other bridesmaids by the door... Well, he had taken the first opportunity he could to speak privately with her and apologise for what he had done. She had given him one of her glassy trademark smiles. "Honestly, Hugo, I couldn't care less. I was only angry with you for appearances' sake. You know I used you just as much as you used me. I was desperate for a way out, and you gave me one. So...thank you, I guess?" She had patted him lightly on the chest, then nodded past him to the room beyond where Amelia had been talking to her mother. "Besides, all's well that ends well, right? And by the way... Hurt her again and I'll kill you. Clear?"

And though he had felt he was being let off rather too easily, he hadn't argued. There was never any point arguing with

321

Cassie. Long experience had taught him that. Now she caught his eye and gave him an only partly-sarcastic look of encouragement, thumbs up.

He acknowledged her with a nod, even that small motion made difficult by the tension in his body. He checked his watch again.

Three minutes past eleven.

Where *was* she?

This was the other reason he had been happy to choose a new wedding venue. He had bad memories of the Conyers chapel. Minutes ticking by and Amelia not turning up…

"*Psst!*" came an entirely unsubtle whisper from the woman standing next to Cassie. Evie. Grinning, she mimed throwing up, clearly noting how green he probably looked.

Hugo gave his sister a flat look while their mother, ever the one to care about appearances, hastily turned in her seat, gesturing at Evie to behave. His father nodded at him, his blue eyes steady and reassuring, and for a moment Hugo felt as he had as a boy, when his father had seemed an omniscient god-like figure, bending the world to his will with one word. There had been something reassuring in that steady command, as much as Hugo had chafed against it. Perhaps one of the saddest things about growing up was realising that one's parents knew no more than you did and were just as likely to get things wrong.

Last autumn, Hugo had been assessed for dyslexia and dyscalculia. He had been diagnosed with the former, but not the latter. But the assessor had suggested that he be assessed for ADHD, which had taken Hugo by surprise, until he spent some time reading up about it online and had felt the back of his neck crawl with the strangest sense of being seen. It was him, down to a T. And the diagnosis had been confirmed.

He had forwarded both diagnoses by email to his father without any accompanying comment. And the only reply he'd had was, "I see."

Well... Fine. If his father wanted to add those two things to the long mental list he kept of Hugo's flaws, then so be it. They still loved each other, even if it was imperfect and awkward. All he really cared about was that Amelia didn't mind. In fact, she found his diagnoses sort of fascinating and spent ages reading up about them in her usual diligent way, without ever attempting to swamp him with information or suggestions. She had let him come to terms with it in his own time, listening and reassuring by turns. And she had been... She always was... Just absolutely perfect.

And now she was...

Late.

Six minutes past eleven.

For the first time in his life, he thought he might faint.

"What if she doesn't come?"

The words broke from him unbidden, though spoken so low that only Roscoe, his best man, and Jay, his groomsman, could hear him.

The two men exchanged a glance, then Jay said, "I didn't quite know how to tell you this, but when I was talking to Amelia yesterday I spotted a one-way ticket to Spain sticking out of her handbag..."

Hugo's heart stopped. Then he realised Jay was laughing. "Jay, you absolute di—"

Given they were in a church, it was just as well the sudden sound of the organ cut off the end of that sentence.

"Too soon?" asked Jay, but Hugo ignored him, because everyone was getting to their feet, looking back towards the large wooden doors that were beginning to open...

Hugo faced the vicar, heart pounding. But he couldn't help it. He had to see her. She was Amelia. How could he ever not want to look at her?

He turned, and there she was, on her father's arm. So beautiful his heart stopped again.

He breathed her name to himself, hardly realising he did it. She met his eyes and smiled the brightest smile he had ever seen.

Then she walked up the aisle towards him, and finally, and forever, became his wife.

Thank you so much for reading. I hope you had fun! I would be so grateful if you could leave a review on Amazon. It makes a huge difference.

Want to know what happens next? Get a free bonus scene when you sign up for my newsletter: www.rachelrowan.com

Thank you

Thank you so much for reading! If you'd like to sign up for my newsletter and get some freebies (like a bonus scene set on Hugo and Amelia's wedding night!) visit www.rachelrowan.com.

If you liked the book, could you help spread the love? Leaving a review on Amazon is incredibly helpful to us indie authors. We have no marketing budget (and, in my case, no marketing skills!) so we really do depend on word of mouth. Posting about it on social media or recommending it to your friends is also incredibly helpful.

Do stay in touch to find out about new releases—follow me on Amazon, or Instagram, or join my newsletter. Or email me just to say hi! I'd love to hear from you!

Email: rachel@rachelrowan.com

Instagram: @rachelrowanwriter

Website: www.rachelrowan.com

Thank you again for reading! I hope to see you here again at the end of the next book!

Have you tried...

There are lots more stories in the *Entitled Love* world:

The *Entitled Love* novellas:

<u>Uncommon</u>

Sparks fly in this fish-out-of-water Pretty Woman-style story in which a playboy Earl meets his match.
- Paid-for fake dating

- Rich boy x poor girl

- Twist ending (and of course it's a happy one!)

<u>Unspoken</u>

She's the only woman he's ever wanted—and the one woman he can never have.
- Brother's best friend

- Friends-to-lovers

- Grumpy x sunshine

Untouched

A socially awkward young woman asks her playboy neighbour to teach her everything about men—including how to be touched...
- Bedroom lessons

- Opposites attract

- Virgin x experienced

Unwanted

After losing his inheritance, a disgruntled viscount is forced to live with the best friend of the woman who ruined his life...
- Enemies-to-lovers—with a twist

- Only one (warm) bed

- Mystery, mistrust, and suspense

All available on Amazon and Kindle Unlimited. Plus, get a free short story when you sign up for the Rachel Rowan newsletter: www.rachelrowan.com

Acknowledgements

I finish every book feeling more humble than I did before. It would honestly be impossible to write without the support of so many people.

My husband, who keeps our whole life on track and does more than his fair share of parenting when mummy is distracted and working (frantically) to meet her deadlines. And who listens, or at least pretends to, when I'm talking about made-up people yet again.

My children for their patience, and for looking over my shoulder at my sales dashboard and telling me the numbers are small. I take your raw honesty as *encouragement*, darlings! You can pay for my therapy when you're older.

Charis. You get a special shout-out. You are there for me in so many ways as a fellow writer, reader, admirer of hands, and general crazy thirsty person. You make this sometimes lonely job far less lonely. Thank you for tirelessly propping up my fragile esteem!

Libby, my editor. The most professional, conscientious and smart person I've had the privilege to work with. You make my books so much better and I'm not sure I could do this without having you in my corner. THANK YOU.

My beta readers—you put up with this story in its raw form and found enough to love to keep me going with it when I was ready to burn the manuscript in despair. Thank you for your time, wonderful insights, and encouragement!

Last, and very definitely not least: YOU. The reader. Anyone who has ever read this or my other works and made this entire exercise in madness seem worthwhile. Thank you from the bottom of my heart. You're who I'm writing for. So thank you for being there.

Now, onto the next book...

Printed in Great Britain
by Amazon

34262226R00192